Your SPARKLE CAVALCADE OF DEATH

ROBERT SHIARELLA

This is an original publication of Metamorphic Press

Cover and Interior Art by StrikingImages.com
Amara as Miss Queen O'Hearts —www.amaradanceproductions.com

ISBN: 978-1-951221-15-7

Metamorphic Press Edition printing November, 2020
First published by The Viking Press, 1974

Published by:
Metamorphic Press
PO 151 Box
Tenafly, NJ 07670
metamorphicpress.com

Proudly Printed in the United States of America

DEDICATION

To Jon Koons, With Great Appreciation,
for his adopting my brain child after it was unjustly
made an orphan decades ago.

PART ONE

Friday, August 4

DING A LING A LING A LING A LING A LING

Fila Noogie pulled the pillow over her ears and waited for the alarm to run down.

A LING A LING A LING A LING

"Okay, okay..."

a ling a ling a ling a...

She let the pillow fall away, yawned and opened her eyes. Over head, a roach meandered across the ceiling and disappeared behind a strip of gilded molding. Rolling her head to the side, she regarded the inert bulk of her husband, sleeping in his shorts beside her. "Hey, Bozo." She reached out, grabbed the rubber tire of flab at his waist, and squeezed.

"Whazzit," rasped Lewd Noogie.

"Get your head outta bed." Languidly, Fila ran her hands across her silk kimono, first cupping her jello breasts, then caressing downward to her zaftig thighs. Raising her buttocks, she hiked up the hem of the garment until she lay naked to the waist; then she rolled over to her stomach and reached out toward the night table, where she kept a rectal thermometer and an open jar of Vaseline. Grasping the thermometer, she dipped it into the petroleum jelly, then held it out behind her and slowly inserted it between her buttocks. Wiping her fingers on the bedsheet, she blew the hair out of her eyes, checked the clock and hummed a few bars of "Yes, Sir, That's My Baby." Realizing that her husband still lay motionless beside her, she reached out and jabbed him in the ribs. "Hey, ace. Drop your cocks and grab your socks."

"Mup. Mup."

Fila watched the clock's second hand sweep upward... *four...three... two... one... kapow.* She plucked the thermometer from her fundament and read the mercury level with one eye closed. "Ninety-seven... point... NINE!" She bolted upright in bed and snatched her basal temperature chart from the floor. "Hot shit! Fila's laid an egg!"

She flung thermometer and chart to the floor and pounced upon her cataleptic mate. "Lewd!" Straddling his legs, she began tugging down his boxer shorts. "C'mon, Boze, baby— ol' Fila's fertile!"

"Mff." Her husband felt himself being rocked from side to side as the shorts were peeled from his flaccid frame. "Chrissake, Fi." He covered his face with her pillow.

Fila left the garment tangled round his pasty thighs and beheld his shriveled manhood. "Huh-boy, spaghetti and meatballs." She sandwiched the lifeless organ between her palms and rolled it briskly back and forth, blowing on it like a Boy Scout lighting a fire. "Ah-ha! Results!"

Lewd lifted the pillow from his face and muttered, "I hafta take a leak."

"Leak, schmeak." Fila shinnied up his trunk and mounted him at the waist. "C'mon, girls, rise 'n' shine!" She began to swab the dampening folds of her vagina with the head of his turgid bone. "We'll show that nasty old Fertility Institute, won't we, big fella?" She flopped down suddenly, driving Lewd's kazoo clean up to her cervix.

"Woof!" Lewd felt a sharp pain in his bladder.

"Oooo," gasped Fila, abruptly glutted. She ground

herself against him, gyrating her pelvis, feeling him scramble her eggs. "Ooo-hoo." Easing forward, she unsheathed all but the blunt tip of his slippery saber. "Come on in, girls... the water's fine." Then she flopped down hard again.

"Ow."

Piston-like, she began to rear up and crash down with great deliberation. "Sock ["Ow"] it ["Ow"] to ["Ow"] me!"

"Ow!"

Fila pumped faster, poking her tongue from the corner of her mouth and gazing beneath her at the shiny pillar vanishing and reappearing at the cleft between her thighs.

Her husband raised a corner of the pillow that covered his face. "I... uh... hafta... ow... leak."

Fila upped the tempo; now the action at her nether region became a soggy blur, causing her to toss back her head and close her eyes. "Ohhh... yesss... innn... dee... dee... doo..."

Lewd's bladder was really aching now. Reaching up, he grabbed his wife's pendulous breasts and tried to pull her from him.

"Zow!" she crooned, assuming the gesture to be prompted by passion. "Gimme it! Blow your nuts! I want it! I need it!" She slowed her rhythm and began driving down on him with powerful relentless thrusts. "Gotta have it!"

"Ow!"

"Gimme!"

"Jesus, ow!" Lewd tried to buck her off with desperate heaves, but she was glued to the saddle.

"Now!" she demanded. "Pump it home!" They fell sideways on the bed; she wrapped her legs tightly round his waist, keeping him hilted, though he tried to scramble away from her. "Good... to the last... drop!" she gasped in triumph, her muscular legs squeezing his torso dry as though he were a giant tube of toothpaste.

"Goddamnit, ow!" bellowed Lewd, breaking her leglock

and heaving her across the bed as he rolled away in the opposite direction. Each thudded to the floor on a different side of the bed, and as soon as Lewd hit the carpet he was on his feet, staggering toward the doorway, clutching his belly in huge folds. "Crazy bitch," he gasped, lumbering from the room.

"Yow," sighed Fila, dreamily, lying on the floor. She hiked her knees up to her chest and locked her arms around them, gazing into space with misty eyes. "I'll just hold myself like this a bit to give the girls a little break. Okay, ladies, its downhill all the way, now... swim, two, three, four... kick, two, three, four..."

From the dining room came a resounding crash, followed by a volley of curse words and the sound of fabric tearing, which meant that Lewd had tripped over the telephone cord again, sending their terrified kitten up the cloth-covered wall.

Fila was unperturbed. She lay there peacefully, listening to the slam of the toilet seat, followed by the trickle of her husband's urine, most of which was doubtless being deposited on the bathroom floor. Lewd returned to the bedroom. Ignoring his wife, he squinted at the clock, then sat on the edge of the bed, crossed one ankle over the opposite knee and began picking the dead skin from the bottom of his foot. He peeled off a flake and studied it briefly, trying to decide whether or not to eat it. Letting it flutter to the floor, he began to pull on his socks.

Curled in a naked ball, Fila began to sing gently. "On the baby's tinkle or the baby's knee, where will the baby's dimple be?..."

Lewd stood up and climbed into his uniform trousers. "Dunno why you're so hot-boxed for a friggin' kid."

"The Noogie name must live on!" his wife proclaimed.

"You're the only hope it's got, Bozo, baby. Your brother's dead, and his kid sure ain't gonna get married."

"Huh." Lewd put on his shirt. "That kid, that Corbin.

Something funny about that kid."

Fila played with the fringe on the bedspread. "The Noogie ancestors... are up the crick. Their only hope is old Lewd Noogie, with his all-girl, Step-'n'-Fetchit sperm."

"Can it, Fi." He snapped on his black bowtie, stuck his subway conductor's hat on the back of his head, and started off toward the bathroom again, realizing he'd forgotten to shave. "Get up off the floor," he said in passing. "You look like some kinda animal." Loping through the dining room, he tripped over the phone cord again.

Fila listened to the water running in the bathroom.

"I'll just lie here a bit," she told herself, still holding her knees against her chest. After several moments, she shifted uncomfortably, digging the pieces of a broken thermometer from the carpet between her shoulder blades. Lewd returned and put on his uniform jacket. His jaw was decorated with little pieces of toilet paper. Standing over her, hands on hips, he muttered, "G'wan, get up. I din't shoot. I din't come inside ya." Then he left for work.

Fila lay unmoving. She heard the door slam, heard the elevator come and go, heard its faint hum as it carried her husband to the street, eight floors below. Finally, she looked in her hand and found that she still held the bottom half of the broken thermometer. Carefully, she upended it over her vagina and tried to tap its contents into her. "Quick, Silver," she whispered, but nothing came out of the broken glass tube. Releasing her knees, she sat upright and looked between her legs; there was not a trace of semen. Then she got up, poured herself half a cereal bowl full of vodka and sat down at the telephone.

Morning was always the roughest part of the day for Corbin Noogie. They stood at his apartment door, he and the middle-aged man he had just spent the night with. Now it was time to say good-by. The man looked around the room one final time.

"Got everything?" Corbin's casualness was forced.

"Yeah, I think so," said the man, too loudly; then he flashed a quick, embarrassed smile.

Last night in Segger's Bar the man had been a dead ringer for Corbin's father; now he was just a middle-aged stranger. Corbin unlocked the door and opened it. As the man moved toward the threshold, Corbin held out his hand and the man shook it briefly, as though he feared the contact.

"Nice meeting you," Corbin told him.

"Same here." The man's gaze avoided Corbin's eyes.

This was the time new friends made sure they had each other's telephone number and address. But last night had been a dream and now it was morning. "Well, so long," said Corbin Noogie.

"Good-bye." The man stepped through the doorway and started down the stairs, never looking back.

Corbin closed and locked the door, then leaned against

it, looking around the single room that was his home.

The window shades were always drawn, yet somehow morning found its way inside. Here, last night, had stood a magic castle; now it was only a bedroom with a queen-sized bed. In the dark, one could not see the Vaseline footprints on the walls, or the shelf lined with penis-sized, battery operated vibrators and rubber dildos, black and white, in graduated sizes, coated with grease and pubic hair

Last night, that little mirrored cabinet atop his dresser had been the door to Wonderland; today it was just a closet full of copouts: narcotics, psychedelics, pep pills, sedatives, hypnotics, tranquilizers, volatile organic solvents-jars and vials of pills, capsules and spanchules, powders, herbs and spices, in every color of the spectrum.

The telephone rang.

Corbin looked at it for several moments, then pulled himself together, sat down on the edge of the bed and lifted the receiver.

"Corbin?"

"Who's this?"

"Aunt Fila. Listen, are you alone?"

"Oh, hello, Aunt Fi. Yeah, I'm alone-why?"

"I've got a proposition for you."

"What kind of proposition?"

"How would you like to help me make a baby?"

Gonna be a real bitch in the tube t'day. Lewd Noogie stood at the sidewalk counter of the Aida Pizza Shoppe, eating breakfast. Not a breath of air was stirring on this humid August morning, and a reddish haze of pollution blanketed the sweltering city. *Hope I get a air conditioned train.*

Lewd munched a wedge of pepperoni pizza, washing it down with cherry Coke. He watched a pert brunette prance by with knockout legs and a walk like a majorette. *Eatin' stuff.* He tracked her undulating buttocks till they were out of sight, then zeroed in on a tall blonde with a pouting, sensual mouth. *Nice chin to rest a pair of balls on.* Peeling off his jacket and unbuttoning his collar, he left the counter and strolled toward the train yard. *Stupid twat.* He shook his head, thinking of his wife. *Someday I'm gonna punch that crazy cunt the fuck dead.* He poked a stubby finger into his mouth, digging a piece of pepperoni from between his teeth.

Crossing the street, he passed a group of little girls on their way to school. One caught his eye. *Looks like that little frog snatch, used ta live on the fifth floor.* The image of eight-year-old Trudy Odelette loomed out of the dark recesses of his mind— little Trudy, robed in a billowing nightgown, fresh and fragrant from her Saturday night bath, her mouth like a little flower, her—

"Squeeze a few grapes last night, Noogie?" "Huh?"

"You look hung over... you sick or something?" A fellow train conductor, Clifford Koulats, had fallen into step beside Lewd. "Hell, if you're sick, take the day off."

"Mokay." Lewd didn't like this Koulats character.

The two crossed the street together and entered the train yard. "I never get sick, myself," confided Koulats. "Number One, I don't drink— and Number Two, I get plenty of fresh air. That's all there is to it."

Clifford Koulats' uniform was neatly pressed, his shirt freshly starched and ironed; he looked as though he'd just stepped out of a Sears catalog. "Last night, for instance, Constance and I took in the park concert. Nothing like a good cellist on a fair summer evening, I always say."

As they entered the terminal, Lewd tried to recall what Constance Koulats looked like. *Big tits* was all that came to mind, and the fact that he'd tried to take off the top of her bathing suit at the annual beach party a few years back.

They walked into the office of the stationmaster, Max Berlitz. "Maybe you'd better send Noogie home, Max," Koulats grinned. "He looks a little under the weather."

Lewd scowled. "He's fulla shit."

Berlitz looked up from his clipboard. "Christ, Noogie, you look like you been run over by a train. Don't you ever clean that uniform?"

Koulats patted Lewd on the back. "Long as he shows up, Max. Noogie's irreplaceable, you know. His train's the only one that makes a stop at Lewd's Landing, isn't that right, Lewd?"

"Suck off, Koulats."

Max Berlitz scribbled on his clipboard. "Let's see, Cliff, you take the eight-oh-three. Noogie, you go out on the seven-forty-six... and for Christ sake, fix your tie."

As Lewd peered at his reflection in the stationmaster's window and adjusted his tie, Koulats slapped him on the back and headed off toward the men's room, probably to comb his hair or brush his teeth. Clifford Koulats would get an air conditioned train for sure. He'd even been written up in the News a while back; the paper had dubbed him "The Singing Conductor" because he constantly entertained his riders with bursts of melody over the P.A. system, and kept them amused with station announcements such as "Next stop, Laurel Avenue— ladies' underwear, sneakers, auto loans..." Lewd never announced anything on his train. *Let the bastards sleep through their stop.*

At seven-forty-six, Lewd Noogie boarded his train and mopped his face with a dirty handkerchief. The train was not air conditioned. He poked his head through the compartment window, flicked the levers which closed the train doors, and began his run for the day.

Corbin Noogie stepped from the elevator and stood before the door to his aunt's apartment. Nervously, he fixed his hair, adjusted his clothing, then took a deep breath and pressed the buzzer.

Footsteps padded toward the door and it swung open before him. "Hello, Aunt Fi."

"Hiya, han'some." His aunt was completely naked. She winked and toasted him briefly with a cereal bowl filled with what looked like water.

"Gin?" he guessed.

"Wad-ka." She lifted the bowl to his lips and poured a good ounce into his mouth.

His eyes widened as he swallowed; then he licked his lips and cleared his throat. "Thermal breakfast."

"I a-dore your outfit," Fila cooed, tracing a finger tip down the front of his white pullover.

"Yours is much better for this weather."

His aunt hooked her finger over the top of his belt buckle and led him inside, closing the door. "How's tricks at the network? You still an usher?"

"Not an usher— a page." Watching her naked buttocks jiggle and bounce, he followed her down the hallway into the living room.

Fila spread herself out on an ancient tufted-velvet sofa and watched her nephew reacquaint himself with the room, which was festooned with a bizarre collection of antiques, junk and high camp.

"Hey, do you know there happens to be an entire live Siamese cat on your wall?"

"That's Kippur. My husband keeps everyone climbing the walls around here."

"How is Uncle Lewd?" His aunt just shrugged. He watched her balance her cereal bowl on her stomach, clasp her hands behind her head and raise her foot high into the air, contemplating her painted toenails. In the silence that followed, Corbin seated himself in a velvet easy chair across from her and took the opportunity to study her huge breasts and the dark red bush at her groin, wondering what it would be like to ball her.

She seemed to read his mind. "How's your love life? Got a steady boy friend?"

"Currently," he said without emotion, "I'm playing the field."

"Bet you play every position, too." She lifted the bowl, swung her feet to the floor, took another swallow of vodka and slapped her thigh resolutely. "Now then— let's get down to business, shall we?"

"Aw, come off it, Aunt Fila. What's all this about, really?"

Fila looked him square in the eye. "Corbie, baby, I explained all that on the phone."

Corbin dismissed it with a wave of his hand. "You don't expect me to fall for all that freaky shit, do you? I mean, it sounds like just another one of your bad-taste jokes ."

Fila put down her cereal bowl. She got up, walked over and stood directly in front of him, fists on her hips, feet planted squarely apart. "Listen, asshole, do you know how long I've been breaking my box to have a friggin' kid?— how many temperature charts I've worn out?— how many fertility doctors I've hounded— MDs, gynos, shrinks?— how many of those wonder drugs I've had pumped into me? For three years I took baking-soda douches to make sure I'd have a boy— then I found out that fart I'm married to only squirts out girl seeds. Tempus fugit, baby— I'm thirty-nine years old, and Uncle Lewdy's fifty-three. All of which boils right down to this: I need some potent jism, and I'd prefer to keep it in the family— and that means you, even if you are as gay as New Orleans at Mardi Gras." She blew a strand of fire-red hair away from her eye. "Now, does it still sound like a great big joke to you?"

Corbin's gaze fell away from hers, drifted down across her naked body and finally settled in the faded Oriental rug.   "No, I guess not." Her somber mood dissolved at once.

"Well, let's have at it, then."

Doing a little dance-turn, she padded from the room. "Sorry I can't offer you a bona fide piece of tail," she called, "but you probably wouldn't be able to find it anyway. Besides, I've been married fourteen years— fourteen faithful years, believe it or not— and I don't want to spoil my record now." She returned with a small glass vial in her hand. "Unless you want to count that Transit Authority beach party a couple years ago. I spied old Lewdy feeling up this bitch behind a sand dune, see— so, just for kicks, I dragged her old man into the weeds and sucked him off. C'mon, baby." She took his hand and led him toward the bedroom. "Boy, was he a stuffed shirt. I bet it was his first head job. But, we didn't ball or anything-so it doesn't count, right? I mean, it was just for laughs, get me?" She held up the glass vial. "Just like this is."

Lewd's train roared through the sweltering underground darkness, each car crammed with patiently baking passengers on their way to work. Alone in his tiny cubicle, Lewd stuck his head through the window as far as he could, but the steady blast of hot air offered little relief.

The train screeched into the Horkbunt Street stop, and he opened the doors, thinking enviously of Clifford Koulats in his air-conditioned eight-oh-three. *Lucky prick.* He felt somewhat placated when he managed to flick the doors shut an instant before a well-dressed businessman could climb aboard.

The next station was Havlick Square, an express stop, which meant that Lewd had to open the doors on the other side of the train. Lumbering out of his compartment, he bulled his way through the edgy standees, drawing looks of disgust in his wake.

As he entered the other compartment, his train ground to a halt; another local was still in the Havlick station ahead, so Lewd's rig had drawn a red light between stops— just as had happened in this exact spot, twenty years ago, on his first run as a conductor.

He dropped the window and poked his head outside. His train was halted at an abandoned subway platform, one that had been closed more than forty years ago, when the city subway system was revised. On the dirty tile wall, a mosaic sign identified the stop as 91ST STREET, but subway folklore now referred to it as Lewd's Landing.

Nearly two decades ago, rookie conductor Noogie's train had stopped at this spot for a red light, and Lewd— overeager and determined to do a top-notch job— had mistakenly flicked his levers and opened the doors at the abandoned platform.

Perhaps it would not have been so bad had Lewd not tried to justify his action by insisting that there had actually been a passenger on that platform, waiting for the train. Hence, a clincher had been added to the legend: the beautiful, mysterious Lady of Lewd's Landing, who had boarded the train and ridden away.

Shoulda kept my fat-ass yap shut. He peered up and down the platform, but all was dark and quiet.

Unaccountably, the memory of little Trudy Odelette crept back into his consciousness. *She'd be almost fifteen now, and blonde. That little whore. Wonder where they moved to?*

His train began to move again, pulling away from the platform, leaving Lewd's memory floating in the quiet darkness. Accompanying the fading memory was the tiny fragment of a dream which Lewd had left behind before he'd fully realized that it was there. *A baby girl*, the dream began. *A daughter. To fool around with.*

But by now, of course, his train was nearly out of sight.

Virile, naked buttocks revolved kaleidoscopically before Corbin's eyes. Heavy breathing, barking breaths began to permeate the atmosphere, thick with the smell of sex.

He tossed his head from side to side upon the pillow, thrusting his pelvis skyward as the relentless fist pistoned up and down along the rigid length of his throbbing penis.

"That's my baby... come for Momma," Fila cooed, kneading his testicles with one hand, pumping his organ with the other, flicking her tongue across its silken, ruby tip. "Momma wants it. Momma wants her baby's creamy come."

In one of his hands Corbin held a Benzedrine popper, a booster rocket to enhance his blast-off. Suddenly he raised it to his nose and snapped it open, sucking in deep lungfuls of its acrid vapor. He sped toward the heavens like an arrow, buried his face in the loins of God, tried to suck the nectar from the sacred font. Inhaling another draught of medicated vapor, he somersaulted toward Eternity, about to sire a child that was his Dad, was God; spasms shook his fragile frame, his delicate mouth gaped, distorted, and the breath caught in his arid throat.

His fountain gushed its milky treasure into Aunt Fila's little vial, half-filling it with microscopic life. There were a few whimpers, and then peaceful, joyous silence.

Crouching over his jerking organ, Fila squeezed the last reluctant droplets into her glass container, then snapped the lid on tight. "Wow." She clasped the warm receptacle, gazed at it with awe, touched it to her cheek.

Slowly coming to his senses, Corbin raised his head and looked at his aunt, who smiled, held the vial up for him to see, then bent down and reverently kissed his genitals. When she was through, Corbin sat up awkwardly and swung his feet to the floor, away from her. "Well... I guess I'd better run along. I've got a ten-o'clock call."

Fila laid her hand upon his back, then suddenly said, "Wait a minute," and scrambled from the bed.

As he climbed into his pants, she scampered to the living room, warming the vial between her palms. Soon she returned with a ten-dollar bill, which she held out to him.

Corbin backed away, offended. "Christ, Aunt Fi, you don't have to—"

"You take it, baby." She stuffed the bill into his trouser pocket. "That's the token payment to remind you of our deal." She held up the vial. "They're all mine now, understand? If I plant a kid it belongs to Lewd, and I don't ever want him to hear different."

Corbin nodded, looking at the floor. "Sure. What do I care?"

Fila cupped the vial in her hands and gazed at it, wide-eyed. "How many d'you think are in here?"

"I guess around four, five hundred million."

"Wow." She licked her lips. "And it only takes one."

She snapped out of her reverie. "Hey, dollface, you run along now— I got to get busy. These little tadpoles are fragile, you know."

She took her nephew's arm and walked him to the door. Facing him, she put her hand flat on his chest and smiled. "Thanks, Corbie."

"That's okay." He put his hands in his pockets and blushed.

She opened the door and Corbin stepped out into the elevator well. Impulsively, despite her nakedness, she rushed out and threw her arms about his neck, kissing him hard on the mouth. "Wish me luck, honey."

"I do. I really do."

Fila raced back into the apartment and began to swing the door shut.

"Aunt Fila?"

She peeked out at him.

"Ah, if it doesn't... take... this time, we can try again—if you want."

Fila grinned. "You're aces, baby. It's a date." She blew him a kiss and closed the door.

Standing there alone, waiting for the elevator to arrive, Corbin moved his hands within his pockets, cupping them around his testicles.

Inside the Noogie apartment, Fila marched with bridal cadence down the hallway toward her bedroom, her hands pressing her ample breasts together, warming between them a small glass vial which contained, alive, the Noogie Family Tree.

PART TWO

Wednesday, May 1

At precisely four-thirty a.m., old Merlin Trump opened his eyes and gazed into the darkness overhead. Those people moved. Lifting the sheet that covered him, he slowly swung his feet to the floor and sat up on his army-surplus cot. "Wowsie man." He shook his head gingerly. "The old Chiefie has a doozie of a headache, Labor Gang." He eased his feet into his slippers. "Ain't it?"

Merlin sat motionless a few minutes, eyes closed, then gently lowered himself to his knees beside the cot, folding his hands for prayer. Tacked to the wall he faced was a large theatrical poster featuring the full-length portrait of a beautiful, blonde belly dancer in action:

THE INTOXICATING LOVE GODDESS OF EXOTIC DANCE!
The Sizzling, Sexational
·· MISS QUEEN O'HEARTS ··

Gazing at this poster in the dark, the old man prayed.

> *"Hail, Mary, feelin' good,*
> *The Lord is whiskey.*
> *Bless Art now against women,*
> *And blessed is Toy Boat*
> *If you kindly please, Chiefie.*
> *Hunky-Dory, mothers are good;*
> *Pray for us swimmers, now,*
> *And after hours if we're deaf, Amen."*

Merlin kissed his right thumbnail, touched it to his forehead, chest, left and right shoulder, then quietly climbed to his feet. For a moment he stood silent in the cool, spring darkness, his body unmoving except for his thumbs, which flicked out of his fists as though he were idly shooting marbles from the hip. Finally his eyes began to glitter, and he grew alert. "Tidy up." At once, he began the daily ritual of cleaning his attic workshop.

The old man made his bed in total darkness, then trudged to his work area, collecting several reference volumes from the oak table and returning them to the bookshelf. Owl-like, he scrutinized the titles: *The Compleat Catalogue of Cocktails, Wines and Spirits; The Encyclopedia of Tasmanian Herbs and Spices; Miracle Cures with Raw Fruit and Vegetable Juices; An Analecta Incunabulum of Potions, Lotions, Notions and Incantations.*

Moving to his workbench, Merlin polished the copper body and cistern of the small alcoholic still, inspected its copper tube and coiled worm, and set a low flame beneath its boiler. He dusted the juice extractor, the blender, and the stoneware beanery, then tidied up the supply shelves, which were stocked with test tubes, beakers, Bunsen burners and other pieces of lab equipment, plus measuring, cutting and serving implements; cooking utensils; racks of bottles filled with various oils, herbs, spices, vitamins, minerals and occult compounds; and assorted curious odds and ends.

He shuffled over to the twenty-foot, hand-carved

mahogany bar, and collected the soiled lo-ball glasses, cocktail shaker and other implements left there from the previous evening. Carrying them to the double sink behind the bar, he filled both basins with scalding water, one soapy and one clear. Leaving the glasses and silverware to soak in the soapy water, he sponged the top of the bar and all the stools, shook each of the three empty cuspidors over the wastebasket near his bed, then polished them with paper towels; finally, he sponged down the five wooden aging kegs in their rack at the end of the bar.

The room was filled with gray, predawn light as he returned to the sink and plunged his hands into the steaming water. "Wowsie man." With great deliberation he scoured each item, swished it around in the hot rinse water, then soaped and rinsed it a second time, before setting it to drain upside down on several paper towels spread upon the bar. When he completed the washing, he dried and polished everything with paper towels, restoring each object to its assigned niche behind the bar. He drained the double sink, scrubbed both basins with powdered cleanser, rinsed them with hot water and wiped them dry with paper towels.

His habitat now in perfect order, Merlin ambled to his cot and slowly peeled off his faded polo shirt, tattered trousers and boxer shorts. Neatly folding the shirt and trousers, he left them on the bed and crossed over to the shower stall, his undershorts in hand. Stepping into the stall, he pulled the curtain closed and turned on the water, which was freezing cold. "Mandalay." Stoically, he waited until the hot water rose from the basement, four floors below.

He lathered himself twice from head to foot, then scrubbed his shorts. As he was soaping himself a third time, the morning sun rose directly outside his garret window, casting its rosy rays upon his shower curtain. The old man peeked out from the corner of the curtain, into the brilliant sunlight. "Hotsy-totsy, that's the ticket... I'll be with you in a jiffy." He rinsed himself, turned off the water and rubbed his body briskly with a threadbare towel.

He dressed slowly, then went behind the bar, opened the small refrigerator and got out a box of Fig Newtons, from which he took two. Breaking each into four pieces and spreading the morsels on a paper towel, he sat at the bar and methodically gummed them down with toothless jaws, every fiber of his being absorbed in the breaking of his fast.

His meal completed, he spread several newspaper pages on the bar, and piled in the middle more than two dozen soiled paper towels. The wastebasket near the bar yielded another dozen, and the one by his cot five more. Folding the newspaper over the soiled towels, he rolled up the wad into a nice, neat parcel. He fished a length of old twine from a drawer, tied the package tightly and tucked it under his arm. Moving to the antique cash register behind the bar, he rang up NO SALE, removed a one-dollar bill, then trundled over to the front bay window and gazed into the street below. Farther up along the block of aged townhouses he could see the paperboy's wagon parked on the sidewalk. "Shake my leg."

He trudged over to the door and peered out through the peephole. "Who's there?" No one answered. He unhooked the chain, took the bar off the police lock, slid open the bolt, and unlocked the latch. Easing the door open without a sound, he peeked down the spiral stairwell cautiously before stepping out and closing the door behind him, locking it from the outside with a small padlock.

His little parcel of trash tucked under his arm, old Merlin slowly descended the winding staircase to the third floor of the venerable Trump mansion, trudging past the silent statuary and the empty rooms, then down the staircase to the second floor, where his family slept. The first door on his right was his daughter's room, and the sound of running water told him she'd begun her day. Next on the right came an empty bedroom, and after that was his son Arthur's room; Arthur was still asleep. On Merlin's left was the master bedroom— his wife's room. He paused at the door and gently touched a finger to its surface three times. "Thalia, my queen?" There was no response from within; there had been none for the past twenty years. *Must still be asleep, God bless her.*

The old man moved along to the resplendent spiral staircase and gradually descended to the main floor. He paused at the foot of the stairs to catch his breath, then shuffled down the hallway to the front foyer, where he peered out the window through a corner of the curtain until the paperboy wheeled his wagon up to the stoop and rang the doorbell. Merlin placed his parcel upon the window seat, then unlocked, unbarred and unchained the huge oak door, easing it open just a crack.

The paperboy, a black youngster of eleven years, was substituting for the regular boy on the route. Seeing a suspicious eye peering out at him from behind the townhouse door, the lad held out a copy of the *Daily News Gazette*. "Murray says I gotta ring your bell. Here's your paper, mister."

The eye regarded him a moment, then whispered, "Watch your foot, the Feds are hot."

The boy shifted his weight from one tennis shoe to the other, and sniffed loudly. He consulted a small notebook, then checked the house number again. "Are you Mr. Trump?"

"Shhhhh!" The oaken portal eased open another foot, and anxious eyes darted back and forth, casing the street. "Mum's the name." The man beckoned the lad to come inside.

Reluctantly, the youngster crossed the threshold, discovering his customer to be a very short, very thin old man with luminous eyes and unkempt silver hair hanging down over his ears. The old man was smiling broadly, and only three teeth were visible in his entire mouth.

Merlin closed the door momentarily, put a finger to his lips, then eased the door open again and said quite loudly, "Trumps, you say? Why, Golly Neds, m'boys she said-those people moved!" He shut the door, grinning triumphantly, then winked at the paperboy and whispered, "Little pitchers have big ears, ain't it?"

The boy shrugged. "Here's your paper, mister."

"Good boy! Good boy! You're a gentleman and a scholar!" Merlin patted him lightly on the head. "Now, let's have a little drink to celebrate, ain't it? Name your poison."

"I'm not very thirsty."

"We got fresh farmer's buttermilk, cold celery tonic— good for the kidneys— or how's about a nice raw egg in half a glass of Pilsner beer?"

"Murray said you'd gimme a dollar for doin' an errand."

"Errand?" Merlin's eyes lit up. "Golly Neds, that reminds me while you're at it, do the old Chiefie a little favor, too, if you kindly please." Trudging to the window seat, he picked up the parcel of garbage. "This is a little present for a friend of mine down the block, as the saying goes." He winked and tucked it under the boy's arm. "Just slip it into the trash basket down at the corner, m'boy— better yet, go down two blocks to the one at Silverman's Drugstore— that way it won't clutter up the neighborhood." He stuffed a dollar into the boy's dungaree pocket. "Merry Christmas, you're a good egg, and macaroni spa-get."

The lad grinned shyly. "Christmas don't come in May."

"You don't tell me? Can you de-magine that?" The old man winked and tapped the package. "Don't let anyone see you— they might try to pull a fast one." He tiptoed to the door, eased it open a bit and checked the street. "Coast's clear." Allowing the lad to squeeze through the narrow opening, Merlin peered out after him and whispered, "Watch your foot."

The boy hopped down the cement steps, checked the dollar in his pocket, then grabbed the handle of his wagon and headed off down the street. "So long, Mr. Trump!"

"Shhhhh!" The old man stuck his head out and said as loudly as he could, "I'll see that he gets the message! Those people moved, you know!"

Re-securing the front door locks, Merlin fished the morning mail from the door box and carried it down the hallway to the suit of black armor standing at the foot of the stairs. "Here she be." He lifted the metal face mask, inserted the letters halfway and clamped them in the iron man's mouth. Then, newspaper in hand, he started upstairs. Part way up the thickly carpeted staircase, the old man paused before a large, ornately framed painting on the wall. It was the portrait of a small, dapper man with an equine nose; his hair was dark and slicked straight back with brilliantine; his ears were large and stuck out too far; dark, bushy eyebrows hovered like rainclouds over sunny eyes; a sinister mustache did not quite hide his winning, foxy smile. One could imagine it to be the portrait of the younger Merlin Trump, but it was, in fact, the likeness of his father, Icarus "Chickette" Trump, who had been ventilated by the Feds during Prohibition.

Chiefie, m'boy, are you thriving? Merlin grasped a corner of the huge, gilded frame and tilted it aside several inches. Hidden behind the picture was a rusty old .45 automatic pistol. Returning the portrait to its original position, Merlin winked at his father and whispered, "Do the best you can, that's all you can do."

He continued up the staircase until he came to another wall decoration, this one a massive architectural rendering of a vast industrial complex. A huge neon sign on the roof of the main building read

Trump Distilleries

and displayed beside it a mammoth bottle of Queen

O'Trump Rye.

"Those people moved," whispered Merlin, his finger to his lips, as he resumed the climb toward his attic workshop.

By the time he'd mounted the final flight and approached the top-floor landing, his daughter was waiting for him outside the work shop door. "Toy Boat, my door-ter," chortled the old man, "are you thriving?"

The woman smiled and nodded. She was thirty-eight years old, and her name was Toy Boat Trump.

"They locked you out, did they?" Her father handed her the morning paper. "Here, hold this, Labor Gang— we'll have 'er open in two shakes of the lamb's tail, as the man said." He took a key from a nail by the door, unlocked the padlock, opened the door and ushered her inside. Then, sticking his head out and peering down the hallway suspiciously, he eased the door shut and secured all three locks.

Toy sat on a barstool, unfolded the newspaper, and laid it before her on the counter. Despite the fact that her long, flaxen tresses were pulled back and tied severely at the neck, she still bore a striking resemblance to Miss Queen O'Hearts, the blonde belly dancer in the poster over Merlin's bed: Her eyes, though devoid of make-up, were just as sensuous and blue; her cheeks, though lacking the rosy blush of the peach, were every bit as cherubic; her lips, though not enhanced by a strawberry hue, were just as moist and impishly bowed. Even her modest house dress, with its neck high collar and ankle-length skirt, could not completely camouflage the lush contours that lurked beneath. One could imagine the poster to be a likeness of a younger Toy Boat Trump, but it was, in fact, a portrait of her mother, who had vanished twenty years ago without a trace.

"Macaroni spa-get." Merlin was puttering around his worktable, preparing for the day's experiment. "Go to 'er, door-ter, my ears are glued."

Toy Boat took up the paper and read the headline out loud:

"CAPITAL PUNISHMENT GETS DEATH SENTENCE"

Merlin inadvertently tipped over an empty cocktail shaker, which clattered on the table top. "Excuse my French." He motioned for his daughter to continue reading.

"Seven months from now, at one minute past midnight New Year's Eve, capital punishment will become unconstitutional in the United States.

"In a special nation-wide referendum yesterday, the controversial new amendment pulled out an unexpected squeaker victory, eking out barely enough votes to gain ratification by the necessary three-quarters majority of the fifty-five states."

Toy paused, listening to a hot-water pipe rattle in the wall; it meant her brother was awake downstairs.

Assuming his daughter's throat to be dry from reading, Merlin left what he was doing and poured her a glass of prune juice. "No charge." The old man returned to his worktable.

Toy took a sip, then continued reading:

"Previous to yesterday's vote, this paper's renowned Straw Hat Poll indicated that nearly seventy percent of American voters are against the abolition of capital punishment. Despite apparent public opposition to the measure; despite opposition by many of this nation's most respected lawmakers; despite the opposition of virtually all United States law enforcement officers and agencies, the bill will become law the first of next year.

"Thus it appears that the earlier, much contested Supreme Court decision has prevailed through yet another public trial. However, the Twenty-Eighth Amendment to the United States Constitution may be destined to become the most unpopular federal amendment since Prohibition."

"Sugar!" Merlin hurried toward her, showing great concern. "You don't tell me? Prohibition again, is it? Golly Neds, we'll have to shut down the factory!" He peered over her shoulder. "Wait till your mother hears about this one. She'll raise the roof."

Toy did not explain to him that the new amendment had nothing to do with Prohibition. She never spoke except when reading directly from the newspaper. Throughout the past seventeen years, she had not uttered a single syllable of her own devising. As far as anyone could guess, Toy Boat Trump was a voluntary mute.

"Seaweed," sighed Merlin, patting her on the top of the head.

"Tighten your belt, door-ter, there's lean years ahead." He squinted at the front page. "What else she say?"

"When informed of the election results late last night, Warden Tully Keyster of the Achen State Penitentiary commented. 'It's a geeking shame.' Keyster, perhaps this country's most outspoken critic of the new amendment, then addressed himself to those young voters who were responsible for killing the death penalty yesterday: 'Bunch of slime-faced punks,' he explained. 'Wait till it's their kids getting raped and murdered'…"

"Read the TV page," Merlin suddenly suggested, "then we'll get the show on the road." He shuffled back toward his worktable, flicking his thumbs out of his fists.

Arthur Trump descended the spiral staircase to the main floor of the Trump mansion. Dressed in a gray DaVinci sweater and Houndstooth-Baskerville slacks, he paused before the suit of black armor his mother had given him over two decades ago, on his twenty-second birthday. A small brass plaque on the exhibit's base read:

> ENGLISH ARMOR, BRUNSWICK BLACK 1413 A.D.
> BLACK ARMOR WAS USED IN BATTLE UNTIL 1413,
> WHEN IT BECAME A SUIT OF MOURNING.

Extracting the daily mail from the iron man's jaws, Arthur looked through the stack of letters and selected three, discarding the rest by raising the armor face mask and shoving them down the black knight's throat. The metal shell was nearly filled with junk mail.

Slipping the three letters into his hip pocket, Arthur proceeded toward the rear of the house, through the dining room, into the pantry and down the cellar steps.

A single bulb splashed eerie light throughout the underground chamber, casting shadow-phantoms everywhere. Arthur paused on the final step and looked around. *Mommy?*

Turning to his right, he moved past the stationary tubs,

the washer dryer, and the hot-water heater, stopping beside the quiet gas furnace. It was a compact heating unit, clean and silent— unlike the sooty, roaring Titan which had stood there in his childhood. Satisfied he was alone, Arthur slipped into the darkness between the furnace and the coal bin. The furnace clicked on; its gas flame erupted quietly and the blue metal pipes began to crackle with heat.

Thirty years ago, these daily expeditions had been much more exciting. Then, this corner of the basement had been the domain of a mammoth coal-eating octopus with an inferno in her belly— a rumbling, slumbering monarch radiating maternal warmth— and the journey into her shadow had been a return to fetal bliss.

In a dark corner directly behind the little furnace, Arthur reached to the concrete floor and picked up an empty glass jar. Unzipping his fly, he fished out his penis, closed his eyes and began to urinate into the vessel, enjoying the delicious feeling of relief which swept over him as he felt the jar turn warm in his hand. To Arthur Trump, a successful urination was like getting away with murder.

Jar in hand, he eased out from behind the furnace and poured the vessel's contents down the floor drain. He rinsed out the jar, returned it to its dark corner, then went back to the sink and washed his hands. Moving toward the north end of the basement, he approached the long workbench standing against the north wall, its pegboard, shelves, and cupboards stocked with an impressive array of hardware and other supplies necessary for the maintenance of the huge Trump mansion. Lifting a flashlight from the workbench counter, he clipped it to his belt then pushed aside an old electric motor which sat on one of the shelves. Behind the motor, the workbench was fixed to the wall by a heavy bolt. Grasping the head of the bolt, Arthur slipped its foot-long shaft from the cinderblock wall and laid it on the shelf beside the motor; then he stepped to the side of the large cabinet and leaned his weight against it. The bench, mounted on hidden trolleys, began to move along the basement wall, exposing a huge iron door concealed behind it. The door was caked with rust and festooned with corroded locks which had not been secured for decades. Arthur grasped its massive iron ring and pulled; slowly, the door swung open on well-greased hinges.

Flashlight in hand, he stepped into the cool, musty darkness behind the iron door. The light darted across long, silent rows of wooden wine racks, down dank narrow aisles paved with cobblestones. The air was tinged with a subtle blend of mold and fermented grapes, though the high oaken racks had long been devoid of bottles. The perfect silence was interrupted briefly by the far-off roar of a subway train rumbling through the bowels of the city.

Closing the door behind him, Arthur bolted it from the inside, then moved to the small wooden desk to the right of the door, where he switched on the desk lamp and set down his flashlight. Circling behind the desk, he took the three pieces of mail from his hip pocket and sat down. Spreading the unopened letters on the desk top, he reached for his pipe rack and selected an exquisitely carved meerschaum, mellowed to a cinnamon hue, which he packed and lit while studying the writing on the three envelopes. Each was directed to a "Mr. Archie Thomas" at the Trump address.

The one Arthur elected to open first had been labeled by machine, its return address a post-office box in New York City. Slitting the envelope, he withdrew the enclosures and perused them one by one. First was a form letter congratulating him on becoming a member of CLUB WHOOPIE— The Correspondence Club for Sexual Sophisticates. His membership included a year's subscription to *WHOOPIE!* magazine, and the current issue was also enclosed.

Arthur leafed through the small publication, which was crammed with provocative photos of lascivious ladies, each accompanied by a carefully worded advertisement appealing for partners in perversion. One photo caught his eye; it depicted a voluptuous vixen, clad only in her honey-blonde curls, her ruby lips wet and pouted, her hands cradling pendulous breasts, offering them to the reader. The ad beneath the photo read:

> Hedonist mother of boy-girl adolescent twins wants help on juvenile discipline from other far-out parents. I want my kids to be as cultured as I am. Diverse instruction encouraged: nudism, Polaroid, French & Greek Arts, bondage, witchcraft— you name it. Our trained German shepherd is VERY FRIENDLY. Husband transvestite. Gay gals & docile men especially welcome. Be discreet first.

Arthur circled the ad with red pencil, then closed the magazine and spun his chair to face the metal filing cabinet behind the desk. Digging his keys from his pocket, he unlocked the cabinet and pulled open the bottom drawer, which was half filled with back issues of sex correspondence magazines, erotica brochures and catalogs, pictures of blondes clipped from nudist publications, and other related material. Stored in the back half of the drawer was a Polaroid color camera, flash attachment and telescoping tripod. Filing the newly arrived periodical, he closed the drawer and turned back to his desk. The second envelope was hand-addressed, from a Ms. Barbara Rosner in California. Carefully he slit the cover and withdrew a handwritten letter, along with two small packets covered with cardboard and tape.

Setting the packets aside, he smoothed the letter out

before him, then stood up. Unfastening his trousers, he slid them down to his ankles, along with his underpants, and tucked his shirttails underneath his sweater; baring himself from the waist down. He lowered himself into his chair again, clasped his half-hard penis and began to stroke it as he read the woman's letter:

Darling Lover Man,

Your fabulous letter was here when I got home from the office yesterday so, I laid right down on the bed and read it. Oh My Darling Archie Baby, your such a hot sexy lover!!! Nobody ever said such fabulous words to me, not even my husband, Steve. Do you really think from my pictures that I am the sexiest most luscious woman, in the Universe ??? Well I am even sexier in person!!!

As I read all those sexy naughty words (I LOVE THEM!!!) telling me all the fabulous things you want to do to me when we get together, I just got so wild and sexy I had to slip my fingers under the legband of my pretty silk panties and, rubbed my little clitty till I came three times!!!

And when I look at the fabulous picture you sent, of your big stiff prick, I get so sexy I could die!!! Right now, I'm writing with one hand and rubbing Miss Clitty with the other ...darn it!!! . ..see what you do to me, you naughty man you!!! (Your really fabulous, though, I was just kidding!!!)

How I wish you were here right now, so that you could stick your fabulous prick in my juicy

quiff and cum deep up inside my nice warm cunny and make me pregnant with a little boy just like you.
Would you like this, Lover???

Please excuse me, Archie dear, but I'm so hot I think that I'm going to cum right now!!!

Arthur's penis loomed at full erection now, and his fist pumped it rhythmically as his eyes glazed and drifted up from the letter, his mind conjuring the woman's image before him. He saw her seated at a writing table, her blonde tresses tumbling down across her fragile shoulders, her sensuous body adorned by a crisp, white c-thru blouse and a soft leather scanti-skirt. Her graceful right hand held a ball point pen, while her left hand crept down to her milky thigh, dipping under the hem of her skirt, snaking beneath the yielding elastic band of her white silken panties and slithering through the honey-downed lips of her gasping quiff. Her hungry gaze was glued to the blurry photograph of a man's naked torso; the man was holding a Polaroid camera, taking his own picture in a full-length mirror; his hips were thrust forward, brandish ing an enormous, unhooded erection. The woman teetered on the edge of a swoon, eyes half shut, tongue lolling between wet strawberry lips; she slouched in her chair, frigging Miss Clitty for all she was worth.

Leaning back in his chair, Arthur continued to stroke his penis with relentless abandon. Swelling ominously, the head of the engorged member blushed deep crimson and began to sizzle with electric ecstasy. At the last possible instant, he forced himself to release his grip, closed his eyes and held his breath until the current dissipated, leaving a dull ache in his glutted testicles. Then, regripping his still rigid organ he began to generate another charge, as Ms. Barbara Rosner's letter continued:

........There, you naughty boy you, made me cum just thinking about you. I just love it when you call me your Queen. But I would still love it if you called me Barbara, or Babs, or just plain Cunt. Please write again real soon and tell me more fabulous things we will do when we meet, of course I would never let you do these things to me, without my husband Steve's permission. If he says will you be glad?

Then we could go up to your place and you could pump me in your bathtub, while I stick my tongue inside your nostrils. Have you ever had this done to you???

Enclosed, please find a pair of my panties I have just been wearing, they are a little wet, thanks to you!!! But, I hope you won't mind. That reminds me, have you been able to find me that pair of rubber panties, I need for my collection??? I hope so.

I hope next time you send more pictures of your hot sexy body and your prick thats nice and hard just for me. And, this time I hope you can get your face in the picture.

Write lots of naughty words and really make me hot, lover, and I'll send you more pictures and maybe come to visit you as a reward. Would this make you happy???

Until next time, write soon, soon, soon!!! cause I LOVE YOU!!!

Love ya,

Babs (Your Queen)

Arthur set the letter aside and opened the larger of the two packets the woman had enclosed, withdrawing a pair of white silken panties. He spread the garment on the desk and gazed with wonder at the light moisture stain in its crotch. Leaning over, he touched his nose to the stiffened spot and sniffed; then he kissed it gingerly.

Turning the panties inside out, he draped them over his pulsating erection, then opened the remaining packet. Inside were three snap shots, which he spread out and scrutinized meticulously, burnishing his penis with the silken garment.

The first showed Barbara Rosner standing in her living room, clad only in her bra, panties, garter belt, stockings and high heels. She gazed provocatively at the camera, hands on hips, golden tresses in erotic disarray, glistening lips pursed and petulant.

In the second photo, the lady languished upon a double bed, sans everything but stockings and garter belt. Her hands were cupped beneath her smallish breasts, and her head was propped up with a pillow, so she could observe the action down below, where her husband, Steve, held her legs spread-eagled, his mouth glued to her wet, sexy cunny.

The final snapshot had also been taken in the Rosner bedroom, this one shot from mattress level, looking from the foot of the bed toward its headboard. Steve Rosner's huge, hairy legs and buttocks were suspended over his wife's smooth, tanned torso. His thighs were planted far apart, her calves draped over them, and her finger tips were dug into his buttocks. Clearly visible was the underside of his thick, slick penis, nearly hilted between the flared, voracious lips of her bursting blonde bush.

Snatching up this photo, Arthur reared out of his seat and pushed the chair away with the backs of his legs, his right fist clasping the white silk panties around his throbbing member. Facing the full length mirror on the wall beside the desk, he began to jerk spasmodically as he whipped his fist up and down on the silk-cloaked organ, urging it to eruption, his impassioned gaze dancing alternately from the photo in his hand to his image in the mirror.

Peering at the photo, he saw his own swollen penis buried to the hilt in that gaping, blonde vortex. With every stroke of his fist he saw the people in the picture move, saw his glistening ramrod ooze out of the sucking lips, then plunge completely home again, pubes grinding mercilessly against pubes, curly brown hairs entwined with moist, blonde ringlets.

In the mirror he saw the woman's silken panties impaled upon his stabbing weapon; he saw her pelvis pumping up and down, pounding his loins sadistically.

He glanced at his face and did not recognize himself, saw only twisted features and tortured eyes, lost, bewildered, crying out God help me, and then The Demon took complete control, pulled the plug, blew his mind, ignited his bowels, shot mini-lightning through his loins. The eyes in the mirror went dead as the helpless creature behind them slipped away, sucked downward through the thundering breast, swept by a blazing torrent that smashed it against the crumbling groin, where it fought in desperation to remain within, lost the tragic battle and was ejected into exile, shot from the body in hot, fierce volleys.

When the nightmare was over, Arthur Trump found himself standing half-naked before a full-length mirror, a pornographic photo in one hand and a pair of soiled panties in the other. Clasped within the moistened woman's undergarment was a pathetic stump of flesh that was part of his own being. He wiped the shriveled member with the garment, then wadded up the wisp of silk and threw it to the floor, quickly hiking up his trousers to hide his shame.

Tossing the photo to the desk top, he grabbed his jet-flame pipe lighter, knelt down and directed a spout of fire at the crumpled silk. The material turned brown, then leapt into blue flame which devoured the garment voraciously, except for the spot that was soaked with squirming sperm. Snatching up a letter opener, he turned the material over to make it burn more completely. Dark, acrid smoke billowed from the smoldering pyre, where half a billion prospective human beings were being ceremoniously exterminated. When the flame died out, he scooped the ashes onto a piece of paper and tossed them into the wastebasket.

Overcome with revulsion, he next pounced on Barbara Rosner's letter, wadding it up and stuffing it into the ash tray on his desk, along with the photos she had sent. He flicked the wheel of his jet-flame lighter and a column of fire shot out two inches in the air. Slowly, he lowered the lighter toward the ash tray. The tip of flame snuck downward, began to nibble at the corner of one photo, turning it slightly brown, and then, reluctantly, he drew the flame away again. Picking up his pipe, he used the fire to relight that instead.

He drew several puffs deep into his lungs, staring at the papers in the ash tray, wanting to destroy them, not wanting to destroy them, and already knowing what he would do. Finally he set his pipe aside, took the photos from the tray, smoothed out the letter and carried the material to the filing cabinet.

Opening the second drawer, he glanced at the labels on the many manila folders filed there. The back portion of the drawer was packed with sex manuals, pornographic novels, blue movies, a water-heated rubber vagina, and a penis-shaped cordless vibrator.

Closing that drawer, he opened the top one, which was completely filled with manila folders. Finding the one labeled BARBARA ROSNER, he opened it up and added her most recent correspondence to the file, which contained all her previous mail, plus carbons of all his letters to her.

The third letter still lay unopened on his desk. Glancing at the return address, he began to open it, then decided to save it for later, slipping it into his desk drawer, which he also locked.

Sinking back into his chair, Arthur puffed on his pipe and gazed into the cool darkness between the wine racks. A subway train rumbled by far away. In the days of Prohibition, this secret cellar had housed the best-stocked private collection in the country. Now, all it held were empty racks and the soundless roar of darkness. This was the dungeon to which Arthur Trump had banished a man named Archie Thomas, for the hideous crime of perversion.

Arthur's pipe went out.

He arose, switched off the lamp, left the wine cellar, replaced the workbench and the long iron bolt, then climbed the stairway to the main floor. Pausing at the dining-room table, he took out a wad of crisp new bills and placed two twenties and ten fives on the table top, the twenties for his sister's household expenses, and the fives for her to slip into their father's cash register.

Then, quietly, he left the house.

"Don'ja be 'fraid, m'boys she said— we back you hup!" Merlin Trump crouched over his laboratory worktable, his bright eyes peering at the clear liquid dripping from the bubbling copper still into a small glass beaker. "First, we douse the fire, if you kindly please. Then we remove the distillate... so!" Lifting the half-filled beaker, he held it up to a ray of sunlight and scrutinized its contents.

His daughter sat at the bar, her pencil poised above the page of a voluminous logbook which contained the chronicle of Merlin's thirty-eight-year search for an alcoholic beverage which would not provoke a hangover.

Merlin watched the sunlight scatter rainbows through the crystal clear alcohol. "This morning," he announced, somewhat grudgingly, "the old Chiefie awoke with a splitting headache."

Toy had the logbook opened to the previous day's experiment. At the bottom of the page, she printed neatly, ENDEAVOR # 12,080 – UNSUCCESSFUL. Turning over to a fresh page, she printed in large letters at the top: ENDEAVOR # 12,081.

"Today's gimcrack," Merlin presented the beaker with a small flourish, "will concern, m'boys she said, a potent but tasty aqua vitae derived from the essence of..." he paused for effect, **"Fo-enugreek!"**

His daughter wrote in the logbook, FENUGREEK WHISKEY. Merlin hurried behind the bar, set out a cocktail shaker and poured the contents of his beaker into it. "Mandalay!" He selected a bottle from the scores that stood behind the bar. "And now, Labor Gang, to handle the Constipation side of the bargain..." he poured a few ounces of golden liquid into the shaker, "Good Old Olive Oil!"

He peered into the silver shaker, then sniffed it gingerly. "She needs a dash of something, or she won't sell." Moving from behind the bar, he carried the cocktail shaker across the room to his supply shelves. "This is going to be tricky, m'boys." Carefully, he began to peruse everything he had in stock.

As she waited for her father to continue his list of ingredients, Toy leafed idly through the logbook, glancing at the previous entries. Those written in her handwriting went back all the way to ENDEAVOR # 5347, an experiment featuring peanut butter and dandelion wine, conducted twenty years ago. Before that, her father had worked alone in his lab, until her mother's disappearance; then Toy had volunteered to come up each day and help him. She had long since given up wondering about the value of his work; it was enough to know she was helping her father, and she felt useful.

The entries at the front of the book had all been logged by her father. She leafed through them with wonder, realizing that the very first endeavor had been catalogued nearly thirty-eight years ago the year Toy Boat was born.

"Honey!" announced Merlin, triumphantly. "That's the ticket!"

He scurried over to his honey rack.

Toy's finger tips gently touched that first page of the logbook. All she really knew about the year of her birth was that it was the year of her father's nervous breakdown. Merlin had not left the Trump mansion in the past thirty-eight years.

"Tasmanian Leatherwood Honey!" proclaimed the old man.

"Your mother's favorite! Hotsy-totsy!"

It always amazed Toy when she realized how little she knew about her parents' lives before her birth. She knew that Merlin's father had been a bootlegger during Prohibition; that he had been killed by federal agents, and that Merlin had inherited the racket. Then he had met Thalia. Toy glanced across the room at the large poster displaying her mother as an exotic dancer. After her parents' marriage, Prohibition had ended and her father had gone straight, building Trump distilleries. During the plant's construction, Arthur had been born; then, five years later, Toy. Merlin's illness had occurred at that time, and the new distillery simply drifted into bankruptcy. What had happened, that year of her birth, to change her father's life so drastically, so tragically? She had never found out, and yet, somehow, she felt responsible.

"Now we're cookin', door-ter, and that's for darned sure!" Merlin came to the bar and peered over her shoulder until he was sure she'd turned back to the day's experiment and had her pencil ready. "Fo-enugreek Whiskey— four ounces. Good Old Olive Oil— two ounces." He watched her write it down. "One tablespoon Tasmanian Leatherwood Honey. One pinch-clove." He opened the little refrigerator behind the bar, withdrew two eggs and emptied them into the mixture. "Two eggs, raw-to settle the stomach."

Toy looked away as he did this, feeling nauseated.

"And… no ice," Merlin instructed her, "…very important." He put the top on the cocktail shaker, shook the mixture expertly, set a hollow-stemmed goblet before his daughter and filled it to the brim. "That'll be eighty-five cents." He rang up the sale on the cash register, took out a five dollar bill and set it beside the drink in front of her.

"Keep the change," he smiled, then drank the cocktail down without pausing for a breath.

"And this," announced the uniformed guide, "is Television Studio 7-A, the largest studio in the BBS Building." The guide waited for his forty followers to file into the narrow room and cluster before the long expanse of glass overlooking the giant hall. "Nicknamed the Granddaddy Studio, it was from here that the late Pietro Scartelli conducted the BBS Symphony Orchestra on the radio more than twenty-five years ago."

The guide strolled behind the tourists as he continued his spiel. "Studio 7-A is a full city block long and three stories high. Because of the subway trains which run beneath the building, the room you are now looking at is actually floating suspended within a bigger room, to keep the studio from vibrating when a train goes by down stairs." He paused behind the tour group and leaned against the back wall, folding his arms across his chest. The name tape on his jacket read NOOGIE.

"The cameras on the studio floor are all color cameras, of course; the pedestal cameras cost seventy-five thousand dollars each, and that dolly unit— the one that looks like it's mounted on a little crane with wheels— is worth well over one hundred thousand dollars."

Corbin paused in his presentation. He had not been paying attention to what he was saying, and now he had no idea what point he had reached in his recital. His attention had been absorbed by one of his tour members, an attractive gentleman in his late forties, who bore a striking resemblance to Corbin's father.

To avoid possible repetition, he skipped ahead several paragraphs. "Some of your favorite programs have originated from this studio, including *Your Sunday Songfest*, *Nippsy Nero's Comedy Hour*, *The Wedding Game—* and, if any of you were watching the election returns on BBS last night, Gunther Bowman and Monty Trent sat right over there in that anchor booth. Down on the studio floor, you can still see the tote board which lists the final vote on the amendment to abolish capital punishment."

Grumbling, the gathering began a brief exchange of opinion on the controversial amendment. Corbin took this opportunity to ease up beside the gentleman in whom he was interested, to study his profile. The man glanced at him and smiled pleasantly. Corbin smiled back and continued his speech, silencing the group. "As you can see, the stagehands are striking the election set right now, and are getting ready to set up one of the most popular shows on television, *The Pastel Penthouse*."

Several females crooned with delight, and everyone rubbernecked more intently at the myriad of personnel and equipment below.

"Don't bother looking for him now, ladies— Art Pastel won't roll in till just before the show tonight." Passing behind the handsome stranger, Corbin lightly brushed the man's buttocks with the back of his hand, as if by accident.

Suddenly he thought of his Aunt Fila. It had been many months since he'd sold her his semen, and he hadn't heard from her since. "Okay, ladies and gentlemen, this way, please. You'll notice along the walls here are pictures of Art Pastel, each marking a milestone in his seventeen-year career with the Blue Broadcasting System. This one shows Art emceeing his very first television show, *Doodle Room*... then we have these photos of him on the set of the *Miss O.K.-U.S.A. Pageant*... and of course *The Pastel Penthouse*. Over here is the dust jacket of his bestselling book, *You Said It, Not Me!*

Now, if you'll just continue along this corridor, folks, we'll pay a visit to TV Master Control."

Corbin fell into step with the man who reminded him of his father. "Where you from?"

"Killeen, Texas," the man drawled. "Up here for the Tin Convention."

"Bring the family along?"

"Naw. I'm a widower, champ."

"I'm sorry to hear that. Say, how'd you like to see The Pastel Penthouse tonight?"

"Why, hell, that'd be terrific. I watch it all the time at home— d'you really think you can fix me up with a ticket?"

"Hell, I'll put you on the Reserve List"— Corbin's voice began to emulate the man's accent— "get you a seat right down front."

"Why, that's real friendly of you, champ! How much do I owe you?"

"Not a cent— the seat's on the house. I'll be working the studio myself tonight, so all you have to do is go to the Main Hall Information Booth no later than ten o'clock, and tell them you're my guest. My name's Corbin Noogie."

"Mine's Cantrell— Wes Cantrell. Mighty obliged to know you." They shook hands. "Tell you what," said the Texan, "if you got some time after the show, I'd be mighty obliged if you'd let me buy you a drink, champ."

"No kidding? Why, that would be just perfect."

Arthur Trump sat in his black and gray Kenita-Delmer sedan, gathering courage to make his move. The auto was parked at the curb in the center of town, and the streets were filled with Wednesday matinee-type women. His auto windows were rolled up, the doors locked.

Across the sidewalk from him sat a gaudy dress shop called Felicity Frocks. There were no dresses in the window, however. Instead, the showcase was festooned with every manner of bizarre undergarment: uplift brassieres, padded brassieres, c-thru brassieres, bras with no tips so the nipples stuck out, pasties which covered nothing but the nipples— some adorned with tassels, others with glass gems. There were black-lace panties with gaping slits at the crotch, panties that left the buttocks exposed, padded panties with foam-rubber hip and buttock expanders; bikinis as small as three bottle caps, c-thru negligees of floral lace, body stockings in erotic designs, lingerie fashioned in every material from lace to leather— in black and scarlet and kelly green, canary yellow, "ultra" violet, electric orange and royal blue; garments adorned with sequins, tassels, rhinestones, beads, ruffles, frills, bows and imitation pearls; fish-net stockings and hi-spike slippers with dear-glass heels. Somewhere in that vast array of frothy female ornamentation, reasoned Arthur

Trump, there was bound to be a pair of rubber panties for Barbara Rosner's collection.

Unfortunately, Arthur could not bring himself to enter the store and make the necessary inquiry. *Hello, maybe you can help me. I need to buy a gag gift for an office party, and I was wondering if you might have a pair of lady's rubber panties in stock.* There were two female customers in the store now; he'd have to wait until they left. *I need a pair of rubber panties for a theatrical production.* The two customers came out of the store and walked down the street. Arthur put his hand on the door handle. *Hello, I'm wondering if you could help me. I have a friend who collects undergarments...* He released the door handle and sat back. He could phone the store instead— or perhaps items could be ordered through the mail. He slipped the key into the ignition, but did not turn it. The store was still empty. Two minutes and it could be over and done with. He took the key from the ignition and put his hand on the door handle.

Two teenaged girls stopped to look into the store window. He put the key into the ignition and started the engine. *Oh. Archie Lover, I've looked everywhere and I just can't find a nice pair of rubber panties.* The girls walked off, giggling. He turned off the engine, took the key from the ignition and put his hand on the door handle. *I wonder if you could help me. My wife's an invalid, you see, and she has to wear rubber panties.*

With a tremendous effort, he swung the car door open and stepped to the sidewalk. Closing the door, he started toward the store entrance. Suddenly, it seemed that everyone on the street was watching him. As he approached the store, he veered off and began walking rapidly along the street. People were staring at him— he knew it. Soon, they would begin to close in on him, and the thought terrified him. In desperation, he turned and darted into the next shop he came to.

Arthur found himself in a rundown antique shop. The long, narrow room seemed crammed from floor to ceiling with tarnished, rusted and dusty relics. Halfway down the aisle, he decided to retreat to the security of his auto again, but when he turned around he found his way blocked by a huge elderly woman with white hair and a hearing aid.

"Can I help you?" she shouted.

"Ah, thanks... I'm just looking," grinned Arthur, helplessly, and he continued toward the rear of the store.

Two female browsers suddenly appeared from behind a pile of debris. Glancing about, Arthur noticed a narrow staircase leading to the second floor. A sign beside it stated LARGER PIECES UPSTAIRS. He ascended the staircase quickly and was relieved to find that there was no one on the second floor. Having proclaimed himself a browser, he felt he now had to spend a respectable length of time looking around before he could leave. He took his pipe from his pocket and put it into his mouth, leaving it unlighted.

The room smelled of antiquity. It was a storage vault for memories, a meeting place for many random pasts, and Arthur felt a mixture of uneasiness and awe— somewhat the same as he felt inside a church. Stacks of furniture, artifacts and oddities lined the room. Slowly, he strolled down the central aisle, pausing before an old carved mantel piece, upon which was set a handmade scale model of a four-masted sailing vessel named the *Tia Melinda*.

He placed a finger to her hull and stroked a bit of the dust away. "Toy Boat," he whispered softly, and smiled. "Toy Boat, Toy Boat, Toy Boat, Toy Boat, Toy Boat."

On Arthur's fifth birthday, Agnes the Maid had taken him down town to see a radio program called *Whose Birthday is Today?* Because it had been his birthday, Arthur had gotten on the show, and the master of ceremonies had played a little game with him.

Arthur, can you say the words "toy boat"?

Toy boat.

Perfect, Arthur! Now then, if you can just say the words "toy boat" five times, very quickly, without making a mistake, we'll give you a real nice prize. Think you can do it?

Uh-huh.

All right... Ready— Set— Go!

Toy boat. Toy boat. Toy boat. Toy boat. Toy boat.

Wow! Listen to that articulation! Little Arthur here is going to make a fine announcer someday, aren't you, Arthur?

Uh-huh.

For his prize, Arthur had been awarded a beautiful miniature microphone, and he had announced into it all the way home: *Good morning, ladies and gentlemen, toy boat, toy boat, toy boat, toy boat, toy boat.*

When he and Agnes had returned home, his father had been on the telephone, talking to the hospital. Arthur's baby sister had been born, right on his birthday, and the hospital wanted to know what name to put on the certificate. *Name, ain't it? What's her mother think?... She don't, eh? Well, then, let's see... we'll call the little lady...*

At that very moment, Arthur had marched past his father announcing into his new microphone: *Toy boat, toy boat, toy boat, toy boat, toy boat.*

Arthur's reverie was interrupted by the distinct feeling that he was being watched. He wheeled about and surveyed the dimly lit room. From the shadows across the aisle, he saw a pair of eyes peering out at him. Two dark eyes, unblinking, pupils blacker than Death, framed in rings of alabaster white and set in the horror of red, raw flesh.

He rolled aside a creaky, ball-and-claw-foot table, edged his way around a gutless grandfather clock and lifted away the corner of a threadbare, faded tapestry.

Before him stood a man: His feet were planted squarely, a shoulder's width apart; his arms were at his sides, held outward slightly from the body; his hands were open, palms facing forward; he seemed to be saying Please. His eyes, so threatening initially, now revealed themselves to be frozen with anxiety. His body was devoid of flesh, devoid of sinew, stripped of every particle of protection. Before Arthur, defenseless, stood the Inner Man.

His bones were sallow ivory; his lungs, metallic blue; his liver looked like half a giant, ripened plum— one end resting on the saffron-yellow bubble of his stomach. Green was his colon— sun bleached, grassy green— and it curved about and held in place the pink, serpentine mass that was his small intestine. And, in the center of his chest, if you bent so you could peer up underneath his rib cage, there beat a heart of cherry red.

Arthur and the man looked at one another a long time.

"Can I help you?" someone hollered.

Arthur turned to see the shop owner wheezing toward him down the aisle, limping.

"Thought you was gonna bring the plaster down on top of me, the way you been movin' everything around up here."

"Sorry if I disturbed you," Arthur blushed. "Ah, could you tell me how much he... this is?"

"Huh? Oh, that. That there's some kinda medical school dummy, or some such animal. I'm gonna hafta have a hundred dollars for that one, y'know.

"Will you accept a check?"

"That's a real, genuine human skeleton, y'know, and those organs are handmade cherry wood, I think— hand-painted, too."

"A hundred dollars certainly sounds reasonable," admitted Arthur. "I'll take it."

"Huh? Well, I paid sixty for it— maybe ten, eleven years ago, and it's been standin' around here takin' up space ever since. Not much demand for these contraptions nowadays, I guess— you a doctor or something?"

Arthur nodded politely. "That's right."

"Yeah? Maybe you could take a look at this knee of mine some time. It..."

"I'm not that kind of doctor, ma'am." Arthur nodded toward the Inner Man. "Does he come apart?"

"Huh? Just leave him set right where he is," shouted the lady, motioning Arthur to follow her downstairs. "My brother'll haul it down and give it a good cleaning for you. These stairs'll be the death of me yet. **Roy! Roy! Where are you?** Never around when you need 'im." She led Arthur to the counter and began filling out a receipt. "You got a car?"

"Why? Don't you deliver?" Arthur became terrified at the thought of having to carry the bizarre creature on the street himself.

"Huh? Hell no, we can't afford it. **Roy!** Damn. Listen— you come back in an hour— we'll have it ready for you then."

Arthur hedged. "I won't be back downtown till after dark."

"We're open till nine o'clock. You say you had a car?"

"Yes. I'll come by this evening, then. Ah, will your brother load it into the car for me? I've got a bad arm."
"I guess," said the woman, looking him over. "You look like a decent young fella." She leaned toward him across the counter and looked at him intently. "Say, ain't I seen you before somewhere?"

"I don't think so." Arthur opened his checkbook. "How shall I make this out?"

"Huh? Might as well make that out to me, Delores Dubitsky, with a 'y.' Say, I know who you look like! You look just like what's-his-name! Oh, hell, I can't think of it— you know who I mean."

"I know," nodded Arthur, embarrassed. "It happens all the time. He's a cousin of mine."

"No lie?"

Arthur tore off the check and handed it to her. "Here you are, Mrs. Dubitsky— I'll be back before nine this evening."

The lady looked at his check. "Okay, Doctor Trump— how come it don't say Doctor on your check?"

"Ah, I'm a Ph.D.," explained Arthur .

"Huh? Well, okay, you drop back later— no hurry, mind. That wooden fella's been waitin' for you fourteen years— another day or two won't make no difference to him."

"Macaroni spa-get!"

Merlin Trump shuffled into the dining room for his evening meal. "Arthur, m'boy she said!" The old man patted his son on the shoulder as he passed.

"Hi, Dad." Arthur was already seated in his place at the foot of the long oaken table. "How are you feeling today?"

"Feelin' good, Chiefie-Weefie. No use complainin', as the man tells us." Merlin gave a toothless grin and winked. He had just emerged from the kitchen, and carried a small paper plate containing a single scrambled egg blanketed with black pepper, a small serving of watery leftover spinach and a piece of whole-wheat toast, burned black. His place was at the head of the table, but he set his plate at one corner instead, and sat down before it, on the very edge of his chair, poised as though he might have to take flight at any moment.

He looked at the kitchen door, waiting for Toy Boat to come in so they could begin eating. Picking up the pepper shaker, he shook another layer of dark grounds over his plate. "Arthur, m'boy, are you thriving?"

"I'm fine, Dad— how's your work coming along?"

"Jim-dandy, m'boy— right on the old beam, and that's for darned sure. Fo-enugreek's the ticket— fo-enugreek and honey, and eggs, and Good Old Olive Oil." Merlin broke his toast in half and set the pieces on his plate. "So to speak ."

He looked at Arthur and winked. "Arthur, m'boy, you're a gentleman and a scholar, and don't forget **that**. You hang on to that job, palsy-walsy. College grad-u-ates are walking the streets. Jobs are scarce, and..." his voice drifted into a stage whisper, **"...stay away from girls.** Listen to your father. Don't have anything to do with them." He paused. "You don't bother much with girls, do you, Arthur?"

"Not much."

"Goood boy. You keep away from them, m'boy. Girls are dirty, Arthur— they pootsy. They go to the bathroom, they make pee-pee and cucky, and they don't wash their hands. So, don't you have anything to..."

The kitchen door swung open and Toy emerged with a tray.

Merlin changed the subject in his usual manner. "Those people moved, Arthur. You know those people across the street? Well, I hear they moved— isn't that right, door-ter?"

His daughter smiled and set the tray in the center of the table. Merlin winked at Arthur and put his finger to his lips.

Arthur had not seen his sister all day. They glanced at one another and smiled shyly.

"Don'ja be 'fraid— we back you hup!" Merlin watched his daughter dish out food for her brother and herself. "Ah, excuse my French," he said, politely, "but did everybody wash their hands?"

Toy and Arthur nodded. Toy handed Arthur his plate, then sat down.

Merlin carefully broke his burnt toast into quarters and placed them back on his plate. "Well, old Labor Gang." He cleared his throat and began flicking his thumb out of his fist, shooting imaginary marbles into the air. Without reaching for their silverware, the three sat quietly for several moments before Merlin ventured once more to break the silence. "Ah, where's your mother, Art?"

"She went out shopping this afternoon," Arthur

answered, matter-of-factly. "She said she might not be home till late this evening."

Toy looked intently at her plate, unblinking.

"What d'you think?" Merlin turned his knife over a few times on the table. He picked up a piece of toast and set it in another position on his plate. "Should we wait for her a bit, or...?"

"Let's eat," suggested Arthur, gently.

Twenty years ago, Thalia Trump had gone to the cellar for a bottle of dinner wine, and had never returned.

On the floor of BBS Studio 7-A, cameraman Bernie Wasno opened the side panel of his color camera and peered into the complex piece of electronic equipment. "Holy fuck." Closing the panel, he crossed the busy studio floor and mounted the iron staircase leading to the 7-A control room.

Inside the control room, Wasno found Technical Director Gene Russelton chatting with Ralph Goliones, Stage Manager of Pastel Productions. "Hey, Gene," the cameraman announced casually, "my camera's fucked up."

The tech director swiveled in his chair to face him. "Would you care to be a bit more specific?"

"No image, no readings-zilch."

Russelton swiveled toward his control panel; Monitor Number Three did not show a test pattern. He reached out and punched up Camera Three. Immediately, the Master Monitor went black as well. "Check the I-O?"

"Gotta be worse than that," drawled Wasno. "Couple of the components are brown— you know, the circuits are all scorched." Ralph, the stage manager, listened to the men's conversation with growing concern.

"Kee-ryst," he sighed, putting down his coffee cup, "that's the dolly camera."

"Better call Engineering," suggested the cameraman.

Russelton climbed to his feet. "I better take a look at it first." He followed the cameraman to the doorway, then stopped and looked back at Goliones. "Where's Monteczuma?"

The stage manager glanced at his watch. "Should be here any time now."

"He better be. This could be trouble."

Ralph Goliones watched through the control room window as Russelton and Wasno descended the iron staircase and moved to ward the crippled camera. "Camel shit," he whispered. *More grief*. He watched a young man climb the metal staircase and poke his head through the control room doorway.

"Pardon me, but do you know where I can find Roland Monteczuma?"

"He's not here yet," said the stage manager. "Do you expect him soon?"

"What d'you want him for?"

"My name's Neal Kroutch. I'm supposed to start work here today."

"Well, pull up a chair. Rolly'll be along pretty soon."

"Thanks." Kroutch sat in the tech director's chair.

Goliones continued to gaze toward the studio floor. "You must be Pastel's new lackey."

"Personal Assistant," the young man corrected.

Ralph suddenly looked at Kroutch with fear: Maybe the kid was one of Pastel's relatives or something. "You know Art Pastel?"

"No, I haven't met him yet."

The stage manager breathed easier. "Who hired you?" "Mr. Monteczuma."

Ralph looked back toward the studio floor and shook his head. "You poor son-of-a-bitch."

"Why do you say that?"

Goliones watched a burly stagehand tromp up the staircase toward the control room. "What kinda job you have before this?"

"I just graduated from Southwestern, with a degree in Radio and Television."

"You poor son-of-a-bitch."

The stagehand stuck his head through the doorway. "Tell Pastel not to fuck around with his chair too much."

"What chair?" asked Ralph.

"The one on stage."

"What's the matter with it?"

"One of the legs is cracked."

"So get another chair."

"Can't."

"Why not?"

"Our dinner break starts in two minutes."

"Do it after your dinner break."

"Can't."

"Why not?"

"The warehouse'll be closed."

Goliones walked over and stood before the husky stagehand. "You mean to tell me that in the middle of the show tonight, Pastel's chair might **fold**— with him in it?"

"It'll probably be okay. Just tell 'im ta take it easy."

"Yeah?" The stage manager ran his hand through his hair. **"Who's** gonna tell him to take it easy? You?"

"That's not my job, pal."

Ralph began to pace the floor. "Kee-ryst! Pastel's gonna blow his fuckin' gourd, man!"

The stagehand shrugged his shoulders. "Tough shit." He looked at his watch. "I gotta go, I'm on my dinner break."

"Goddamn it!" Goliones erupted. **"What am I supposed to tell Pastel?"**

"Tell 'im to go suck himself," suggested the stagehand, as he lumbered off to dinner.

Goliones continued pacing. "Kee-ryst!" He found himself looking down at Kroutch's anxious face. "You wanna know why you're a poor son-of-a-bitch? 'Cause **you're** the one who's gonna tell Pastel about his chair! And I'm a poor son-of-a-bitch because I gotta tell him about that fucking camera! We're both poor son-of-a-bitches—" he pointed toward the doorway where the stagehand had stood—" but not **that** lucky motherfucker! He belongs to a goddamned **union**! You and me, we belong to Assholes Incorporated!" Ralph still pointed toward the doorway, where a tall black man had magically appeared.

The black man clamped a slender cigar between his teeth and smiled."I see you've begun orientation on our new staff member."

"Rolly! Jesus Christ, am I glad you're here!"

"Problems?" He extended his hand toward the young man. "Hello, Neal."

Kroutch stood up. "Nice to see you again, Mr. Monteczuma."

"Problems?" complained the stage manager. "I'll say we got problems! A camera's on the fritz, Pastel's chair's all fucked up—"

"What's the matter with the camera?" asked Monteczuma.

"Shit, we don't know for sure, yet— Gene's lookin' at it now— but the stagehands tell me they can't replace Pastel's chair before air!"

"It's broken?"

"One of the metal legs is cracked, and it's liable to go at any—"

Gene Russelton strode into the control room, his face ashen.

"Camera Three's kaput. I just hope we can fix it before air."

Monteczuma glanced at the monitors. "The dolly blew?"

"Yeah," sighed the tech director. "If it was one of the other units, we could replace it— but this is the only dolly in the building." He picked up the telephone and dialed three numbers. "Hello, Engineering? This is Studio 7-A. We got an emergency camera problem— get somebody up here, pronto, okay?"

"Kee-ryst," sighed Ralph Goliones. "My ass is had."

Monteczuma was wearing a pullover sweater and tie; he shucked off the tie and unbuttoned his collar. Sinking back into his chair at the control board, he pursed his lips about his small cigar and shot a column of blue smoke into the air. "Gene, you and your boys get to work on that camera right away. Do the best you can, okay?"

"Right," said the tech director, darting from the control room.

Monteczuma looked at Neal Kroutch. "Neal, find yourself a copy of the yellow pages and dig up a metal-working shop that'll send someone over to spot-weld that chair before air." He pointed at a desk near the end of the control room and Kroutch headed toward it. Monteczuma locked his fingers behind his head and squinted at Ralph through the smoke from his cigar. "Let's run the dress with just two cameras and try to rough out an alternate shooting script as we go along. That'll be better than playing it by ear if we can't fix Number Three by air time."

"Yeah," muttered Ralph. "Jesus Kee-ryst, yeah, okay Rally, what ever you say. Same time for dress?"

"We'll run the dress at eight-thirty instead of nine, if you can rustle everybody together." Ralph bolted for the doorway and Monteczuma called him back. "Don't get uptight. I'll handle Pastel, if necessary— okay?" A look of relief swept over the stage manager's face. "Okay, now shag ass."

Monteczuma swiveled around to face the control board. The Number Three Monitor was black. He picked up his mouthpiece and announced, "Everyone please be advised that dress rehearsal will now take place at eight-thirty instead of nine o'clock. All crew chiefs and department heads report to the control room, please— panic stations, as usual." He put down the headset, glanced at the clock, shook his head and smiled.

It was the beginning of another routine Wednesday evening for Roland Monteczuma, Show Director for Pastel Productions.

11

Arthur Trump stood before the full-length mirror in his bedroom. He wore a green mohair jacket, black silk shirt and trousers, black shoes and a white silk tie. Protruding from his breast pocket was a black silk handkerchief, which he arranged carefully for several moments before plucking it out and replacing it with one of white silk.

Stepping close to the mirror, he smiled broadly, examining his teeth to make certain no foreign matter was trapped between them. Satisfied, he left the room and started downstairs.

Near the bottom of the spiral staircase, he met his sister coming up. Their eyes did not quite meet as they nodded and smiled awkwardly. "Well, I'm off," ventured Arthur.

Toy smiled again and nodded, gazing at the steps before her.

Continuing quickly to the main landing, Arthur pivoted around the banister and crouched at the side of the black suit of armor. Peering over the metal shoulder, he gazed at his sister as she moved away up the staircase.

Despite the high collar she always wore, the long sleeves, the full skirt that reached well below her knees, the low-heeled shoes— despite the modesty of her attire, she could not hide the fact that she had her mother's body.

She moved like a dancer, with natural grace, and as she mounted each step, her hips undulated with hypnotic sensuality.

As she continued her ascent, Arthur knelt lower and looked beneath her skirt. She wore no stockings; her calves were straight and full and smooth, and flawless white; the backs of her knees were deliciously hollowed; her thighs were firm and supple and ripe, and seemed to glow from within with a pale, white light.

She vanished round the staircase curve, and Arthur remained crouched on the floor beside the hollow metal man. Something sizzled in the center of his chest, and he found it difficult to breathe. His penis began to swell, tangling itself in his bright cotton britches. He looked at his watch. It was too late to visit the cellar, so he pulled himself together and quietly left the house.

The small desk lamp clicked on in the basement wine cellar. Its feeble light groped through the somber darkness, casting the dim shadow of a woman on the stone wall. An unlighted pipe protruded from the woman's mouth.

Holding her brother's meerschaum pipe gently between her teeth, Toy crept behind his desk and settled lightly in his chair, just as she did every Wednesday evening after Arthur left for work. Her hands reached out un-commanded, caressing the smooth desk top, touching the things his hands had touched. She did not smell the damp and musty scent that filled the room; she just smelled Arthur there— the hint of licorice that marked his special blend of pipe tobacco, the subtle spirit of his cherry cologne.

She swiveled round in his chair and let her gaze caress the filing cabinets behind the desk. She took his pipe from her mouth and brushed its bowl against her cheek, as she'd seen him do so many times. Carefully she set it down in the exact position she had found it. Leaning toward the filing cabinets, she took hold of one of the drawer handles and slowly pulled it. It was locked, as usual. The desk drawers were locked as well.

What was stored inside these drawers? She had never had a glimpse within, and yet she had decided long ago that Arthur's work down here had something to do with solving the riddle of their mother's disappearance. These drawers were full of clues, she thought. Arthur was conducting his own investigation, and someday the mystery would be solved.

If only she could help him— remember some crucial, forgotten fact; but it was no use— she knew she could not. Despite the twenty years that had gone by, the day their mother vanished was still minutely detailed in Toy's mind; but details added no illumination to the basic facts:

It was the summer of her eighteenth year, June 29th, a Thursday, and it was raining. Arthur was away in the army. Merlin puttered in his workshop during the day. Toy was helping Agnes in the kitchen when her mother returned from shopping, wet and in an awful mood. Thalia complained bitterly about the bills in the mail, and her dwindling bank account; she expressed exasperation at Merlin's weird behavior, and chided Toy for not going out with boys; she called their home a "mausoleum," from which she longed to get away— to Europe, perhaps, or South America— though God knew where she'd get the money. Depressed and disgruntled, she went down to the cellar to select the dinner wine, and never returned.

Thalia Trump had vanished from their lives in a single, shattering instant— a completely meaningless occurrence, so incredible, so unexpected, that suddenly it seemed that she had never really existed at all— except to Merlin, of course, who was still not aware that she was gone.

To Arthur, who had not been informed about the disappearance until his discharge from the army two months later, the mysterious happening must have appeared even more unreal. And so, Toy reasoned, each day he came down to this room, the room from which their mother had vanished, and tried to find the door that wasn't there, the secret passageway between two walls, the trap door that swung open into nothingness, the hidden set of stairs that led to— where? His eyes, his finger tips had memorized this room each stone, each stick of wood, the depths of every crack that might just lead to the void that once had swallowed up a human being. Was he getting closer to the answer? Had he found it already? His desk and files had always been closed to her. Leaning over, she peered into his wastebasket, which contained nothing but the remnants of a burnt rag. All she ever found in there were charred remains.

And what was the full-length mirror for? She didn't like mirrors much.

Easing herself out of his chair, she set it back in the exact position she'd found it, so he would never know his private sanctuary had been violated.

Things could have been so different between her and Arthur; they could now be sharing secrets, talking to one another, loving one another like normal siblings. But no, seventeen years ago she had gone and ruined everything.

Now they'd be strangers forever.

Kee-ryst, is he gonna be pissed. Ralph Goliones huddled in the dark freight entrance to the BBS Building, dragging nervously on a cigarette. *That goddamn camera don't get fixed for air, he's gonna blame me sure.*

Each Wednesday, at precisely nine p.m., the stage manager waited downstairs for Art Pastel's arrival, to drive his auto to the parking garage. Each week, the star arrived at a different entrance; tonight, Ralph had been instructed to be at the freight entrance. No one but Roland Monteczuma, Ralph and Art Pastel was privileged with this information; severe security precautions were necessary because of Pastel's neurotic fear of people.

Ralph gazed at the luminous dial of his watch. *Nine-fifteen. Where the fuck is he?* He eased his head out of the shadows and peered up the street; Pastel's auto was not in sight. He then surveyed the sidewalk, making certain no reception committee lay in ambush. *All I need's those fuckin' Animals to show up. He'd have my ass for sure.*

One particular group of fans made it their lifework to haunt the studio entrances, hounding the stars for everything from autographs to handouts. Such characters were known as "Eighty-Sixes" to BBS personnel; in Studio 7-A they were affectionately referred to as "The Art Pastel Fan Club"; Ralph Goliones called them "Animals"; Art Pastel called them "freaks." These people had learned by experience that Ralph was the key to Art Pastel's arrival point. Thus, the stage manager was left with the difficult task of remaining out of sight from the street, while at the same time watching the street for his boss's arrival.

He lurked in the darkness, sucked on his cigarette and watched pedestrians pass by, feeling like some kind of pervert in an alleyway. *Well at least the son-of-a-bitch chair is fixed. I don't know how Rally does it. That son-of-a-bitch is made of iron. Eleven years he puts up with this shit— I been here two and it seems like a miracle.*
With the exception of Monteczuma and Goliones, no one had ever worked for Art Pastel as long as two years before getting fired.

He poked his head out and peered up the street. Still no sign of Pastel's car. As he withdrew into the shadows once again, he heard a ghoulish giggle drift from somewhere down the street. His heart stopped. "Oh, for Jesus Kee-ryst Almighty, **no**." He tossed his cigarette away and jogged toward the origin of the sound.

"Hiya, Ralphie."

Goliones froze. Huddled out of sight beneath a portico was a group of five grinning Eighty-Sixes. "Oh, Jesus God," he sighed, glancing nervously up the street. "Goddamnit, you Animals get the hell outta here before I call a cop!"

The group grinned back at him complacently. Two of its members were over eighty years old— gaunt little ladies, one black, one white; the BBS Staff had nicknamed them "Chocolate and Vanilla Granny."

"Beat it!" shrieked the stage manager.

"It's a free country," cackled Chocolate Granny.

"And we're a citizen," Vanilla Granny added, "so fuck off, Ralphie boy."

I'm dead, thought Ralph Goliones. Frantically he dug out his wallet. "I'll give you son-of-a-bitches five bucks to drag your asses outa here!"

"How 'bout a ticket for the show, Ralphie?" cooed Fat Suzie, a sleazy, pasty-faced fat girl with yellow teeth.

"Where's Nastel?" A tall man with a harelip and tiny close-set eyes waved a notebook in the air. "I wanna get Nastel's john henry."

The last member of the group was a pudgy teen-age boy with lifeless eyes and a huge portable radio propped upon his shoulder, blasting boulder music in his ear. The boy giggled ghoulishly.

The stage manager snatched a twenty from his wallet. Suddenly, Vanilla Granny poked a gnarled finger up the street. "Here he comes!"

Ralph spun as if punched, just in time to see the black-and-gray sedan cruise by and pull up to the building. Desperately he sprinted toward the car, hearing the vultures flap along behind him. The weird pack of curious creatures leapt, limped and waddled down the sidewalk, like an attack force from Hell.

"Shag ass!" Ralph spat over his shoulder. Running backward, he emptied his wallet and held all his money out to them.

Art Pastel was already out of his car by the time his stage manager arrived to open the door. The star's face was masked with fear as he watched the gang of ghouls descend upon him, their faces laced with sleazy grins.

"Jeez, Mr. Pastel," Ralph panted, "I'm awful sorry— I dunno how they found out, honest to God I don't!" He held out his hands palms skyward. "I was just tryin' to chase them away!"

Pastel's steel-gray eyes riveted Goliones to the pavement.

"Hiya, Artie!" Fat Suzie tried to paw the star's sleeve with flaccid fingers.

Pastel jerked his arm away. "Keep your rancid sweat off me." He strode toward the building.

Chocolate Granny followed close on his heels. "How 'bout a ticket for the show, sonny boy?"

"Two! Two tickets!" rasped Vanilla Granny. "You got Toby Tyler on t'night! I wanna see 'im!"

Ralph wedged himself between the star and the Eighty-Sixes, shouting, "Leave 'im be, will ya?" Seeing Vanilla Granny grab for Pastel's coattail, he delivered a sharp karate chop to the old woman's arm.

"Yow!" howled Granny. **"You keep your fuckin' paws offa me, you rat-assed bastid!"**

Dead Eyes listened to his portable radio and giggled ghoulishly. "This way, Mr. Pastel, sir," said Goliones.

Pastel motioned him out of the way. "Park the car, greaser." His voice trembled with emotion. "You're washed up." As he reached the doorway, a tattered notebook was thrust before his face.

"Hey, Nastel," said Harelip good-naturedly, "how 'nowt givin' nee your ol' john-henry?"

Pastel ducked away from the dirty pages. "I don't sign my name for freaks." He bolted through the doorway out of sight.

His fan club tried to follow him, but its path was blocked by a security guard.

Mummy-like, Ralph plodded toward the sleek auto,

with Vanilla Granny in hot pursuit. **"Nearly busted my fuckin' arm!"** she screeched, holding the assaulted appendage in her other withered hand. **"Where's the Pigs?"** She peered up and down the street. **"Call the Pigs! I'll see your ass rots in the box, you rat-assed woman beater, you!"**

The stage manager climbed into the car, gunned the engine and wheeled Pastel's auto round the corner toward the parking garage. His hands were shaking. "He didn't fire me. He was just pissed, is all. Rolly'll take care of things—he'll know what to do. Those Christ forsaken leeches. I hope I busted the bitch-whore's arm. It'll be okay, if I can just get that camera fixed for air."

Suddenly, Ralph was aware of someone sitting beside him. "Jeesus!"

Swerving the auto wildly, he jammed his foot on the brake, causing the man beside him to flop forward and strike his head on the padded dashboard. "Kee-ryst!" Ralph reached over to help the man sit up again.

He froze at the touch of the cold hard figure. Waves of fear washed over him. He sat the man upright on the seat, where he was bathed in the pink light of a street lamp. "I'll be Jesus Christ! It's some kinda goddamn dummy! A goddamn body without no skin!"

Ralph Goliones breathed a sigh of relief. The Inner Man was not a threat to him.

In his plush office, Art Pastel stood in the center of the room, sucking on a cigarette and gnawing the cuticle of his little finger as he solemnly studied the large poster cards propped against the sofa on the floor before him. He scowled and searched his fingers for another shred of skin to tear at. "Christ shit!" He paced the room several times, then strode to the door and yanked it open. **"I want Monteczuma!"** he bellowed into the quiet hallway. **"Now!"** Crashing the door shut, he paced about frenetically until he heard a quiet knock. **"Get your ass in here!"**

The door opened slowly and a young man stood uncertain on the threshold.

Pastel backed away defensively. "Who the Christ are you?"

The young man swallowed hard. "I... I'm Neal Kroutch, sir your new assistant."

"Well, what the Christ do you want, boy? Where the hell is Monteczuma?"

"He's running... He told me to tell you he's rehearsing the run-through and could I take care of whatever you wanted." Kroutch twisted his college class ring and felt tiny blooms of perspiration burst upon his forehead.

Pastel leaned his fists upon the desk top and lowered his head, speaking toward his brown desk blotter. "You know what you can do for me, boy? **You can stay out of my Christing way. That's your job around here— to stay the Christ out of my sight— because the next time I so much as see your ass, I'm gonna shit-can it, is that clear?"**

"Yessir!" Tears filled Kroutch's eyes.

"Now get lost!" Pastel suddenly lunged around his desk and kicked the first poster card with all his strength. It careened across the room and chopped into the young man's knees, sending him hopping backward into the hall. **"And take these goddamned cue cards with you!"** The star booted another card; it flipped into the air, half-torn, and flopped to the carpet, face down. "Shit!" shouted Art Pastel. "These... jokes... are... **shit!"**

The assistant glanced desperately up and down the hallway, trying to decide whether to bolt or pick up the scattered cards. With a lunge that sent Pastel retreating behind his desk, Neal re-entered the office and darted about, gathering mutilated cards, pawing at the moisture which blurred his vision, and sniffing loudly.

Pastel ignored him, pouring himself a tumblerful of gin and downing half of it before he heard the door close behind him and footsteps scamper away down the hall.

An overwhelming fatigue settled over the star, forcing him to sink into his upholstered chair and close his eyes. He yawned widely, took several deep breaths, then hammered his fist on the arm of the chair several times. Sitting up, he opened his desk drawer, removed a small vial, popped two green-and-black capsules into his mouth and washed them down with a swig of gin straight from the bottle.

Sitting back, he became inert once more, then yawned again, feeling a slight cramp beginning to gnaw at his intestines.

The house had stood for more than a century, providing shelter for three full generations of the family. Now, as Toy Boat Trump, current mistress of the quiet mansion, moved with feather footsteps through the dimly lighted rooms, she realized that she was not alone. As she tiptoed across the faded splendor of the living-room rug, transparent figures stepped aside to let her pass: second-rate ancestors who could not afford the luxury of reposing within golden frames upon the wall.

Quietly she padded up the spiral staircase, remembering the time Arthur had opened the bottom banister pole for her and showed her the rusty shotgun concealed within. All the windows of the house were glazed with bulletproof glass; the doors were lined with armor plate; there was an arsenal hidden behind the library shelves; the ping-pong table in the game room contained a hideaway roulette wheel. The entire mansion was a relic from the days of bootleg bourbon and bathtub gin.

As she reached the top of the stairs, moved along the balcony and down the hallway toward the master bedroom, the house grew uneasy about her. Heating ducts popped and crackled, water pipes thumped and grumbled at her passing and the floor boards murmured beneath her feet.

Silently she stood before the master bedroom. Far

away overhead, an object thudded and rolled across the wooden attic floor, the sound drifting down as though from another world.

She laid her hands upon the mahogany door, then closed her fist around its polished brass knob. The old house held its breath. She turned the knob, eased the huge door open, and stepped into the fragrant aura left there by a woman named Thalia Trump.

Ralph Goliones mounted the stairs two at a time and stumbled into the 7-A control room. "Rolly! Kee-ryst, am I in deep shit!"

Monteczuma was munching on a sandwich. "Yeah?"

"Pastel just canned my ass! Those fuckin' Animals jumped him downstairs, so he shit-canned me! What the Christ am I gonna do, Rolly?"

"I'll talk to him."

"Would ya? Jesus, thanks Rolly— I'd appreciate it!" The stage manager looked at the control board, and his face paled again. "Camera Three's still dead?"

"That's right."

"Shit, man, then so am I."

The show director took a swig of coffee. "Look, Ralph, that camera's not your responsibility, it's mine. Now, why don't you stop shitting your pants and get down to the studio floor so we can finish this run-through?"

"Yeah, sure, Rally— thanks, thanks a lot!" Ralph left the control room and started down the stairs, bumping into the Musical Director, Ulloch Tugg.

"Vut ees?" The bandleader stood at attention before him, wiggling his little mustache in annoyance. "We 'hearse? We not 'hearse? I'm not having all night, keed."

"Yeah, yeah," said Ralph. "Get back on the floor, Ulloch — we'll pick it up right away."

Tugg spun about and marched down the stairs like a wooden soldier, his metal cleats clacking on the iron staircase. "Son... beech... bastar."

Crossing the studio floor, the stage manager noticed Neal Kroutch, with cue cards under his arm, wandering about as though in a trance. "Hey, Kroutch, get your ass in gear. We got a run-through to finish and—" Ralph looked closely at the young man's face. "Jesus, fella, you look like you just sat on a high-tension wire— your lips are blue!"

Kroutch ran a trembling hand through his hair. "Oh, boy — what am I gonna do, Mr. Goliones? Mr. Pastel just raked me over some thing fierce. Oh, boy— I mean, he really hates my guts!"

"Yeah? Well, welcome to the club, kid."

Kroutch's eyes were red-rimmed, his face ashen. "I mean, he told me to stay out of his sight! How can I be a man's personal assistant if I have to stay out of his sight? And he— boy, was he hacked about the opening monologue, and he..."

"And he kicked the cue cards all over the goddamn room." Kroutch looked wide-eyed. "How'd you know?"

Goliones pointed to his cheekbone. "See this scar? It's from a flying cue card."

The young man looked in awe. "No kidding?"

"Shit, I wish I had a dime for every cue card I've dodged in that mother's office." Goliones started walking Kroutch toward the cam eras.

"Holy Jeez, though-d'you think he's gonna fire me?"

"Did he say you were fired?"

"Well, no, but..."

"Then don't sweat it. You just had a little operation, is all. You'll be okay."

"Operation?"

"Sure. Pastel just tore you a new asshole. I got another one myself today. Guess I got about fifty assholes by now." He patted the youngster on the back. "C'mon, you got to stand in for shit-face Pastel while we finish the run-through."

"But, what about these cue cards?" Kroutch held them out anxiously.

"Let the writers worry about them— you've seen enough action for one day." The stage manager looked at the Number-Three Camera, dismantled on the studio floor, and shook his head. "If assholes wuz purple hearts, we'd all be Audie Murphys."

The smell of sweet, red strawberries. That's what the first breath was always like in her mother's room. Toy Boat closed the door with reverence and stood within the shrine. Fresh cut strawberries and heavy cream— that's what her mother had always been to her, just as her father was the scent of sweet whiskey and brilliantine.

Eagerly, the other senses rushed to satiate themselves. Her eyes were dazzled by the beauty of lavender silk and gossamer lace; her hands reached out to revel in the wonder of things smooth and cool, things soft and quick to warm; and her mouth— her fingers fluttered to her mouth as she tasted a pungent memory.

She stood before her mother's vanity table. Beside it sat a walnut chest which held the clothes Thalia Trump had worn when she was "The Queen." When Arthur and Toy were very small, they were sure their mother had really been a queen, and often she let them come up and watch her don her royal robes, and she had danced for them. But as they'd grown into their teens, the queen had held court for them no longer, so Arthur had taken to peeping at her through the keyhole, and Toy had watched him from her room across the hall. And then the queen had vanished. Toy, the golden-haired princess, had turned eighteen, looking so much like a young Thalia that she couldn't help but wonder what she'd look like in her mother's finery. So she had snuck up here, opened the walnut chest, peeled off her clothing, and dressed herself in the awesome, exotic costume of a belly dancer.

The adventure had proved so wonderful she'd returned there very often, and soon she'd begun to dance just like her mother, watching herself with wonder in the mirrored wall, hoping her brother was crouched outside, peeping through the keyhole.

For three whole years she had dressed and danced in her mother's room, breathless with the thought that Arthur might be watching, but never knowing if he was or not.

And then, one day in spring, she had suddenly found out.

Art Pastel sucked savagely on his cigarette and pulled the smoke deep into his lungs. The inhalation turned into an expansive yawn, his mouth gaping widely, his head rolling far back on his shoulders. His neck was sore and stiff with tension; his eyelids were heavy, and all he wanted to do was sleep.

His watch told him it was just nine-thirty-one hour before air.

Leaning far back in the soft chair, he rested his head and closed his eyes. Automatically, his hand moved up his trouser leg and squeezed the bulge of his genitals. Opening his eyes, he glanced across the room to make sure the door was locked; then he unzipped his fly and dug out his flaccid penis. Stroking it gently, he watched as it rose to full erection; then he stood up, unfastened his trousers and pulled them off, along with his underpants, draping the garments neatly over the back of the chair. He took off his jacket and hung it on a hanger by the door; then, tucking his shirttails up under his undershirt, he stood naked from his waist to his shoes.

Quietly, he tiptoed across the carpet toward the door leading to his private dressing room. Dropping to his knees before the closed portal, he turned the knob slowly and eased it open just a crack. The room was dark and empty. On his hands and knees, he crawled inside. Careful not to make a single sound, he climbed up on a straight-backed chair, then mounted the counter of his make-up table. Lifting the chair from the floor, he placed it on the counter and stood upon its seat.

This brought his head just even with the foot-square grille of a ventilator mounted high on his dressing-room wall. Peering through this metal grille, Art Pastel looked down into the dressing room of his all-girl dance troupe, the Penthouse Pixies.

All ten of the young dancers were in the dressing room, getting ready for the show. All had long, blonde, curly hair. The room was filled with chatter; some of the women applied their make-up, others fixed their hair; all were in various states of disarray— some dressing, some undressing, others simply lounging about, half-nude.

Art Pastel's dry tongue rasped across his parched lips. With one hand he clasped a water pipe to steady himself; with the other he clasped his erect penis and began to pump it slowly, his eyes devouring the creamy feast below. Sweeping his gaze across the sea of golden waves, silken flesh and delicious strawberry lips, he finally riveted his attention upon one luscious creature who was facing his way, apparently withdrawn into a reverie as she slipped out of her street clothing and prepared to don her dance costume. Shucking off her blouse, she reached up behind to unhook her bra, her tongue protruding from the corner of her scarlet mouth.

Pastel pressed his face against the metal grille and held his breath, waiting for the garment to fall away.

Watching herself in her mother's mirror, Toy Boat slowly let the bra straps slide from her shoulders. Holding her hands beneath the pink, silken cups, she slowly lowered them away from her chest, unveiling the perfect twin globes of her milk-glass breasts. Now they had begun to sag a tiny bit with age, but they had certainly been flawless that day when she was twenty-one and Arthur twenty-six. Unfastening her skirt, she slowly let it slip downward across her softly rounded hips, her supple creamy thighs, to lie in a heap at her delicate feet. All she now wore was a pair of pink bikini panties.

Her hands moved up across her smooth, flat belly, cupped the luscious ripeness of her honeydew breasts. Looking past her graceful image in the mirror, she watched the tiny keyhole in the door across the room. Smoothing her hands down over her rib cage, she dipped them beneath the pink silk waistband, and paused before delivering the ultimate revelation.

Art Pastel's body began to tremble violently and his breath erupted in convulsive jerks as he watched the blonde Pixie slide her dainty panties down, revealing her gorgeous mound of Venus.

A strangled whine squeaked from his aching throat as he pressed his face harder to the grille, thrust forth his hips and pumped his turgid penis with desperate urgency.

The dancer stepped out of her panties, straightened up and pensively assessed herself in the mirror. Her body was awesome, flawless; she was a golden-tressed goddess, to be worshiped and adored. Pleased with her aspect, the lady smiled. Then she picked up the bottom portion of her costume and began to step into it.

The costume was of Turkish design, quite similar to that worn by a belly dancer.

Toy Boat was twenty-one again.

Natural, naked and glorious, she stood before the mirrored wall and tossed her honeyed curls across her ivory shoulders, a golden waterfall splashing over milk-stone rocks.

He was there, watching. She knew it. She had seen the door move.

Her naked breasts rose and fell rapidly; her nipples were hard and pointy; her heart pounded away at her breast bone, as though trying to find a way out of her body. She felt dizzy, giddy, scared, euphoric. Would she faint? Would she dance? Should she laugh? Should she cry?

She pirouetted before the mirror, arched her back and let her hair swing out behind her; in front her breasts thrust outward, as did her luscious honey mound.

Dipping down, she raised the lid of the walnut chest. She plucked up a lavender-and-gold gossamer costume. Turning toward the mirror, she held the garment up to her body and examined her reflection. She began to hum, and her supple body swayed. The garment seemed to cling to her of its own volition, as her hands danced over her ribs like fragile moths, fluttering to her downy breasts, and there they lit, as though attracted by a flame. Her face lifted, turned toward the ceiling and her flaxen curls cascaded down her back. She stepped, she swayed, and slowly turned until she faced the open door-and then she froze.

A mad, desperate creature came crawling toward her across the lavender carpet. Terrified, she shrunk back toward the dressing table, clutching the scanty costume to her breast.

Oh!

Her brother scuttled to her feet, his eyes wild, wide and pleading, his mouth opening and closing convulsively, emitting a strangled squeak from his constricted throat.

His icy fingers entwined about her ankles and slithered up the insides of her legs. She heard a voice that sounded like her own gasp *No, no Artie... please*.

She thrust out her hands to push him away, and the gossamer costume tumbled from her breast, fluttering over her brother's head as he pressed his face against her churning belly.

Oh no... oh, please, no...

Her legs snapped shut and pinned one of his probing hands between her knees, while his other hand tobogganed along the frozen slope of her body, up over her hips, across her rib cage and plunged into the bank of her swinging, spongy breast.

Oh!

Her hands came up to peel the kneading fingers away; her knees relaxed, and suddenly his other hand darted upward, capturing the golden fleece.

Oh, God!

Her legs collapsed from under her and she slumped against him, watching her mother's costume fall away from his face as he darted upward, his voracious mouth engulfing one of her swollen, hard nipples.

Oh, please.

Welded together, they sank to the carpet, her hands flopping helplessly beside her on the floor, as his mouth and hands dragged her through a labyrinth of ice and fire.

Oh, Artie... Artie please.

Animal sounds erupted from her brother's throat. He had a thousand hands, and they were everywhere. His mouth devoured her, sucking at her greedily, trying to suck her soul out of her body from every opening to which his desperate lips attached themselves. First one rubber nipple, then the other— then down across her stomach, where his tongue tried to unlock and open her navel— then down and down, and she clutched at his head, trying to push him away, felt his hot, excruciating mouth take full possession of her golden tabernacle, then found herself pulling his head closer to her, felt herself being drained, disarmed, defeated, until all she knew how to do was lie there quietly and be devoured, whispering

No, Artie, no... we mustn't.

His body slithered up on top of hers until his breath was hot against her throat, sweet with the smell of gin. She heard the clink of his belt buckle and ominous buzz of his fly.

Oh, Arthur, darling... we mustn't... it's wrong.

And yet her arms encircled him, her thighs drew wider, inviting the inevitable thrust.

INCEST.

The word lashed at her, stabbed at her, tried to worm itself inside her body and inject its ugly venom. Once, twice the serpent struck and missed its mark. Desperate with terror, she grabbed her brother's hair and wrenched him away from her, bucking her body and throwing him off.

Groaning, whining, he clutched at her again, pleading, demanding, pawing at her, pulling her to him, trying to mount her again.

Frantically, she lashed her hand across his face.

He froze, stared at her stunned, and started to cry.

Her heart melted instantly and she was overcome with love, compassion. He rolled away from her and she went after him, clutching his wretched head to her breast, crying, kissing his eyes, his mouth, his chin, his throat, his hands, his chest— then suddenly there it was in front of her: all his need staring at her, beseeching her from the tiny, single eye of the pulsing penis lying pitifully along his belly.

Without a moment's hesitation, she advanced impulsively, captured the throbbing monument between her loving lips, devoured all his burning need, ingested it, and claimed it for herself, forever.

Quaking uncontrollably, Art Pastel closed his eyes and clung to the water pipe to keep himself from falling as his pumping hand enticed him toward ecstasy.

Toy Toy Toy Toy Toy

Fireworks ignited before his face; the midnight sky was etched with streaks of strawberry red, creamy white, lavender and gold.

Mommy always rewards a good boy.

Lightning jumped from toe to toe; Mommy flashed her angelic smile and touched the hardness that his body made for her against his will; Thalia and Toy Boat and silken strands of honeyed hair; a pleading, starving mouth, begging for the life that lurks within, until a heart, engorged with love, explodes with a rampaging torrent of white-hot lava, which thunders down against the dam, gathers terrible, delicious momentum, and bursts into the universe.

Toy collapsed to the floor of her mother's bedroom, her throat convulsing in a series of helpless gags that brought the bitter taste of bile to her mouth. Only a tremendous effort prevented her heaving stomach from complete eruption, and for several minutes she lay there pale and shivering, gulping air with burning swallows that brought more tears to her red-rimmed eyes.

Toy, she heard her brother whimper, *Toy, so help me God, I deserve to be struck dead for this.*

And she had not had the strength to tell him it had been her fault, not his; that she'd provoked him knowingly, had tricked him into making love to her. She had not told him, had not spoken, and the very next day Arthur had been chosen master of ceremonies of his first network television program: Just when he'd demanded punishment, he'd been handed supreme good fortune and success.

She spread her palms upon the thick carpet, pressed her face against it and clamped her quivering lip between her teeth.

Forgive me, Arthur. Forgive my stupid, selfish mouth.

Ever since that terrible day, seventeen long years ago, Toy Boat Trump had not uttered a single word of her own devising.

In the 7-A control room, Show Director Roland Monteczuma was making a few final notes on a sizable sheaf of papers. "Okay now," he turned to the tech director, "we shit-can the dolly shot in the middle of Toby Tyler's song. Camera Two can zoom in from the other side of the bandstand— a slow zoom, instead— got it?"

"Right." Gene Russelton made his own notations.

Through his headset, Monteczuma suddenly heard his stage manager's voice burst in. "Hey, Rally! Great news!"

"We've been pre-empted."

"Nope. Camera Three's operational! Circuit's replaced and it's ready for air! Man oh man, how 'bout that shit?"

The director sank back into his chair and flipped his pencil into the air. He and Russelton looked at one another and smiled; both men calmly picked up their voluminous notes and dropped them into the wastebasket between them.

"Great, Ralph," Monteczuma said into his mouthpiece. "Clue everybody in— we're back to the original script. Air in... twenty-nine minutes."

"Right, Rolly. God damn, what a lucky-assed break. Hey, you get a chance to talk to Pastel about me yet?"

"Not before the show, Ralph— I'll talk to him later, when he's more human."

"Whatever you say, Rolly. Thanks a lot!"

The show director took off his headset, lit a slim cigar, leaned back and closed his eyes.

Downstairs in Studio 7-A, the BBS pages were ushering the members of the Pastel Penthouse audience to their seats.

12

Son-of-a-knee-sock. A large wad of paper towels in hand, Merlin crawled across the floor of his attic workshop, dabbing up a puddle of spilled alcohol. *The little lady sees this, she'll raise Cain, and that's for sure.*

He rubbed the planks dry, then slowly climbed to his feet, shuffled to the wastebasket and discarded the soiled towels. "Everything's hotsy-dory, Labor Gang— no need to climb on your high horse, ain't it?"

The old man carried the wastebasket across the room and upended it over a newspaper spread on the bar. *Pootsy*. Carefully wrapping the newspaper round the soiled towels, he tucked the parcel under his arm, trudged to the door and unlocked all three locks. Easing the portal open a crack, he peered outside and whispered, "Wreck o' the Hesperus." Then he crept into the stair well and locked the door from the outside with a small padlock.

"The heat's on, as the old Chinaman tells us. Bad-egg Pro-hibition's in the machinery again, chiefies, but the old King Fish ain't licked yet, and don't forget *that*." He slowly descended the winding wooden staircase. "Shut down the factory, that's the ticket. Back to the good old days— bootleg hooch and easy speaking. Haw! How's that for a gimcrack?" *Shhh! Someone's coming!* "Those people moved, you say? Well, well, well, can you de-magine that?"

As he reached the third-floor landing, he met his daughter coming up. "Thalia, my queen!" he beamed. "It's only the little lady, boys! I ask you: Is she the most beautiful girl in the world, or ain't it?"

His daughter smiled and held up the evening paper.

"Good girl! Good girl! Chiefie needs it for tomorrow's garbage, and I thank you kindly." He showed her his trash package, patted her lightly on the shoulder, then ushered her past him with a gentle flourish. "Beautiful, beautiful." He watched her ascend the staircase toward his workshop. "Just like the day I married her."

Forgetting he'd been heading in the opposite direction, Merlin followed his daughter back up the stairs and found her waiting for him at his door. "Don't be 'fraid, door-ter, we back you hup!" He unlocked the padlock with the key hanging by the door, then hesitated, squinting at her suspiciously. "Are you alone?"

His daughter nodded.

"It pays to be ignorant." Merlin opened the door and showed her inside. Toy sat at the bar and laid out the evening paper as her father set his parcel down, took a sheet of old newspaper from behind the bar and began to line the wastebasket with it.

Toy read the evening headline out loud:

"WORLD RECORD! WOMAN GIVES BIRTH TO NINE LIVE BABIES!"

"No foolin'?" Merlin poked his head up from behind the bar. "Ah, excuse my French, door-ter, but you don't look so hot, if I don't mind saying so. Did you move your bowels today?"

Toy looked at her paper and nodded uncomfortably.

Merlin set a shot glass on the bar and poured her a jigger of olive oil. "Little physic, that's the ticket." He returned the wastebasket to its place and began sponging down the bar, while Toy resumed reading.

Beneath the banner headline was the large photo of a bewildered man holding five cigars, and a nurse smiling at him. The caption read:

> "Subway conductor Lewd Noogie can't believe his ears as nurse informs him that wife, Fila, has just presented him with nine-re peat. NINE-male heirs. Dad is in shock, but mom and boys are doing fine."

Merlin shuffled around the bar and peered at the man's picture. "Wowsie man." He returned to the sink to wash his hands.

Toy turned the page.

> "This afternoon at Midtown Hospital, the pretty wife of a city subway conductor gave birth to nine hale and hearty baby boys, thereby establishing a spectacular new world's record for multiple live births. With her present phenomenal confinement, Fila Noogie, 40, who resides with her husband, Lewd, at 1472 Dorago Avenue, has more than offset the disappointment and frustration of nearly fifteen childless years of wed lock. At 3:18 p.m., the exhausted stork delivered the ninth fragile fledgling to the crowded Noogie nest, and the living legend was complete. Thanks to…"

"Mandalay!" Merlin rubbed together his freshly cleaned, pink hands. "God bless the little buggers, and I don't mean Mayberry." He set two lo-ball glasses on the bar, poured three fingers of blended whiskey into each, lifted one and toasted: "Long life, healthy happiness, and macaroni spa-get!" With a single tilt, he emptied the glass, held its contents in his mouth a moment, then washed it down with the second glass of liquor. His face screwed up in mock agony and he swallowed several times before he could finally rasp, "Wowsie man," his eyes red-rimmed and watery. Leaning his elbow on the bar, he looked at Toy seriously. "Them little youngsters... are they thriving?"

His daughter nodded and pointed to the paper:

> "Thanks to an ingenious new incubation device, all nine minute males are very much alive and kicking, though they are by no means out of danger at this time. The highly sophisticated incubator, developed by..."

"Hold your high horses!" Merlin suddenly exclaimed. "Hotsy-totsy, Labor Gang— the Chiefie's got it!" He hurried to his work bench and began rearranging things. "King O' Trump Cocktail, Number Twelve-thousand-oh-and-eighty-two!" He spun about and faced his daughter, waiting until he held her full attention. **"Rock-and-Rye...and BABY OIL!"** He grinned at her and raised his eyebrows shrewdly. "Ain't it?"

Toy Boat nodded her approval.

Merlin wagged his finger at her. "Smooth as a baby's bottom! if I may be so kind, and excuse my French. Sleep like a baby! No morning misery! Baby oil's the old gimcrack, door-ter!" He rushed to his supply shelves. "Baby oil... baby oil... Golly Neds, hope I'm not out of it."

Toy glanced at her wristwatch, saw that it was late, and leafed through the newspaper until she found the radio-TV listings for the day. " 'Ten-thirty,' " she read aloud. *"The Pastel Penthouse."*

Merlin looked over at her. *"The Pastel Penthouse?"* Immediately he forgot what he'd been doing and hurried toward her. "You don't tell me? The Pastel Penthouse? It's Wednesday in the p.m., is it? and make no mistake?"

His daughter nodded and pointed to her watch.

"Golly Seaweed, we better shake a leg, ain't it? How's the coast? Are we too late?"

Toy smiled and shook her head.

"Wowsie!" Merlin shuffled quickly toward the door. "We better get down to the old tee-vee, P.D.Q...." He hesitated and looked back at his daughter "Or not? D'you think we should, palsy-walsy?" He flicked his thumbs out of his fists.

Folding the paper, Toy nodded and climbed from her stool. "You're the boss!" announced the old man happily. *"I'm* not the boss— *you're* the boss! And make no mistake about that!" He opened his bureau, withdrew a clean but tattered sweatshirt and pulled it over his head. "Watch your foot, Labor Gang— good old Arthur's on the tee-vee tonight!"

"Oh jesus god," whispered Art Pastel, through clenched teeth. He sat upon the toilet in his private bathroom, arms folded across his belly, his body doubled over with pain. Cringing in the semidarkness, he cowered helpless as searing cramps staggered through his belly in relentless waves. As the current torture subsided, he grabbed a lighted cigarette from the rim of the sink and sucked on it, then took a swig of gin from the bottle at his feet.

Suddenly, the demon clamped his innards in its jaws again; he gasped and folded over; the tile floor wobbled and distorted before his eyes; nausea welled up in his throat.

There was a knock at his office door. From outside, a muffled voice called, "Mr. Pastel? Five minutes to air, sir."

The star forced himself upright on the toilet seat. Miraculously, the pain began to subside. He wiped himself, got up and washed his hands. Turning on the light, he studied his reflection in the bathroom mirror; his face was pale, but the make-up covered it. Fleetingly, fresh pain wandered through his bowels, then subsided, like a warning.

Moving to his office, he slipped into his trousers and jacket, checked himself in the full-length mirror, then walked to the door and paused, yawning broadly. Then he unlocked the door and stepped into the quiet hallway.

Trudging along the dimly lit corridor, the star felt as though he were moving through water. He yawned again. His eyelids were heavy; his body weighed a million pounds— and yet, his head was weightless.

He was a little boy again, awakening in the night and feeling very lonely. He was four years old, climbing from his little bed, walking out into the silent hallway, past his father's quiet room, padding through the darkness to his mother's door, where he gently turned the knob and found it locked. And there were noises in his mother's room. Squatting in the hallway, he listened at the door, and heard his mother and father humming funny songs inside. And the bed was going squeak squeak squeak. Having a fight? Playing a game? His mother and father hummed together very loudly— then everything was quiet. Climbing to his feet, he moved along the hallway toward his room again, but this time, as he passed his father's bedroom, he stopped and stood there, looking at his father's door. Fear possessed him. He sat down on the carpet and he quietly began to cry. Inside his father's bedroom, he could hear his father snoring.

Art Pastel found himself backstage in Studio 7-A. He heard the director's voice announce over the P.A. system: "Thirty seconds, everyone— stand by."

How long had little Arthur sat there in the middle of the hall, listening to his father's peaceful snoring, his tearful gaze fixed unblinking through the darkness toward his mother's bedroom door?

"Fifteen seconds," said the stage manager, on stage. "Break a leg, everybody."

Art Pastel set his jaw, closed his eyes and held his

breath. The pains were gone now, as usual; only the customary terror remained. He felt the countdown click away inside his head: *five... four... three... two... one...*

On stage, the orchestra erupted into the show's theme; on the screen of the backstage monitor appeared the logo **THE PASTEL PENTHOUSE,** superimposed over a long shot of Studio 7-A. The music faded somewhat, but the announcer still had to shout to be heard above it. "Hey, America! There's a party tonight— in *The Pastel Penthouse!* Your host, of course, is Mister Television Himself— **Art Pastel!**" The music swelled, then faded slightly once again. "Art's guests tonight are— Toby Tyler, Oleg Kobelesko, The Aquarian Era, Scarlet Tuloon, Ulloch Tugg and the BBS Orchestra, and me— I'm Freddy Fredella." The picture dissolved into a shot of the grinning, bald announcer. "Hi, everyone! Art'll be with you in just one minute— after this important message from the Cundelini Cracker Company!"

The screen faded into blackness, then a puff of white smoke appeared, revealing a man dressed as a Buddha and holding a box of crackers. In the studio, the TV sound was turned off during the commercial, and Pastel could hear the announcer urging the studio audience to "Give Art a really boffo welcome when he comes on stage."

Alone in the backstage twilight, Pastel clenched his teeth and shook his head with intense determination. *You can't make me. You can't make me do it.*

A trumpet fanfare sounded. "And now, all you Pastel Penthouse Peeping Toms—" the announcer shouted, "glue your eyes to that keyhole, 'cause **here comes The Man With The Magic Smile!**"

I will not. The star prepared to make his customary leap through the curtains. *I will not make pee-pee for you.*

"Ladies and gentlemen— **Mister Art Pastel!**"

When Mister Television smiled, heaven and earth belonged to him.

"Love ya, Party Peepers!" The star bounded across the stage, basking in his thunderous ovation for several moments before raising his arms and shouting, **"Are we gonna have some FUN?"**

"YES!" roared the studio audience.

"You said it— not me!"

One hundred thirty million Americans squirmed and giggled with delight.

"Haw!" Merlin slapped his thighs and peered back toward his daughter. " 'You said it-not me!' Wowsie man! The boy's funny, ain't it?"

The old man sat on the edge of his easy chair, his face just a few feet from the screen,the volume set so low that the sound was barely audible. Toy sat motionless in the semidarkness, alternating her gaze between the image of her brother on television,and the face of her father illuminated by the colored light from the screen.

"Welcome to Uncle Artie's Penthouse," Pastel announced with a roguish grin. "And a special welcome to all you lovely ladies out there. This show is designed just for you, you know: We put your husband to sleep, so you can watch the late show in peace!" Women across the country chuckled knowingly and looked at their mates. "And, believe me, ladies, the movie's worth staying up for tonight. It's the world's first combination musical and horror show-called *Demons Are a Ghoul's Best Fiend!"*

"Haw! Mandalay! The boy's funny!" insisted Merlin. "A chip off the old block! Shhh!" he put a finger to his lips and turned back to the screen.

"Speaking of combining music with horror," Pastel continued, "let's say hello to the old Penthouse Terror-Ulloch Tugg!" The audience applauded as the bandleader's face appeared briefly on the screen and was quickly replaced again by Art Pastel's. "We get a lot of letters asking if Ulloch's originally from Transylvania— but actually, he's a very rare breed of Hungarian-Spaniard. Ulloch's father, Pablo, was Budapest's most famous flamenco dancer, until he developed bad kidneys and his doctors told him he'd have to wear foam rubber heels or he'd kill himself."

"Haw!... What'd he say? Something about foam rubber." Merlin reached out and touched the volume control, but the change was imperceptible. "You tell 'em, Arthur, m'boy!"

"Ulloch was raised on gypsy cooking, and that's why he looks half dead. A gypsy fixed me an Alka-Seltzer once, and it gave me heart burn." Pastel suddenly danced toward the audience and picked up a cue card propped there for him to read. "Well, folks, I could keep boring you with this phony cardboard comedy, but tonight I've got something better to talk about." He tossed the poster away, leaned against the railing in front of the audience seats, and winked at four ladies sitting in the first row. The ladies winked back and blew him kisses. "Maybe some of you haven't heard the fantastic news yet, but just this afternoon over at Midtown Hospital, a woman gave birth to *nine* baby boys!"

The audience gasped in disbelief, then burst into spontaneous applause.

"Can you believe it? *Nine* babies! More than have ever been born at one time before— alive— in the entire history of the world! And, thank God, so far all the babies and their mother are doing just fine." The audience buzzed with excitement; Pastel raised a hand to quiet them down. "The name of the couple who's been gifted with this fantastic blessed event— is *Noogie*. Now, I don't know if any of you folks in the studio noticed as you came in, but one of our own BBS pages right here tonight has the name NOOGIE printed on his uniform!"

Necks craned everywhere; people at the rear of the studio began to *oooh* and *aah* and point excitedly at a uniformed young man standing petrified against the wall.

Pastel shaded his eyes and peered toward the back of the studio. "Yep, there he is, folks! Come on down here, Mr. Noogie!"

The page stood transfixed until two other uniformed lads urged him forward and sent him marching stiffly down the aisle toward the studio floor.

Pastel met him at the bottom of the stairs. "Here, turn around and face that camera, so all the folks can get a good look at you. Now, what's your first name, Mr. Noogie?"

"Ah, Corbin... sir."

"Married, Corbin?"

"No."

"Well then, let's hope you're not the father of those babies, eh, folks?" Laughter and applause. "How old are you, Corbin?"

"Twenty-eight." The young man's face was ashen.

"I don't suppose you're any relation to the couple who just had those nine babies, are you?"

"I... I don't know."

"You don't know?"

"This is the... first I've heard of it."

"No kidding?" Art Pastel was delighted. "Well then, Corbin, let me ask you this: Do the names Lewd and Fila Noogie mean anything to you?"

The young man's head jerked upward as though he'd been hit with an uppercut. He swallowed with difficulty and looked back toward the floor again. "They're my... my uncle and aunt."

"Wow! Well, Corbin, let me be the first to congratulate you: You just got yourself nine brand new cousins!" The audience shrieked and applauded as Pastel pumped the young man's hand and slapped him on the back. As soon as things quieted down, Pastel put his arm about the page's shoulders. "Well, Unc, how's it feel?"

Corbin smiled weakly. "I... can't tell you how it makes me feel."

"Nine babies!" Pastel marveled. "What d'you call nine babies, anyway? Let's see... quintuplets, sextuplets...then what?— septuplets, I guess..." He held up eight fingers, "octuplets..." then added a finger, "**novuplets!** THE NOOGIE NOVUPLETS!" The audience cheered. "I don't know if you realize it yet, Corbin, but your family name is gonna be world-famous! What do you say to that?"

Corbin Noogie said nothing.

Pastel waved his hand back and forth before the page's eyes; the young man looked at him blankly and raised his eyebrows: "I beg your pardon?"

Pastel winked at the camera. "He's still in a state of shock, folks. Corbin," the star grabbed his hand again, "the best of luck to you— and when you see those proud parents, tell 'em the whole country loves 'em, and that we're all praying that those beautiful little boys pull through these first crucial weeks. Will you do that for us?"

Corbin Noogie nodded. "Yes," he whispered quietly, then added, "...thanks."

"Good boy! God bless you! Ladies and gentlemen— **Corbin Noogie!**"

The studio resounded with applause as the star strolled back to center stage and turned to the camera. "I've got a little surprise for those Noogie tots, folks, so stick around— we'll be right back after this word from the people who pay the bills here in the Penthouse."

Art Pastel's face faded from the screen, and as the commercial came on, Merlin turned the sound off completely, as he always did when his son was not on camera. As the screen showed a tiny Oriental man skating across a shiny kitchen floor, the old man sat flicking his thumb from his fist. "Toy Boat, my door-ter— those people moved, I hear. By and way, excuse my French, but you're not looking quite so hot, if I may say so myself. Have your bowels been moving hotsy-totsy?" Toy nodded gently.

"Olive Oil, that's what the old ticket is— little raw eggy

in a glass, or a fresh fig-there's a full case in the fruit cellar. Your mother can get it while I watch this program, would you please, my queen? Thank you kindly and macaroni spa-get. Shhh— we'll discuss it later, I'm trying to watch Arthur on tee-vee."

The commercial ended and Art Pastel returned to the screen, this time standing near the bandstand beside Ulloch Tugg, who was seated at his piano. "Let's see, Ully, do you know the song, 'You're My Bouncing Baby Boy'?"

Tugg shrugged. "You sing heem, I'll play heem, keed."

"Good. Let's do that one, only I'll sing it as 'You're My Bouncing Baby **Boys'** and dedicate it to those wonderful little novuplets over at Midtown Hospital!" Big applause.

Merlin shook his head, grinning. "Arthur, you're a gentleman and a scholar. Where's Thalia? **Thalia? Come here and listen to this!**" The old man looked around and spotted his daughter across the room. "Oh, there you are, my queen. Arthur's going to sing to the little babies! **Toy Boat! Agnes! Come here and listen to this!** Shhh!" He turned up the volume imperceptibly.

> *"I used to think that I was happy,*
> *But now I know I was wrong.*
> *You came along and called me Pappy,*
> *Made me sing a different song.*
> *Like shiny pennies from the skies,*
> *Tears of joy now fill my eyes*
> *For my bouncing baby boys..."*

Merlin began to cry. He shook his head slowly, and tears trickled down across the wrinkles in his cheeks.

> *"Once upon a time you were a gleam in*
> *Your Daddy's ever-lovin' eyes.*
> *Now it's come true, what I've been dreamin',*
> *Wouldn't tell you any lies.*

I'm the proudest guy on earth
Since the day Mommy gave birth
To my bouncing baby boys."

Merlin wiped his eyes with a paper towel. "The boy's a saint." He looked across the room at Toy and shook his head. "Thalia," he said, his voice breaking with emotion, "our little boy's a saint."

Corbin Noogie stood at the rear of Studio 7-A, his arms folded across his chest, as heads kept turning from the audience to look at him. His eyes stared straight ahead, unseeing. Inside, he seethed with emotion.

Novuplets! I didn't even know she was pregnant!

A moment ago, on stage, he'd been offered the chance to proclaim his fatherhood to the entire world. Now, the moment was gone; now, he knew, he would be silent forever.

Novuplets!

He was a god. He was a clown.

"You can take a break now, star."

Corbin flinched and looked beside him, where another page stood, not bothering to whisper while a boulder-music group crashed through its number on stage. "I have a Second Stay," the page explained. "I'm relieving you."

"Oh. Sure... okay." Noogie headed for the studio doors; several people grinned and waved as he left.

Outside, the halls were silent and empty, and he couldn't feel his legs as he plodded to the elevator well and pressed the DOWN button.

Novuplets.

The elevator doors opened and he stepped inside. "Three, please."

"You got it," yawned the elevator operator, and the car descended. "What's new?" the man asked him, sleepily.

Corbin looked him squarely in the eye. "I am the father of

nine baby boys."

"No shit?" The elevator halted at the third floor and the car doors opened. "Watch your step."

In the control room, Monteczuma had his eye on the clock. "Let's put this mother in the can," he said into his headset. "Ralph, give Pastel the speed-up— we have one minute to sign off."

On the studio floor, the stage manager caught the star's attention and twirled his hand in the air as though turning a small crank.

"Well," Art Pastel smiled into the cameras, "I can see by the cop at the door that our time's about up..."

"Cue theme," directed Monteczuma, and the orchestra began playing softly.

"...so until next week, good night— God bless. And don't forget to say a little prayer for the Noogie Novuplets!"

"Hit the APPLAUSE sign," the director ordered, and the audience erupted into resounding applause. "Theme up... ready Camera One... take One. Ready to super Camera Two... super Two. Roll the credits... cue Announce."

"This portion of *The Pastel Penthouse* has been brought to you by the Hinkle Home Products Company, makers of Cundelini Crackers and Sparkle Wax. Art Pastel's fashions by Mister Esteem, Unlimited. This has been a Pastel Production, in association with the BBS Television Network. Stay tuned for more frantic fun, coming up next on 'Sniffer and Me'— the zany adventures of a blind German shepherd and his seeing-eye owner."

"Five seconds," the director cautioned. "Keep hitting that APPLAUSE sign... aaand... Bingo. That's thirty, everyone — thanks for a fine job." He pulled off his headset, climbed out of his chair, picked up his jacket and briefcase, waved at his control-room staff, then strode directly from the studio. As soon as his image faded from the studio monitors, Art Pastel made a beeline for his dressing room, head down, speaking to no one. In the quiet of his office, he drank three fingers of straight gin, then locked the suite securely and hurried toward the back of the building, where a freight elevator awaited him.

As Pastel stepped into the waiting car, he saw that there was another passenger aboard: Roland Monteczuma.

The show director nodded but did not smile. "Ralph tells me the Eighty-Sixes hassled you tonight. I'm going down to help him handle them."

The elevator operator closed the car gate with a clatter and flipped the handle; the car sank silently.

"That greaseball's through, you know," said Pastel, looking at his shoes. "I shit-canned him."

The three men continued their descent in complete silence. The operator stopped the car about a foot below the first floor landing, yo-yoed several times and finally yanked open the metal gate.

Pastel strode from the car, with Monteczuma close at his heels. Zigzagging around piles of huge burlap sacks stuffed with the building's daily production of trash, they moved to the doorway at which the star's auto was waiting. Pastel pressed his hand against the door frame and peered outside apprehensively.

Monteczuma pushed the door open and led the way. "Should be okay this time— Ralph's on the other side of the building, creating a diversion."

The star's Kenita-Delmer stood waiting at the curb; there was no sign of the Eighty-Sixes. Pastel quickly jumped in behind the wheel and locked his door; Monteczuma climbed in on the passenger side and, in answer to the star's withering gaze, said simply, "How 'bout dropping me at the train station? It's on your way."

Pastel gunned the engine, shoved it into gear and sped away. The pair motored several blocks in silence, then the director turned to observe the wooden figure sitting between them. "Gonna use him on the show?"

Art Pastel lit a cigarette. They rode on a few more blocks, and this time Pastel broke the silence. "Call a production meeting next Thursday— three o'clock."

"New project?"

"I want to do a special on those Noogie brats. Get on it right away. Get them under contract. Schedule the old man next week on the 'Penthouse.' "

"We'd better shoot some footage right away," suggested Monteczuma. "Maybe some of those kids will die."

"I hope so." Pastel tossed his cigarette butt through the wind wing. "Better human interest." He pulled into the train station, stopped the car and lit another cigarette. "About those freaks. I don't want it to happen again. Do something about it."

"I'm not your security officer." Monteczuma opened his door. "While we're at it, Ralph Goliones is a good stage manager. I want to hang on to him."

"Ralph Goliones is a stupid greaseball, " said Pastel, not looking up at Monteczuma. "And his ass is fired."

"If he goes, I go."

The star's face shot around and their gazes locked. Pastel's jaw muscles twitched. His gaze bore into the director's cool, confident eyes, then faltered and fell away. Roland Monteczuma got out, closed the door and strode off into the terminal.

"Doosy the spinnaker, and raise the roof!" Merlin stood in the bow of a silver sailboat, knifing through the troubled waters of an amber sea. "We're pulling a fast one in front of the wind, and that's for sure!" Giant mounds of mashed-potato clouds nestled on the sea around him, some pink, some green. The whistling wind was a visible thing, a swirling mist of lavender that filled his silver sail and wafted through his silver hair. "The coasty's clear, and thank you kindly!" Captain Trump steered his course with a silver cord that stretched from his hand to the tiller astern. "The

King Fish is coming, My Queen, she said!" A shabby pigeon fluttered overhead, across the jet-black sky. A strawberry dolphin leapt from the whiskey sea, plucked the fowl with needle teeth, somersaulted over the mainmast of Merlin's craft, and landed in a tin of Good Old Olive Oil. "Macaroni Spa-get! It's Mandalay, and there she be!" A gold-and ivory island rose on the horizon, and the old man's speeding sailboat sprang toward it. "The Good Old Land of Milk and Honey! Can you de-magine that?" A monstrous obstacle suddenly rose from the sea ahead of him: an enormous playing card-the Queen of Hearts-a queen with radiant face, for she was with child. "Thalia, My Queen!— Are you thriving?" The card slid out of the sea and soared into the heavens. The Queen let out a playful giggle and a golden infant blasted from her belly like a circus clown leaping through a paper covered hoop. The baby became a yellow stone that plummeted to earth with blinding speed, crashed into the sea and dispatched massive waves toward Merlin's silver sailboat. "Don'ja be 'fraid, m'boys she said!" He felt the craft begin to heave beneath him. "We back you hup!" The vessel rocked violently. Merlin dropped his silver cord, reached out to capture the lavender breeze, and fell into the amber sea.

The old man toppled from the barstool he'd been sleeping on, and thudded to the floor of his workshop.

A single candle flickered from its perch atop the cash register, casting eerie shadows all across the room. Merlin sprawled motionless for several moments, his eyes half opened. *No damage done, m'boys.*

In slow motion, as though he were submerged in water, he rolled to his stomach, flexed his arms and legs, then slowly climbed to his hands and knees. "Everything's totsy-dotsy, Labor Gang." He swam to the bar and tried to pull himself up, but he toppled backward instead and thumped to the floor again, giggling. "Oh, wowsie man. The old Chiefie's feelin' good tonight. One too many, as the pot said to the kettle."

He rolled over slowly twice, and this time, with the aid of both the barstool and the bar, he managed to climb to his feet, beginning to giggle again, shaking his head from side to side and pawing at the spittle trickling down his chin.

Upon the bar sat a nearly empty fifth of Rock 'n' Rye, beside which was an equally depleted bottle of baby oil. "Hunky-dunky." Merlin closed his eyes and stood in silence for a long while before raising his head suddenly and deciding, "Golly Neds, it's past my bedtime." He leaned across the bar. "But first, m'boys, she calls for a teensy nightcap, and so forth." He groped for the whiskey bottle, knocked it over, and caught it before it rolled off the bar. "So to speak." He poured the contents of the bottle into his glass, presented a brief toast— "Don't let the bedbugs bite"— then swallowed down the amber liquid. "Little wrench," he gasped, washing it down with a mouthful of baby oil. "Ahhhhh…" He thumped his glass down on the bar. "Those bedbugs moved."

He trundled toward his tiny cot, collapsed halfway, and crawled the rest. Pulling himself up to a praying position, he raised his head so he could gaze at the poster tacked to the wall:

THE INTOXICATING LOVE GODDESS OF EXOTIC DANCE!

The Sizzling, Sexational

•• MISS QUEEN O'HEARTS ••

Thirty-nine years ago, Merlin had learned that his beloved wife was carrying another man's child, and his mind had snapped.

"My Father, who is Art in Heaven…" *he's making a list, checking it twice…* "Holy Mother, married to God…" *gonna find out who's naughty and nice…* "pray for us swimmers now, and every hour on the hour…" *and the goblins will get you if you don't watch out . . .*

Eyes closed, the old man's head lowered slowly to the cot. The candle behind the bar flickered, then went out.

Softly, Merlin Trump began to snore.

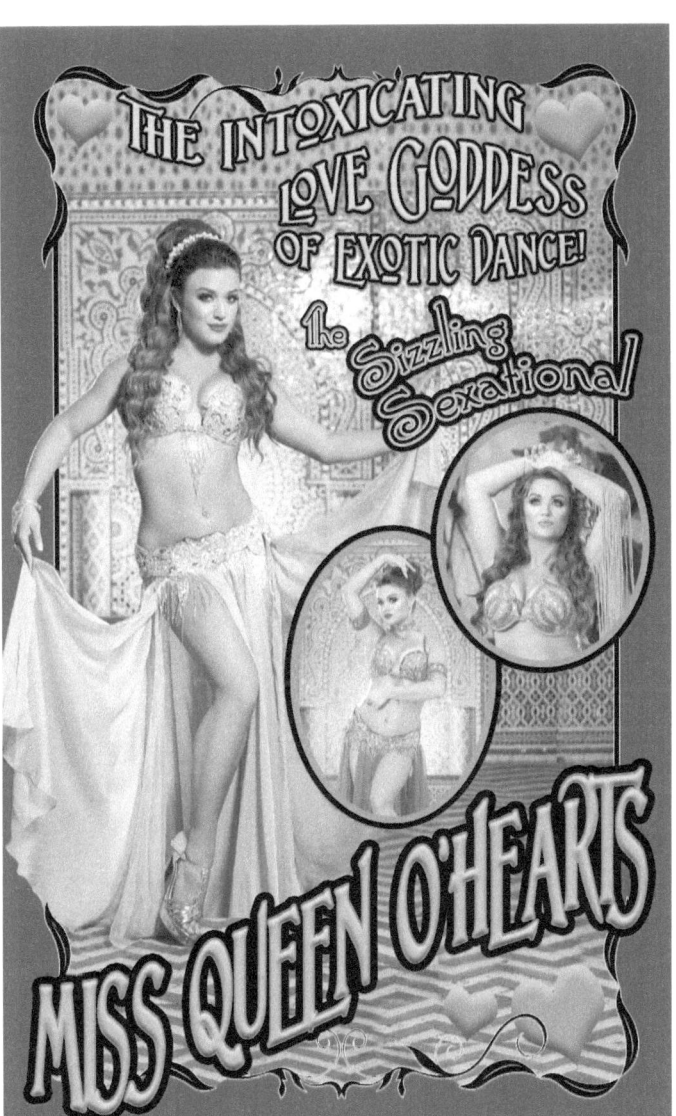

PART THREE

Wednesday, May 17

13

Scum fag mother of a geek.

Tully Keyster slammed his desk drawer and shot to his feet. His mind was seething. Chomping his fat cigar, the warden crammed his fists into his jacket pockets and lumbered back and forth across his office, polluting the air with acrid billows of smoke. Pausing at the window, he scowled into the prison yard below, where lines of convicts shuffled toward their evening meal.

Someone knocked at the door and Keyster spun his huge frame to face it. "Yeah?"

An elderly guard poked his head through the doorway. "Fucilla's outside, Warden."

"Well, kick his buns in here!"

The warden strode to his desk, sat down and busied himself with paperwork. The door opened and a short, thin convict, his face ashen beneath a mop of curly black hair, was ushered inside. The young man stood before the desk, turning his cap in his hands, waiting for Keyster to look up. Finally, the convict cleared his throat. "You... ah... wanted ta see me, Warden?"

Keyster continued signing papers. When he spoke at last, he did not look up. "What do you got to say for yourself, Fucilla?"

The young man thought a moment. "About what,

Warden?"

"**CRUMB PUNK SON-OF-A-SLIME-SNAKE!**" Keyster roared to his feet, driving his fist down on the desk.

Fucilla dropped his cap.

"**LISTEN, YOU CREAM PUFF WIENIE-BEATER,**" the warden charged round his desk and descended upon the terrified convict, "**DON'T TRY TO SHYSTER ME, OR I'll FLOG YOUR NATES SO GODDAMN HARD YOU'LL BE DUMPIN' IN A THUNDER MUG FOR A CHRISTING MONTH!**"

Wide-eyed, Fucilla back-pedaled until he hit the wall, then groped frantically behind him for the doorknob, but couldn't find it. "**I dunno what you're talkin'!**" he shrieked. "**I'm clean, I tell ya! I wanna see the chaplain!**"

"**YOU'LL SEE THE CHICKEN-MOTHER CHAPLAIN!**" thundered Keyster. "**HE'LL GIVE YOU THE MOTHER-JUGGING LAST RITES, AFTER I GET THROUGH PUTTIN' THE KIBOSH ON YOUR DUNG-BEETLE HORNIES!**" The warden grabbed Fucilla by the lapels, wrenched him off his feet and heaved him toward a straight-backed chair several yards away. Dead on target, the convict landed squarely on the chair, which collapsed at once, the momentum sending him skidding across the floor on the wooden seat, coming to rest against the wall beneath a photo of the first electric chair.

"It's a frame-up!" whined Fucilla, shielding his face with his arms.

Glaring at the prostrate convict, Keyster rocked back and forth on his heels, his fists clenched at his sides. The physical contact seemed to have relieved the warden of some excess emotion; when he spoke again, his voice was under control. "Okay, fart, we'll play A B C." He shifted his cigar to the other side of his mouth, chewed on it a while, then asked casually, "Where were you at four-fifteen p.m. on the afternoon of May seventeenth of the current year?"

"Jeez, Warden... gimme a break, will ya?" Fucilla cringed behind his arms. "How'm I s'posed ta remember back that far?"

Keyster squinted down at him through blue-white smoke."You dunderhead pansy— **today** is May seventeenth!"

The convict peered between his arms and grinned meekly. "Oh. T'day?"

The warden dragged a chair over and sat backward on it, straddling the seat with his beefy thighs and resting his elbows on the wooden back. "Where were you at four-fifteen today, Fucilla?"

"I wuz right here, Warden."

"Right where, butt-hole? Right here in my office?"

"Naw, Warden, I mean I wuz right here in stir... I din't go nowheres."

"You bet your sweet crabs you were at Achen State, Nancy," the warden agreed, "and you'll be here till your gourd rots, too, if you don't start leveling with me."

The convict wiped his face on his jacket sleeve and laughed nervously. "Oh, I getcha! You wanna know where I wuz in stir at..."

"Four-fifteen this afternoon."

"Right. Four-fifteen. Let's see... well, I... ah... guess I wuz out inna yard with the guys."

Keyster flicked his cigar ash at the convict. It hit him in the center of the forehead, burst into gray powder and cascaded down across his nose and cheeks.

"Heh heh," grinned Fucilla. He did not wipe it off.

"You were in the prison yard at four-fifteen?"

"Yeah, I wuz inna yard... I guess ."

"You weren't working in the garden behind my house?"

"Oh. Hey, yeah-how 'bout that!" Fucilla's face lit up with recognition. "I wuz inna garden back of your house, Warden."

"And what were you doing in the garden, Fucilla?"

"Well, I wuz pullin' weeds, I guess... somethin' like that."

Warden Keyster crossed his arms over the back of the

chair and rested his chin on his wrists. "Now, listen carefully, Fucilla. While you were pulling weeds in the garden behind my house at four-fifteen p.m. on the afternoon of May seventeenth, did you have visual contact with any person or persons?"

"Huh?"

"Did you see anybody?"

"When? T'day? Naw, I don't think so, Warden... Why?"

"I'll ask the questions, Fucilla, if you don't mind." Keyster puffed on his cigar a moment, then slapped the back of his chair decisively. "Listen, Fucilla— you're levelin' with me, I'll level with you. The Gar Mountain Public Schools let out at four o'clock every afternoon. Some of the kids walk past my house on their way home. You didn't happen to see some kids today, did you, Fucilla?"

The convict knitted his brows in thought.

"Come on, Fucilla, you don't have to bust your nuggets to remember back a couple hours, do you?"

"Naw, Warden, I guess not. Well, there mighta been a couple of kids... but I din't pay no mind, know what I mean?"

"Sure, sure. Tell you why I'm askin' Fucilla..." Keyster leaned forward, his tone growing confidential. "Some of them kids... well, sometimes they see a con in the garden— they make a crack or something. Now, some of those young girls... they know a con don't get no nookie, see...? So they'll kinda wiggle their butts, or give you the big come-on, get me... just to get your gonads in an uproar."

Fucilla sighed. "Yeah."

"Some of those girls can be real tinkle teasers," frowned the warden, "real bitches."

"Yeah . . . bitches."

"Things like that happen, I wanna hear about it, Fucilla. I gotta look out for my cons— see that nobody diddles with 'em, get me?"

The convict was impressed with Keyster's concern.

"Sure, Warden— you're a real square shooter."

"Thanks, Fucilla, thanks for your vote of confidence." The warden got up, gave the convict his hand and helped him to his feet. "Here, Anthony— sit here." The young man sat down on the chair Keyster had just occupied, while the warden pulled up another and sat down beside him. "Now then... what about it, Anthony, son?" Tully Keyster asked softly. "Any of those little bitches try to put a bump in your jeans today?"

A slight glaze covered Fucilla's eyes. "Yeah, Warden... one did."

"There, you see? I was right, wasn't I?" The warden placed a paternal hand on his shoulder. "Which one was it? What'd she look like?"

Fucilla shook his head. "Gee, Warden, I dunno who she was. I mean, this wuz my first day out of the walls in a couple years, I guess. But anyway... there I wuz... crawlin' around them daisies or p'tunias or what-have-ya... an' I looks up an' there's this little bitch standin' by the fence, givin' me the eye, y'know?"

"Wigglin' her butt, I bet. What'd she look like, Anthony?"

"Kee-ryst..." Fucilla swallowed. "Like, she was a walkin' ad, y'know? *Come An' Get It*, y'know? I mean, this long blonde hair, an' a sweater looked like it was painted on, an' a pair of them c-thru-slax, so thin you can see her business end... I mean she was really lookin' for action, y'know?"

"What'd she say to you, son?"

"She din't say nothin'!" The convict was gesturing enthusiastically, his forehead beginning to perspire. "She just looks away when she sees me eyeballin' her, y'know, like I wasn't even there? An' she kinda struts back and forth along the fence, pretendin' ta pick flowers just so's I can get a good shot of her snatch when she bends over. Wow. I mean it wuz like *Come An' Get It*, y'know?"

"Really nice stuff, was she?"

Fucilla mopped his brow with his sleeve. "Yeah."

"Really made your gourd groan, did she?"

"Warden," the convict confided, "I'd chance an ass full of buck shot just to climb over the wall for a sniff at her bicycle seat."

"I know how you feel, son," sighed Keyster. "By the way... just for the record, did you happen to say anything to her?"

"Only what she wanted ta hear."

"And what was that, Anthony?"

Fucilla grinned at the warden. "I tol' her ta make tracks before I stuffed my cock up her crack!"

Warden Keyster Tully drove his massive fist into Anthony Fucilla's face. The blow knocked the convict over backward in his chair, and almost before his back hit the floor he was snatched to his feet again, another wicked punch flattening his nose and sending him reeling across the room, where he tumbled over the warden's desk and landed on his head in Keyster's chair. Powerful hands hiked him to his feet; rock-hard knuckles plunged into his belly, driving his breath out with a loud whoosh. A double-handed rabbit punch on the back of his neck propelled him toward the floor. A sledgehammer upper cut reversed his direction and flipped him backward, crashing him against the bookcase. Seven volumes of the State Penal Code toppled from the shelf, thudding down upon his head and shoulders.

Warden Keyster stood wheezing over the unconscious convict bleeding quietly on the floor. "How d'ya like them apples, sow jugger?" He stood with his full weight on one of Fucilla's hands. "What say, maggot vomit?" Keyster walked to the door and opened it. "Rosencrantz!" The elderly guard came into the office, accompanied by two younger officers.

The young guards lifted Fucilla by his arms and dragged him toward the door, while Rosencrantz began to tidy up the room.

Keyster sat at his desk and watched the men haul their burden away. "Toss the scab-mouth in The Hole for thirty days. His trustee status is revoked, his parole's denied, and his buns is generally in a sling for the duration of his stretch."

Just before the guards closed the office door behind them, Keyster added, "Oh, and when the rag-licker comes to, tell him that little girl he saw was my daughter— my little Jen. That'll frost his heehaw."

The setting sun had just dipped behind the high, ivy wall as Keyster began his evening stroll across the deserted prison yard. The upper windows of the ancient cell blocks still reflected the sunset's rosy glow, and the warden paused in the gathering dusk to enjoy the colorful patterns.

Keyster's College, he grinned with satisfaction. *Get your sheep skin from this little mother, you got yourself an education.*

He lit a cigar, jammed his fists into his suit-jacket pockets, and continued his stroll across the broad expanse of concrete. *Be a while before that maggot gets another hardon. Horning off at my Jenny, pure as the driven snow. The gink mouth. Wish to gourd he'd been two feet taller and a hundred pounds heavier— we 'd a had us a real good time.*

The warden found himself standing in the center of the concrete baseball diamond at one end of the prison yard. *Reminds me. Call a practice tomorrow— Tully's Torpedoes. Cotta keep the cup from those cream puffs at Zenobia.* His foot prodded at the painted white mark that designated the pitching rubber. *Too bad Lexanovsk y hadda burn. That mother could sure throw a baseball. Some game he gave Zenobia last year... pulled him outta the Death House to pitch, the day before he fried. The kid threw that ball like there was no tomorrow.*

Keyster resumed his stroll. At the edge of the baseball diamond, a football blocking dummy sat in quiet darkness. The warden eyed the padded rig, then crouched before it, touching the knuckles of his right hand to the ground in the set position . "Hut," he whispered, "Hut... **Hut.**" He sprang forward, crashing his shoulder against the padded surface with the full force of his 263 pounds. The heavy blocking sled lurched backward several yards with a loud screech.

Suddenly, Keyster found himself bathed in white light. He straightened up and squinted toward the blazing spotlight atop the wall.

"Thought it was you, Warden." a voice called down. **"Just wanted to make sure."**

Darkness enveloped Keyster once again, but a glowing red spot continued to hover before his eyes. "Leech pus. **Hey, Casey! It's as dark as a clam's ass down here... turn on the yard lights— I'm goin' home."** The prison yard lit up with greenish light.

Instead of heading toward the gate nearest his house, as he usually did, the warden now found himself walking in another direction. On the west wall of the penitentiary stood a pair of massive iron doors, and Keyster carried the only set of keys that would unlock them. As he turned each key and heard the bolts click open, a wave of emotion washed over him.

What is it?— twenty-three? Yeah. Twenty-three times I cracked these doors... in nine years. He shook his head. Another couple months, they might as well brick the mothers up. Swinging open one of the huge doors, he stepped into the cool darkness, closed the door and locked it once again.

The warden stood in the dark a moment, then flicked a switch and illuminated the barren, fifty-foot passageway which led to still a second set of massive iron doors. *The Last Mile.* He strolled along the concrete corridor, listening to the echo of his footsteps. *Not the same, walkin' it alone. No con bawlin'... no chaplain makin' with the mumbo jumbo. Creepy.* He gazed around him. *Probably be takin' guided tours through here in a couple years. Look, folks, here's where Rhino DeBussy vomited on the floor... and over there's the exact spot Tallulah Masheen told the chaplain and all the guards they could have a shot at her crotch if they'd let her live. Boy, them were the days.* The warden unlocked the second set of doors with reverence— *It's the end of an era, by squat—* and swung the metal portals open.

Before him spread a spacious chamber, two hundred feet long and nearly a hundred feet wide, with a forty-foot ceiling. Decades ago, when the convicts had farmed, built roads, dug cesspools, etc., this expansive structure had served as a heavy-equipment garage— and soon it would probably become a garage once more— but presently it enjoyed a much more awesome designation: Tully's Playpen.

Somber walls of granite block stood windowless on every side. Near the middle of the gray expanse of concrete floor, several rows of folding chairs sat in neat formation around a small platform made of rough plank-wood. Above the wooden platform, descending from the lofty ceiling on a long black wire, hung a bare electric bulb, which was always lit. It was the sole illumination in the gloomy hall, and directly beneath it, in the center of the plank-wood dais, sat "The Devil's Throne"— Achen State Penitentiary's electric chair.

Uncle Tully's Widow-maker. Warden Keyster walked slowly toward the execution platform, his crepe-soled shoes making eerie squishing noises on the polished concrete floor.

Brooding on its rough-hewn dais, The Chair held out its oaken arms, patiently waiting to administer the embrace of eternity. Keyster mounted the low platform and ran a finger over the chair's polished seat, to be certain that no dust had gathered there. *Tighten your belt, man-eater. Looks like you're in for a couple lean years.* The warden sat down in his electric chair.

Yessir, chalk up one for the pansies. My Death Row's as empty as an old maid's cranny. Never thought I'd live to see capital punishment get muff-canned. Fought it till my buns broke. Well, its no skin offa my squat. They'll see, the scum bags. I give this leeching law a year... then they'll be shippin' beef up here so fast I'll have to fry 'em piggyback.

He climbed to his feet and strolled from the platform. *Yeah, this room is full of memories. Twenty-three burns in nine years... and the seven years before that, while I was Chief Security Officer, musta cooked another fifteen, twenty. Some electric bill.* He walked toward the north wall. *A lotta tough cookies been baked in here. No matter how big they are when they walk in, they all fit in the same size hole when they leave.*

Warden Keyster stood before a large circuit breaker bolted unobtrusively to the wall, and closed his fist around its handle. *Yessir. You can be the slimiest cream-puff runt, or the meanest son-of-a-bull dagger in the world... The Chair ain't partial to nobody. When you sit up there, and Tully Keyster pulls the switch on you...* he slapped the handle downward, driving the metal contacts together... *you shit your pants.*

Keyster shoved his fists into his suit-coat pockets and walked toward the massive iron doors. Before he left the huge death chamber, the warden paused and gazed once more at the sullen chair, dwarfed by the lofty granite walls around it. *Well, I still got seven months before that sow-suck law takes over. Maybe time for one last cookout, just to shut the place up in style. I'll have to shop around— see if I can't find me some beef to barbecue.*

"Anita! Jenny! I'm home!" Warden Keyster stomped through the front doorway of his house, and was immediately attacked by an enraged Pomeranian named Bromberg, who came charging out of the kitchen, barking insanely and snapping viciously at the warden's ankles.

YAP!YAP!YAP!YAP!YAP!YAP!

"G'wan, beat it, ya little maggot, before I kick your nuggets up your smut-crack!" Keyster booted the tiny ball of furious fur halfway across the foyer, sending the terrified canine streaking for the kitchen once again, where it retreated under the stove and continued barking hysterically.

"Gink bastard mutt." Tully poked his head into the living room. "Anita?" He looked up the staircase. "Jen?"

A terrible din erupted from the back yard-a chorus of booming roars emanating from the outside pen where Tully kept his six Doberman pinschers. "What in the…" Keyster lumbered into the kitchen and headed for the back door. "Man comes in from a hard day…" He swung open the screen door. **"WHO GOES THERE?"** Suddenly, his wife rushed by him into the house. "Anita! What the squat…"

Ashen-faced, Anita Keyster stood at the sink, holding her heart. "Tully Keyster, those horrid animals are going to drive me to my grave!"

"Oh, for fag sake, Anita." He poked his head outside and bellowed, **"NO!"** The barking ceased at once. "What were they barking at, anyway?"

"They were barking at me, that's who they were barking at! If they could get out of that cage, they'd have torn me to shreds!"

"Oh, for the love of..."

"Do you know that my heart stopped out there? Well, it did! The way those fiends attacked me..." She turned to the sink and began to wash her hands.

"Come off it, Anita, that's impossible! Those dogs know you. Why should they... Wait a minute— what's that?"

"What?"

"That sweater you got on. That don't look like one of yours."

"No, it belongs to one of Jenny's friends. I just threw it over my shoulders while I took out the garbage..."

The warden exploded with laughter.

"Tully Keyster, this is nothing to laugh about!"

"Now, now, calm down, my dear. The dogs thought you were someone else— they smelled that sweater!"

Anita Keyster was not impressed. "Well, isn't that wonderful? In my own home, I have to choose my clothing to please some horrible animals. Tully, you take those beasts back behind the wall, where they belong."

"You won't say that when one of them cons gets to runnin' around loose. Them Dobermans can hear a con fart from half a mile."

"Tully Keyster, you mind your language in this house."

"Yeah, yeah— sorry. Had a tough day, I guess. Let's drop the whole clam, okay? Is dinner ready? I'm starved."

"It's been ready nearly an hour. How come you're so late?"

"I stopped to visit a friend." The warden picked up the evening paper. "Where's Jen?"

"She's having dinner at a playmate's house."

"Yeah? Which playmate?"

"I don't know for sure... Nancy Webster, I think, or Darlene Sonnet— now, Tully, don't start making a big fuss. The girl's a teenager now, and it's only seven o'clock in the evening."

"Oh well, yeah, sure it is... and it's only dark out already, and we're only a gonad's throw from the state pen!"

"Tully."

"Okay, okay, but do you know what happened today? No? Well, I'll tell you. That patsy-faced geek-con working out in our garden spilled his roach-slime hornies on our little girl, that's what!"

Anita Keyster gasped. "He . . . **what!"**

"Spewed his maggot muck at our little Jen! Made 'er cry, the louse sweat! Paid for it with his blood, too— you can bet your snatch on..."

"Tully!"

"Okay, I'm through, I'm not gonna say another word."

"If you'd speak plain English instead of that gutter language..." Anita was concerned and shaken. **"Now, what did this convict do to Jenny?"**

"The dirty clam vomit... Okay, okay, he threatened your daughter, and he used disgusting and abusive language— is that the King's English for you?" Tully buried his face in the paper.

"He *said* something?" Anita sighed with relief. "My God, I thought he *raped* the girl or something!"

"Oh, no. *Today* he didn't rape the girl, today he just smut mouthed her. Maybe *tomorrow* he'll rape her, if it's a nice day."

"Well, what did he say?"

"I don't want to talk about it. Are we gonna sit here and eat dinner, or is that our lousy breakfast in the oven over there?"

Mrs. Keyster served the meal without another word. Her husband propped the newspaper against his beer can and shoveled spoonfuls of beef stew into his mouth as he read, emitting an occasional grunt.

Anita finally said, "I wish you wouldn't read at the table."

"Huh. Yeah, well, it's not exactly a tonic for my stomach, I'll tell you that. This here rag's fulla the same old snake snot. Lookit how wonderful we are, world— no more executions. Make a decent man want to vomit."

"Tully, I'm trying to eat my dinner."

"Huh. Well, me too... what is this stuff, anyway?"

"Beef stew, and what's the matter with it?"

"Huh."

Anita placed her napkin on the table. "Are you going to start about my cooking again?"

Tully shoved a huge hunk of meat into his mouth and shook his head. "I can eat prison cookin', I can eat anything." Glancing at his wife, he saw that she was on the verge of tears. "Aw, look, Neet, don't pay no attention to me tonight. I'm not myself, what with this here new law, and that business with Jen and the con— it's got me a tad tense, I guess. Sorry.

"Anita's face softened; she picked up her napkin and returned it to her lap. "I'm an old grouch myself, today, You'd think I was going through my menopause again."

"Huh. The whole world's going through some changes, I'll tell you that. Look at this... this broad just had nine brats— the Noogie No-vump-lets. I'd shoot myself."

Anita smiled. "Their father's going to be on Art Pastel's show tonight."

"Remind me to miss it."

"Eat your stew," his wife said.

"Nine boys. Wouldn't that frost your dingus? They'll probably grow up and form a rape gang. What time you say Jen was due home?"

"Soon, dear."

"I could call her girl friend's house... maybe she wants

me to drive over and pick her up."

"If Jenny wants a ride, she'll call us."

Tully turned the page of his paper. "Did you see this? 'The History of the Electric Chair.' Already it's history. What d'you bet some museum will get the hots for my toaster? Stick it between the dinosaurs and the last outhouse." He pulled a cigar from his lapel pocket and began to unwrap it.

"You haven't finished your dinner yet, dear," his wife reminded him.

"Huh? Oh, yeah." He laid the cigar beside his plate and picked up his fork again. "Sure hate to be walkin' the beat today, I'll tell you that." He rearranged the food on his plate. "Gives me the willies, what's happenin' to this world today. That's why I'm worried about that little girl of mine. I know what can happen..."

"Don't get yourself worked up again, dear."

"No, no, don't worry, I'm not climbin' on any soapboxes— but, scab-muff-it, it's the truth, it's how I feel." He sliced a piece of potato with his fork. I'm tryin' to be a good dad to that little girl— busted my heehaw to get to know her and understand her... and I've done a helluva good job, too, I'm proud to say." He shoved the cigar into his mouth.

"You said you were hungry, Tully bear," soothed his wife.

"Right." He slipped the cigar into his pocket and reclaimed his fork. "Good stew," he remarked, stirring it briskly. "She tells me she's thinking about doing some sort of religious work when she grows up. The maggots and goons out there are just waitin' to get their slimy hands on a little saint like that. I gotta look out for her."

"Your stew's getting cold, Tully."

"Yeah, okay, the subject's closed. This girl friend of hers— she a nice girl?"

"Eat your dinner, dear."

"Sure, sure, you win. I'm not gonna say another word." Warden Keyster consumed three slices of carrot, one piece of meat and a potato wedge, then looked up at the wall clock over the sink. "Almost seven-thirty. It's a school night, you know."

15

"Ahhh... miso, miso, miso, deva... karoo, karoo, karoo..."

Young Jenny Pye Keyster lay sprawled upon her back in the spring sweet meadow grass, her naked body pinned to earth beneath the warm and comforting weight of the man who lay on top of her, incessantly thrusting his stiff, slippery penis deep inside her churning cooze.

"Ohh, miso, miso, deva-doll... this moth is really feezed..." She rolled her head from side to side and brushed away the matted hair from her perspiring brow.

The man stilled her head in his hands and bit her mouth, then slobbered down across her chin and began to lick her neck.

Aflame with rapture, Jenny gazed up at the starry sky and watched the universe revolve around her. Hiking her knees up to the man's slender rib cage, she locked her ankles at the small of his back and squirmed her hips deliciously as he hilted her again and again, forcing luscious waves of ecstasy through her quivering innards.

"Ahhh, yes..." she sighed, "that's quick... that's near... that's floral, tidal, treble..."

The cosmos began to whirl above her; then, deep within her being, another universe prepared to burst into creation. Her breast began to flutter; she gulped the cool night air in desperate draughts. Her hands caught at her lover's hair and popped his sucking mouth from her bruised and swollen nipple; she glued her lips to his; her mouth was hot and dry, but his gurgled moisture like a mountain spring; she probed her parched tongue into his bubbling well and swabbed up irrigation for her arid throat.

"Karoo, karoo," she panted urgently into his mouth, "...oh, curd me, curd me, curd me..." Her hands slid down across his back and began to knead his thrusting buttocks.

"Uh," the man grunted. "Oh... uh." He pistoned into her with greater frequency.

"Curd me... curd me... curd me..." begged the frantic girl, her hand cupping his testicles and milking them with gentle insistence.

"Oh— oh," the man gasped suddenly, his bewildered eyes bugging in his head. He sank the full length of his sizzling shaft into her demanding depths, ground his pubes desperately on hers and began to shudder uncontrollably. "Oh— **oh**," he pleaded into her ear with slobbering urgency. "Something... **God!**"

Jenny felt a lava geyser spurt its molten elements inside her, scalding her entrails again and again. She gaped her mouth and uttered an extended cry of absolute silence as she saw the universe implode outside her, and felt a universe explode within. It was another Genesis.

Chaplain Ryder Levitsky lay motionless on Jenny Keyster's naked body, listening to the throbbing hammer of his heartbeat. Though he suspected that his dead weight was becoming a bit uncomfortable for the young girl to bear, he could not bring himself to face her at the moment, so he continued to sprawl upon her hot, moist flesh, his face buried in her fragrant hair. The Catholic priest held his breath as he felt her gentle hands glide across his goose-fleshed buttocks. His spent penis shriveled with guilt and backed out of the warden's daughter like an intruder who has found himself in a forbidden room. *Dear God*, thought the Chaplain of the Achen State Penitentiary, *what have I done?*

The young girl sighed and picked some strands of flaxen hair from the corner of her mouth. "Deva-doll," she whispered, brushing his earlobe with the tip of her tongue, "I can't breathe."

With great effort, Levitsky extracted his face from her damp tresses and raised himself away from her. Their perspiration-soaked chests parted with an embarrassing sound of cellophane tape peeling from its roll. The priest blushed.

" 'Scuse me..." He climbed across her out-turned thigh and rolled to his back in a patch of wild flowers. The night had a thousand eyes. *You have disgraced your sacred vows. You have committed statutory rape. You Have Fucked the Warden's Daughter.*

"Miso, deva," Jenny sighed, lying languid in the tall grass.

The chaplain's eyes stared dumbly at the sky as his fingers discreetly routed an itinerant ant he felt detouring through his pubic hair. *Now I've really done it.* He wanted to run away, to leap and bound gazelle-like across the moonlit meadow— but all he had on was a pair of black socks. *Get dressed. Sit up.* He did not move.

Jenny Keyster lounged in drowsy contentment as the universe revolved with awesome precision overhead. The immutable hum of the cosmic dynamo resonated within her breast, lulling her with its soothing vibrations. A mosquito lighted on the tender tip of her left nipple; she wished it away, and it obeyed.

Her companion suddenly sat up, coughed self-consciously and rummaged through the grass at his feet. She watched him shake out his T-shirt and squirm into it. *Cute*, she thought sensing his mortification. She sighed dreamily. You'd think it'd be tougher, getting a priest to screw you. She felt she should reach out to him, cuddle him, explain to him... but instead she turned her radiant face toward the stars again.

   Later, she decided. *I'll smooth him in an eon... when my balloon comes back.*

Warden Keyster closed his study door and paused to bite the end from a new cigar. *If it don't fry your aitchbone*, he mused, reflecting upon the events of the day. Ambling to his desk, he picked up a miniature replica of an electric chair and turned it over in his hand. MERRY CHRISTMAS TO THE GAR MOUNTAIN MONSTER, read the inscription, FROM FOWLEY, POCK AND RHINO— THE BOYS ON DEATH ROW.

Keyster smiled. *Never let it be said them cons don't have a sense of humor.* The warden flicked a lever at the side of the chair and a tiny flame shot out of its seat. He lit his cigar, sat down and fished a bundle of letters from the inside pocket of his suit jacket. "What a day. No time to look at my squatting mail." He opened one of the letters.

Dear Warden Keyster,

I did not vote for this rotten amendment. I have served as a witness at seven of your executions. You have been doing wonderful for all us decent people. I am sick as you about this lousy law. If I can do something, let me know. I am in your corner all the way.

Your friend,

OLIVE PONTEVECCHIO

Keyster lowered the letter and squinted toward the ceiling. *Pontevecchio, Pontevecchio... oh, yeah— she's that wrinkled old snatch, the one always brings popcorn to the burns. Sorry, Cranny, get your jollies somewheres else— the show's over.* He tossed the letter into the wastebasket.

Nine-thirty. His gaze shifted from his watch to the study door. The house was silent, except for the faint sound of the TV program his wife was watching in the living room. Nine o'clock that little girl oughta be home school nights. He puffed his cigar and opened another letter.

GAR MOUNTAIN POLICE ACADEMY
•founded 1889•
—Respect for Law is Taught by Example—

Dear Warden Keyster:

This June 25, our academy will present coveted police shields to 143 deserving cadet patrolmen.

We, the academy administration, the graduating class, their families and guests, would be pleased and honored if you would consent to deliver our commencement address at this ceremony. On this most important day of a young policeman's life, the thoughts of a revered criminologist such as yourself would serve as inspiration toward a long and outstanding career in the field of law enforcement.

May I phone you next week to discuss this matter with you?

Sincerely,

F. CHATMAN TACK

Supt., GMPA FCT/gfy

"Well now," the warden beamed; he flattened the letter on his desk and reread it. "...'revered criminologist,' huh?...

'inspiration toward'...'' He sent several billows of blue-white smoke rolling across the desk top. *This... is a real joint jerker.*

Keyster floated to his feet. "Yes**sir** ." He lumbered about the room, smacking his fist into the palm of his hand. *I'll inspire the dugsuckers.* He found himself standing before a faded photo on the wall— a police academy class picture, shot thirty-seven years ago. There, in the third row, seventh from the left, stood a six-foot-four-inch, muscular young patrolman, his proud, stern face steeled with the patented Keyster "don't-fuck-with-me" expression. *A real rock stamper, I was. Get-out-there-and-bust-the-goons, make-the-world-a-better-place... Then you find out you're the only fuzzball in your leeching precinct that ain't on the take.* "Gives you a bit of a turn." He smiled and shook his head. *Yessir, men, they pin a silver shield on your tit, and all of a sudden you're supposed to be God Almighty* — "A sawbones, a boy scout, a nose wipe, politician, head shrink-and a clam-assed computer all rolled into one."

Keyster chomped his cigar and resumed pacing. "And remember this: It's the uniform that swings the weight, not the guy inside it. Take off that blue suit and you're lower'n a worm's wong."

He caught a glimpse of his reflection in the darkened window. "See these duds? I've worn a business suit seven days a week for the past nineteen years, but till I was thirty-eight years old I clam-near never had one of these things on my body. I wore a patrolman's uniform eighteen years... yessir, I earned this business suit. Now I could walk into a cell block naked as a maggot, and the cons would shiver." He sat down at his desk and read the police academy letter a third time; then he sat back, stared at the ceiling and nodded. "You send a snot-eared cadet out on the beat thinking people are pure as the driven snow, he's gonna come back to the station house with his night stick up his bum-hole."

"Better dump me at the corner— I'll walk the rest."

Chaplain Levitsky pulled the car to the curb and switched off his headlights. For several moments, they sat in silence; the priest had not uttered a word since mounting Jenny in the meadow, and the girl had decided to respect his wish for silence— but now it was time to part, and there were things which must be said.

When she laid her hand upon his sleeve, she felt him stiffen. "You're feezed, aren't you?" she inquired gently.

The priest began to cry.

"Hey," Jenny cooed, taking him in her arms, "hey there..."

Levitsky clamped his fists between his knees and buried his face into her shoulder. "Oh Jenny Jenny Jenny," he sobbed "what have I done?"

"Hey there, hey hey," the girl consoled, petting his hair. "Every thing's espee, everything's sleek..."

"What have I done...? What have I done...?" the chaplain blubbered against her sweater, gradually becoming aware that his chin was brushing the top of her downy breast.

"Hey now... smooth up, deva-doll, everything's floral..."

"...What have I done...?" His face sank deeper into the gossamer softness, and the bulge in his trousers began to swell. *Oh God!* he realized, desperately, *See! The vortex! The trap!* Estimating the location of her unsuspecting nipple, his mouth suddenly gaped, engulfing a generous portion of the tender breast.

"Oh wow," gasped Jenny, lifting his head away gently but firmly, "that's crambo, deva— you better turn your head on." She plucked the handkerchief from his lapel and dabbed at the spittle on her sweater.

The priest pressed his forehead against the dashboard. *There. See? I'm a sex fiend.*

Jenny laid an understanding hand upon his back. "Forget it, blue bird. Don't cry."

Levitsky sniffed loudly, then fell silent, thrilling to her touch upon his spine. When he spoke, his voice was devoid of emotion. "I'll be crucified for this, you know."

"Don't be silly. It was my light bulb, not yours."

"Light bulb?" The chaplain raised his head and gazed through the windshield toward the sky. "What light bulb?"

"Light bulb— you know— idea. All this was my idea, not yours, so stop macing yourself... if you want to mace somebody, mace me."

The priest looked at her quizzically, then returned his head to the dashboard. "What have I done?" He sighed.

"Look, that's crambo," Jenny insisted. "Thirty years from now, are you gonna regret more the things you did or the things you didn't do?"

"I took advantage of you."

"How?"

"You're just a child." Through the trees he could see the illumination of the penitentiary searchlight as it made its ceaseless rounds. "You're only fifteen."

The girl wrinkled her nose. "What difference does that make? Besides, I'm not fifteen anyway."

Levitsky stared at her. She's not fifteen! She's twenty-one! A consenting adult!

"I'm thirteen."

Chaplain Levitsky envisioned Warden Keyster's massive fist swinging toward his face like a giant steel wrecking ball.

Jenny propped her feet against the dashboard, saw how the priest's eyes began to widen as he gazed at her moonlit c-thru-slax, then lowered her legs again. "Thirteen years old-what does that mean? In biology, Miss Hawkins told us that every seven years, every cell in our body is new . . . which means that next year I start my third body. So, what's thirteen years old? My name? Omee, so my name's been around thirteen years— and your name's been around — what?— fifty?"

The priest looked offended. "I'm only thirty-eight."

"Omee. So you've been Ryder Levitsky longer than I've been Jenny Keyster— that means you raped me?" She captured several strands of her long blonde hair, drew them across her face under her pert nose, then let them drop.

"Ever cabob a moth before?"

"Huh?"

"Am I the first girl you've ever fucked?"

The chaplain's head snapped as though he'd been slapped. "Why— What kind of language— you shouldn't... *once*! Just this once, in thirty-eight years! You gotta give me a break on this!"

Jenny quieted him with a hand on his cheek. "Well, I've done it lots of times."

Levitsky gazed at her hopefully. "You have?"

"True-tell," she smiled, "so we're even— you're twenty years up on me and I'm twenty fucks up on you."

Thoughts floated sluggish and vague behind the chaplain's eyes. "You mean you aren't... weren't... a..."

"Cherry? Karoo, no," Jenny laughed, "not since sixth grade. A high-school boy skewered me— I made him do it, just like I made you."

"You... made me?" Ryder Levitsky felt like a very small boy.

"That's the supertruth." She swung the car door open, the light went on and the priest turned his face away from her. "I thought it would be sleek to have you curd me. There wasn't anything you could do to stop it— you're a man."

The priest waited until she got out and closed the door putting the light out. "Buy why?" he beseeched her, quietly. "Why me?"

Jenny leaned in the window and regarded the distraught clergy man with her wide and innocent eyes. " 'Cause I thought it would be sleek, you being a priest and all." She waited to see if he understood, but he seemed only to grow smaller in his seat. "I mean, you've got God's power of attorney, grab? You forgive sins for Him. You're closer to God than anyone else I know, and I want to get tight with Him, too— so I decided that having you inside me would be like having God there, grab?"

The chaplain's face screwed into a smile of bitter irony. "And now," he pronounced, in his best sermon voice,"you see what folly it was."

"Folly?" Jenny was surprised. "Deva-doll, it was megabliss!"

"It... it was?" He was flattered, in spite of himself.

"Sacrosupernova!" Jenny bubbled. "So thanks a lot, okay?" She blew him a kiss and began strolling away.

You're welcome. He almost said it aloud; now he watched her walk away toward the corner. I'll be your pony, she'd whispered to him in the meadow, and you be my Ryder. He switched on his headlights and put the car into gear, noticing that the lights shone directly on the young girl's back as she moved away from him.

She turned and waved. The light was brilliant on her body; it seemed to dissolve her c-thru blouse and slacks, leaving only a tiny black bra, wispy bikini panties, honey-golden hair and skin like the alabaster Madonna in Saint John's chapel.

His tongue dipped into that satiny navel. His fingers distorted the flawless symmetry of those awesome buttocks. Her creamy luscious thighs swung open and slithered round his eager body. *This isn't happening, you see. This, and back there in that meadow— they're just like all the others.*

Images of past erotic fantasies tumbled from the shadows of his mind: his head up Jenny's dress, burrowing between her legs as she cringed in the confessional; violating Anita Keyster from behind in a crowded subway car; swinging on a playground swing while Monsignor Maywine ran back and forth beneath him, sucking his penis;

lying naked in the prison yard, his knees hiked up and tied to his chest, as every inmate lined up before him, each holding a monstrous erection in one hand and a jar of Vaseline in the other...

I'll confess, and that'll be that. You'll see. Just like all the other times. I'm losing my mind.

He watched Jenny drop her hand and disappear around the corner. *She's thirteen years old, and I'm a Catholic priest.* Suddenly he tromped on the gas, sped to the corner and screeched to a halt. "Jenny! he hissed, urgently. "Hey!"

She scampered out of the darkness and thrust her golden head through the window opposite him.

The chaplain placed his elbow on the back of the seat and casually laid his head in his hand. "You... ah... you won't tell your father about... this, will you?"

"Daddy?" She was amazed. "Are you moonblind? If my daddy found out about us, he'd murder you with his bare hands!" She stared at him wide-eyed and very seriously for a moment, just to be certain he understood the importance of her words; then she flashed him a friendly smile and sprinted away into the night.

Tully picked up the phone and dialed ten numbers. "Hello, who's this— Warden Park? I just called to ask if you knew that Park spelled backwards is Krap."

The Warden of Zenobia State Penitentiary laughed. "Keyster, you old bull, how's it goin'?"

"Well, no lie, Krappy, this amendment's got me madder'n a raped snake. listen, Lonnie, here's why I'm callin'— you wouldn't happen to have any cons in your Death Row, would you?"

"Hell, Tully, you know as well as me there's not an execution order outstanding in the whole country."

"Huh," Keyster nodded. "Wish I hadn't burned those three I had last year— but I thought I'd better get rid of my inventory before they put me out of business. Vulture vomit. What about outside the country? Think I'd have to pay duty if I import a condemned con? I got seven months till this law goes into effect, and I want to have one last burn before I lock the old Playpen."

"Sure..." Warden Park's voice cracked; he cleared his throat. "I'll keep my eyes open for you, Tul."

"You do that, Lonnie— and don't worry about how I'll get him transferred to Achen State. You just find me the beef, I'll put my brand on it." The study door opened and Tully saw his daughter enter the room. "Well, nice talkin' to you, Krappy. Give me a call next week and we'll set a date for an interprison ball game." He hung up without waiting for Lonnie Park's response. "There's my little girl!"

"Hi, Daddy Bear!" Jenny all but disappeared in her father's vast embrace.

Tully pawed the blonde head gently. "How's my muffin?"

"Omee!"

"You didn't walk home in the dark did you?" "Huh-uh-my friend's father drove me."

"Yeah? Next time you bring him in and let me get a look at him. What's he do?"

"When?"

The warden held her away and squinted at her. "What's he do for a living?"

"He works for the church," the girl explained innocently. "I think he sells Bibles or something."

"Huh." He held her between his huge hands as though she were a piece of fluff. "Sellin' Bibles don't make him a saint, Jen. He's just another salesman, and all salesmen got hornies the size of this house."

"Oh, Daddy."

"Mark my words. He tries something funny, you let me know." Tully peered at the c-thru outfit she had on. "Say, ain't that material a tad skinny?"

"Oh, Daddy," his daughter reached up to straighten

his tie, "don't be such an old fuss." She strolled around his desk, out of the light, so he could no longer see through her clothing. "Did you have an omee day today?" She nosed through the papers on his desk.

"Huh. I had a day would give a maggot the GIs." His hands felt his pockets and glanced about the room."Now, where the squat did I leave my cigar?" He unwrapped a new one and shoved it into his mouth, leaving it unlit. "Yessir, a real grub sucker, this has been. Well, at least you'll be glad to know I fixed that con with the squat juice mouth."

Jenny's eyes widened. "Who?"
The warden chewed his cigar and watched that familiar expression sweep across his daughter's face. Just like her old lady, he thought, knowing he was about to encounter that mysterious, incomprehensible phenomenon he'd grown to refer to as "bitch morality."

"Daddy, who did you fix?"

"Ah, I had a little talk with that Fucilla fellow— you know, the one who shot off his yap to you in the garden."

Jenny's face was white. "Deva, Daddy, you didn't hurt him, did you?"

"Naw." His gaze faltered and fell from hers. "Course not."

"Daddy I told you that poor man didn't do anything wrong!"

"Nothing wrong?" Warden Keyster's ears turned red. **"For scab sakes, Jen, the man is a scum bag! Ebie Faber saw the whole thing from his watch post on the wall! What am I supposed to do-just stand around and wait for my daughter to get raped in my own ragging back yard?"**

The young girl's eyes brimmed with tears. "You hurt him! You did!"

Tully lunged toward her viciously, veering off at the last instant and attacking a large unabridged dictionary on the end table near his desk. **"MOTHER OF A CLAM!"** He delivered a roundhouse punch to the tome's thick spine; the heavy book shot five feet horizontally through the air, struck the side of a metal filing cabinet with the sound of an Oriental gong, then thudded to the floor, its binding ruptured in three places. **"For the love of squat, Jenny, nobody has to tell me how to handle cons! That son of a snake told me what he said to you! Any roach goes around vomiting that kind of puke outa his yap— he gets his face changed, it's as simple as that!"** He held his arms away from his sides, his palms toward her. "What am I,Jen, some kind of a brainless ape that goes around opening heads for the fun of it? Have I ever lifted a finger to you?" He jammed his fists into his jacket pockets. "I let a con get away with a stunt like that, I'm washed up. What he did to you, he did to me at the same time— he knew it, you know it, I know it— and tomorrow every chicken-mother in stir will know it too. I shoulda killed the slime weasel, but I didn't want to make a big thing out of it."

Jenny's chin was on her chest; a golden curtain of hair hid her face from Tully's sight. "He couldn't help it," she said softly, "it was my fault."

"Your fault?"

"I let him look at me." His daughter's voice was just a whisper. "He only wanted love."

"Young lady, you watch your language! I know roach well what he wanted, the grease-wart! If I hadn't a put the kibosh on that son of a fag snake, nine'll get you ten he'd a been waitin' for you tomorrow with his wong out!"

"TULLY!"

Keyster turned to find his wife standing in the doorway, livid with anger. Simultaneously, the Pomeranian shot across the carpet to ward him like a furry bullet and caught hold of his pants cuff. **"Shag ass, you little hair fart!"** Tully tried to pull his leg free, but the dog's teeth were firmly implanted in his trousers, so he tried to step on the tiny animal with his other foot. **"You turd mouth..."** Bromberg, sensing impending doom, released the warden's pants leg and sped to his mistress' side, where he continued to hurl abuse at the object of his ire.

The warden met his wife's withering gaze. "Well, hell's eels, Anita, the little maggot was tearing my suit!" His wife was too furious to speak, the dog kept shrieking at him, and Jenny's head was still bowed, her fragile shoulders heaving gently. Throwing up his hands, Tully decided to retreat. "All right, okay, I'm sorry, forget it, the subject's closed on both sides, I'm not gonna say another word." He patted his daughter's shoulder. "Everything's over and done with let's forget the whole shebang and go watch TV... what say, muffin?"

Jenny sniffed, raised her head, forced a smile and nodded. "That's my little girl!" The warden laid his arm gently around her shoulders and walked her to the study door; he ushered her through ahead of him, trying to ignore the burning gaze of his wife.

"**Tully Keyster...**" Anita hissed, leaving the rest unspoken.

"I know, my dear, I know," sighed Warden Keyster, motioning for her to precede him through the doorway. When she was gone, he switched off the study light and paused, gazing into the darkness. *I got to learn to keep my yap shut.* He shook his head and stepped out of the room, swinging the door shut behind him. When he plucked the fresh, unlit cigar from his mouth, he saw that half of it had disappeared.

"**Hey, America! There's a party tonight— in** *The Pastel Penthouse!*"

Tully lowered his newspaper and scowled at the television set. "Rag." Then he ducked behind his paper again; he had learned long ago to keep his yap shut about Art Pastel.

"**Hi, everyone— I'm Freddy Fredella.**" The announcer

grinned.

"Art'll be out in just one minute— after this important message from the Cundelini Cracker Company!" The screen faded to black; there was the clash of an Oriental gong, a puff of smoke and then a genie appeared, holding a box of soda crackers.

The warden glanced over at his daughter, who was curled up at one end of the sofa, staring blankly at her homework in her lap. "Muffin, how d'you expect to get any work done out here?"

Jenny looked up at him with the same blank expression. "Huh?"

"I want to know how the grease you're gonna learn anything," repeated Keyster, louder than necessary, "with all that racket in your ear!"

His daughter's eyes widened slightly. "What racket, Daddy?"

Tully squinted at her suspiciously. "What racket. The TV, for squat sake. What racket."

"Karoo, no, Daddy Bear— I need it for my homework."

"What're you studyin', dramatics?"

"Math."

Tully looked at his wife, who smiled; Anita didn't mind them talking during the commercials or when Art Pastel was not on the screen. The warden swung his gaze back to Jenny. "For math you need the television going?"

"Sacro, Daddy," Jenny lifted her homework paper. "This scene is like crossing the great water— I mean, math is an entire other realm." She nodded toward the TV. "I need to hear Earth Mother humming to keep me from slipping right out of my conch."

Warden Keyster turned to his wife. "And you say you can't under stand the muffing way I talk!"

"Shhh!" hissed Anita, watching the commercial end; her tiny Pomeranian, lying in her lap, growled at Tully and bared its teeth.

"And now, all you Pastel Penthouse Peeping Toms— glue your eyes to that keyhole, 'cause here comes The Man With The Magic Smile!"

Keyster narrowed his eyes and watched Art Pastel leap from behind the studio curtains and bask in a thunderous ovation. *Homo Fart*. He glanced at his family: Jenny still gazed blankly at her home work; Anita stared entranced at the roguish face of Art Pastel. *Mister Big Shot. If he ain't a cow fag, then I'm a clam's uncle*. From his wife's lap, two little coal-black eyes continued to monitor his every move.

"Hey there!" The Man With The Magic Smile shouted, **"Are we gonna have some fun?"**

"YES!" roared the studio audience.

Pastel walked right up to the camera lens, his eye filling the Keyster television screen. **"Hey, Peeping Toms— got your eyes on that keyhole?"**

Anita Keyster smiled and nodded her head.

The camera dollied back until Pastel was visible from the waist up; he grinned suggestively. "Okay, voyeurs— I mean *viewers*— keep your peepers peeled and **watch us do it!"**

Tully bit through his cigar. *Wonder what it'd cost me to shove my foot through that picture tube.*

"You said it— not me!" accused Art Pastel.
The studio audience howled and Anita Keyster grinned with delight.

"Hey, we've got a whale of a show tonight— oh, before I forget, I want to send out a great big smooch to all of you gorgeous dolls who wrote in to say you liked that little song I did for the Noogie Novuplets last week!" He reared back and blew a big kiss at the camera. "The response was so great, we decided to record 'You're My Bouncing Baby Boys' on Whirl Records and it should be available at your local stores in a couple weeks. [Applause] Don't get me wrong, folks— I just sing the song, I don't want any credit for the birth of those kids! [Laughter] But there is someone here tonight who does deserve a lot of the credit! What say, everybody, how 'bout a real Penthouse welcome for America's sexiest male animal— **the father of the Noogie Novies— LEWD NOOGIE!"**

"Oh!" gasped Anita Keyster, excitedly. Even Jenny looked up from her homework .

Tully watched the curtains part, revealing a tired-looking man in a wrinkled subway conductor's uniform. You poor sap, thought Keyster.

The picture on the screen alternated between Lewd Noogie's bewildered face and a shot of the audience on its feet applauding and cheering, while Ulloch Tugg and the BBS Orchestra blared an up tempo version of "You're My Bouncing Baby Boys."

Art Pastel shook Lewd's hand warmly, then led him upstage to a pair of upholstered chairs, where they sat down. The music ended, but the audience's wild applause continued until the star raised his hands and asked for silence. Pastel looked at the camera then, and nodded thoughtfully. "You know, we can all count ourselves fortunate to have lived in a year when so many wonderful and important things have happened in this great land of ours: The Noogies' incredible blessed event, the long overdue and equally blessed end to capital punishment—"

"WORM TURD!" Tully Keyster was bristling.

"*Tully!*" snapped his wife. Bromberg shot from her lap, streaked across the floor, and speared the warden's pants leg with his tiny teeth, growling furiously.

"I don't give a muff-squat!" Keyster shouted, kicking at the dog and jabbing his finger toward the TV. **"That homo roach got his bung-hole where his mouth should be! Mother of a wet clam, decent little children got to listen to—"**

"Jenny, leave the room!" Anita ordered.

"What for?" Jenny asked.

Bromberg bounced away from the warden's swinging

foot and again charged at him, barking hysterically. Keyster crumpled his newspaper into a wad: "**...and if that little hunk of crap doesn't zip his mangy yap, I'm gonna ram it back to his cuck-hole!**" He raised the wadded paper, but instead of throwing it at the dog, he flung it at the television set.

Anita snatched the dog from the floor and cradled it protectively.

"There, there, Bromby darling..." She glowered at her husband. "Tully Keyster, you apologize for that remark!"

"Inna pig's squat I will!"

Jenny witnessed the repartee with faint amusement. The television set had become completely disregarded, when suddenly during a lull in the Keyster quarrel, this exchange was heard emanating from *The Pastel Penthouse*:

ART PASTEL: Well, Lewd, how does it feel
                    to be the father of nine baby boys?
LEWD NOOGIE: Lousy.

Anita Keyster quickly forgot her argument with her husband; the television set once more commanded her attention. Jenny also stared at the screen. Only Tully and Bromberg remained immune to its spell; the two glowered at one another in the center of the room.

Art Pastel was a bit rattled by his guest's remark, but recovered nicely. "Ha, ha! Well, you're lousy with kids, that's for sure!" The audience followed Pastel's lead and took the entire exchange to be a joke. "But seriously, Lewd, I'll bet you and the little woman are proud as punch to be the parents of the only set of *novuplets* in the entire world, aren't you?"

Noogie shrugged. "Fila maybe. Me, I'd as soon had a little girl, or none at all."

There were shocked gasps from the studio audience.

Anita sat down slowly, biting her lip and shaking her

head.

Jenny's eyes were very wide; "Unwow," she said.

Even Warden Keyster stood staring at the set.

Art Pastel bobbed to his feet. "Well, thanks for dropping into the Penthouse, Mr. Noogie. Good luck and good night."

"And good riddance," added Anita Keyster.

There were scattered boos from the studio audience as Lewd Noogie rose and loped away; but mostly there was silence.

PART FOUR

Thursday, May 18

17

by LA MONIQUE

THROUGH THE TUBE, DARKLY

Thursday, May 18— Pastel Penthouse Peeping Toms really got an eye-full last night— and a gut-full, too. We boob-tubers thought we were gonna get a gander at the proud poppa of nine new baby boys— but what did we see instead? Some animal called a LEWD NOOGIE: You pull its chain and it says, "I wish those kids were never born." NOW HEAR THIS, LEWD NOOGIE: WHEN TWO-HUNDRED-MILLION IRATE AMERICANS GET THROUGH WITH YOU, YOU'LL WISH Y-O-U WERE NEVER BORN...

Fila Noogie lowered the newspaper to her lap and gazed toward the ceiling of her hospital room. "Zow." She closed the paper and scanned the front page. First time in a week we didn't make page one. "Oh, Bozo, you really busted my chops this time," she said to the empty room—then she remembered that the room was far from being empty: there were nine other human beings there with her.

She glanced across the room toward the large glass-and-metal cube humming peacefully in the morning sunlight; the device was called a "fourpee"— *Pythia Post-Parturition Pod*— and it was absolutely the last word in infant-life monitor-regulating controlled-environment systems. Gingerly, she swung her newly painted toe nails from the bed, got up and tiptoed halfway across the tiled floor before she froze in awe.

There, snoozing cozily within the complaisant mechanical womb, snuggled nine minute beings, just eight days old.

One, two, three, four, five, six, seven, eight, nine. She snuck up to the humming, airtight compartment and pressed her nose to the warm glass. Two, four, six, eight, nine. Slipping her hands beneath the waistband of her pink satin pajamas, she spread her palms across the wrinkled surface of her now deflated belly, stroking the furrowed pasture while her eyes beheld its wondrous harvest. "Wow."

Behind her, the door swung open and the head nurse, Tina Limones, breezed in with the morning medication. Her greeting was the same as every other day, but this time she did not smile. "And how's our celebrities today?"

"Aces," said Fila, still gazing into the Fourpee.

Mrs. Limones moved with exaggerated efficiency as she set the pill container on the bed tray, along with half a cup of water. "You catch the Art Pastel show last night?" She examined the medical charts in her folder.

"Uh-huh." Fila watched the number-three mini-baby poke its fist in its eye.

Nurse Limones let a reasonable interval pass before speaking again, and this time her casual tone was betrayed by just a touch of emotion. "You saw your... husband, then?"

Fila straightened up. "Yep, I saw him all right." She winked at the novies, then strolled to her bed tray and glanced at the pills, but did not take them. Her hands were still inside her pajama pants, and when she stood with her feet planted apart, she looked like a cowboy.

The nurse arched her eyebrows coldly. "My-my, we're certainly treating all this pretty lightly, aren't we?"

Fila shrugged. "What'm I supposed to do," she climbed onto the bed and hiked up her feet to see if the nail polish had dried, "beat my head against the wall?"

"Well, for openers," Mrs. Limones bristled, "I'd tell that — man ta get lost, and then I'd make one hell of a statement to those people outside, and I'd tell them..."

"Wait a minute!" Fila tossed her red tresses away from her face and studied the nurse quite seriously. "What people outside?"

"My God, you mean you don't know that there's hundreds of people picketing out front, right this very minute? The National PTA, the American Mothers, the..."

"Whoa now— hold on!" Fila scampered to the window, though she knew it did not face the front of the building.

"You mean they're demonstrating out there— against my Lewdy?"

"You're damn right they are, and if I wasn't on duty I'd be out there too."

Fila was enthralled. She craned her neck at both sides of the window, but could see no indication of the crowd gathered at the hospital entrance. "What's their beef?"

"They want you to divorce that... *him*... or they want those babies taken away from him somehow. And there's a bunch of reporters out there, too— newspapers, radio, TV— they want to know what you're gonna do to protect your children."

"Wow." Fila sank into a chair.

The nurse watched her awhile, then strode to the door and looked back impatiently. "They're not gonna wait forever, you know."

Fila bobbed to her feet, wandered to the bed table and screwed a pink cigarette into her holder, she lit up and pulled a great mass of smoke into her lungs.

"Well?" prodded Limones.

"Yeah... yeah, okay..." Fila's mind was in high gear. "Tell them... tell them I'll be down in a couple minutes to make a statement." She paced across the room and leaned against the Fourpee, deep in thought.

Nurse Limones went halfway out the door, then remembered something and returned to plunk a sheet of paper on the bed. "Here's the form for the babies' names. It's been over a week now— about time they had names, don't you think?"

"Huh...? Oh, yeah... okay."

The nurse breezed from the room, and Fila wandered aimlessly about, waiting for the pieces to come together in her head. Sucking at her cigarette voraciously, she moved to the bed tray, dumped the water from the paper cup and refilled it with vodka from a bottle she kept in the bedside cabinet. Shoveling her morning pills into her mouth, she washed them down with the vodka, feeling her tension dissipate as the warmth flowed through her body.

There was a knock at the door, but Fila didn't hear it. The door opened quietly. "Ah... hi, Aunt Fi."

Fila spun around. "Corbin!" She flew to him and flung her arms about him gratefully. "Jesus, you don't know how happy I am to see you!"

The young man patted her awkwardly. "How are you?"

She sprang away, her hands clutching both his arms. "Baby, I don't know my asshole from an armadillo, and you're the only person on earth I can talk to about this! Come over here and sit down. Where've you been, for

Christ sake? Why haven't you come to see me? I've been..."
She noticed him staring across the room toward the Pythia
Post-Parturition Pod, and her frenzy drained away. "Oh,
Corbin," she whispered tenderly, "darling, forgive me... how
could I be such a selfish clit? I completely forgot you
haven't even seen them yet." Gently, she took his arm and
led him over to the Fourpee.

Corbin Noogie laid his palms upon the warm glass top
and gazed down at the tiny infants snoozing in their pod.
He closed his eyes; his mind ran away; he felt himself
sinking, rising, floating; and to keep his consciousness, his
sanity, he opened his eyes again and focused on the nine
baby boys.

He felt his aunt's hand settle on his stomach, slide
down across his fly and cup his testicles tenderly. "Sugar,"
she whispered, "you got the hottest, sexiest, manliest,
most atomic-powered jism in the whole mother-lovin'
universe!" Seeing her nephew's eyes swell with tears of
pride, she smiled and stepped softly into his embrace,
slipping her arms about his neck. "Thank you, baby," she
whispered, and pressed her wet, open mouth on his, gently
spearing him with her sexy tongue.

He was like a baby in her arms— awkward, innocent—
and he received her probing kiss with fear at first, an alien
anxiety that was quickly swept away by the waves of
pleasure that her tongue evoked. Her tongue was strong
and hard, just like a penis, and soon his eager lips were
grasping at it hungrily, and he tried to suck it down his
throat with all his might.

"Auh!" Fila gasped, trying to extricate herself from his
frenzied quicksand mouth. *"Augh!"* She tried to push him
away, but he sucked harder on her tongue and she saw
stars explode before her eyes. **"AAAUG!"** Finally, with one
hand she grabbed the long hair at the back of his head,
pulled back with all her might and viciously smacked her
other palm against his forehead, driving his voracious

mouth away with a loud pop.

Corbin staggered over to the bed and sat down, holding his head, while Fila hurried to the mirror to survey the damage. "Christ, baby," she mumbled, examining the root of her tongue, "you got a mouth like a plumber's helper." She wiggled her tongue about until she was satisfied it had not been injured. "Take anything, but don't take my tongue."

Corbin gazed sullenly at the humming Fourpee. "Did you hear what Uncle Lewd said on TV last night?"

His aunt came away from the mirror and sat beside him on the bed. "That's what I have to talk to you about, baby. It's my move now, and I don't want to fuck it up."

Corbin got up and paced to the Fourpee, grinding his fist into the palm of his hand. "Why? Why do they have to grow up thinking he's the father? It's... not fair."

"Now, sugar, you got to take the bitter with the sweet. Remember, if it hadn't been for my Bozo's slow sperm, I wouldn't have needed to engage your services."

"And you wouldn't have had them," Corbin whined, pointing to the pod.

"Camel crap. I coulda used Quasimodo's come and done the same thing. It was my egg that did the trick, buster, and don't forget it."

"I'm still the father!"

"Shhh!" Fila hissed. "Look, smart-ass, if you want the whole world to know about it, why don't you just run outside and tell all those reporters, for Christ sake?"

Corbin looked at the floor. "You know I'd never do that."

Fila softened. "Aw, I know it, sugar lamb," she went to him and pressed her cheek to his, "and I'm sorry for putting you down like that, but you shouldn't bad-mouth your uncle. If anyone's got to stab him in the back because of all this, then it's got to be me and no one else, get me?"

Corbin sighed, shrugged his shoulders and turned away from her, peering down at the babies. "I think he knows they're not his."

"Bullshit."

"He's got to," Corbin insisted. "Why else would he say the things he said last night?"

"Corbin, he said them because they're true. A lot of people hate their kids— the only thing different about Lewd is he admits it."

"But, doesn't he even suspect something? I mean, his sperm is mostly full of females, and you just had nine boys!"

"Look, take it from me," Fila assured him, "all my Lewdy figures is that Fate just gave him another rap in the nuts, like it's been doing all his life."

"It's not fair," said Corbin softly, looking at his sons.

Fila moved to the bed tray and put a fresh cigarette into her holder. "Listen, honey, there's a crowd of people out there waiting for me to make my play, and I want to be sure you're in my corner before I dive in." She lit her cigarette and blew the smoke toward the floor. "I'm going to file for a legal separation."

Corbin's eyes widened. "You... you're going to leave Uncle Lewd?" A tremendous weight began to lift from his shoulders; if Corbin couldn't be the novies' father, nobody could.

Fila poured herself another slug of vodka. "Corbie, I got no choice. It's a crummy thing to do, I know, to sell Lewdy out, just because I had nine kids for laughs and he doesn't think it's funny... but those brats are worth a fortune, and if I try to haul Bozo along for the ride, he's liable to queer the whole thing." She downed her drink, then noticed that her nephew's face had clouded ominously.

"You don't love those babies either," he said bitterly. "You're just using them for what you can get out of them. You're as bad as he is!"

Fila shrugged. "Nobody's perfect. Besides, those brats

coulda done a damn sight worse than me for a mother, so don't feed me that crap. I've acted like a good wife for fifteen years, and I'm gonna act like a good mother for the next fifty— and that's a damn sight better than most of those hypocrite broads out there on that picket line can say. Sure, I'm lookin' out for myself, too. If you hadn't come along with your ten-dollar bottle of baby seeds, l'da spent the rest of my life counting roaches and watching Bozo pick dead skin off the bottom of his feet. Look, I know I'm no saint— none of us are— so we gotta make the best of a shit situation, right? So what do you want for those kids? The best money can buy? Or do you want them to grow up in the same house with Lewd Noogie? He could lose his temper, baby— he could hurt them."

"I'd kill him!" Corbin lurched toward her, eyes blazing.

Fila realized she'd oversold her case. "Hey... easy, baby..." She put her arms around him and felt him quivering with rage. "Hey... don't go off the deep end on me now... we gotta stay cool about all this."

"If he **ever** laid a hand on those babies..." Even his voice was quivering.

"There, there..." Fila patted his back, soothing him, "...you leave everything to Mama. Pretty soon, your mean old uncle will be out of our lives, and everyone will start to think of you as a second father to my kids."

She felt the rage drain out of him as though a stopper had been pulled at his feet; his body ceased shaking and he raised his head slowly, his hopeful eyes searching hers.

"Trust me, lover," Fila pleaded gently, then she kissed his cheek and led him toward the door. "Be a good boy and run along now— sneak out the back way while I get dressed. Lewd's due soon, and then I have to go down and talk to those reporters."

Corbin was smiling weakly now, and docilely allowed himself to be ushered through the doorway and into the hall.

Alone in her room again, Fila poured another slug of vodka and prepared to improvise her statement to the press. Poor Lewdy. But then, there was that unfortunate fact of nature: In order to make something clean, you have to make something else dirty.

Morning rush hour was over, so Lewd Noogie had no trouble getting a seat on the Hamilton Avenue Bus. He was glad he could sit down, since it was a half-hour ride to the Midtown Hospital, and he hadn't had much sleep the night before.

Upon returning from the BBS Television Studios, he had entered his apartment to find the telephone ringing, and had shared this conversation with a shrill female voice:

"Hullo?"

"You prick bastard!"

"You cock-sucker!"

(Click)

No sooner had he hung up than the phone had rung again, and this time a man's voice had told him, "You touch a hair on one of them kids and you get a can of bug spray in bote your eyes."

"Yeah, well c'mon over, I'll be waitin'," Lewd had told him, "and bring a friend, 'cause you're a rat's asshole and your fuckin' mother's the major cause of clap in this city!"

The phone rang again as soon as he'd hung up, so he'd let it ring awhile, and then he'd ripped the wire out of the wall.

Before he had finished undressing for bed, someone had rung the buzzer from the downstairs lobby. Lewd had thrown on an overcoat, stuffed a tire iron in one pocket and a butcher knife in the other, and had gone downstairs; but no one had been there when he had arrived.When he'd returned to his apartment, the downstairs buzzer had rung again. Then, during the night, someone had smeared shit on his front door.

Now, as he sat on the Hamilton Avenue Bus and gazed bleary eyed out the window, he contemplated catching a few winks before he got to the hospital. Today, he was working the four-to-midnight shift on the subway; unless he copped a few Zs sometime before that, he wouldn't be worth much on the train.

Slouching down in his seat, he rested his head against the window and closed his eyes, conjuring up an image of a gorgeous dancer he had seen at the Art Pastel show the previous evening. He watched her do some bumps and grinds for him, only this time he was alone with her in his dressing room, and this time he reached out and sank his eager fingers into her luscious naked waist, drawing her toward him, pressing his hungry mouth against her soft and silky belly... His eyes came open.

Shifting position on the seat, he crossed his arms over his chest and closed his eyelids again, reconstructing the scene where he'd left off. The dancer's belly smelled sweet against his face... he dipped his tongue into her quivering navel, felt her hands run through his hair... His eyes were open again, and he was thinking of how no one backstage had spoken to him or even looked at him after his on camera interview last night.

Fuck 'em, he decided, and doggedly closed his eyes again, but in a moment they popped open of their own accord, and he remembered the harassment he'd received at home last night. *Fuck them, too.*

He decided not to sleep— *Prob'ly miss my stop anyway* — and elected instead to patrol for beaver.

Three teen-agers got on at Catalpa Street, and one, a petite brunette with an ass like a basketball, had on c-thru-slax. She can sit on my face any day, thought Lewd. He focused his gaze on the pale shapely calves clearly visible through the diaphanous material, then he caressed his focus upward over the creamy flesh, the nubile thighs, to the taut silken contours of her pouting pussy-filled panties, imagining his slippery probing tongue snaking beneath that yielding elastic leg band and gliding down the milky gulch where thigh meets torso, soft as a puppy's belly, and into the musty virgin forest where the cockpit was hidden... but suddenly he realized he was not looking at the young girl any longer. Instead he was staring out the window, focusing on nothing. *What's up?* He decided it was nerves, due to lack of sleep.

A young woman was seated across the aisle. Her legs were crossed, and her skirt had ridden three-quarters of the way up her bare, well-proportioned and well-tanned thighs. He imagined himself slipping out of his seat and kneeling before her, sliding his trousers down to his knees, hiking her skirt up over her naked hips, easing her off the seat and impaling her slowly, inch by inch, until... he found himself gazing at an ad for a hemorrhoid preparation.

Chrissake. He shut his eyes. *Fuckin' eightballs... expect a guy to turn cartwheels 'cause his bitch drops a fuckin' army of brats. Bad enough I gotta put up with her, I need nine more on my back. Well, that's how I feel, so fuck 'em all...* his eyes were open again, and he was looking at the young woman across the aisle, only this time he wasn't looking at her legs— he was looking at her eyes. And her eyes were looking at his eyes.

Lewd Noogie never looked at eyes. His gaze spun away and locked in on the girl with the c-thru-slax. Only this time he wasn't looking through her slacks, he was looking through her eyes— and her eyes were looking through his eyes.

He glanced quickly out the window. *Is my fly open?* He rubbed his forehead with his hand, shielding his eyes so he could check out his zipper, but he saw only his wrinkled subway conductor's uniform— nothing unusual.

Looking up again, his gaze was immediately arrested by the sinister eyes of a fat woman with a mustache. Everything had changed overnight. Now the world was full of eyes.

He shut his eyelids tightly, but it didn't help much; he still knew they were all watching him. *Fuck 'em. It's a free country. Fuck 'em all.* Nevertheless, Lewd Noogie realized that it would be a long time before he could nap in public again, or leisurely savor the succulent secrets of an unsuspecting snatch.

Ralston Hutsut, ace correspondent for *The Daily News Gazette*, sat atop a low stone wall outside the Midtown Hospital, enjoying the balmy spring morning and watching the picket line pass by.

"Well, feeze my bubble— the gag rag sent its top garbageman today."

Hutsut turned to discover Levi Cuffe, a youthful reporter from an anti-Establishment paper, strolling toward him. "Anything big enough for the Daily Fuck is big enough for me," Hutsut drawled, thoughtfully studying Cuffe's weird clothing and shaven head. If anything disturbed him about this irreverent kid it was the certain knowledge that nothing Hutsut could write about him could disturb Cuffe's life in the slightest; and that was power, no matter how you looked at it. Hutsut raised an eyebrow. "What's your Pussy Paper interested in around here, anyway?"

"Pussy, Lem— just pussy." Cuffe dug beneath the hem of his leather skirt, scratched his balls, then hiked himself atop the wall beside the News reporter. "Picket-Line Pussy- that's why I'm here, Lem. A blouse gets thermal on a picket line. I mean, you put your nanny on a picket line, she'll get horny." He nodded toward a petite brunette nurse who happened to march by just then, chanting LYNCH LEWD! "Right now, I'm waitin' for that to heat up. Whose ass you after?"

Hutsut smiled thinly. "Lewd Noogie's."

"Why, Lem? Your ciphers feezed with the little Taurus Brothers?"

"My... *what?*"

"The Taurus Brothers, Lem— don't you grab astrology? The nine brats. Your readers bored with them already?"

"Hell, no— not till yesterday, anyway. Those little pricks coulda kept us in copy for years." He saw a protest poster he hadn't noticed before and copied its message into his notebook. "Shit, their old man's been bad-mouthing his kids all along, but we've been covering it up, just to keep the story alive. Then the dumb son-of-a-bitch gets on the tube last night and blows the lid clean off. As it stands now, we can't print a word— no happy family stuff, no background copy, no first-person bullshit— nothing. That bastard queered the biggest story of the year for us, and somehow he's gonna pay for it with his blood."

Suddenly, a tremendous roar arose from the demonstrators. They broke ranks and converged upon the spot where a city bus had just stopped to discharge passengers. Green-suited policemen linked arms and formed a tiny pocket of space in the center of the mob. From their perch atop the wall, Cuffe and Hutsut could see a lone man inside the ring of cops— a man wearing a blue uniform cap.

The man stood dumfounded for several moments. Then his police made buffer began wedging through the mob toward the hospital steps, the man lowering his head and trudging stoically through the din and flying debris. A beer can arced through the air and bounced off his shoulder; he stopped and glowered into the crowd, but this resulted in his being pelted by various other items, so he just lowered his head again and climbed the steps. At the top, the police ranks opened up and admitted the eager reporters. Several microphones were thrust before the man's mouth, and a volley of unintelligible questions was fired from every direction.

"Lemme 'lone," he muttered, shouldering his way through roughly.

Suddenly he was staring right into the face of Max Berlitz, his subway supervisor. " 'Lo, Max." He was grateful to see a friend's face.

"Lewd Noogie?" inquired Max Berlitz, loudly.

Lewd forced a smile, "How ya doin'?"

"Lewd Noogie?" asked Berlitz, louder.

Microphones were thrust between them, and Lewd wondered what was going on.

"LEWD NOOGIE!" Berlitz announced again. **"My name is Maxwell O. Berlitz, Subway Dispatch Supervisor, and Secretary of Local One-thirty-one of the Brotherhood of Sub-Surface Transit Workers!"**

Lewd was perplexed. "What the hell ya doin', Max?" Berlitz shoved an envelope into his face. **"This letter..."** He held it up for the cameras, then shoved it into Lewd's face again. **"...This letter is signed by Hogan P. Donnegal of the Transit Authority, and has the full approval of the Brotherhood! You're a lousy father! You're a lousy conductor! You are hereby fired!"** Berlitz smacked Lewd's conductor's cap from his head and tore two buttons from his uniform jacket before Noogie crumpled the letter in his fist and rammed Max Berlitz in the mouth.

In the resulting confusion, Lewd managed somehow to slip into the building, to safety.

Max Berlitz was helped to his feet and he began daubing his mouth with a handkerchief as pandemonium reigned about him. The television newsmen muscled in and thrust their microphones to catch his words.

"...see that bastard pays with a hell of a lot more than just his job, get me?" Berlitz was proclaiming through bloody lips.

"Mr. Berlitz... Mr. Berlitz..." one commentator pleaded for recognition. When Berlitz saw it was TV, he gave it all his attention. "Mr. Berlitz, let's get the events as they happened. You just served Mr. Noogie with his severance notice, is that right?"

"**That is right!**" Berlitz hollered breathlessly. "**In a special session last night, by telephone, the Transit Authority and the BSSTW jointly agreed to can this bum as of the moment he was served with the paper this morning, just a minute ago, which I just gave him, and then he hit me in the mouth!**"

"Wait just a second, Mr. Berlitz. Let's get this straight, now. You fired Lewd Noogie— why?"

"**Because he's a lousy conductor! He always was a lousy conductor, he always will be a lousy conductor, and he does a lousy job, and that's why he's fired!**"

"Sir," the commentator prodded, "doesn't this action have something to do with Noogie's attitude toward his nine babies— the things he said on television last..."

"**NO! NO! NO!**" Berlitz insisted. "**No, this has nothing whatsoever to do with any matters outside of his work as a subway conductor. No! We been thinkin' about cannin' his ass a long time now— we just decided to do it, and that's all there is to it now, get me?**"

"Well, sir, I think you'll agree that some people will quite understandably infer that since the action was taken last night, right after Mr. Noogie's appearance on..."

"**I don't think people will care why we canned his ass. I think they'll be happy we did it— though I stress that this action was not taken because of anything but the bum's work.**"

"What was there about Noogie's work that was, as you call it, lousy?"

"He was a lousy conductor."

"Could you— ah— be a bit more specific?"

"Okay, you want the truth, I'll givitaya. He was a slob, for one thing. He never looked like nothin' but a bum, which he is, and he never smelled too good, neither, if you want to know the truth. He was not courteous to riders. He was not thought of too highly by his fellow employees— and not to mention that he was nuts."

"Would you care to elaborate on that last point?"

"Sure. The man was *nuts*," Berlitz explained. "He always done nutty things, far back as I can remember. His first day on the job, I knew he was a nut. That was twenty years ago, and he ain't changed since. Listen to this: First day on the job, the jerk opens his doors at an abandoned station— and then he swears up and down that a gorgeous dame got on. Can you beat it? Is the guy nuts?"

"Well," smiled the reporter, "that certainly is interesting, Mr. Berlitz. Now then, you just served Lewd Noogie with his dismissal papers. What happened next?"

"You saw it. The jerk slugged me— right here. I don't have to put up with that kind of funny stuff— not from an employee, I don't. See what I'm tellin' you? He's nuts."

"Do you plan to take any other action as a result of this attack?"

"I'm gonna request that the sergeant here place that jerk under arrest for assault and battery, and I also intend to sue the jerk for causing me embarrassment out here in front of all these people and many members of my own union, and ladies too. Before we get through with that jerk, he'll wish to God he never was born!"

When Lewd ambled into his wife's hospital room, she was waiting for him. Fila stood with her back to the humming Fourpee, leaning with her elbows on top of the pod, like a torch singer at the piano. Her long auburn tresses cascaded over her shoulders and down across the shimmering surface of her satin pajamas. A blue cigarette smoldered in her long silver holder. She watched him intently as he entered, but she did not speak.

Lewd looked like the Sad Sack. His hair was mussed more than usual; two buttons were missing from his wrinkled uniform; his hat was gone. He did not speak either, but instead just shuffled to the bed and sat down, his back to her.

Fila peered at his unmoving hulk until her blue cigarette burned down to the nub; then she ejected it from the holder and ground it into the tile floor with her pink satin slipper.

With great deliberation, she unbuttoned her pajama top and let it slip from her shoulders to the floor. She was now naked from the waist up, and her pendulous breasts jiggled as she kicked off her slippers. She loosened the waist of her pants, let them slide down her legs, then stepped out of them and flicked them away with her rose-hued toenails. She stood naked a moment, eyeing herself in the mirror, then walked to the dresser, selected a pair of gray pantyhose, sank into the chair and pulled them over her legs. Next, she donned bra and panties in matching gray, and a pair of gray shoes— low heeled and not too stylish. She slipped a simple gray dress over her head— it was waistless and the hem dropped to just a bit below her knee; the sleeves were long and the neck was high. She scrutinized herself in the mirror again, then began pulling her long sexy tresses back severely and pinning them into a bun behind her head.

"I lost my job," Lewd said softly, his back to her.

She stopped styling her hair and looked at him in the mirror. "When?"

"Just now. I hit a guy, too."

She turned and looked at the back of his wrinkled blue jacket. "Who?"

"Max Berlitz."

Fila turned back to the mirror and studied her eyes for a moment; then she slowly raised her eyebrows and finished fixing her hair.

As she turned away from the mirror, she noticed the piece of paper the nurse had left on the bed for her. Quickly, she went to the night table and got out a book entitled Naming Baby. She laid the paper and book atop the Fourpee, looked down at the nine sleeping infants, then shrugged and started leafing through the book, writing down the first two names listed under each of the first nine letters of the alphabet.

> Aaron Abbott Noogie
> Bailey Bainbridge Noogie
> Cadby Caddock Noogie
> Dacey Dag Noogie
> Eachan Earl Noogie
> Fabian Fabron Noogie
> Gabriel Gable Noogie
> Hackett Hadden Noogie
> Ian Ignatius Noogie

She snatched up the paper, crossed the room and stood before her husband.

He slowly raised his head and looked up at her. "Where you goin'?"

"I'm playing for big stakes now, sugar," she told him gently, "so I'm putting you out to pasture before you hurt yourself. Kiss mother bye." She bent down and planted a wet kiss across his thin lips.

"Y'mean... we're all washed up?"

She smiled. "You guessed it, Bozo." She walked to the door, then turned back and looked at him one last time. "I guess I should apologize for all this, but after fifteen years, why start doing the right thing now?" She blew him a kiss. "Adios, lover. "Then she was gone.

After several minutes, Lewd climbed slowly to his feet and stood there quietly, unmoving. He wasn't thinking anything, but eventually he just shrugged and turned to look across at the pod that housed the Noogie Novuplets. Slowly, he started across the room toward the space-age incubator, not noticing his wife's pajama bottoms on the floor in front of him.

His feet got tangled in the satin garment, and he found himself pitching forward. First he tried to jerk a foot free to put it between his falling body and the rising floor, but both shoes were tightly secured within the satin folds. Next, he instinctively swung out his hands to break his fall. Unfortunately, the floor was not the first thing he hit.

As he pitched forward, the crown of his head connected forcefully with the front window of the Pythia Post-Parturition Pod. There was no pain. He heard, more than felt, the loud crunch of contact, then slipped peacefully into black unconsciousness, tumbling loosely to the floor.

As he watched a great red eagle swoop and take him on its back, soaring through the black air as thick as water, his ears were blissfully insensitive to the high-pitched whine the ruptured Fourpee now emitted, and the terrified screams of nine tiny souls, as they watched the myriad of lightning-jagged cracks in the window at their feet, and saw their cozy cubic world begin to darken with a cold, chalky mist.

18

The vast editorial room of the Daily News Gazette was a bedlam of frantic activity; the world's largest picture newspaper was on a Special Edition Deadline.

Ace reporter Ralston Hutsut stepped from the elevator and paused on the threshold, relishing the pandemonium. Grinning with exhilaration, he threaded his way across the busy room to the door marked EDITOR-IN-CHIEF, and went in without knocking.

Stella Kelly Braun sat behind the huge desk of her battlefield command post and rapped out orders like a teletype machine. She was surrounded by editors, and all the lights on her conference phone were blazing. "...all it's worth, and that goes for every swinging Richard here. I don't give a shit if you're Sports, Town and Country, or Want Ads, got me? You find an angle that fits your format! Charlie, you're Travel— do a ditty on the subway system. Gert, you're Home Improvement— Fila was an interior decorator before she got married. I want to see NOOGIE on every page! Okay, get the lead out— deadline all departments, one-thirty p.m." The crowd exploded like a football huddle and disappeared. Stella Kelly Braun punched off all the people who'd been listening on the conference phone, then swiveled to face Ralston Hutsut. "What happened down there?"

The reporter flopped into a chair, pulled off a shoe and dumped out a small pebble which had been bothering him. "Looks like the asshole tripped and hit his head on the incubator. The thing went haywire and the kids choked. The head nurse comes in and finds him staggering around the room— the pod's shattered and full of smoke. She screams her ass off and runs for help. When Noogie sees what's happened, he panics and makes tracks.The hospital was sealed off, and he was finally flushed out by accident— a spic delivery boy took some meat to the deep freeze and found him in there covered with frost."

Miss Braun spun to face a large storyboard at the side of her desk. On top, in twelve-inch letters, was the word EXTRA, in red. Beneath were listed several staff submissions for the headline of the special edition, already set in type. She considered them each in turn:

NOVUPLETS SLAUGHTERED!

"Not bad, but too impersonal."

DAD MASSACRES NOVUPLETS!

"The law would have our ass for that."

LEWD LIQUIDATES LADS!

"Still libelous, and too cute."

NOVUPLETS FROZEN STIFF!

"Redundant, though I like the way it ties in with him being found in the deep freeze."

LEWD COOKS KIDS!

LEWD BOILS BOYS!

"Both still too cute, but I like the implication he was gonna eat them. Were they cooked or frozen, by the way?"

"Neither. Asphyxiated."

"Shit. Our clowns won't even know what that means. 'Suffocated' is better... or 'smothered'. What did you say before, 'choked'?"

"How 'bout 'strangled'?"

"Great! Perfect! NOVUPLETS STRANGLED. You never picture anyone strangling all by himself— there's always that pair of hands wrapped around his throat. But it still isn't right for the banner, though— too impersonal, like 'slaughtered,' and it looks funny in caps." She took a swig of cold coffee and tossed the paper cup into her wastebasket. "Oh well, shit, what does it matter? If we want to serve those kids up cooked or frozen, we'll do it. We got to crucify Lewd Noogie... but we got to be sure we don't end up on the hot seat with him. We got to be... subtle." She scribbled on a sheet of canary bond. "I don't suppose the kids bled at all?"

"No, but he did. Cracked his skull."

"Then there was blood in the room, right? here, give this to Lou on your way out— that's the banner and the blurb we're gonna launch with." The phone on her desk buzzed. "Get to work on that lead story," she told Hutsut as she picked up the receiver. "Let's get Noogie's ass and kill this new amendment with the same shot!"

The reporter left her office and picked his way through the tumult of the editorial room, his mind already constructing the lead sentences of his front page story. He paused at the Copy Desk. "Hey, Lou, Stella says we're going with this banner and blurb. Set it up, okay?"

"Right, Ral."

Hutsut glanced at the sheet before turning it over to the copy chief.

NO MORE NOVUPLETS !!
All Nine Strangled During
Crazed Dad's Blood Bath

"That," declared Ralston Hutsut, "is subtle."

19

Toy Boat placed the tray of soiled dinnerware on the kitchen counter and began filling the sink with hot, sudsy water. While she waited for the basin to fill, she took the newspaper from the tray and spread it open on the counter.

Next to the front-page photo of the dead babies was a picture of Lewd Noogie, his face covered with blood, his hair white with frost. *God forgive him*, thought Toy, fighting down a chill and a slight feeling of nausea. She paused to shut off the running water, then returned to the news.

> Aaron Noogie dead. Bailey Noogie– dead. Cadby and Dacey and Eachan Noogie– dead. Fabian, Gabriel, Hackett and Ian Noogie– all are dead.
>
> A single, fleeting week of precious life, and now, nine tiny souls are doomed to everlasting darkness.
>
> Stunned, a nation cries out in sorrow. Outraged, its people cry out for vengeance.

The article, bylined Ralston Hutsut, then offered a recap of the events leading up to "the defenseless infants' deaths by strangulation— most painful and terrifying of all ways to die." The capsule chronology was limited almost exclusively to the words and actions of Lewd Noogie: His "expressed hatred" of the babies on Arthur's television program; his "savage threats to telephone callers"; his "brutal, unprovoked attack upon Max Berlitz, a close friend for some twenty years." The article continued:

At exactly 10:30 a.m. today, Mrs. Fila Noogie left her healthy, happy babies in their room and appeared at the entrance to Mid town Hospital, making this tearful announcement to hundreds of demonstrators and members of the press: "Due to certain recent events and other circumstances of long standing, I have decided— for the welfare of my children— to institute separation proceedings at once."

She implied that she was seeking a separation on the grounds of cruel and inhuman treatment, and that she feared for the safety of her boys and herself.

While the shaken mother was delivering her emotion-packed statement, she was unaware that her husband was prowling through the hospital to the room where the helpless babies lay unprotected.

At 10:45, head Nurse Tina Limones was drawn to the room by "what sounded like a fight." Nurse Limones, hysterical and near collapse, described the scene to this reporter: "It was horrible. There was the pod, all smashed and covered with blood-the babies were quivering, turning blue-and there was this... this madman, jumping around, with blood smeared all over his hands and face. When he saw me-oh, God, I swear it he smiled! I just knew I was next– so I screamed and ran."

The nurse summoned security guards and hospital aides; when they arrived at the novies' room, the infants were dead and the father had escaped. Building exits were sealed immediately and a hospital-wide manhunt began, with more than 200 police and other volunteers combing every inch of the vast medical complex.

Then, at 11:45 a.m., just one hour after the gruesome demise of the nine innocent tots, Lewd Noogie was cornered. Acting on a hunch, 16-year-old Jesus Bodega, a grocery delivery boy, searched the huge hospital deep freeze. There, huddled between two sides of frigid beef, Bodega found the desperate ex-subway conductor, his face a frozen mask of fear and hate.

Meanwhile, outside the hospital, news of the tragedy had reached the throng gathered there, and there was crying in the streets. Windows were smashed; passing autos were overturned; three nearby buildings were set ablaze; 27 demonstrators were placed in custody and six policemen were treated for minor injuries at the hospital emergency room.

Lewd Noogie, chained hand and foot, was taken from the building in secret by ambulance, police officials fearing he would be lynched by the crowd without first receiving a fair trial.

The kitchen door eased open and Arthur poked his head in. "Hi... I, ah... I was just looking for the paper."

Toy instantly folded the newspaper and carried it across the room to him.

"Hey... no," her brother protested, "you finish looking

at it. I can wait."

She smiled, shook her head gently and pressed the paper into his hands.

"Well... if you're sure."

She closed her eyes, smiled and nodded.

"Thanks. I'll give it back as soon as I'm through." He smiled, then stood there a moment, uneasily gazing at the floor until finally he just backed through the doorway and let the door swing shut between them.

Toy walked slowly to the sink and began to dunk the soiled dinnerware into the soapy water, first scraping the food scraps into the garbage disposal. She picked up her brother's plate and held it a while, gazing with affection at the remaining bits of lima beans and mashed potato he had left. Gently, she pushed a finger into the cool, soft potato, then lifted it to her mouth and licked it clean.

PART FIVE

20

Tuesday, July 25

"All rise."

Everyone in the crowded courtroom came to his feet and watched Judge Harrison Farrell enter and take his place at the bench.

"Be seated," announced the court clerk.

Though the trial was just beginning, most members of the jury already looked tense and exhausted. The task of selecting the jurors had dragged on through weeks of tedious examinations; it had not been easy to find twelve men and women completely free of bias concerning the indictment of Lewd Noogie for the murder of his nine sons.

The defendant was not yet present in the courtroom. His lawyer, a young court appointed counsel named Barney Orchard, sat alone at the large defense table, nervously arranging papers.

The prosecution table was surrounded by a battery of state and district attorneys, all of whom appeared poised and confident.

Fila Noogie sat in the first row of the gallery— black dress, black hat, black veil— dabbing her eyes from time to time with a black handkerchief.

Across the aisle from her sat two full rows of busy reporters, some scribbling in notebooks, some sketching courtroom scenes on large sketch pads. The remainder of the room was occupied by those members of the general public who had braved several days on line outside the courthouse, and then been lucky enough to find space for themselves inside the courtroom before the doors had been closed. A dozen policemen lined the walls, and two hundred more were deployed throughout the building and its surrounding area.

Judge Farrell glanced over some last-minute paperwork, looked sternly about the courtroom and banged his gavel to silence the chatter. "This court will come to order. Now, we are all very much aware of the sensational nature of this trial. Until today, both the public and some representatives of the press have been acting in a manner— shall we say— not entirely compatible with the laws of justice in this great land of ours. I trust that this will not be the case in our courtroom. In fact, I demand it. The defendant will enter this room presumed to be innocent until proven guilty beyond a reasonable doubt. You ladies and gentlemen of the jury remember that." He turned his attention to the gallery. "And if there is any sort of commotion in this court of law, we will not hesitate to clear the room of all spectators and conduct the administration of justice behind closed doors." He waited for his message to sink in, then nodded to the bailiff. "You may bring in the defendant."

There was some shifting around in seats, but then the silence became absolute, as everyone's attention zeroed in on the door at the front of the courtroom. After what seemed like an eternity, the portal swung slowly open with an eerie creak.

Four uniformed policemen were first to enter the room. Lewd Noogie was next. He wore a gray prison suit with black work shoes, and his wrists were handcuffed before him. His complexion was very sallow, and a nervous smile twitched across his face. Behind him walked the bailiff, who was in turn followed by four more cops. The procession lumbered across the room toward the defense table.

Suddenly, someone in the gallery unleashed a terrifying howl. Two hundred people all gasped in unison and snapped their heads toward the source of outcry. A man had stood up in the aisle at the second row of the gallery. He was aiming a gun at Lewd Noogie.

"HIT THE DIRT!" someone shouted, and everyone in the room seemed to fall away as if swallowed by the earth, leaving Lewd standing all alone in the center of the room.

The assailant stared wild-eyed at him. "YOU MURDERED MY FATHER— FOREVER!"

Lewd just stood there, a scant twenty feet away, looking down the long barrel of what seemed to be some sort of antique dueling pistol. His eyes darted left and right; suddenly he spun and dashed for the doorway he'd just come through, but he stumbled over the body of one of the cops lying on the floor.

The assassin's antique weapon went off, the explosion resounding throughout the room with the resonance of a nuclear detonation. Lewd Noogie sank to the floor.

The gunshot triggered the crowd to animation. Everyone seemed to have the same intention: to get as far away as possible from the man with the gun. Almost all the patrolmen in the gallery crouched behind benches with their revolvers out, but the gunman was in the center of the courtroom and the room was jammed with people, making it dangerous to shoot at him.

The assailant remained in firing position several seconds after discharging the single-shot pistol; then, with great deliberation, he wound up like a baseball pitcher and heaved the weapon fiercely at Lewd's prone body. It arced through the air and thudded into the back of a reclining policeman, who said, "Ow."

Now that the assassin was devoid of his weapon, a dozen blue suits converged upon him in a savage wave. But then, quite unexpectedly, the man reached into his coat and whipped out another pistol identical to the first. The police charge instantly became a frenetic retreat, the terrified cops scratching, kicking and biting to get out of the gunman's way.

The man waved his new pistol in the air and shouted in exaltation toward the ceiling: "I'M COMING, DAD!" He pointed the weapon at his face, closed his lips around the end of the barrel and slid it into his mouth. His legs seemed to give out and he sank to his knees, hovering momentarily before falling forward to his elbows, clutching the pistol with both hands, barrel upward, his head bobbing up and down on the long, steel shaft.

Several cops began creeping toward the crouching figure, but before they could get close enough to pounce, he gurgled in ecstasy, sucked the gun barrel deep into his throat, and pulled the trigger. This time the detonation was muffled. A spray of blood and bits of bone exploded upward from a gaping hole in the nape of his neck.

Pandemonium reigned. Women screamed hysterically and fainted dead away. Men shouted meaningless exclamations and turned away, nauseated. The gunman remained crouched on the floor an amazingly long time before slowly toppling over, flat on his back in the aisle, surrounded by a growing pool of oozing red.

One young cop, who had huddled frozen with fear behind a back row of benches, now hurled himself down the aisle and kicked the empty pistol out of the dead man's hand. Drawing his service revolver, he stood over the stiffening corpse, aiming the weapon with both hands, shuddering uncontrollably. **"Okay, you bastard,"** he rasped, his breath huffing out in short jerks, **"on your feet."**

By this time the judge had gotten up from behind his massive bench and stood in disheveled robes, whacking his gavel on the wood block over and over again. **"Clear the courtroom! Order in this court! Arrest that man! For the love of God, this is a court of law!"** But no one paid any attention to the judge.

The cops responsible for guarding Lewd Noogie had scrambled to their feet and were fluttering about in consternation. Finally, they managed to locate the defendant, who had crawled beneath the prosecution table and huddled up with his prosecutors for protection. Grabbing him by the feet, the cops dragged him out into the open and frantically searched him to find the source of the blood dampening his gray uniform. Lewd was in great pain, but he was conscious and the wound was not serious. Relieved, the officers stood him on his feet. The assailant's bullet had lodged itself deep in Lewd Noogie's right buttock.

Fila was lying curled up on the front row bench where she'd been sitting when all the commotion had begun. Hearing the gunman scream behind her, she had spun around, seen him and immediately ducked behind the back of her seat. Throughout the ensuing incident, she had lain there, terrified, fearing he would kill her as well, but he had not seemed to notice her. When he had shot himself, not three feet away from her, the spray of blood and bone fragments had swept over her, and still she had remained motionless, wondering how, in the light of these developments, she could most effectively react.

Now, when she felt the hands of concerned citizens hooking beneath her arms and helping her to her feet, she committed herself to a course of action and launched it with great gusto.

The corpse of the assailant was ringed with blue

uniforms. Fila grabbed one of them and spun it aside, then gazed upon the dead man's face with horror and screamed.

The courtroom din subsided at once; every head turned to tune in on the woman's words, which, when they came, were projected quite well enough for all to hear.

"CORBIN!" she howled. "CORBIN NOOGIE!" Fila ripped off her hat and veil, staggering to the rail and pointed a finger of damnation at her hapless husband. "**HIS nephew! His whole family's crazy! They're ALL murderers!**"

A hush fell over the courtroom. All that could be heard were the soulful gasps of the weeping ex-novie mother, as every eye in the place trained itself upon the forlorn figure of Lewd Noogie, standing there before the judge's bench, his shackled arms twisted around behind him, holding his wounded buttock.

21

Friday, September 8

Anita Keyster relaxed in her favorite easy chair, reading the latest issue of Screen Secrets magazine. Her feet were propped upon a footstool, and Bromberg curled snugly in her lap. The house was quiet; Jenny had finished the dinner dishes and had gone out, so Anita could rest in peace until her husband came home to be fed.

The article she read was entitled "I Tried to Hook Art Pastel— With Jail Bait!" It was written by a seventeen-year-old girl named Melanie Marlowe, who claimed to be a secretary for Pastel Productions. The story told of the young virgin's determination to make her boss seduce her, and Anita was nearing its thrilling climax.

It was megabliss! Alone with HIM at last! Parked at Lover's Leap in his sleek red XKE!

The night air twined through my waist-long tresses like excited fingers as I gazed at his masterful profile in the moonlight— that black curly hair, those dark, sexy eyes, that dazzling smile and powerful Leo chin...

Suddenly he smothered me in his muscular embrace and glued his sweet, demanding lips to mine. It was no use, I was his eternal slave.

Relax! I told myself. Let the waves of burning desire sweep away your schoolgirl fears!

A tiny nose burrowed beneath Anita's magazine, and when she raised her book, Bromberg put his front paws on her bosom and licked her face. "What do you want, you little monkey? Can't you see I'm trying to read?" The dog whined, and she finally realized that his concern was with the fact that she was crying. "Oh, you little precious, do you think Mommy's sad?" She stroked his silky body and his tail beat at the pages of her magazine. "Mommy's just reading." She patted his head, then raised the magazine and resumed the article.

Suddenly, Arty tore his mouth from mine and held me at arm's length. "It's... it's no good, kid," he whispered, gently.

Had he sensed my fear? In utter abandonment I threw my arms around him and begged urgently, "But, Arty, darling, I love you! I need you!"

He shook his head sadly. "No you don't, kid. You're just dazzled by all the bright lights and fame. Oh, maybe you don't understand it all right now, but someday you'll look back on all this and thank me. You're a wonderful kid, Melanie— and that's why I've got to let you go."

At this point, Anita paused to blow her nose, which provoked her high-strung Pomeranian into such a violent expression of concern she was forced to put down the magazine and make a fuss over him. "You little love bug." Bromberg leapt to the floor and eyed her excitedly, his ears straight up and just the tip of his tail wagging.

"Does he want to go out?"

"YAP!"

"Just let mommy finish this story."

"YAP! YAP! YAP! YAP! YAP!"

"Oh, you little pill." Turning back to the start of the magazine article, she carefully tore out the full page photo of Art Pastel.

"YAP! YAP! YAP!"

"Okay, okay... give me a chance to get up, will you?" She climbed to her feet, photo in hand, and went to the kitchen, where Bromberg waited impatiently at the screen door. "You're a little monkey, that's what you are."

"YAP!"

"Shhhh." She opened the door for him, but he froze at the threshold, wanting her to go out with him. "Oh, for heaven's sake— go on, you little coward." But Bromberg would have none of it. Anita peered into the ominous backyard darkness wherein resided Tully's six vicious Doberman pinschers. "Well, you can just stay inside, then."

"YAP! YAP! YAP! YAP! YAP!"

Moving to the pantry, she took down a large cardboard box from the top shelf. "You can just yap your darn fool head off." She opened the box, which was filled with hundreds of photographs and clip pings concerning Art Pastel. To these she added the picture from Screen Secrets, then returned the box to its shelf.

"YAP! YAP! YAP! YAP! YAP!"

"Oh, you little dickens! You're giving me a headache!" She threw a sweater over her shoulders, opened the screen door and stepped outside, a quivering Bromberg glued to her heels. The night was cloudy; there was no moon— still the dogs did not bark. They were asleep, she decided, glancing nervously toward their kennel. She walked softly into the thick grass, waiting for her Pomeranian to get up enough nerve to leave her side and go do his business. The Dobermans did not even growl. Had they gotten out of their pen? Gingerly, she took a couple steps toward the kennel, but she was still too far away to see the black dogs in the dark.

"Hi, Mommy!"

Anita gasped and clutched her bosom. Bromberg, in the midst of doing his business, scampered to her on three legs. "Jenny? Where are you? You scared me half to death!"

"I'm sorry, Mommy. I'm in here."

Her daughter's voice seemed to be coming from the kennel. "Are you...?" Anita stepped closer to the wire fence. "Where...?" She peered into the dark enclosure and slowly discerned Jenny's form, sitting on the earth inside the dog pen. "Jenny Keyster!" She hissed frantically. "Are you in there again? You come out of there this instant!" She glanced anxiously at the wooden hut where the dogs slept. "If those beasts wake up and find you there, they'll tear you to pieces!"

Jenny giggled. "Oh, crambo, Mommy, hush... they're not sleeping, they're right here."

As Anita's eyesight became accustomed to the dark, she began to see the huge black dogs, all curled up round Jenny like pups around their mother. "What in the world... How in the... Oh, I wish your father were here!" Bromberg had by now approached the fence himself, growling, his hackles up. "You git," Anita told him, "before you get eaten alive. And you," she addressed her daughter, "what are you doing in there, anyway, Miss Keyster?"

"It's omee here," Jenny explained, putting her finger on one of the dog's noses, and getting it licked.

Anita sighed and shook her head. "Between you and your father and those dogs, I'm going to find an early grave."

"Isn't Daddy home yet?"

"I suppose he's in the city, nosing around that courthouse, They expect a verdict in the Noogie case tonight. I sure hope that man gets the chair."

"Miso, Mommy, how can you be so maroon? That poor cipher."

"I don't care, that's how I feel. Besides, your father has his heart set on frying him— I don't want to see him disappointed."

Jenny sat in silence, petting a dog's belly, then she asked softly, "Mommy, if I killed somebody, would Daddy want to fry me, too?"

"What? Why, what a question! Of course not, dear— he loves you!"

"Oh."

"My, the things you children think about. Your father would rather die than lift a finger to either of us, and you know it."

Jenny tossed her hair away from her face. "Oh, I grab that, Mommy... and I just love old Daddy Bear something tidal... it's just that, well, killing people... Oh, crambo, I don't know."

"Some people deserve to die." Mrs. Keyster fell silent then, and took in the dark sky. Autumn was in the air, and she crossed her arms over her bosom to ward off a chill. She watched the full moon peek through the clouds, then become swallowed again. "Oh, I know what you're trying to say, dear, about your father's work. If you were a little older, you'd understand. The best thing to do is just not think about it." Her voice became wistful. "When I married your father, I was forty-six years old... six years older than he was, even. I had plenty of time to express myself before I married him... and my life was nothing to brag about. Your father may be rough around the edges, but he's a good man and heaven knows he loves us more than anything in the world."

Bromberg raced toward the back door, yapping maliciously. They heard the front door slam then and Tully's voice call, "Anita?"

"Now, there's your father. Mind you, don't be bothering

him with this kind of nonsense now, you hear? He's got enough on his mind without all this."

"Sure, Mommy."

"Are you coming in now?"

"I'll be in in a sec."

Tully called again from inside.

"Here I am, dear!" Anita and Bromberg went into the house.

Jenny sat on the ground in the kennel, listening to her parents greet one another in the kitchen.

"Where the leech were you, Neet?"

"I was just out..."

"If this little butt-sucker doesn't let go of my pants cuff..."

"Brombie, you be still now."

"Never mind the little fart! Mommy, we're in business!"

"Business, dear?"

"You bet your buns we are! The jury's in! Lewd Noogie's gonna fry— right here in Tully's Playpen!"

"Really, dear? That's wonderful!"

"Wonderful? For sweating out loud, it's terrific! He fries on New Year's Eve!"

"I'm so happy it all turned out the way you wanted it to, dear!"

"C'mon, Mommy, let's have a good stiff belt to celebrate! Hot clam! What a party we're gonna have! Where's Jen? C'mon, let's go in the living room and get some hooch!"

Jenny Pye sat crosslegged on the earthen kennel floor and soothed the dogs, who had become animated at the sound of Tully's voice. When the Dobermans were settled once again, and her parents were safely on the other side of the house, she said casually, "You can come out now."

Presently, a dark form stuck its head out of the doghouse, listened intently to the warden's voice reverberating faintly through the house, then studied the reclining canines, all six of which regarded the intruder with great interest. "Will they attack me?" whispered the crouching form.

"Uh-uh. C'mon over."

Chaplain Levitsky crawled out of the wooden hut and cautiously approached the dog-surrounded girl.

"You're getting your omee black suit all dirty," Jenny said softly.

" 'Sokay. Nice doggy." He squatted two feet from the nearest Doberman, a nervous smile etched upon his face.

"Well, I guess I'd better be running along."

"But I don't even know what you're doing here."

"Yeah, well..." the priest sighed, "I was in the neighborhood, so I thought I'd just drop by and say hello."

Jenny shook her head slowly. "Deva, are you moon-blind? Why didn't you come to the front door? If I wasn't here these dog-oes would have browned you out."

"Yeah. Thanks." He peered at her in the darkness; she was wearing a white shirt and dungarees, and her long golden hair cascaded over her shoulders, picking up tiny rays of light where it seemed no light existed. He picked up a stone, decided it might not be a stone after all, and dropped it. "I... ah... haven't seen you for a couple months now. Where you been hiding yourself?"

"Oh, around. Has it really been that long?"

"Nine weeks." Levitsky edged a bit closer to her, but the dog nearest him raised its head and let out a low growl.

"Hush." Jenny ushered it out of the way so that the priest could approach her unmolested.

Levitsky crawled to her side and sat down. He picked up a twig, but it turned out to be a tail, so he put it down. "I've missed you."

Jenny leaned over and kissed him gently on the mouth; then she held his hand and they sat in silence until the dogs became so accustomed to having him there that one laid its head on his leg.

Ryder caressed her tiny hand. "Not only that, but it's been over sixteen weeks since... since we..." He raised her hand to his lips and kissed it. It smelled of dog. She kissed his hand in return. He studied her face in profile— so finely sculptured, framed in gold. He reached out and touched her hair.

"They're gonna fry him," she said quietly.

"Who?"

"That man— that cipher who killed his babies." She looked at him quickly. "Are you glad?"

"No... why?" Her hair was silky soft, despite the fact that it was a bit dusty.

"Everyone else is." She traced the line of a pointed Doberman ear. "Will you be there?"

His hand crept through her hair and touched her neck. "Where?"

"When they fry him."

"I guess. Last rites." He started to slip his hand around the back of her neck, but something cold and wet obstructed his progress: it was the nose of a concerned dog, so he carefully withdrew his hand from her completely.

"Does it hurt?"

"What?" His gaze roamed over her face and down across her throat.

"Frying."

"Some."

The shirt she wore was unbuttoned at the neck. In fact, the first three buttons were undone, and he could see the left side of her collarbone and the smooth white skin of the top of her chest.

"How much?"

"I don't know."

"I bet it hurts a lot," Jenny decided. "I bet it hurts a whole lot. Unwow." She leaned over and rested her head in her left hand, her elbow on her knee.

Levitsky saw the blouse front fall away from her chest. Carefully, he leaned toward her and peered into her shirt. Her naked left breast was clearly visible. The breath caught in his throat.

"Huh?" Jenny asked, in reverie.

"Nothing." He leaned closer. It was her breast, all right. Proud and pert, the small creamy orb hung from her slender body with astounding grace.

The dog resting its head on the priest's leg pricked up its ears and intently watched what it assumed to be some small animal stirring in the man's trousers.

"Maroon," sighed Jenny, "all that omega pain... and someday my poor Daddy Bear'll have to pay it all back. Crambo."

That single, naked tit was the most beautiful object Ryder Levitsky had ever seen. The underside was sheer perfection of form; the arc of its profile carved an incredibly flawless curve through space; the bulging crescent of pale ivory glowed luminous as the moon; it seemed at once to be as smooth and firm as milk-glass and as soft and supple as whipped cream. Wonderstruck, he sat before this awesome apparition; tremblingly transfixed, he set about to etch this vision eternally in his mind, as his blooming bone burrowed beneath his BVDs.

Jenny was lost in the karmic ramifications of her father's lifelong glee at making people suffer. The realization of what he was setting himself up for in his future lifetimes appalled her. What could she do to help him? How could she make him see the light? As she pondered this great problem, she completely lost the awareness of where she was and who was with her.

Meanwhile, Chaplain Levitsky continued to be lured by the marvelous magnetic mammary. As he hovered closer, he soon was able to perceive the sublime summit of that magnificent mound. *My God, it's her nipple!* His heart fluttered and his breath rasped in and out in short jerks. Nothing in the universe could rival the impact of beholding the pink pinnacle on that divine dug. All the wondrous treasures of the world lost their luster in the presence of that splendid pap, that staggering, spellbinding, exquisitely sculptured crown of fabulous flesh which capped the precious peak of Jenny Keyster's left titty. Jutting out in sultry, sensual silence, it sang its siren song.

Mesmerized, Father Levitsky watched his quivering hand drift out across the celestial void toward the alabaster globe. Would it vanish as he grasped it? Would the world end? Would Jenny Keyster smack him in the mouth? His timid hand drifted through the opening of her shirt; the soft, cotton garment brushed the back of his hand as it approached the shimmering, sacred spheroid. Then, with a sigh, he captured it. His hand cupped the underside of the glorious orb, hammock-like, and the contact astounded him. His brain reeled, and there was a sweet burning sensation deep inside his hammering chest. He had reached out to sample earthly pleasure, and had touched, instead, the face of God.

Jenny took no notice of what he was doing to her; her reverie was unassailable.

The priest held his breath and swept his thumb in a slow arc up across her silken nipple, as the dog in his lap studied the powerful heartbeat of the strange animal in the chaplain's trousers. Levitsky leaned toward Jenny's open shirt front until he was just a few inches away, watching his ecstatic fingers caress the miraculous flesh. Saliva drooled out of the corner of his mouth, and he knew it was time to be suckled. Ignoring the canine chaperones altogether, he slipped his left hand round her back and with his right released her breast and peeled away the shirt front.

Bending her backward, he lowered his face to the ivory orb. The tender nipple touched his nose; his closed lips brushed across the sleek surface beneath. The gentle essence of her, a subtle blend of the earth and dishwashing detergent, blessed his nostrils. He parted his lips; his timid tongue crept out and tasted the yielding underside of the sweet young breast; the flesh was honey-luscious, salty-sweet. His questing tongue crisscrossed over the downy bulge until it glistened like a creamy bubble, then he licked upward to the silky circle round her nipple and traced the curving border without crossing it. Here, the priest hesitated, taking note of the full dramatic import of what he was about to accomplish. *Now. Now, I'm going to suck Jenny Keyster's breast.* And then, with reverence he fastened his moist lips around the entire tip of the young girl's bosom, and drew it deep into his mouth.

Jenny's reverie was punctuated by the odd sensation that she was tilting backward. Was she going into a trance? But then she felt the mouth closing over her left breast, and she realized she had not been paying proper attention to her guest. She looked down and saw the chaplain's mouth firmly glued to her chest; she tried to ease him away, but that didn't work, so she cuddled him in her arms and rocked him back and forth. "Oh, deva, I'm sorry. I'm such a light head... but look, you've got to stop that."

Levitsky sucked harder. His tongue skated frantic figure eights over the tip of her tit, and her delicate little nipple began to rise to the occasion.

"Uhhh, ohhh deva-doll," Jenny sighed, "you got to retro before we go into free fall... please stop..." She lowered her lips to his ear and whispered, but the delicious waves of pleasure compelled her to alternately plead with him, then dip her tongue into his ear. "Please..." she entreated, probing her wet tongue among the furrows of his ear, "please stop..."

Father Levitsky reached down between her legs and kneaded her coozy through the coarse denim. He was vaguely aware of some commotion going on around him, but he was too possessed with desire to be concerned.

Suddenly, the back of his jacket collar was clamped in a vicious bear-trap grip, wrenching him from the young girl's breast and smashing him to earth with cyclone force: the air was blasted from his lungs; he was enveloped by the ferocious din of snapping teeth and savage growls, stifled by the fetid stench of tepid doggy breath. When he returned to his senses, he found himself flat on the ground with two huge dogs standing on his chest looking him straight in the eye, and several other canine mouths attached to various parts of his body.

"Shhh..." Jenny was soothing the beasts, "hush now." They soon stopped growling, but it was a few moments more before she could coax the two off his chest. "They thought you were hurting me."

Her breast was still exposed, and feebly he reached for it, but a dog pounced upon his hand and held it menacingly in his mouth.

"Hush," Jenny soothed, "shhh."

"But I want to!" the prostrate man beseeched.

"I know you do, deva-doll, but I can't let you do that, grab? Even the dog-oes know it wouldn't be right."

"Why not?" He watched her gingerly remove his hand from the dog's jowls.

"Because you're a priest."

"It was okay before... why not now?"

"I didn't know any better then." She tugged the dogs away from him; he crawled to her and put his head in her lap, inching his hands toward her crotch. "Oh, crambo," she sighed. "It's all my fault, letting you get this thermal." His mouth lunged at her lap, but a dog butted him sharply and he fell flat on his back beside her. "There now," Jenny cautioned, "don't move any more and they won't bother you."

Chaplain Levitsky began to cry.

She leaned over him, deeply concerned. "Miso, bluebird, don't cry." She laid her head on his chest and heard his thundering heart beat. "Poor baby... you're all adrenal." Her hand lightly cradled the bulge at his crotch, and he gasped. "I'm sorry, Ryder-diter, but I just can't let you curd my conch." Suddenly she had a brainstorm and sat up. "I know what!"

Levitsky felt her hands at his fly, and lay very still.

She opened his zipper, reached inside and pried out his throbbing organ. Grasping the stiff member gently in her hand, she began to pump it slowly up and down.
The priest closed his eyes and reached for her breast, but grabbed a cold nose instead, so he crossed his hands upon his chest and passively submitted to his fate.

Jenny continued to piston her fist along the rigid warmth of his impassioned penis. "You see, I thought I could get closer to God through you, butterfly... but all I really did was push you farther away from Him. Now you're trying to get back to Him through me... but I can't let you, 'cause I know it doesn't work." She watched one of the Dobermans sniff at the hot piece of meat she was massaging. The dog took a whiff of the beet-red head and began licking it.

Ryder felt something soft and moist on his bone. Was she going to suck him off? He dared not open his eyes, for fear she'd quit. Her warm little fist continued to stroke him and the eager satin tongue lapped deliciously at his most sensitive spot until he felt the sweet fire ignite in his chest again and sweep agonizingly down toward his loins. He held it there, wanting to savor the occasion as long as possible, but soon he could control himself no longer, so he wadded up all the prurient thoughts, all the sexy dreams, and all the obscene fantasies he'd suffered over that past sixteen week eternity, and fired them into the cool night air, stuffing his coat sleeve into his mouth to keep from hollering.

The surprised Doberman backed away from the spitting member and looked perplexed at Jenny, a glob of semen fastened to its nose. Jenny grinned and continued to pump the pulsing organ, catching as much of the seminal fluid as she could, so it wouldn't get all over his suit. She milked him completely dry, then took out his hanky and cleaned up everything, carefully putting his flaccid penis away and closing his trousers.

"Thank you," he whispered.

"You're welcome. Only don't misunderstand why I did it... all this sort of thing is flooy, grab? No more."

"You're wonderful."

Her father's voice bellowed from the other side of the house. **"Jen? Jenny?"**

Levitsky scrambled to his knees and scuttled toward the kennel door, where he commenced fumbling with the latch, trying to get out.

Tully's voice grew louder as he approached the kitchen. Jenny crept over to the kennel door and unlatched it. Her breast was still exposed, but the priest seemed to take no notice of it now. As soon as the door was open, he sprang outside and thundered through the backyard toward the penitentiary. By the time Tully got to the back door, the yard was quiet and Jenny was walking toward the house, her clothing neatly rearranged. "I'm coming Daddy Bear!"

"Muffin, do you know what time it is? Anyway, you're missing all the fun! We're having a rat-fag celebration!"

22

Saturday, September 9

Roland Monteczuma breezed along the corridor of the BBS Building and entered a door marked PASTEL PRODUCTIONS CONFERENCE ROOM. Inside, a din of frantic chatter ceased at once and a roomful of faces snapped in his direction. "At ease," the director smiled.

Relieved that it was not Pastel, everyone resumed the nervous chatter. Ralph Goliones waited until Monteczuma was seated next to him at the conference table, then leaned close and asked softly. "What's the scoop on this meeting, d'you know?"

Monteczuma opened his briefcase and took out several sharp wooden pencils and a large yellow note pad. "Well, the grapevine says he's gonna fire the whole staff."

Goliones' eyes rolled toward the ceiling. "I know what the grapevine says... I want to know what you say."

"Why speculate? We'll know for sure in a couple minutes."

Ralph drummed his fingers on the table top. "A guy likes to have a chance to defend himself."

Monteczuma closed his briefcase and set it on the floor beside his chair. "Since when does Pastel have to call a staff meeting to take a bite out of your ass, Ralph?"

He glanced around the room, making a mental roll call. Seated with himself and the stage manager at the long table were the twelve other principal staff members of Pastel Productions: four writers, two talent coordinators, a unit manager, musical director, tech director, assistant director, associate producer and the coordinator of sponsor relations. The perimeter of the room was lined with various secretaries and production assistants, their miniature tape recorders prepared to capture everything that was about to transpire.

"Where's Neal Kroutch?" asked Ralph.

"I told him to lay low for a while." A sudden hush fell over the room, and Monteczuma glanced toward the door as Art Pastel entered, head bowed, hands in his pockets, and marched straight to the head of the table.

You could hear a pin drop.

When the star finally raised his head, he did not look directly at anyone; instead, his gaze focused upon the clock at the rear of the room. "I am going to air a special program this New Year's Eve, from eleven to twelve-oh-five. The concept of this show will be twofold: to ring in the new year, and to televise the execution of Lewd Noogie. Aside from this electric chair gimmick, the show will go roughly the same as last year: celebrities, dancing, a lot of schmaltz, flag-waving— crap like that. Okay, that's it, now get your asses in gear and work out the details." Art Pastel put his head down and strode from the room.

For a long time, everyone just sat and looked at each other in stunned silence. Then, since the tape recorders were rolling, making it impossible for anyone to express his astonishment audibly, there was a flurry of strained facial expressions and hand gestures, and the passing of several hastily scribbled notes.

Finally, the associate producer climbed unsteadily to his feet and cleared his throat. "Well…" He licked his lips, "this is a pretty tall order." He glanced at Roland Monteczuma, who was jotting quick notations on his yellow pad. "But I'm sure, if we all pull together as a team, why everything's going to be a piece of cake... right, Rolly?"

Monteczuma climbed to his feet, making a few final marks on his pad. "Okay now, let's see..." He glanced over his notes, then tossed his pencil away and turned his attention to the flabbergasted faces gathered round the conference table. "I think the first thing we have to do is forget about all the reasons why this show can't be done. Sure, other than the usual problems of going on location, we can expect a lot of political static on this baby... so, Merv, you and I will really have to do a job on the FCC to get this thing in front of the cameras. We'll also need clearance from the Governor, and that won't be easy, either.

"Gene— you, Merv, and me will run up to the state pen, check their facilities and get the warden's cooperation. Ron, you get busy setting up that time slot, and this time make the deal include a world-wide hookup, 'cause this mother's gonna be the show of the century if we can pull it off. Also, you line up the sponsor for this one— I see it as a package deal offered to the network complete. Monty, Ace, we'll need big names in the audience— stars, politicians, athletes— as well as headliners for the show itself... find out who's available so we can cast as soon as we get a script. Hear that writers? We'll hammer out a rough outline as soon as we can, but meanwhile, brainstorm some possible bits and knock off some snappy promos— you know the kind of thing we need. Ralph, I need a rough schedule by tomorrow— rehearsals, sets, costumes, transportation, make-up, dancers, equipment, zot-zot-zot. Ulloch, we need music— not just plain, vanilla orchestra, but, like the man said, something schmaltzy... see what you can come up with. We'll talk about the score as soon as we get an outline. Anybody's got nothing to do, check with me. And for Christ sake, stop looking like you don't know what's coming off... this is just another show— the problems are bigger, but so are the rewards. With a ton of effort and an ounce of good taste, we can parlay this little hour into a big fat Emmy Award, and bonuses all around. Okay now, let's see some sparks fly. If you got a question, don't ask me — I need a whole hell of a lot more answers than questions right now. Remember, we got more than three months to mount this baby so let's get it done in two and take Christmas off for a change. Okay, talk's over— let's see some action." He waved everyone out of the room.

During the exodus, Ralph Goliones sat slumped in his chair, watching the director pack his briefcase. "Ho-ly Kee-ryst. The son of a bitch is off his nut. We'll never pull this crazy mother off... then he'll shit-can us for sure."

Monteczuma snapped his briefcase and headed for the door. "Tell you what, Ralph— you run down to the unemployment office and sign up if you want to..." He paused in the open doorway and stuck a slim cigar into his mouth. "Me, I got a show to put on the air."

Electrifying Clean!

SPARKLE
Wax

Shines and Beautifies
All Wood Surfaces

Sunny Citrus

27 FL OZ (1 PT. 11 OZ)

PART SIX

Sunday, December 31

23

Eleven members of the Pastel Productions staff milled about uneasily before Sub-Surface Gate A, deep in the bowels of Achen State Penitentiary, awaiting the arrival of Tully Keyster.

In charge of the unit was Assistant Director Marc Chonkey; accompanying him on this assignment were a motion picture cameraman and assistant, a sound man, a light technician, two grips, a production assistant, two women from the wardrobe department and a make-up man.

There was little conversation; two armed guards scrutinized the group at all times, and closed-circuit television cameras maintained a silent vigil.

In the midst of the deep quiet, Georgie the make-up man giggled nervously and rolled his eyes. "This place is unreal."

Marc Chonkey leafed through the papers on his clipboard. Everyone else alternated between trying to appear casual, and glancing apprehensively from armed guards to TV cameras, to iron bars.

At last they heard footsteps approaching; two men appeared at the end of the corridor and strode toward them. One of the men looked like a walking mountain, and Chonkey recognized him at once as Warden Keyster. He was accompanied by a clergyman.

"Morning, rag-lickers," Tully beamed. "Been waiting long?"

Eleven heads wagged from side to side in unison. The assistant director stepped forward and extended his hand.

"Warden, I'm Marc Chonkey... we met the other day."

"Yeah, sure, how are you, Chonkey?" Keyster squeezed his hand until the man's smile began to wilt. "First off, take a real good look at all your lackeys here— make sure you don't see no strange faces."

Chonkey scanned the assemblage carefully. "Yep, these are all my people, Warden." He nodded toward Ryder Levitsky, "Except him, of course."

"He's clean," Keyster grinned at the chaplain, "more or less." Everyone laughed politely, except the priest. The warden peered at each face in turn, training a particularly withering gaze upon Georgie the make-up man. "Okay, let's go see my prize specimen. Open up, Malenbower."

There was a buzzing sound, then a loud click, and the heavy gate swung open. Keyster stepped through first, then stood beside the guards, watching the others file by. He glanced at his watch. "Some catering fags should be here soon... Chef Somebody-or-other. You guys got his name on your sheet. Be sure to hustle them through, get me?"

With the gate securely locked behind them, Keyster led the group down the concrete corridor. The only sound was the echo of twenty six feet clopping along, which caused the warden to survey the gathering once again. "Sure takes a lot of leeches, just to take a couple pictures."

The assistant director smiled. "Yeah, well, you know unions."

"A bunch of grub-sucks, these unions. Well, I think this little movie's a good idea, anyway— *The Con's Last Day on Earth*— give the folks at home a peek behind the scenes. Well, here we are." They had reached the end of the corridor and were now standing before Sub-Surface Gate B.

"This, folks, is the entrance to Death Row."

The only thing unique about Sub-Surface Gate B was that, unlike the gray bars typical to Achen State, this section's bars were black. The effect was subtle but sufficient.

The gate glided open, permitting the group to pass through, then it slipped soundlessly back into place. The visitors now found themselves in a windowless corridor of solid concrete, indirectly lighted. On the right, stretched out before them was a row of twelve cells, their bars also painted black.

Marc Chonkey whistled softly. "Get a shot of this, Toby."

The camera whirred.

They walked along the corridor, Keyster and Chonkey in the lead. "My first eleven holes are vacant right now," the warden's tone was slightly apologetic, "but this time next year we'll have to put in triple-decker bunks, sure as God made green maggots. This show tonight is gonna usher in a new era. Well, here's our cream puff."

Two armed guards faced the bars of the twelfth cell, keeping constant surveillance of all activity within.

Chonkey nodded to his cameraman. "Keep rolling."

A bright light was directed into the cell and the camera lens moved up to and between the bars. Inside the austere cubicle sat Lewd Noogie, looking older than his years, very thin and very tired. He squinted into the brilliance of the camera lights, and smiled weakly. Warden Keyster laid his arm across the cell bars and pressed his forehead to his wrist, studying his prized possession. "I thought I was gonna knock heads with a real kick-ass when they shipped me this one. Look what turns up."

The bright lights faded and the camera stopped grinding. "Warden, it'll ease the congestion a lot if we let the wardrobe and make-up people do their jobs first and clear out of here. What do you think?"

"Yeah, sure." Keyster nodded to one of the guards, who

stepped to the cell door and placed a small electronic device against the lock while his partner stood by him with pistol drawn.

The warden entered the cell and strolled over to the condemned man's bunk. "How's it going, cream puff?"

A nervous, fearful smile twitched across Lewd Noogie's lips.

Keyster glanced toward the group outside the cell. "Okay, you costume people, come on in— he's not gonna grope you."

Two elderly women entered meekly, bearing some black garments and a sewing basket; they were followed by the slender blond Georgie, who carried a green metal tackle box filled with stage make-up. Tully poked at the clothing the women carried. "He's gotta try these on, is that the idea?" He tossed the garments into Lewd's lap.

"Here, Nancy, time to get measured for your party suit."

Lewd stood uncertainly and looked around for a place to undress in privacy, but even the toilet was fully exposed. Keyster shook his head. "What's the matter, big shot? Scared to show your dirty jockeys? Okay, okay, all you people turn your backs, so Nancy here can drop his drawers."

Everyone turned away while Lewd removed his prison suit; both guards, however, continued to watch the condemned man carefully, and Georgie the make-up artist peeked out of the corner of his eye.

While Lewd was changing, Keyster noticed the chaplain still standing outside the cell. "Levitsky, for the love of muff, get your aitch bone in here and start makin' with the mumbo jumbo. Don't you want to get your picture took?"

The chaplain entered the cell, nervously leafing through his Bible. "Crab sake, man, you're supposed to be saving this man's soul— that's what I pay you for." Seeing that Lewd had his new trousers on, Tully nudged one of the wardrobe mistresses. "Okay, Granny, do your stuff." He frowned at

Georgie. "You too, muff-buster— but remember, I got my eye on you."

The two elderly women knelt at the condemned man's feet and began pinning his black trousers, as the priest read aloud from the Bible. *"OH LORD my God, in thee do I put my trust; save me from all them that persecute me..."*

The camera whirred.

Georgie opened his tackle box on Lewd's bunk and began to flit around the condemned man, testing a dab of pancake here, a touch of eyeshadow there, muttering, "My dear, are you serious? I mean, this face..."

"OH LORD my God, if I have done this; if there be iniquity in my hands..."

"Ow."

Everyone looked at Lewd Noogie, who grinned sheepishly.

"Did I stick you with a pin?" inquired one of the wardrobe ladies. "Sorry."

" 'Sokay."

"Let the enemy persecute my soul and take it; yea, let him tread down my life upon the earth, and lay mine honor in the dust. Se'lah."

"Excuse me, Chaplain." The assistant director walked into the cell. "I'm sorry, but this scene strikes me as a bit sacrilegious. I'm afraid we'll have to shoot something else."

Keyster strolled over to Marc Chonkey. "What's next?"

The A.O. consulted his clipboard. "Well, I thought it'd be a terrific scene if we could shoot the prison doctor giving Noogie a physical checkup on his last day alive. You know, the irony..."

"Not on your muff, buster."

"Why not?"

"The law says a condemned man's gotta be in top shape before he can fry. Let a sawbones check 'em over and they'd all come up with leprosy the last minute. Reminds me of old Cookie Gazinta. Got hisself appendicitis three hours before his date with the thunderbolt. I tried to hush it up, but the slut-mother couldn't even walk." There was a clattering sound from the other end of the corridor. "That must be the chow."

"Yeah... so what happened with this guy, Gazinta?"

"We hadda haul the chicken-weasel to the infirmary so they could slice his gut. He mends in a week and we fry him the day he gets released. Gazinta never was too long on luck. Even his murder rap was a fluke... he robbed this dame's house— get me— tied her up and gagged her, only she couldn't breathe out of her nose on account of a head cold, so she croaked."

The camera was grinding again and everyone turned to watch the arrival of the caterers. "The condemned man ate a hearty meal," somebody muttered.

An impressive parade marched ceremoniously along the corridor. At the head of the procession, impeccably attired, was a resplendent maitre d'hotel, who announced with a flourish, "Mesdames, monsieurs... Chef Miro Poperin, du Chateau Royale!" He bowed and deferred to the personage behind him, a tall, massively built man with luminous eyes and a huge handlebar mustache. The chef wore a spotless white uniform and a high mushroom hat; he flashed a disdainful smile and nodded: "Zut."

The procession swept into the cell, maitre d' and chef followed by a brace of gorgeous mademoiselles— a strawberry blonde and a leggy brunette— both breathtakingly clad in scanty c-thru waitress costumes; the brunette wore a golden key and wine cup round her neck, nuzzling her ample cleavage. Behind them marched two young men in white— a busboy and a kitchen aide— pushing a large stainless steel combination steam table and service cart.

With great aplomb the maitre d' supervised the setting up of a folding table and the placement thereon of a genuine Verasoie table cloth, a complete table service of

Couteux silver and a place setting of Trevierge china and Memchose crystal. Warden Keyster looked on in amazement; the camera whirred; Lewd Noogie changed back to his prison suit behind a blanket held by two guards. Preparations complete to his satisfaction, the matre d' turned to the chef. "Maestro?"

"Zut."

The maitre d' approached the suspended blanket, behind which stood the guest of honor, and cleared his throat respectfully. "Monsieur... s'il vous plait?"

The blanket dropped away, revealing lewd Noogie buttoning his fly. His feet were bare on the cold concrete; his gray hair was disheveled; a few dabs of stage make-up remained on his gray face. The maitre d' led him to a straight-backed wooden chair before the splendid table, and lewd sat down.

Instantly the catering unit burst into a flurry of efficient activity. The chef flung open steam compartments as his assistants manipulated crockery with great dispatch; the maitre d' hovered over Lewd, making sure that all went well, as the wine stewardess wiggled over to the table and presented a bottle of Dom Luic Cordon '64 for lewd's approval, and the sultry waitress served up the first toothsome remove: *"Fraises Liberte!"* Announced the maitre d' proudly— plump, giant strawberries, hollowed out and stuffed with pink Balboa caviar, then topped with Balalaika vodka. *"Viola!"*

The champagne was poured, the Fraises Liberte unveiled before the condemned man, and then there was a respectful pause as everyone awaited the guest of honor's ceremonial entrance into the fabulous land of haute cuisine.

lewd Noogie smiled apologetically. "Ah... I'm not very hungry, I guess."

There were a few giggles from the TV crew; the maitre d' looked shocked; Chef Poperin raised one eyebrow and peered at the condemned man: "Zut?"

The maitre d', upper lip quivering, bent over stiffly and respectfully addressed lewd's right ear. "But surely monsieur weeshes to zample zuch tres delicieux art culinaire?" He appealed to the master chef with a grandiose sweep of his arm. "Maestro!"

The chef swept away one stainless steel lid with a flourish and introduced the mouthwatering contents beneath: *"Jarret de Boeuf Miro!"*— a succulent shin of braised beef, marinated in sparkling Burgundy and gilded with an edible coating of pure gold leaf, four millionths of an inch thick. Another lid arced upward, trailing savory vapors through the dank basement atmosphere: *"Poireaux Poperin, avec Sauce Perigord!"*— flash-braised Hungarian leeks, smothered in a cognac-truffle sauce and garnished with lemon wheels and fluffs of bitter chocolate. Next: *"Cerises et Chataignes Chef-d'oeuvre!"*— fresh, plump Oriental cherries and Viennese chestnuts, drowned in flaming creme de menthe and served on a frigid bed of white licorice Austrian ice cream.

Everyone's attention swung back to Lewd Noogie, who shifted uneasily in his chair, shrugged his shoulders and flashed another nervous smile. "I'm just not very hungry, is all."

Chef Miro Poperin of the Chateau Royale snapped his head back as if he'd been slapped, his tall hat flopping to the floor. **"Coq suckaire!"** he hissed ominously. **"MOTHAIRE FUCKAIRE!"** His fist came crashing down upon the steam table, sending a large ladle spiraling toward the ceiling. Before the airborne utensil hit the floor, Chef Poperin was out of the cell and striding down the long corridor, his faithful maitre d' close at his heels.

During the confusion that followed, the buxom waitress leaned over Lewd's shoulder, maternally brushing her bosom against the back of his head, her honeyed voice urging, "C'mon, sugar... you've got to try to eat something.

How do you expect to stay alive?"

Marc Chonkey was philosophical. "Well, we got a good beginning on film... we can fake the rest."

The wine stewardess stepped behind the steam table, frowning prettily. "You can't really blame the poor man..." She gazed down at the food compartments. "After all, who can eat junk like this at ten o'clock in the morning?"

Warden Keyster shook his head and smiled. "You sure put up with a mountain of maggots in your job, Chonkey." Moseying over to the table, he picked up Lewd's wineglass, drained it in a single gulp, then held the empty vessel out toward the wine girl. "Here, honey, hit me again. Yessir, this TV is some business. Everyone's a kiss-ass big shot."

Marc Chonkey stood in the center of the cell, studying the shine on his shoes. "Warden, wait till you meet my boss."

An elderly man and his young female companion stood in the entranceway to Tully's Playpen, gaping in awe at the rampant activity that permeated the great hall. Shouting workmen wheeled handcars piled high with heavy cartons; carpenters swarmed over an unfinished structure nearby, their tools filling the air with the sounds of combat. At one end of the enormous arena, musicians tuned their instruments in dissonance; a mob of little choirboys raced about, shrieking; gigantic stacks of folding chairs were heaped about the floor, a small army of workers setting them up in jagged rows. High overhead, in the vast web-like network of steel girders, people scurried to and fro, rigging countless lights and hanging giant netting crammed with colored balloons.

The woman clutched her escort's arm. "Oh, Hink— are you sure we're in the right place?"

"Hush, Deirdre. I'll soon get to the bottom of this."

At the west end of the hall, plumbers assembled temporary comfort stations, as stagehands draped black curtains around the huge BBS Mobile Control Trailer, from which a young man now exited and strolled toward the couple, smiling and extending his hand. "You folks must be from Sparkle Wax!"

"You're damned right I am," the old man bristled, "and I

want to see Linus Sutherland, pronto."

The young man's face went serious. "I'm afraid that will be impossible, sir. Mr. Sutherland is in a sanitarium."

"What? Why, that's preposterous! I just spoke with him yesterday!"

"He collapsed on the set late last night... overexertion, I guess. He was doing a bang-up job, too."

"Poor Mr. Sutherland!" the young woman lamented. "He was such a sweet man, wasn't he, Hink?"

"Yes..." the old man was clearly disarmed, "yes, he was."

The young man's face turned optimistic. "I'm sure he'll be back to his old self in a month or two. Meanwhile, I'm the new man in charge of Sponsor Relations, and I'll be glad to help you out in any way I can. My name's Neal Kroutch." He offered his hand again, and this time the old man took it.

"Well, Kroutch, I'm Bailey Hinkle, Jr., President and Chairman of the Board of Fyzberger-Castel, makers of Sparkle Wax, and this is my... assistant, Deirdre Bartell."

Kroutch exchanged greeting with Miss Bartell, pretending not to notice that her nipples were quite visible through her c-thru outfit. Deirdre Bartell was a knockout brunette, the leggy show-girl type, and couldn't have been much over twenty years old; her boss, whose arm she clutched quite pointedly, was at least sixty years her senior — very tall and very slender, and obviously very well preserved for his years. Hinkle was not to be trifled with today.

"Look at this place— a shambles! No wonder Sutherland collapsed! We can't possibly be ready in time without him— it's less than ten hours before we go on the air!"

"We're right on schedule, Mr. Hinkle. Things always look like this the day of the show."

"Nonsense! I've been buying time on network shows for years, and..."

"Yes, sir, but this is location work. It's not as simple as a studio show. Believe me, as setups go, this show's in better shape than most."

Hinkle frowned. "Well, if you don't mind, I'd prefer to find that out for myself. Where's Art Pastel?"

"Mr. Pastel? Oh, he's a hard man to track down, sometimes— very busy. Listen, would you folks care for a glass of champagne?"

Deirdre Bartell lit up. "Oh, that would be megabliss!"

The three crossed the hall toward the long bar table, Hinkle shaking his head. "Kroutch, do you have any idea what this disaster is costing me?"

"An awful lot of money, sir, I know. The cost of things these days, it's disgraceful. That's one of the reasons we wait till the last day to do a lot of this work— it's cheaper. Would you folks like to get rid of your coats?"

"We'll keep 'em," Hinkle grumbled. "There doesn't even seem to be heat in this old barn. C'mon Deirdre... after you've had your champagne, we're going to pay a visit to Mr. Art Pastel."

Overhead, a voice spoke from a loudspeaker: "Maintenance, report backstage right away— some trouble with one of the organ motors. Tech staff, stand by— we'll pick up cue one-fifty-seven and run it straight through to one-sixty-two. Go to your earphones, please."

"That's our technical director," Kroutch explained. "Right now, they're running through a tech rehearsal— camera cues, sound, lights, that sort of thing. Next is dress rehearsal— that's when the show director, Roland Monteczuma, takes over. So you see, though things may look disorganized..."

"Where's Roland Monteczuma now?" Hinkle asked.

"I believe he's out to lunch." They arrived at the bar and Kroutch addressed one of the waiters. "Listen, these people are the sponsors of the show. Would you open a bottle of champagne for them, please?"

The waiter eyed them suspiciously. "No champagne till the party starts."

"Look, you don't understand These people are VIPs. Oh, where's the champagne? I'll get it myself."

The man scowled and crossed his arms in front of his chest. "It's outside in the snow, and that's where it's stayin' till the party. That's our orders."

Kroutch sighed, turned to the sponsors and shrugged. "Well, I guess that shows you how well we're watching your pennies, Mr. Hinkle. If you folks will excuse me a minute, I'll find this fellow's supervisor and shake loose a bottle for you." He pointed toward where the men were setting up the folding chairs. "Just have a seat, and I won't be a sec." He headed off across the floor.

Bailey Hinkle addressed the barman. "Admirable, this frugality. But why? Are you afraid there won't be enough for the guests?"

The waiter scoffed. "Are you kidding? There must be a thousand bottles out there."

Hinkle blanched. "For six hundred people? A thousand bottles of wine, for only six hundred..."

"That's nothing," the man confided, "you should see the eats. They'll be feedin' the prison for a month."

The technical director spoke over the P.A. system again: "That's thirty, everybody... take a one hour break—dress rehearsal starts at exactly two-forty-five."

Bailey Hinkle zeroed in on the Mobile Control Trailer. "You wait here, Deirdre."

"Now, don't get all adrenal, Hink." She watched him stalk away.

"Remember your condition."

As Hinkle approached the BBS trailer, the door opened and the technical director stepped out, followed by an elderly man in cover alls. "Now, let me get this straight," the director was saying, "our auxiliary generator is big enough to do the whole job, right? But your people went and hooked it up to the prison generator, and now you're telling me that both generators can't put out what one generator alone could?"

"Well, yeah," affirmed the chief electrician, " 'cause they got 'em rigged up parallel, which means they both gotta run at the same speed, and that prison unit's pretty old."

"Okay, okay, so why did they hook them up like that?"

"Because I wasn't there lookin' over their shoulders."

"When did all this happen, anyway? We've been using power here all week."

"Last week sometime."

"And you just noticed it?"

"You can't be everywheres at once."

The director shook his head and sighed. "Is it too late to change it around the way it should be?"

"Prob'ly. I mean, maybe we could do it in time, but we'd hafta shut everything down while we worked ."

"Meaning no power for the rest of the day."

"Right."

"And maybe no power for air, either." "Right."

Bailey Hinkle had heard enough. "Just a moment, here! Do I understand you to say that there isn't going to be any electricity for the program tonight?"

Both men eyed him indignantly. "Who are you?" asked the tech director.

"I'm paying for this fiasco, that's who I am, and I want to know what the devil this is all about!"

The director noticed the VIP tag on the man's lapel. "Oh, I wouldn't worry about it, sir. It's just routine."

"Routine?" Hinkle gaped.

"All in a day's work." The TD turned to his chief electrician. "So what happens if we leave the generators set up like they are?"

"Should be okay, I guess."

"You worried about when the chair goes off?"

"Naw. Couple thousand volts ain't nothin' compared to what we're already using for our equipment."

"In other words, there's probably nothing to worry about?"

"Prob'ly."

The TD smiled at Bailey Hinkle. "See? He just wants me to tell him not to change it, so I'll be responsible if something goes wrong."

"Look," said the electrician, "if you want me to go ahead and switch the hookup…"

"Leave it the way it is," the TD decided. "Only, if we go out of here tonight carrying candles, I'll be looking for your ass, Wenkowski."

The electrician shrugged. "You can't hurt me… I got seniority." He moseyed off across the hall.

Bailey Hinkle, who had been standing by, speechless, found words at last. "Young man, what's your name?"

"Gene Russelton." The tech director held out his hand, but Hinkle disregarded it.

"For the love of God, man, didn't you hear what he just told you?"

"Sure, but you gotta know how to interpret these technical guys… they're all prophets of doom. Look, already today," he began to count off on his fingers, "my construction people promise me the bandstand's gonna collapse… the plumbers say we won't be able to flush the johns… the caterer threatens to take his men and split… my sound engineer thinks there's a short somewhere… the stagehands have voted not to work within thirty feet of the electric chair… and my chief electrician tells me we'll be ringing in the New Year with a brief candlelight service. Listen, I only hope dress rehearsal goes this well. Now, if you'll excuse me, sir, I'd better run along and see if they're gonna be able to get the curtain open in time for the show."

Gene Russelton strolled off toward the stage, as

Hinkle's beet-red complexion slowly faded to chalk-white. Seeing his pallor, Deirdre Bartell hurried to his side. "Now, Hinkness, look at you— you're all adrenal!" She led him to a stack of folding chairs and set one up for him.

Just then, Neal Kroutch appeared with an open bottle of champagne and three goblets. "Presto!" he grinned. "It wasn't easy, but— Why, Mr. Hinkle, are you all right?"

"This is preposterous!" fumed the old man. "Listen, you, I want the cold, hard facts about this generator business!"

"Generator business? Ah, let's see..."

"And the toilets, and that curtain, and I want an exact count of each and every bottle of champagne on the premises!"

"Yessir." Kroutch fished a small notebook from his pocket. "Yes sir, uh-huh... gener—"

"Now you listen to me and listen good. I want to see Art Pastel, and I want to see him pronto, understand me? Because if Art Pastel isn't out here in five minutes flat, your job isn't going to be worth a plugged nickel!"

"Yessir, Mr. Hinkle, right away, sir." Neal Kroutch hurried off toward the backstage area, his face pale.

"C'mon, Hinkness— simmer down." Deirdre picked up the bottle Kroutch had left on the floor. "Let's have something cool to drink." She poured two glasses of champagne, fetched another chair from the stack and set it up for herself; then the pair sat in ominous silence, sipping their wine and watching the hubbub all around them.

"What d'you think you're doin' wit deez chairs, buster?"

Bailey and Deirdre looked up to find two burly workmen standing at their side. "What does it look like we're doing?" Hinkle snapped. "We're sitting down."

"Oh." The first workman looked at his companion. "They're sitting down."

The second workman put his hands on his hips. "I don't suppose you happen to be a member of Local Eight-eight-eight, huh, buddy?"

"Of course I'm not, you blundering idiot."

The first workman stuck out his jaw menacingly. "Look, Mac, nobody handles deez chairs unless they're a member of Local Eight-eight-eight, get me?"

Hinkle regarded him stiffly. "Now see here, my good fellow, do you know who I am?"

"I don't care if you're the Queen of Sheba, deez chairs go back to the stack *as was*, or we report the infraction to the union steward."

The old man rose, trembling. "I happen to be the sponsor of this show!"

"Yeah? Well, unless deez go back to that stack, you're gonna be sponsoring it widdout chairs, get me?"

"Why, you impertinent clot!" the old man yelled.

The workman threw up his hands. "*Oh*-kay, that's it— Breach of Contract." He turned toward the score of people in the midst of setting up the six hundred audience chairs. **"Hey— Eight-eight-eight! Put 'em down-relax! Breach of Contract!"** The men stopped working and sat down .

Bailey Hinkle glowered in the direction Neal Kroutch had gone. **"Where's that goddamned Pastel?"** He stalked off toward the stage. **"Won't show his face, huh!"** Old man Hinkle found himself in front of the bandstand. Musicians were seated on the platform, and a horde of little boys in choir robes clustered round the steps leading from the arena floor up to the bandstand bleachers. Hinkle stopped short, remembering what the tech director had said about the bandstand collapsing. "My God," he gasped, "with all those kids aboard!" The images of endless lawsuits filled his mind, and head lines reeking bad publicity.

He strode toward the podium, upon which stood a short, slender man with slick black hair and a tiny mustache. Standing ramrod straight upon the bandstand, baton pointed at the floor, Ulloch Tugg waited with stoic revulsion for the raucous children to mount the bleachers and settle down.

"Look here, Tugg!"

The band leader opened one eye and peered down over his shoulder. "You talking me, Meester?"

"Listen, goddamnit, I want all these people off this bandstand at once! Don't you realize it's threatening to collapse?"

Tugg's eyes narrowed to slits. "Fugg off, yes?"

"By God, if anything happens to those kids, I'll hold you personally responsible!"

The band leader whirled to face him, stiffly, fists on hips. "Leesen, you old croning, clam down before I'm losing my temperature!" A stray choirboy scampered by the bandstand; as he passed Tugg's feet, the musical director bobbed down and snatched the youngster by the hair, swinging him screaming to the platform and propelling him toward the bleachers with a rap of knuckles at the back of his head. "Son... beech... bastar!" Tugg shot Bailey Hinkle a withering evil eye, then executed a smart about-face, turning once more to his musicians.

The President of Sparkle Wax was livid. Darting to the edge of the platform, he dropped down on all fours and crawled under the apron drapery, disappearing beneath the wooden bandstand.

The children continued to giggle and push as they took their places on the bleachers, and suddenly Ulloch Tugg reached the limit of his patience. "QUAI-YEEET!" he shrieked, leaping from the podium and streaking across the platform toward them. Plowing headlong into the youthful throng, the enraged band leader flailed his arms like windmills gone berserk, raining random blows upon the little heads, driving screams of terror from the ambushed lads. Tugg's swinging arms cut down the tiny bodies like wheat before the reaper's blade, and when the bitter harvest was finally complete, the petrified silence that followed was broken only by an occasional stifled sob.

Tugg stood like a stick before them, his eyebrows

raised, inviting another challenge to his authority. Before him, frozen and saucer-eyed, clustered fifty young boys between the ages of six and ten the most gifted singing voices from all the orphanages throughout the state. This was their first rehearsal with maestro Ulloch Tugg.

The musical director rose to the tips of his toes, then settled slowly back to his metal-cleated heels. "So, babies." His gaze swept disdainfully across the assemblage. "We haff leetle beef-baff from Oncle Ulloch... yes?" He raised his brows and closed his eyes, then his brows came down and his eyelids opened halfway. "These... ees... beeg times. Oncle Ulloch... beeg star. You?" He singled out a random blond head. "Leetle preek."

Beneath the bandstand, Bailey Hinkle thumped a wooden beam, testing its strength. Tugg flashed his hot gaze across the sea of wax like faces. "Who these was?" One hundred anxious eyes darted left and right. Tugg whipped his baton rhythmically against his trouser leg. "Son... beech... bastar. I fine, I keel. Son... beech... bastar."

He pivoted to his left on one heel, took a few measured steps, then spun about and returned to his former position, his relentless gaze spearing face after face. "So, babies.We making rules, yes?" He held up one finger. "Hanky-panky? No. I see, I keel." He held up a second finger. "Talk? No." Additional fingers shot up in sequence. "Geegle? No. Wise guys? No. Peek nose? No. One times fugginup... Oncle Ulloch making babies scream. Twice times fugginup... ees plenty houseless babies where you from. Yes? No?"

Bailey Hinkle crouched in the darkness beneath the bandstand, listening to Tugg's speech overhead. "You crazy son-of-a-bitch!" Tossing his head back, he bonked it on a wooden beam. "*Ow!* Goddamn you!"

Ulloch Tugg sprung into the air several inches and came down staring wide-eyed at the floor. Suspiciously, he surveyed the choir, then the men in his orchestra.

"Goddamn you," the floor muttered once again.

Tugg backed up a few steps, then spun about and strode to the podium, facing the entire ensemble, his mustache trembling. "I fine, I keel." He let his threat sink in as he stabbed his gaze about. "Ho-kay. We 'hearse, no?" Nummer... seesteen, perfec' firs' times, yes?"

Deirdre Bartell had lost track of her employer. Having been intimidated out of her seat, she meandered through the hall, sipping champagne, until suddenly the orchestra burst into song, drawing her attention toward the bandstand. There, just beneath Ulloch Tugg's feet, she saw a white head appear through the platform apron. "Hink!" She ran to meet the crawling old man, helped him to his feet and led him away from the bandstand racket.

"Hinkness, are you moon-blind? What in the world were you doing under there?"

Bailey Hinkle was rubbing his head. "Goddamn that son-of-a-bitch, anyway."

Their path was suddenly obstructed by an enormous man standing before them with his fists jammed into his suit-jacket pockets. "Howdy, folks!" The man smiled amiably, glancing at their VIP badges. "I saw the old geezer here come out from under the stage. Thought it might be one of my goons tryin' to pull a caper."

Hinkle looked him over. "What is this, another union gripe? Listen, mister, I want your name and I want it pronto!"

"Tully Keyster." When that didn't seem to ring a bell, the big man added, "Warden Tully Keyster. This Playpen belongs to me."

"Huh," muttered Hinkle, " 'playpen' is right."

Keyster eyed him suspiciously. "You some kinda inspector or something?"

"Hardly."

"Well, you gonna tell me, muff-mouth, or do I hafta guess?"

Deirdre Bartell was instinctively afraid of Warden

Keyster. She clutched her boss's arm and said quickly, "This is Mr. Hinkle, the President of Sparkle Wax."

"Well, well, well! The promoters of the show, huh?" The warden beamed.

Old man Hinkle scowled, "Side show, that's what the hell it is. Warden, I want to know exactly what you think about the way this program is being put together. No soft-soaping, now— just your honest opinion, straight from the chest."

Keyster glanced around the hall, shaking his head. "You don't see none of my cons working with these eightballs, do you? I bring my boys here to work in the middle of the night, so's they won't be exposed to any bad influences."

"Warden," Bailey Hinkle eyed him sagaciously, "you've got a good head on your shoulders."

Keyster frowned, peering at Deirdre Bartell's visible nipples. "I see your daughter forgot to get dressed this morning."

Hinkle disregarded the comment. "Say, maybe you know where I can corner this Art Pastel fellow. I sent some lackey looking for him half an hour ago, and..."

"Save your shoe leather, pops. I hear the snake won't haul his nates up here till just before the show."

"Do you mean to tell me he isn't even here?"

"Don't it frost your hornies? I tried to get him on the phone last night— one of the guys here called his house for me. And you know what? That Pastel fag fired him."

Hinkle's eyes narrowed. "This fellow— his name wouldn't happen to be Linus Sutherland, would it?"

"Yeah, that's the guy."

"Oh, Hink." Deirdre clutched her boss's arm.

"That confirms it," sighed Bailey Hinkle, badly shaken. "The ship's adrift."

Overhead, a voice spoke over the public address system: "Dress rehearsal, fifteen minutes."

Warden Keyster glanced at the Mobile Control Trailer at

the end of the hall. "Course, I been hearing big things about this black super clam, what's his name, Monteczuma— but so far he ain't stuck his muff outta that kiddy car long enough to show me much."

"Hinkness, look!" Deirdre said suddenly. "It's that Mr. Kroutch!" Neal Kroutch had walked right by without seeming to notice them. "Look here, Kroutch," Hinkle snapped, "you needn't go sneaking around like that. Your little masquerade is over! We know all about Linus Sutherland!"

Kroutch looked at him a moment before recognizing him. "Oh, Mr. Hinkle." His voice was expressionless. "Art Pastel isn't here."

"Yes, yes, we know all about that one, too, you conniving—"

"I tried to get him on the phone for you," Kroutch explained, "and he axed me."

Two men in serving jackets approached from the food storage shed, one pointing at Neal Kroutch. "That's him... that's the guy." The other man confronted Kroutch accusingly. "Are you the guy that copped a bottle of wine from my man here and used abusive language?"

The barman nodded his head."Yeah, that's him awright, Arnold." Arnold, a supervisor, was quite indignant.

"Listen, friend," he told Neal Kroutch, "this man is not some kind of slave, you know— he's a flesh-and-blood human being, who just happens to be paid-in-full member of Local Six-forty-nine of the WBAA. So when you call him a dirty name, you're calling eighty-one thousand, seven hundred waiters and barmen a dirty name, too."

Kroutch looked at him a moment, then said, "Blow it out your ass."

The barman watched his supervisor's mouth drop open, waited a while, then pointed out, "He said, 'Blow it out your ass,' Arnold." Suddenly, Arnold tilted his head back and shouted vehemently, **"In-fraction!"** He spun away and marched across the half. **"In-fraction! In-fraction!"** All serving personnel within earshot stopped in their tracks.

Nearby, the contingent from the National Chair Folders Union continued their sit-down. A passing construction worker was heard to explain loudly, "If there's a wildcat strike, Local Nine-fifty-eight will strike in sympathy."

Tully Keyster clenched and unclenched his fists. "What these pus-suckers need is to see some of their blood on the floor. That'd show 'em who's boss."

A burly workman stepped up to the warden. "Just who the hell d'you think you're mouthin' off to, buster?"

Keyster shoved his chin into the workman's face. **"I'M TALKING TO YOU, YOU GREASE-FAG CHICKEN-MOTHER SON-OF-A SCUM-SLUT LEECH!"**

The man's ears turned red; he stood his ground a moment, then backed off. "Oh-kay, buster... we'll see how you like getting along without toilets!"

Keyster lunged at him, but the man bolted.

"Anarchy!" wheezed Bailey Hinkle. "I won't have these— animals working on my show!" Scattered jeers arose from the gathering crowd of union members, and the old man's knees began to buckle. Deirdre looked about vainly for a chair, then let him sink slowly to the floor, where he sat cross-legged, shaking his head.

Warden Keyster surveyed the grumbling mob of indignant workers, and smiled. This is it. Gonad-counting Time. **"Ya buncha clam assed pantywaists,"** he spat, grinning contemptuously. **"Gangin' up on the old buzzard, are ya?"**

The workers converged upon him instantly. He began to back away, luring them toward the south wall of the Playpen, where a long buffet table was set up. The workers shook their fists, wielded tools and hurled obscenities at him, stalking him boldly, secure in their numbers. As soon as the warden felt his back touch the edge of the table, he spun around and hiked himself upward, standing atop the counter, facing his antagonists." Okay, farts— the honeymoon's over!" The workers stopped advancing. Keyster planted his feet firmly apart, his fists squarely on his hips. **Mean-ass studs, are ya? Walkin' around here, nuggets to your knees, a pack of union shysters lickin' your slimy butt-holes. Well, you ain't nothin' but a buncha nutless Nancys doin' turd-poor work my granny could do better with her muff tied behind her back."**

Incredulous, the workers lunged toward him again, roaring, and the warden was ready. Pointing a massive finger at the biggest, meanest looking bruiser he could find, he growled, **"You're a dead man."**

The worker stopped in his tracks. So did everyone else. The mob was mystified by Tully Keyster.

"Wise up, cream puffs. You're in Keyster Country now, and your leech-suck unions don't cut no ice with me. If any of you snot-chompers think I'm bluffin', drag your nates up here and get your education."

One hundred men and women stood frozen with outrage and dread. Fists clenched, knuckles white, eyes bulging and insane with blood lust, every worker leaned forward ominously, on the verge of all-out assault.

"What's going on here?"

A tall black man walked casually through the scattered groups of livid workers; he wore a pullover sweater, and his hands were in his hip pockets.

The appearance of Roland Monteczuma meant only one thing to the assembled union members: Arbitration. And Arbitration meant Redress of Grievances, Penalty for Default of Agreement, Negotiated Settlement, Reconsideration of Contractual Obligations... in short, *More Money.*

Instantly the workers swarmed around the show director, venting their frustration with hysterical invective. Tully Keyster stood upon his counter top like a Shakespearean actor watching a brawl in the pit. *Clam crap.* He saw the mob's explosive tension gurgle away through a mass of roaring throats. *That black bastard put the kibosh on my big finale.*

Monteczuma made his way to the table and climbed up beside the warden. "Mister, I can't tell you how close you just came to getting your ass torn off."

The workers screamed with glee, rejoicing in their sense of infinite power; they had spared the life of the infidel— but they could, at any future moment they desired, just go ahead and tear the bastard's head off, after all.

Warden Keyster waited for the clamor to subside. "Okay, sow suckers... you played your ace, now I'll play mine." He raised his eyes toward the roof of the arena.
Stationed every twenty feet around the ceiling perimeter of the great hall was a black uniformed prison guard, barely visible, his high-powered rifle at the ready.

You could hear a pin drop in Tully's Playpen.

After a respectable silence, Roland Monteczuma quietly addressed the petrified throng. "Must I remind you people where we are? This man is Tully Keyster, warden of the penitentiary."

"Howdy folks," grinned the warden. "Welcome to my Playpen." There was some shuffling of feet and a few hushed exclamations, but mostly just blank faces directed toward the ceiling.

Monteczuma took this opportunity to make his play. "Now, as for this little misunderstanding with the warden here, I'm afraid he's perfectly within his rights to regulate our conduct while we're at Achen State... though I certainly don't approve of his methods. Also, since he has no legal connection with the network or Pastel Productions, nothing he does can be considered in violation of your contracts. The same goes for that elderly gent over there, who happens to be an investor in the show, and therefore, technically, just a visitor on the set. As far as Neal Kroutch is concerned... well, the man has been fired, fair enough? Now, listen— from here on in, anyone with a gripe should see me personally, is that clear? Okay, what say we all get back to work now... we've got a dress rehearsal in ten minutes, and a million things to finish up before the party starts tonight."

The workers slowly returned to their jobs, buzzing cautiously. Keyster and Monteczuma jumped down from the table, and the director said, "Stick around, Warden... I want to talk to you."

"Sure, okay." Keyster was content to bask in the new atmosphere of respect he now commanded.

Walking over to Bailey Hinkle and Miss Bartell, the director sat down beside the old man on the concrete floor. "Now, what's this I hear about people giving you a hard time?"

"Hard time? *Hard time!?*" Hinkle paused for air. "Packs of wild animals roaming around free... Pastel nowhere in sight... Linus Sutherland fired right out from under my goddamned nose. *Anarchy*, that's what it is, and there's not a goddamned soul around who knows a goddamned thing about it!"

Monteczuma smiled sympathetically. "Well, maybe I can answer some of your questions, sir. You see, I happen to be in complete charge of this production while Mr. Pastel is off the set."

Bailey Hinkle eyed him as though he were a mirage. The old man pointed toward the north wall. "How much champagne is out in that snow?" he asked skeptically.

"Six hundred bottles of Dom Luic Cordon sixty-four," said Monteczuma. "For food we have thirty hams, five beef roasts and six hundred servings each of Strawberries Liberte, some other French dishes I can't pronounce, plus ample coffee and tea."

Hinkle leaned back and regarded the director incredulously; then he fired off another volley. "What about this generator business? The electricians say that—"

"Listen, Mr. Hinkle," the director broke in gently, "do you honestly believe that I and my staff would blatantly ignore a serious threat to the success of this program? Faulty generators, falling band stands— do you know where ideas like that come from? They come from people like the ones you just saw almost start a riot out here."

"Pack of goddamned animals," affirmed the old man.

"So believe me when I tell you there's nothing to worry about. Sure, these workers are unreliable and inefficient, but let's face it, they're all that's available, and it's my job to see they get the work done in the fastest, cheapest way."

"Young man," Hinkle gazed around at the activity in the hall, "my hard earned money is being squandered around this place with the wildest abandon since the fall of the Roman Empire— and nobody gives two damns about it! I want a dollar's worth of value for every dollar I shell out. Where is it? All I want to know is this: What in the name of sanity is all my money buying around here, besides chaos?"

"Well, let's see," the director began, offhandedly, "for equipment— mostly rented from the network— we've got the X-Ten Mobile Control Trailer, four Atlas Vans, an auxiliary generator and five color cameras... that includes one dolly, one handheld job and one ceiling-suspended unit. Then we have two hundred fifty-odd stage lights, plus ceiling grids, a lighting board, two follow spots and two Aircraft P-B Reflectors for outside-the-hall illumination. We're using twelve microphones, six speakers and a sound console, two applause signs and various other minor tech apparatus— all the latest remote control stuff, of course— no wires or cables to clutter up the place. Course we can't forget the two cycloramas... three hundred fifty and one hundred seventy feet long, respectively, each forty feet high... and then there's the six hundred audience chairs and six temporary johns.

"Construction-wise, we've built a complete proscenium stage, seventy-five by thirty... an adjoining bandstand and choir box... coatroom, dressing rooms, storage rooms, buffet and bar tables. Of course, the party decorations, stage decor, etcetera have been donated by various patriotic organizations.

"Our biggest expense, naturally, is for personnel. For the party and audience arrangements, we have fifteen waiters, twenty service and bus personnel, and twenty network pages. For security..." he glanced toward the ceiling, "well, you know all about that.

"Now then— the staff: In the control room with me, there's the assistant director, tech director, switcher, audio engineer and associate producer. Floating the hall, our unit manager, a sound technician and lighting director. Our stage area staff includes the stage manager, three production assistants, a staff announcer, color girl and, of course, Art Pastel, our producer. Toss in the musical director, set designer, costume designer, choreographer, four writers, two talent coordinators and whoever else I forgot to mention, and it comes to a total of twenty-seven on the production staff.

"As for the crews, backstage we have six electricians, four make up people, six wardrobe mistresses, two prop girls, six grips and ten senior stagehands. In the house, six cameramen— one relief and one assistant— two spotlight men, three shotgun mike operators and four tech assistants. On the construction crew: twenty-three carpenters, six masons, four plumbers and nineteen laborers. Throw in a full compliment of assistants and other peons and you come up with an entire production battalion of two hundred forty-six people.

"Finally under the heading of 'Talent,' we list thirty-two union musicians, one organist and fifty choirboys. We have ten dancers, nineteen members of the official execution staff and about, say, fifteen various other performers. Total talent: one hundred twenty eight.

"Add all that up on your pocket abacus and you come up with a grand total of four hundred seventy-four bodies on the payroll for this production. The six hundred members of the audience, fortunately, are ours for the price of just one bottle of champagne and a serving of chow apiece.

"Now, since you aren't just buying the air time for this show, but are actually investing in Pastel Productions to offset the great expense of this spectacular, I feel that you're also entitled to know something else, Mr. Hinkle. We — that is, myself and my highly qualified staff of top-notch professionals— do not just feel obligated to get this program on the air. Each and every one of us is deeply dedicated and firmly committed to making this show a truly creative endeavor, an artistic event whose every on-the-air moment exhibits the ultimate in good taste... to reflect favorably on the name of Sparkle Wax, upon your reputation as a good and decent human being, and upon our high professional standards and the standards of the entire television community." Roland Monteczuma sat back and glanced at his watch, deciding he'd poured it on thick enough.

Transfixed, the old man gazed at the director, his mouth hanging open several moments before stretching into a grateful grin. He reached out and clapped the black man on the shoulder. "Young fellow, if you ever— and I mean ever— take it into your mind to go hunting for a new job, there'll always be a spot for you at Sparkle Wax, y'hear?"

"Mr. Hinkle, I'll remember that."

"You do it!" Hinkle insisted. "You're okay!"

"You sure are!" agreed Deirdre Bartell. Slinking to the side of the director, who was still sitting on the floor, she loomed over Monteczuma provocatively and eased her fur coat open, presenting him with a bird's eye view of her chestnut-crested nest.

Monteczuma glanced up her dress, then returned his attention to the old man. "Tell you what... why don't you folks run along now and leave everything up to me? You can take a little nap wherever you're staying, and be well rested for the party tonight."

Hinkle nodded weakly. "Sounds good to me... I'm bushed. C'mon, Deirdre, our investment's in good hands."

The trio exchanged goodbyes, then Monteczuma strolled over to where Warden Keyster sat on the buffet table. "Tell me, Warden, what would have happened if I hadn't walked in here when I did? Would your men have started shooting?"

Tully grinned. "Couple rounds over their heads woulda done the trick. Too bad you queered it. It'd a been a lesson them crap-lappers woulda never forgot."

"Well, before I forget, let's get one thing straight, Keyster. The men in this hall are my responsibility, and your convicts are yours. If I see you even think about mouthing off to one of my people again, I'm gonna kick your ass so far off this show, you'll be pulling the fucking lever in another time zone, you dig?"

The warden leapt to his feet. "Why, you wart-mouthed clam jugger, I'll..."

Monteczuma squared off and looked him straight in the eye. "Keyster, I've got you pegged. You want to be on that stage tonight so goddamn bad you can taste it. You'd let a Ubangi ram your old lady before you'd fuck up your golden chance to fry that poor bastard in front of a billion people. So don't go shaking any fists or rifles in my face, mister, or your TV debut is gonna be shit-canned, understand me? Now, if you think I'm bluffing, you just try me."

The warden was dying to ram his fist into the director's face, but it was no use; this time the black bastard really had him where the hair was short. Keyster wanted so desperately to be on that show tonight, he *would* have let a Ubangi ram his old lady.

"Our Father, watch Arthur in heaven;
Hollow be thy name;
Thy kindly come, do the best you can on earth,
*   as they say, and in heaven;*
Give us this day our daily paper;
Forgive our past messes, and we forgive and
*   forget, and that's for darned sure;*
Teach us how to watch your foot; And deliver
us from evil omens."

Merlin made the sign of the cross, then slowly rose from beside his cot. For a few moments he stood motionless in the chilly twilight of the unlit room, flicking his thumb out of his fist; then he shuffled to the window and peered out at the gray city lying beneath a cloudy winter sky. "Mornin', Labor Gang." It was late afternoon.

He trudged to the bar and prepared to clean up the mess from that morning's experiment. Lifting a soiled zombie glass, he sniffed at the dregs of this latest concoction, the Hi-wy-an Cocktail: papaya juice, coconut milk, Chartreuse and sake. Merlin had consumed a sufficient quantity of this exotic beverage to render him unconscious for the past six hours; now, he gazed off into space and inwardly assessed his physical condition. "I...

have a splitting headache."

Endeavor # 12,321 was a failure.

As he carried some glassware to the sink, there was a knock at the door. "Oh-oh." He dried his hands with a paper towel and tiptoed to the door; carefully securing all three locks, he pressed his ear to the door and whispered, "Who shall I say is calling?" The gentle knock was repeated. "Sugar!" The old man fretted, "hold on a minute— someone's at the door." He opened the three locks, cracked the door and peered into the stair well.

His daughter was there, holding the afternoon paper.

"Wreck o' the Hesperus... it's Toy Boat, is it?" He swung the portal wide. "Come in! Come in! Have a drinkie!"

Smiling at her father, Toy switched on the ceiling light and sat down at the bar, spreading the paper out before her. Merlin returned to his sink. "Go right ahead, door-ter... don't let the old Chiefie interrupt you." He scoured a solid-silver cocktail shaker as Toy began reading from the front page of the paper.

"TV SHOW OF THE CENTURY TO BE AIRED TONIGHT

"Despite the heated protests of an out raged minority, the countdown continues toward an eleven p.m. blast-off of Art Pastel's New Year's Eve spectacular, which will rocket the execution of Novies murderer Lewd Noogie into one billion homes throughout the entire Free World..."

As Merlin returned some glasses to the shelf, he happened to notice a large daily calendar hanging beside the cash register. The top page read SEPT. 1, and had not been touched in thirty-two years. Carefully, the old man tore off this yellowed leaf, then peered myopically at the page beneath. *February two?* He gaped. "Good old Groundhog Day! Why, can you de-magine that? It's old

Chiefie's birthday!"

Toy shook her head again, but her father did not notice. "Wowsie man! The old groundhog's comin' out of his cave today! Drinks are on the old house, and I don't mean Mayberry!" He leaned toward Toy across the bar, confiding quietly, "I'm thirty-seven years young... but don't tell your mother whatever you do." He hurried to his worktable, chafing his hands excitedly. "Mandalay! This calls for a drop of aqua vitae, m'boys she said!— something special for the holidays!" He paused, one fist on the table and the other on his hip, his tongue at his upper lip and his eyes squinting toward the ceiling. Presently, he slapped his thigh triumphantly. **"Groundhog Cocktail!"** He looked at his daughter for approval. "Ain't it?"

Toy smiled and nodded, reaching for the experiment logbook and a pencil. Under the date, December 31, she wrote GROUND-HOG COCKTAIL: Endeavor # 12,322.

Merlin puttered about his supply shelves. "Groundhog Cocktail she be. See now... what do those little fellows eat, anyhow? Roots, I betcha..." He selected a dusty jar of sassafras, then suddenly exclaimed, "Hotsy-totsy!" Rushing to the refrigerator, he fished out two bunches of fresh carrots, a celery stalk, a golden delicious apple and a sprig of parsley. "That's for sure!" Depositing the produce on his worktable, he perused the spice shelf once again. "Groundhog... groundhog..." He selected jars of sage, cumin and fennel seeds, announcing each ingredient so his daughter could copy it down. Flicking on the electric juice extractor, he then began to feed it carrots and celery. "Wait till your mother tastes this!" he shouted over the whine of the machine. "Golly Neds, door-ter... go ahead with your reading— I won't say another word!"

"Preceding the show will be a gala New Year's Eve ball, attended by six hundred

elegantly attired dignitaries, each of whom
has donated $500 or more to a fund now
totaling over half a million dollars. Of this
money, $ 100,000 is for the proposed Noogie
Novuplet Memorial; another $100,000 will be
awarded to their mother as a pension, and the
remainder added to the Fund for Repeal of the
Asinine Amendment.

"Appearing with Art Pastel tonight will
be..."

"One ounce carrot juice..." The old man began pouring
ingredients into a measuring glass. "Two ounces celery... a
dash olive oil..." Finally, he dumped the entire mixture into
a cocktail shaker, tossed in a sprig of parsley and shook it
briskly. Opening the shaker, he peered inside, added
another dash of olive oil and agitated it again.

"Dad?" Arthur stood in the doorway, an overnight bag in
his hand. He and his sister exchanged shy smiles of
greeting.

"Arthur, m'boy! Are you thriving?" The old man hurried
over to shake his son's hand and pat him on the face. "So
the good old Army gave you a furlough, ain't it?"

"Right. Listen, Dad..."

"C'mon, c'mon," Merlin dragged his son over and sat him
at the bar. "One Hi-wy-an Cockt... ah, whatchacallit?
Groundhog! That's the ticket! **Groundhog Cocktail**, coming
right up for the chip off the old block, m'boys she said!" He
poured a large drink and set it before his son.

Arthur picked up the drink and saluted his father with
it; then he took a tiny sip from the glass. "Why, Dad, that's
really delicious."

"**Macaroni spa-get!**" the old man shouted. "Go get your
mother! *Thalia! Come here!* We're really in the chips this
time, and that's for sure!" He picked up his son's glass and
drained it, while Arthur took six new five dollar bills from
his pocket and laid them on the bar. Merlin spied the bills

and picked them up slowly, shaking his head as he walked to the cash register. "I'll see if I have the change." He brought back a nickel and a dime.

Arthur climbed from the stool. "I have to go now, Dad. I have a show to do upstate... I'll be back tomorrow morning."

Merlin was already busily setting up the final phase of his latest experiment: the field testing of his new concoction by drinking the entire quart himself. "Okay, m'boy, you're a gentleman and a scholar, and don't you forget that!" As Arthur was closing the door on his way out, the old man added, "And don't forget to thank your sergeant kindly for letting you off on the old Chiefie's birthday, God bless 'im."

"I'll do that, Dad." Arthur glanced at Toy. "Bye," he said, and left.

Merlin downed his third Groundhog Cocktail, smacked his lips and squinted at the empty glass. "Those people moved."

Toy folded up the newspaper, preparing to return downstairs. On the bottom of the front page were three pictures. The first was a shot of her brother, and was captioned: At the microphone. The second, of Lewd Noogie, was subtitled: At the chair. The third was of Warden Tully Keyster, and beneath it: At the switch.

26

The front doorbell rang again.

"Yeah, okay, hold your buns!" Warden Keyster was in his study, rooting through the desk drawers in search of his gold cuff links. He wore tuxedo trousers, black patent-leather pumps and a ruffle-front white shirt with French cuffs. His shirttail was out and the French cuffs flopped down over his hands.

The doorbell rang again.

"Will somebody get that smut-damned door, or am I the only roach in this wart-forsaken house?"

"I'll get it, Daddy Bear!" Bare feet pattered down from upstairs and a flash of violet whispered past the study doorway.

"Ah, there you are, you little squat-mothers." Tully fished two loose links from his bottom drawer, blew hot air on them and burnished them on his trouser leg. As he was attempting to stab one through the tiny slits in his shirt cuff, Jenny came into the study.

"The car's here, Daddy."

Tully grunted. "At least somebody's on time around this place tonight. Aw, pig muff— here, gimme a hand with these things, will you?"

"Sure, Daddy."

Tully looked at his daughter for the first time. She wore

a pastel violet gown with sheer violet stockings and no shoes. The gown was full at the skirt and quite short, and its neckline dipped so low that the ringlet tips of her long golden tresses nestled in her youthful cleavage. "Where's the rest of that dress?" asked her father.

"Oh, Daddy, don't be flooy."

"Yeah, well, you put on a sweater over that thing— it's nippy in the Playpen."

"Daddy Bear, this is the style. Isn't it omee?"

"Pretty color. Now see if you can find a purple sweater to go with it, 'cause you ain't getting out of this slutting house without one."

His daughter looked up at him, crushed. *"Oh... Daddy."* She seemed to grow smaller right in front of him— except for her eyes, which ballooned to agonizing proportions and welled with tears.

Tully looked helplessly about the room. "Aw, for the love of... *okay, okay*— wear what you want, for snake sake— freeze your buns off... 'sokay with me— only, would it be asking too much for you to put something on your feet?"

"Daddy Bear," Jenny whined, "it's the style!"

"Bare feet?" Keyster was dumfounded. **"In fifteen inches of sucking snow?"**

"I'll wear boots on the way."

"The floor in that place is *plain unheated concrete!"*

"I know it." His daughter turned away and showed him the bottom of one foot. "See? I'll be megabliss!" Inside her indestructible Eterna Leg-Pet Panting Hose she wore a wafer-thin Nudie Thermo Sole covering the underside of her foot.

Keyster shook his head. "Beats the geek outta me." He let her snap the second cuff link. "When you go back upstairs, tell your mother to shake a bun, the limousine's here. We're gonna drive in through Gate Three."

Jenny's face grew serious. "I... don't think we should do that, Daddy."

"Why not? We got a right to make a grand entrance like all the other big shots."

"Sure we do..." She picked up her father's electric chair cigarette lighter and turned it over in her hand, "only I'm afraid you'll get all... adrenal, or something."

"You mean those fag-slime protesters? They don't steam me none. I *do* want to make sure my boys can handle it, though... so's them maggots don't give the guests a bad impression."

Jenny strolled to the window and gazed off toward where the demonstrators were assembled on the other side of the prison. "Most of them are really floral."

"Who?" Tully strode over to her and pointed into the darkness. "You weren't out there fraternizing with those grease weasels, were you? **By rag, it don't look right, the daughter of Tully Keyster out there rubbin' elbows with lice like that!**"

Jenny took his arm. "See, Daddy? You're getting all crambo already, just talking about it."

"Yeah... okay, I'll simmer down." He glanced at his watch. "You get upstairs and goose your old lady— it's almost seven-fifteen."

"Sacro, Daddy Bear." She scampered from the room.

Warden Keyster looked out at the dark night. "Protesters, my squat." *Lunatic-fringe bull-fag bearded dykes.* Struggling into his suspenders, he turned away and headed back to the desk, looking around for his bow tie. "Now, where in the name of smut did that disappear to?"

Just then, Jenny's excited voice called from upstairs, "Daddy! Come quick!"

"Now what?" Tully groaned. He grabbed his tux jacket and headed for the door.

"Dad-dy!"

"Yeah, yeah— hold your muff!" He found the tie on the floor by the study door and scooped it up as he stepped into the foyer and saw Jenny standing at the top of the stairs.

"Oh, Daddy, it's just crambo! Mommy says she's not coming tonight!"

Tully slung his jacket over the banister and scaled the steps two at a time. "What's the matter with her?"

"She says she's sick!"

He bounded to the end of the hall and burst into Anita's room. Bromberg shot from the bed like a rocket, shrieking wildly and attacking the warden's ankle. "What's this I hear about— **Hey, you little muff-rag, these are rented pants!**" Snatching the screaming creature by its tail, he carried it to the closet, dumped it inside and slammed the door, muffling its outraged, hysterical howling. "Now, get your rags on and get downstairs, Neet— it's almost seven-thirty!"

Mrs. Keyster sat ashen-faced upon the bed, wearing just a slip. "I... don't feel well," she said weakly.

"Just more of your old-age bull-squat. Couple swigs of champagne, you'll forget all about it. Get dressed."

"It's no use, Tully— I just can't make it, and that's that."

The warden studied her a moment in silence. "Just like that, huh? Your old man's big night... getting up in front of all those big squats... the show going all over the God-suck world, and you sit there like it was a policemen's ball. **Fag-nabbit, Anita, I'll be famous overnight!**" He appealed to Jenny. **"The biggest night of my leeching life, and my own wife doesn't want to share the scum bag with me!"**

Jenny sat beside her mother. "He's right, Mommy. You really should be there... I mean, don't you want to be?"

"Of course I want to be there."

Tully paced the floor. "Good squat, Anita, you're the last person in the world I thought would let me down at a time like this!" He searched himself for a cigar, but he had none on him. "Six hundred Nancys pay through the hose to come up here and watch me yank that switch— and you and me are supposed to be on that greeting line when they pull in! What am I supposed to tell them? **The little lady has the** trots?"

Still pale, Anita straightened up a bit and asked quietly, "Will Art Pastel be at the party?"

Tully stopped pacing and eyed her darkly. "How d'you like that? For me she won't go, but for that greased fart, she'll think about it. Well, it so happens Mr. **Fart** Pastel **won't** be at the party, because the fag snake thinks he's Jesus Christ Almighty... so you'll have to wait till he comes on stage to get your jollies off. **Now, are you putting on that dress, or are you going in your drawers?— 'cause, either way, you're going, sister, if I have to drag you by the muff!"**

His wife rose from the bed, smiling thinly. "All right, Tully, you win. I won't let you down... I'll go."

Keyster sighed and leaned back against the closet door, causing the imprisoned Bromberg to fly into another rage. "If all my cons was females," the warden shook his head with bewilderment, "I'd be... wart, I dunno what I'd be."

27

Tully's Playpen glittered like a fairy tale come true. Muted lighting bathed the hall with misty tones of rose and blue; Burgundy curtains graced the walls, lush and regal, festooned with rows of patriotic bunting; miles of rainbow colored streamers looped across the lofty ceiling, their tails fluttering down toward a shimmering dance floor, where splendidly attired couples swirled through the waltz impassioned air.

On the bandstand, an ecstatic Ulloch Tugg swayed to and fro before his mammoth orchestra, waving his baton and humming along with the dreamy music. Elsewhere in the vast arena, empty rows of blue-upholstered chairs waited in subdued illumination, and the stage area remained concealed behind an unlit curtain.

The west quarter of the building swarmed with festive couples, noshing on exotic foods and swilling imported champagne from gleaming goblets ceaselessly replenished by a corps of liveried waiters. A roving azure spotlight danced among the gathered guests, and a beam of silver brilliance played upon the Official Entrance Arch, where late arrivals were being announced over the P.A. system, then greeted by the Official Receiving Line.

"Mr. E. Jarvis Hooper, Head of the Federal Bureau of Intelligence, and wife."

The federal official and his spouse were greeted in turn by Governor and Mrs. Angus Black, Tully and Anita Keyster, Bailey Hinkle and Deirdre Bartell, Mr. and Mrs. Ronny Rolf of BBS, Monty Spiegel of Pastel Productions, and the Guest of Honor, Fila Noogie.

"Dr. Sumner V. Cashewe, President, American Medical Monopoly, and wife." Warden Keyster shook the surgeon's hand. "Welcome to the Playpen, Doc— this here's the little woman."

"Chief Akumba Chimba, Leader of the Black Brotherhood for Bloodshed, and woman." Keyster engaged in an extended hand squeezing contest with the militant black leader, then propelled him along the line without introducing him to Anita.

Anita kept peering at the entrance arch. "Tully, are you sure Art Pastel isn't coming to the party?"

Ignoring her, the warden shook hands with Ignatius A. Hunk, Chairman of the Board of Chemical Foods, Inc. "How's it going, Hunk?"

Keyster mopped his brow and glanced at his watch. "Thank squat it's practically nine," he muttered. "If I hafta pump any more mitts, I won't have enough left to pull the switch."

Dictating into a small tape recorder strapped to her shoulder, the fashion editor for the Distaff Daily newspaper roved the great hall, covering what had turned out to be *the* fashion event of the season.

"Oodles of surprises here tonight," she told her microphone. "Quite predictably, of course, fur ensembles are very much in vogue this year, but what surprises and delights the fashion palate is the dazzling variety of diverse pelts in evidence throughout the Playpen, and the fresh, ingenious ways they've been employed. We see Alaska sable, Baltic tiger, kolinsky, Roman seal, marmink, cony mole..." Stepping up to a chunky redhead all decked out in white, the editor peered at the woman's name tag and held the microphone before her. "Excuse me, Mrs. Rawdon..."

"Why, hell-ohh!" the redhead effervesced, pretending to know the news correspondent.

The editor checked her guest list. "I see you're the wife of Willie Foster Rawdon, National Chairman of the American Gun Association. That certainly is a chicly recherché ensemble you're sporting tonight. Who's your designer, dear?"

"Farley Feigh," confided Mrs. Rawdon, "and I don't mind telling you, he's not cheap."

"I notice it features a sort of *néerlandais* bodice and a bell-flare, honeycomb hoop-skirt, hem-tipped in— is that *lapin de garenne?*"

Mrs. Rawdon blushed. "No, honey, this here's just plain ol' wild bunny rabbit."

"Yes, that's what I said, dear. Now then, the gown itself — a beautiful piece of goods— is it really white leather?"

"One hundred percent buffed white albino doeskin," boasted Mrs. Rawdon, "almost nine whole yards of it."

"And this?" the editor touched the wide band of dark fur circling the woman's waist.

"That's my motorcycle belt," the redhead giggled. "Isn't it cute? One hundred per cent electric beaver, twelve inches wide."

"And, of course, your neckline is *lapin* as well. Now, tell me about your *tres spiff chaussure.*"

"My...?"

"Footwear, dear."

"Oh." Mrs. Rawdon held aside her long skirt, revealing mid-calf fur-trimmed boots. "These are one hundred per cent white-rhino bootees, topped with electric beaver."

Just then, a tall, slender man with shiny black hair approached them, beaming. "Why, look who's here!" squealed Mrs. Rawdon, taking his arm. "This is my man, Willie Foster!"

"Mighty proud," the head of the American Gun Association shook the fashion editor's hand, pretending to recognize her.

"We were just admiring your wife's ensemble," the editor explained, eyeing him up and down. "Pardon me, but is that a *leather* tuxedo you're wearing?"

"Eight hundred bucks' worth," affirmed the sportsman. "One hundred per cent spade black Shammy, and genuine poached alligator boots to match."

"Astonishingly smart," applauded the fashion editor, turning full attention to her microphone. "Shunning lackluster fadmongering, and at the same time avoiding, as well, the restricting limitations of quote formalwear unquote, *comme il faut*, Mr. and Mrs. Willie Foster Rawdon have come up with a matched pair of absolutely fab trend-setting inspirations created by the ultrasmart fashion magician, Farley Feigh, entirely from the pelts of rare wild animals. Look out, Mother Nature— if this look becomes *de rigueur*, it'll be open season on anything with skin. Thanks ever so, Mr. and Mrs. R— and enjoy your gala evening." Clicking off her tape machine, the editor sauntered away in search of another fashion plate.

The BBS Orchestra played the final bars of the "Waterhead Waltz" then fell silent amidst scattered applause as maestro Tugg spun toward the dance floor, grinning. "Ho-kay, lady an' genmans— party start to cook, yes? Nummer-one beeg dances for evesning! Less go, keed-heverybody dancing 'Hanky-Panky'!"

Everyone began to link hands in a snake-like line that overflowed the dance area. At the Official Entrance Arch, the reception line broke up and Jenny ran over to her parents. "C'mon, Daddy Bear, Mommy— let's do the 'Hanky-Panky.' "

"You dance with your mother," Tully suggested. "I gotta see a man over here..."

Anita took his arm. "Now, come on, dear. This is a big night for all of us. The least we can do is dance together."

The warden eyed his wife suspiciously. "You sure pulled a fast recovery, sister." Then he tossed up his hands and grinned. "The 'Hanky-Panky,' huh? How d'you do the muffing thing, anyway?"

"Don't worry, Daddy— just do what we do!"

They got into line, Jenny and her mother on either side of Tully, and as they waited for the music to begin, the warden gazed about the hall with satisfaction. *The old fun house looks okay. Look at that mother floor shine. The cons did a job for me there... middle of the night, scrubbin' their hornies off.* He turned his attention to the begowned and tuxedoed guests. *Nice crowd. Big shots, but not cream puffs. Kinda crowd this place needs.* A bank of brilliant floodlights flashed on briefly near the stage, then faded into darkness once again. *TeeVee. A network show. Oh, it's big.* Music began and Tully was suddenly yanked across the dance floor. "What the...?"

"C'mon, Daddy-skip!"

The warden tried to skip, and was accidentally kneed from behind by his wife. "For scab sake, Anita!"

"Oh, Tully," laughed his wife, "what's the matter— forgot how to skip?"

"Inna pig's squat I have!" The warden began skipping across the dance floor with the rest of the revelers. "I just feel like a horse's ass, that's all."

At the bar beside the dance floor, News reporter Ralston Hutsut conversed with Levi Cuffe, correspondent for the *Daily Fuck*. "Yes sir," Hutsut boasted over his champagne glass, "my paper takes this evening as a personal triumph."

"Floral, Lem." Cuffe unbuttoned the jacket of his black denim tuxedo and leaned against the bar. Squinting at the line of passing dancers, he produced a box of cigarettes and offered one to Hutsut.

"Are those brand-name cigarettes?"

"Espee, Lem— as a matter of fact, they are. However, there's enough liquid hemp in these pineals to bluebird you into supernova till the end of the cycle, grab?"

"Yeah, I grab." Hutsut shook his head. "I don't turn on."

"Lem, you don't even have a switch."

The two observed the dance floor antics awhile, then Hutsut asked casually, "Just what *does* impress you, Cuffe— if anything?"

The Daily Fuck reporter shrugged. "Just conch, I guess."

"Conch?"

"Cunt. For example, latch onto that pony-moth over there, shaking her stuff real thermal. I'd karoo going carnal with that."

"Her? That's Jenny Keyster, the warden's kid."

"Unwow," sighed Levi Cuffe. He watched Tully Keyster's massive bulk slip by, then returned his gaze to the young blonde's shapely legs and firm, bouncing breasts straining to free themselves from the low-cut gown. "Tell you this, Lem— it'd be worth it."

The "Hanky-Panky" ended and the line of dancers broke up, gleeful and exhausted. "That's enough for me," puffed Warden Keyster, taking his wife's arm. "C'mon, Neet, let's make the rounds." He fished two champagnes from a passing tray and off they went.

On the bandstand, Ulloch Tugg wiggled his mustache mischievously. "Eet's go-goes times, folks— juz like deez-go-tex! Heverybodies do dee 'Teekle'!"

Someone touched Jenny's arm and she turned to find Chaplain Levitsky at her side. "Hi!" she bubbled. "Isn't this a sleek bash?"

"Yes, it's quite nice." The priest spoke with forced pleasantness. "You look magnificent."

"Thank. Wanna vibrate?"

"Beg pardon?"

She took his hand. "C'mon, deva-doll, let's dance!"

He let her lead him onto the dance floor, then stood uncertainly, watching her begin to gyrate. On the podium, Ulloch Tugg crooned flatly,

"Teekle, Teekle— oh, so!
Teekle, Teekle— bingo!"

"Don't be such an adverb," Jenny teased. "Vibrate!"

The priest brought his fists up to his chest and began jerking his hips from side to side, awkwardly, as he gazed with wonder at the sun-gold hair, pouring like melted butter over vanilla-sweet shoulders and shimmering down alabaster flesh toward the incomprehensible perfection of those two ambrosial knockers palpitating at the top of her gown.

"I'm going to renounce my vows," Ryder announced loudly, over the music.

"Teekle, Teekle— show how!
Teekle, Teekle— right now!"

Jenny darted at the chaplain and began tickling him mercilessly, as the song demanded.

"Hey!" He tried to fight her off, getting little electric shocks each time his flesh touched hers. "Don't do that!"

"Tickle tickle!" Jenny squealed, continuing the attack.

"Didn't you hear what I said?" Ryder insisted. **"I'm going to renounce—"**

"Omee," Jenny shouted, **"what's it mean?"** She kept trying to get at his ribs.

"It means I want to marry you!"

Jenny grinned. "Deva-doll, I'm thirteen years old! C'mon tickle me!"

"Teekle, Teekle— you'll go!
Teekle, Teekle— loco!"

Levitsky's hands jerked out and grabbed her by the rib cage, his thumbs sinking into the soft outer perimeter of her breasts.

"Deva-doll," Jenny warned, "you're crossing the great water." She pushed his hands toward her waist and resumed her tickling. Ryder would not play ball. Drawing her to him, he pressed the full length of his body against hers and nuzzled the top of her head. Jenny just stood there, peeking out between his shoulder and jaw. "Flooy, she sighed, with resignation.

"Adrenal, gross bodies," a voice boomed beside them, **"where do I sign up?"**

Jenny and Ryder came apart and looked at Levi Cuffe. **"Pardon?"** Shouted the chaplain.

"Mind if I mace?" the reporter yelled.

"What's he talking about?" Levitsky asked Jenny.

"He wants to cut in. You know, dance with me."

Levi Cuffe stepped between them and herded Jenny away from the priest.

"Hey, now," Levitsky objected, **"what's the big... just what do you think you're..."**

They left him standing there alone as they tickled each other across the dance floor.

"Sacra-lotus," Cuffe cooed, moving his probing fingers over Jenny's slender hips, "you're really astral-near."

The flustered girl adjusted his hands. "Bogey maroon, what's feezing you pilgrims tonight? You're as flooy as he is!"

"You mean the archbishop?" Cuffe glanced back toward where they'd left the priest. "He's thermal for you too, huh? Who is he, anyhow?"

"A friend." They were standing still on the dance floor. "Look, do you want to dance, or what?"

Cuffe took her by the elbow and steered her toward

the bar. "Let's get floral on some bubbly."

"I don't drink."

"Tidal." He handed her a goblet of champagne. "Just hold it and behold me then, grab?" He sidled close to her and searched her guileless blue eyes. "My stamen's aimin' for a duologue with you, moth." His brazen gaze explored the vibrant subtleties of her mouth. "Let's sweat together, lunar-pony— feel my curd pumping hosanna behind your navel."

Jenny Pye Keyster nervously sipped at her champagne, and the bubbles tickled her nose. "Golly," she whispered.

Cuffe produced a box of cigarettes and handed her one. "Here, butterfly, this'll put you in arterial free fall."

"Thank," whispered Jenny, taking the offered reefer, but since she didn't smoke, she just slipped it into the bosom of her gown. "I'll save it for later."

Levi Cuffe slipped his hand between Jenny and the bar, where no one could see, and began to knead her firm little buttocks, gently but relentlessly. "Now, cosmic honey-conch," he breathed in her ear, "let's wing outside and nest in the snow, so I can spread your lotus-legs and grab some hair-fusion."

"Ah... karoo," Jenny sighed, laughing nervously. Then she pulled herself together and looked up at him, not without appreciation. "I can't." She drained her wineglass and picked up another, gyrating her buttocks sensuously against his massaging hand. "How 'bout tomorrow?"

The six hundred bottles of Dom Luic Cordon '64 dwindled rapidly as six hundred distinguished Americans floated their inhibitions into exile across a sea of alcoholic effervescence. Shoes were lost, corsages became crushed and wilted, gowns and tuxedos were stained and torn, the dances got livelier and the laughter less restrained.

On the bandstand, Ulloch Tugg whipped his orchestra through a spirited rendition of "Caramba!—The Samba!"

Near the buffet table, Fila Noogie was corralled between two matronly representatives of the Daughters of Dead American Heroes, one of whom was surveying the hall proudly and explaining, "All the bunting and the streamers are ours, my dear— our donation, I mean— and, of course..." both ladies grinned toward the ceiling and announced in unison, "the balloons!"

"Do tell?" Fila squinted heavenward. "Prick-shaped."

"Come again, my dear?"

"I said, they have a pretty shape."

"Yes, they do, don't they?" the first lady agreed. "There are ten thousand, you know."

"In all colors," added lady number two.

"Except yellow, of course," they both harmonized.

Fila raised an eyebrow. "What's wrong with yellow?"

The daughters of dead heroes gasped. "My dear, that's the color of cowards!"

Fila contemplated their line of reasoning and found it flawless; toasting them with her champagne, she downed it in a single gulp. The ladies sipped their drinks. "And, of course, my dear, we're all so perfectly delighted to see you get all that money from The Fund— after all you've been through."

Fila shrugged. "Consolation prize."

"Pardon, dear?"

"Measly hundred grand. Ten Gs a year for ten years— peanuts, compared to what I had goin' for me." She speared a full goblet from a passing tray. "Maybe I'll run up there and sit in Bozo's lap when they throw the switch."

The samba ended. In the control room, Monteczuma switched on the public address system and spoke to the throng in the hall. "Evening, everyone. Hope you're all having a great time. It's now ten fifteen, time to start setting things up for air. The pages will assist you in finding seats with your friends; you'll find party hats and noisemakers on each chair, but please refrain from using them until exactly midnight.

"You fifty couples who were preselected to remain on the dance floor for the opening of the show will take your seats during the first commercial break. Right now, as soon as the rest of our guests are seated, we'll continue with a few preshow activities for your entertainment. Thank you."

Monteczuma leaned back in his chair and a network page thrust a sheet of paper under his nose. The director read it and screwed up his face. "Where'd this come from?"

"Guard phoned it in from Gate Three."

"Run out and give it to Warden Keyster," instructed Monteczuma. "This is his department, and he's good at it."

Keyster led his wife toward the audience area. "Guess I'd better head backstage and get ready, Neet— but first I'll get hold of these ushers and make sure you get a front row seat."

"Really, Tully, I'd prefer..."

"Where's our little girl run off to?" The warden stood on tiptoe and searched the hall. "There she is, by the bar, yakkin' with some grease punk. You wait here— I'll go get her."

"Warden Keyster?" A young page handed Tully a piece of paper. "Mr. Monteczuma said you'd know how to handle this, sir."

Tully read the message through twice before he crumpled it in his huge fist. His brow knitted ominously and his neck flushed crimson. "Get the wife a seat," he ordered, and bolted off through the crowd.

Anita watched her husband disappear. "Is something wrong?" she asked the page.

"A last-minute problem, ma'am. The warden will clear it up in a jiffy. Now, if you'll just follow me, Mrs. Keyster, I'll show you to your reserved seat."

"If you don't mind, young man, I'd rather sit toward the

back," confided the warden's wife. "The bright lights bother me."

The 1200-cc Harlequin-Mandalla prison motorcycle roared down the winding tree-lined road leading from the Playpen to Gate Three by the main highway. Astride the thundering steed, tooling through the frigid darkness, with a cigar in his mouth and fire in his eyes, was Warden Tully Keyster, wearing a tuxedo.

Clam-fag roach-dyke. He poured on the power and banked through the turns, eating up the sixteen hundred feet of cold macadam in twenty seconds flat.

The guards opened the gate when they heard the approach of the cycle, protecting against trespass with weapons trained upon a large gathering of youthful demonstrators swarming about outside. Scores of young women sat smugly on the freezing pavement as guards dragged them aside, one by one, only to see them replaced immediately by substitutes from the milling crowd. The object of the confrontation was a single, late-arriving automobile, surrounded by demonstrators. Some protesters sat blocking the thoroughfare at both ends of the vehicle while others swarmed about it, swaying it on its springs and chanting, "ROCK THE HAWK! ROCK THE HAWK!"

The warden's growling motorcycle came highballing down the roadway toward the open gate; the guards split ranks and the sitting protesters, trapped between the auto and the charging cycle, scrambled for their lives. At least one girl seemed doomed.

Fifty yards short of the gate, the warden kicked his cycle into neutral and began to slow up, though his motor was still raging full-blast. He boomed through the gateway and, at the very last second, locked both wheels and spun the bike 180 degrees, stopping dead in the about-face, his rear wheel less than a foot from the cringing waist of the young girl lying terrified upon the asphalt.

Instantly, the guards formed a phalanx across the road on either side of the cycle, as Keyster hopped off and strode toward the stranded auto, treading right on the back of the prone girl.

The throng moved to aid her, and immediately the prison guards let out a bloodcurdling roar, attacked the crowd with night sticks flailing. Keyster waded through bodies to the auto and began peeling people away, discarding them like the leaves of an overdone artichoke. When he had strong-armed his way to the car door, he leaned over and peered inside, but could see no one. The door was locked and the window tight shut. **"This is Warden Tully Keyster. Is anybody there?"** Mayhem continued to reign about him.

Slowly, within the automobile, a white face began to emerge from near the floorboards. So this, thought Warden Keyster, is the famous Art Pastel. **"Get this tin can rolling,"** Keyster told the white face. **"I'll lead the way."**

The road was clear for the auto now, but head-busting continued around the fringes. Striding back to his still perking bike, the warden shook his head at one of the guards nearby. "How'd you meatheads let a thing like this happen, anyway?"

"Honest, Warden, it—"

"Yeah, yeah." Tully mounted his cycle, revving it up thunderously. "I want to see every swinging son-of-a-sow on duty here in my office nine o'clock tomorrow morning!" With that he popped the clutch and scorched through the gate, Art Pastel's auto screeching along behind.

Barreling up the road toward the Playpen, Keyster glanced back at the car and sneered. The icy wind whistled through his tux, but he did not seem to notice. Let the chicken-mother know who's boss right off the bat. He chewed his cigar and let up a bit on the accelerator. *Watch it, Tully. He's from the Outside... and you could use him.* He glanced back and let up a bit more on the gas, seeing that

Pastel's car was having trouble keeping up. *Sure, he's a cream puff, but he's got pull. You just saved his neck, and he owes you. A TV series, maybe... weekly con-roasts, fat paychecks, kickbacks. Play it buddy-buddy awhile— let him make his move.* The warden putted into the staff lot and indicated Pastel's parking space near the back door. Dismounting, he moseyed over to the star's auto, just as Pastel was emerging, pale and shaken. "Howdy, Art!" Keyster thrust out his hand, but the star did not seem to notice it, so Tully just shrugged and led the way to the stage door. "Lucky I come along when I did, eh? Them Nancy-suckers woulda had you for supper!" He held the door open until Pastel passed through, then followed him closely along the hallway, putting his hand on the star's shoulder.

"Don't touch me," said Art Pastel.

Keyster squinted at the back of Pastel's head, but managed to let the incident pass. "Yeah, sure, you're prob'ly a tad tense after all that excitement. Here, this here's your dressing room." He reached past Art Pastel, and opened the door. "Pretty snazzy, huh?" Tully started to follow the star into the room. "I hear you're well-stocked with hooch, too. What say we pour a couple and— Hey!"

Art Pastel had suddenly turned on the big man and, grabbing him by the front of his ruffled shirt, pushed him off balance, sending him backpedaling out the door and across the hall, where he smacked against the wallboards just as the star's dressing-room door slammed shut and the lock clicked.

Speechless with rage, Warden Keyster scrambled to his feet and hurled himself against the closed door, splitting it down the middle. His next barrage would have reduced the portal to splinters, but before he had a chance to launch himself a second time, four professional wrestlers rushed out of their dressing room nearby and pinned the raving warden to the floor.

PART SEVEN

28

At exactly ten-forty-five p.m. the Playpen audience saw a shiny bald head emerge from between the stage curtains; it wore large black framed glasses and a wide toothy grin as it shouted, **"Hey there, Peeping Toms! Welcome to 'The Pastel Penthouse'!"**

The crowd, recognizing announcer Freddy Fredella, greeted him with friendly applause mingled with the scattered toots and rattles of noisemakers. Fredella stepped from behind the curtains and gazed about the great hall. "Hey! This isn't the Pastel Penthouse— it's the Pastel Death House!" He waved the crowd quiet again. "But seriously, folks, it's a real pleasure to be here tonight, working for our old friends, the people who make Sparkle Wax. That Sparkle's great stuff, isn't it? I not only use it on my floors, y'know..." He buffed his scalp with the sleeve of his jacket.

Locked in his dressing room backstage, Art Pastel sat on the toilet, doubled over, clutching his belly with both hands and rocking back and forth as waves of searing agony rumbled through his innards. "Oh, God," he gasped, snatching up a bottle from the floor and forcing a mouthful of gin into his ravaged stomach. At last the ruthless cramps began to subside and the star's relieved body went limp, preparing to meet the next spasmodic onslaught.

"Now remember, folks," Fredella was saying on stage, "the viewers at home won't have any fun unless they feel that you people here are really enjoying yourselves, you get my point? Fun is contagious. So, when you want to laugh, for example, we want the whole world to hear you. In other words, don't laugh like a lot of people I see." He clapped a hand over his mouth and emitted a stifled nasal wheeze. "Doctors say if you hold a laugh in like that, it goes back down inside and spreads your hips!" The audience laughed so the whole world could hear.

Tully Keyster sat in the make-up room backstage, a baby-pink towel pinned around his beet-red neck, as Georgie the make-up man submitted him to the humiliation of a powder puff. Finally, the warden exploded. **"Okay, nugget-muncher-cut the crap!"** He tore off the towel and bounded from the chair.

Georgie backed off, his hands fluttering near his shoulders. "Now *look*, sugar..."

"Nobody's sending Tully Keyster out there lookin' like some kinda fag maggot, get me?" The warden jabbed a finger in the direction of Art Pastel's dressing room. **"Save your dyke paint for that other fart-slime fairy, leech-licker!"**

Out on the apron of the stage, Freddy Fredella was instructing the audience in the art of applause. "Now, to really sound effective, applause should spring forth spontaneously from your overgenerous hearts. However..." He looked up at a huge electric applause sign hanging from the ceiling. "See that? Well, it says APPLE SAUCE, and that will flash on from time to time— just to help you be a little more spontaneous. Just in case some of you are too sauced to see the sign, some pals of mine will mingle among you with little rubber hoses, and they'll give you a tiny reminder if you forget to laugh and applaud... the bruises'll go away in a week or two." The audience laughed and looked at the three production assistants standing in the aisles, waving little rubber hoses.

Through a doorway far stage left, young choirboys began to file from the wings, walking stiffly and silently past the orchestra to the choir bleachers beside the bandstand.

The announcer noticed them. "Of course, no occasion like this would be complete without a choir of authentic cherubs, so how 'bout a big hand for the Homeless Boys' Choir!" Freddy Fredella glanced at his wristwatch. "Seven minutes to curtain, folks... or should I say **curtains?**"

Far away in the Trump mansion, Toy Boat switched on the television set and prepared to watch her brother's program. She had gone up to Merlin's workshop to remind him of the show, but had found the old man fast asleep, having drunk himself to dreamland on Groundhog Cocktails.

"You couples out on the dance floor," Fredella was saying, "we're counting on you to get the show off to a whiz-bang start, so I want you to really live it up... you can live it down tomorrow. Now, when I introduce Art, let's all let him know how much we really love him, okay?"

A voice drifted down from the P.A. system. "Three minutes till air."

"Three minutes!" Fredella squeaked. "Don't anyone get nervous— just stay calm like me." He wiped his forehead with his tie. "Okay, I've gotta run backstage now and announce the opening of the show... so I want you all to have a ball, make plenty of noise and really hang loose— not a stiff in the place— well, *one*, maybe!" Amidst much applause and noisemaking, Fredella walked off stage left, waving and grinning.

From overhead, the control room announced, "Two minutes."

Fredella's bald head poked out from the wings and added, "Two minutes to go... in case anyone has to!"

The audience laughed and continued to pass empty goblets toward the aisles, where waiters were replacing them with fresh ones filled with champagne. Occasionally, a noisemaker would rasp or blat, and an answering sound would issue from another part of the house. There was much head turning and chatter, and female squeals of laughter. Soon, the director's voice spoke from above again, and everyone tilted his head back to listen.

"We're coming up on one minute to eleven now, ladies and gentlemen, so I'm going to ask Ulloch to begin the waltz. Have fun, everyone, and Happy New Year."

On the bandstand, maestro Tugg poised his baton and closed his eyes, gathering energy. His height increased an inch or two and the volume of his chest expanded. Then down came the baton and the orchestra erupted with a vibrant and sparkling classical waltz, heavy on the brass. The fifty chosen couples began to waltz their hearts out as the lighting in the arena began to dim.

In the control room, Roland Monteczuma and his staff prepared to begin the live transmission. "Break a leg, everyone," he said into his headset. Checking his monitors he saw that all five cameras were riveted on their opening cues, and the Master Network Monitor, which showed the picture going out over the air, carried the BBS station break logo. "Ten seconds-ready Camera Four." The red hand swept upward. "Five, four, three, two, one— fade in Camera Four."

One billion viewers joined the throng in Tully's Playpen; through a camera suspended high above the glittering chamber floor, they looked down upon resplendent couples flowing upon the swirling current of an exhilarating waltz.

"Ready Camera Five..." instructed Monteczuma. "Dissolve to Camera Five."

The overhead view was gradually replaced by a long shot of the entire arena, under richly toned, subdued illumination, with dazzling beams of blue and rose dancing through the smoky haze, igniting the hall with sudden magic.

"Ready Camera Four on title... Cue Announce."

Freddy Fredella's excited voice reached over the strains of the music and into homes throughout the world. **"From the picturesque Achen State Penitentiary, in the heart of the beautiful Gar Mountains, the friendly folks who make Sparkle Wax proudly present...*YOUR SPARKLE CAVALCADE OF DEATH!"***

"Super Camera Four," ordered Monteczuma, and the show title appeared superimposed over the shot of the arena. "Ready Three... Super Three."

"Starring... Mister Television Himself... Art Pastel!"

"Dissolve Camera One."

A handheld camera at the front of the audience began panning the distinguished faces as the announcer continued. "Art'll be out in just one minute, folks— but first, why don't you run out to the kitchen and raid the refrigerator, while we have a word with your vinyl floors?"

"Cue commercial." The director watched the clock tick off the 120th second of the show.

On stage, in the dim light behind the closed curtain, the ten Pastel Pixies took their places for the opening musical number. Ralph Goliones hurried by, frantic.

"Where's Pastel?" he hissed. *"He's not in his dressing room!"* One of the dancers nodded toward the high black grotto sitting center stage; Ralph rushed over and peered inside. Art Pastel was sitting in the electric chair.

"Jeez!" the stage manager gulped. "Ah, sir, Rally would like you to sort of get on your mark, if it's okay. The tape's right over here..." He shined his flashlight on the floor before the platform.

"Fuck off, greaseball, " said Art Pastel.

Ralph clicked off his light. "Yeah, sure." He disappeared at once. Pastel closed his eyes, considering the turmoil within: head spinning, lungs incapable of taking air, bowels churning. The whole world was on the other side of that curtain— watching, waiting. *You can't make me.* He clenched his teeth with determination. *I will not make pee-pee for you.*

The commercial ended. "Fade in Camera Three," said Monteczuma, and the world saw a shot of the stage, curtains closed. "Cue Music." There was an elaborate fanfare, followed by an extended drum roll. "Cue Announce."

"And now... here's the star of our show... Mister ART PASTEL!"

The orchestra launched into "The Pastel Penthouse" theme and the audience went wild as the curtains began to part, revealing Art Pastel standing center stage— humble, handsome and happy.

The scenery around him was breathtaking. Immediately to his rear, on a foot high platform, sat a temple-like black marble grotto containing a dazzling gold-plated electric chair framed with plush draperies in red, white and blue. Atop the ten-foot grotto sat a huge model of the Sparkle Wax bottle, housing an electronic chronometer which flashed the exact time by hour, minute and second.

Behind the grotto, stretching across the stage, were the two hundred ten golden pipes of a tremendous organ, arranged by height into a U-shape across the stage. Driven by thirty-six-horsepower blower motors, the organ boasted a single console with fifty-five stops and a range of five octaves. It was to be played later from backstage by renowned virtuoso Q. Connor Figg.

Above the golden pipes were black drapes, across which, in three foot unlighted letters, were the words HAPPY NEW YEAR. The lower ten feet of the enormous pipes were also masked with black; across the top of this section, in three-foot lighted red letters, were the words AN EYE FOR AN EYE. Topping off this Biblical phrase, spaced evenly across the entire width of the row of organ pipes, were miniature flagpoles bearing the colors of the fifty-five states.

Across the top of the proscenium arch were loops of pleated red-white-and-blue bunting. At stage right was another platform backed by a red wall, on which hung a huge circuit breaker, encircled by the words ACHEN STATE PENITENTIARY. Above the circuit breaker on the wall hung a twenty-foot American flag.

At stage left was a longer platform, backed by a black wall, draped with black. On this wall, under the large black letters R.I.P., were the names of the nine dead Noogie Novuplets, plus the names CORBIN GILBERT NOOGIE and LEWD NMI NOOGIE.

On each side of Art Pastel stood five beautiful dancers, wearing scanty costumes in red, white, blue and black.

The applause continued for a full minute before Pastel moved downstage and stepped upon the stairway leading to the audience, which was the signal for his opening number to begin. The orchestra segued neatly from the Pastel theme into the intro of the first song, and the dancers began their routine.

Art Pastel hollered, **"Love ya!"** and the ovation intensified; then he held up his hands and began singing just as the noise level dropped to the point at which he could be heard comfortably. It was an up-tempo song, penned especially for this show: "Lectrifyin' Lewdy!"

> *"Sparks are flyin' out across*
> *The air waves tonight,*
> *'Lectrifyin' Lewdy's*
> *Generatin' de-light!"*

The dancers wore little lightning bolts on their heads. As the song continued, slug lines appeared at the bottom of the TV screen crediting the various organizations which had contributed to the set decor.

ORGAN
Courtesy of UNITED LEGION OF LABOR

NATIONAL FLAG
Handmade by OLD FOLKS, INC.

FLAGS OF 55 STATES
Courtesy of VETERANS OF LIMITED WARS

"Watt's the hottest item
In the current events?
Lewdy's got us sizzlin'
With high-tension suspense!"

Off in the wings, sitting in the semidarkness, Jenny Pye Keyster gazed at Art Pastel singing on stage. She had fled backstage to escape the romantic advances of Levi Cuffe—to prevent herself from doing something foolish— but still, the spark ignited by his probing hands continued to smolder in her young breast, and now it was becoming fanned to greater intensity by the dynamic stage presence of Art Pastel. "Karoo," she whispered, her wide eyes absorbing the rugged features of the star. "He's somehow sleek."

By this time, Pastel's song had carried him down the steps into the center aisle. As he sang, cameras roved the audience, selecting certain luminaries for the folks at home to see, their identities appearing at the bottom of the screen.

GENERAL MURRAY VON ROSTENBERGER
Vice-Chairman
JOINT CHIEFS OF STAFF

J. WALDO WIELD
President
FEDERAL NUTRITION AND DRUG ADMINISTRATION

Pastel worked his way back to the stage and finished the song where he'd begun it, the dancers forming a tableau around him.

"Turn the juice on,
Hit 'im with a bolt from the blues,
Maine to Tucson,
Powerhouses'll be blowin' a fuse!
'Lectrifyin' Lewdy—
Light our fire tonight!"

The applause was thunderous, and during it the dancers moved off to different parts of the stage, leaving Art Pastel alone in the spotlight. **"Hey!"** shouted the star basking in the roaring tribute. **"I can feel it in the air! We got a house full of Love People here tonight!"** He motioned them to grow quiet. "Save some of that for my guests, will ya?" he pleaded, and the commotion settled down.

The star shook his head, dazed by the audience response. "Folks, it'd take the rest of the show to thank you the way you deserve, so I'm not even gonna try, because I think you're more interested in seeing the show, and we've got a fantastic one for you tonight— you might call it a real shocker! Personally, I don't see what all the fuss is about, except for the fact that this is probably the first time in history that a billion people sat around watching one guy get juiced." Pastel looked across at the bandstand. "I mean, nobody wants to watch Ulloch over there, and he gets juiced almost every night." The outflow of mirth was directed toward the musical director, who bore the brunt of it with his customary bewilderment. "No kidding, folks, how 'bout a hand for the maestro, his orchestra and choir!"

The APPLAUSE sign flashed on and the audience responded with "spontaneous" applause, as Tugg bowed with grinning formality. The TV screen showed the group of young boys, with the superimposed caption:

HOMELESS BOYS' CHOIR
Courtesy of UNITED ORPHANS OF AMERICA

"We'll hear the youngsters sing later on," Pastel announced, "but right now, I know you're all eager to say hello to our Lady of Honor— the woman who's been through more hell in one year than most of us suffer in a lifetime. Let's let her know exactly how we feel about her, folks. Ladies and gentlemen... FILA NOOGIE!"

A rather haggard-looking redhead entered from the wings stage left and was greeted with a standing ovation. Fila's hair was a bit disheveled and her lipstick slightly smeared from necking with one of the wrestlers backstage. Art Pastel took her hand and together they stood center stage while the ovation continued. Fila scratched the palm of Pastel's hand, provocatively.

The APPLAUSE sign stopped flashing and the death chamber gradually grew quiet. Pastel waited until there was complete silence, then took both the woman's hands and told her gently, "They love you, Fila."

"And I love them."

"Fila, you've lost nine little babies in a single, tragic blow. Your nephew, Corbin, is dead. Now, tonight, your husband is going, too. Yet, you manage to bear this terrible, awesome burden like a saint— stoically, humbly, *heroically*." He reached into his inside breast pocket and withdrew an embossed envelope. "Now, Fila, just to show you that our hearts are in the right place, I'd like to present to you this little token of our love and esteem. On behalf of the distinguished guests gathered here tonight, I take great pleasure in presenting you with this certified check in the amount of one hundred thousand dollars. It's not enough to ease the pain of your loss, we know, but at least it will permit you to suffer in a little more comfort. God bless you, sweetheart." He handed her the envelope.

The audience rose to its feet again, cheering and applauding, as Fila gratefully embraced Art Pastel and stuck her tongue into his mouth. Pastel wrenched himself free gracefully and waved the crowd to silence. "And now, ladies and gentlemen, it's time to meet the real star of the show. This man genuinely needs no introduction, having propelled himself to the absolute pinnacle of infamy by committing the single most despicable crime in the history of mankind." A drum roll began. "If I may direct your attention to the large iron doors at the rear of the hall!" The drum roll intensified. "Pre-senting... **the Official Grand Execution Procession!**"

At the west end of the chamber stood two heavy iron doors, each ten feet wide and twenty feet high. Before each was a prison guard in full dress uniform, grasping the large iron ring used to pull the door open. The spotlights swung across the hall and bathed the metal portals with brilliant light. Over the drum roll came a heraldic trumpet fanfare, and the guards began pulling at their iron rings. The huge doors swung open slowly.

The opening doors revealed an impressively proportioned man standing in the center of the areaway, dressed in a tuxedo. His feet were planted firmly apart and his fists were jammed into his jacket pockets. His face was sternly set. The caption at the bottom of the television screen read:

TULLY FRANCIS KEYSTER
Warden
ACHEN STATE PENITENTIARY

With the appearance of the warden, the Homeless Boys' Choir burst into an exalted chord of angelic splendor. When the doors were fully open, Keyster strode forward, heading for the stage, two hundred feet away.

Behind him there appeared two tiny young girls dressed

in scanty black gowns with short ballerina skirts and carrying large baskets filled with lilies, which they began to strew in the path of the procession. At the advent of the flower girls, the boys' choir emitted a more exultant chord.

FLOWER GIRLS
Courtesy of UNITED ORPHANS OF AMERICA

Next to issue from the doorway was a double column of twelve spit-and-polish military men dressed in black uniforms with white helmets, gloves, leggings and rifles. They half-stepped smartly, and as the rhythm of their bootfalls echoed through the great hall, the choir struck a still higher chord, this time joined by the entire orchestra, which struck up a resounding military march.

HONOR GUARD
Courtesy of GUNG-HO GUERRILLA UNIT, USMC

Following the honor guard at a respectful distance came a solitary priest in floor-length vestments, quietly reading from the Bible. The martial music took on the flavor of a religious crusade.

FATHER RYDER LEVITSKY
Chaplain
ACHEN STATE PENITENTIARY

Next to enter the death chamber was the Condemned Man himself. Lewd was dressed in a black silk uniform, the right pants leg cuffed at the knee. On either side of him, one step behind, were two prison guards in their full dress greens. At Lewd's entrance, the magnificent pipe organ came to life, filling the hall with awesome glory. The Condemned Man stopped in his tracks, astounded, and squinted into the brilliant lights until the two guards took his arms and ushered him forward.

LEWD NOOGIE
Condemned Man

The procession was completed by the appearance of an elderly man wearing a black suit and carrying a black bag. He was followed by two young women.

DR. RAMSEY PETTIBONE
Prison Physician

HONORARY NURSES
Courtesy of MEGABLISS MOTION PICTURES

The two lovely young starlets were attired in mini-c-thru nurses' uniforms, with lilies pinned in their flowing tresses.

As the Grand Procession marched across the open section of the chamber and entered the center aisle of the audience area, Art Pastel burst into song on stage, singing new words to the tune he sang every year at the Miss O.K.–U.S.A. Pageant:

> *"Here he comes!*
> *The Condemn-ed Man!*
> *Silken pant leg shorn,*
> *Dressed to kill!"*

Lewd Noogie shuffled down the center aisle watching his feet, trying to avoid stepping on the fresh lilies lying on the floor. Several wilted corsages sailed through the air and landed amidst the pro cession. Toasting goblets spattered the floor with champagne.

"All decked out to meet his maker,
Be he a-the-ist or Quaker!"

Art Pastel stood forward and stage right of the electric chair as the procession mounted the steps and came onto the stage. Fila stood to his left. Warden Keyster glowered at the star and took a place stage left of the chair, leaving room between himself and Fila for Lewd to stand when he came on stage. The flower girls separated and moved to the extreme right and left downstage corners, where they proceeded to throw their remaining blossoms into the audience.

The honor guard marched to the rear of the stage and lined up across the backdrop, beneath the phrase AN EYE FOR AN EYE and the flags of the fifty-five states. The Penthouse Pixies alternated themselves with the soldiers, who struck a smart parade rest and remained motionless.

"Raise your cup in dedication.
Offer a champagne libation,
Toast to Lewd's grave situation!"

Chaplain Levitsky stood stage right of the chair, directly behind Art Pastel. Lewd stumbled coming up the stairs and, when he regained his balance, found himself standing face to face with his wife.

" 'Lo, Fi." He smiled with embarrassment.

"Hiya, Bozo."

Lewd was led to stand between Fila and Warden Keyster; the two guards then moved almost out of sight toward the rear of the black marble grotto. The prison doctor took his place stage left of the chair, directly behind the warden, and the two honorary nurses took places on either side of the chair. Art Pastel completed his song as everyone reached his proper place on stage.

"Hail to Lewdy and his court,
Live it up, your time is short!"

The music crashed to a finish and there was a resounding ovation for the onstage assemblage. Art Pastel let it continue for the proper duration, then waved the audience to silence. "Thanks, folks you're very kind!" He moved out in front of Fila, Lewd, and Tully. "Administering the 'Juice of Justice' here tonight, ladies and gentlemen, the Warden of Achen State Penitentiary!" He indicated Keyster with a sweep of his hand.

Tully stepped forward, beaming. "Howdy, I'm—"

"We'll hear from the warden a little later, folks," Pastel interrupted, "but right now it's time for him to go backstage and limber up his switch-pulling arm. See you later, Warden!"

Keyster hovered ominously over Art Pastel a few moments, clenching and unclenching his fists; then he wheeled about and strode from the stage, steaming.

Pastel placed himself between Fila and Lewd, asking seriously, "Lewd, have you something you'd like to say to your wife at this time?"

Lewd stood holding his hands behind him, looking at the floor. "Just... I'm sorry, I guess."

"Fila? Any words for your husband?"

"Yeah," said Fila, with a twinge of sympathy. "Aces up."

Pastel looked into the camera. "Fila here is going to be one of our Official Witnesses, of course, so now I'm going to ask her to step over to the witness box and take her seat. Okay, Fila?"

"Sure, baby."

"How 'bout it, folks— let's hear it for a great little woman!" The audience applauded as Mrs. Noogie moved across to stage left and sat in the first of the four witness chairs.

Art Pastel threw his arm around the shoulders of the

Condemned Man and addressed the viewers at home. "We'll be right back to chat with our guest of honor here in just one short minute, everyone— but first, let's enjoy a little visit from the Sparkle Sprite!" The camera tilted upward from the shot of Art and Lewd, framing the large Sparkle Wax bottle atop the black grotto. The chronometer in the body of the bottle read **11:20:58**, then **11:20:59**, and at exactly **11:21:00** the picture faded to black and was replaced by a picture of a tiny elf flying through the window of a housewife's kitchen, holding a bottle of Sparkle Wax.

In the dark attic workshop of his mansion, Merlin Trump sat up in bed and gazed about. "You don't tell me?" Swinging his feet to the floor, he slowly rose, then remained still for several moments, squinting at the ceiling and shaking his head. "The old Chiefie feels some thing, mighty strangely."

He shuffled over to the bar and lit a small lamp. "What's up?" The refuse from his present experiment cluttered the top of the bar. Suddenly, the old man's eyes sparkled with alertness. He stood immobile, inwardly assessing his physical condition.

"Golly Neds," he whispered with disbelief. "The Chief does not have a headache!"

He rushed over to the logbook and studied the last entry. "Groundhog Cocktail! Mandalay! We did her!" Smacking the book down, he raised a glass containing the dregs of a Groundhog Cocktail. "The world's first hangoverless libation!" He drained the glass with a grand flourish.

"Hotsy-dory!" Returning to the logbook, he perused the list of ingredients, trying to discern the secret of his miraculous success. "...see now— carrot juice, celery, apple... parsley... sage, fennel, sassafras... Good Old Olive Oil." He pored over the list again and again, then suddenly stopped short. "Hold your horses, here, Labor Gang... I think we're on the tail of something." He read the recipe once more, slowly, then smacked his hand down on the bar: "Got her!" Grinning triumphantly, he held the book in the air and waved it emphatically.

"No aqua vitae!"

Setting the book upon the bar, he laid a finger to the recipe and addressed the room. "There's your answer, Gangie. Haw! Leave it to the Chiefie, didn't we tell you and we thank you kindly? Only a matter of time, m'boys she said! Hot dog! No aqua vitae!"

He opened his clothes closet and took out a business suit he had not worn in thirty-nine years. "This little drinkie will put House O' Trump right on the old map, boys and girls, and don't you forget it!"

Undressing quickly, he stepped into the shower and began to lather up, humming happily.

Back in Tully's Playpen, Governor Angus Black was standing on stage between Art Pastel and the Condemned Man, completing a short official address. "...and that is why, as Chief Executive of the 'Law-and-Order State,' I pledge to continue my never ending battle for Truth, Justice and the American Way!" The hall resounded with cheers, applause and the sound of noisemakers as the Governor waved, shook hands with Art and Lewd, and moved stage left to the Official Witness Platform, where he sat down beside Fila Noogie.

"There goes the next President of these United States, folks!" shouted Art Pastel above the clamor. "Governor Angus Black!" The orchestra played several bars of "Black Is Beautiful."

As the audience settled down, the emcee slung his arm across the shoulders of the Condemned Man, who was very listless and pale. "What's the matter, chum?" Pastel winked at the camera, understandingly. "I think he's a little nervous —aren't you, pal?— a little butterfly in the tum-tum, am I right?"

The Condemned Man smiled weakly and nodded his head. "Well, you just relax and take your mind off your miseries, buddy, because we've got a whale of a show lined up for you. Right now, I want you to meet the other two Official Witnesses chosen to watch your execution here tonight. First…" Pastel danced to the footlights, shading his eyes. "Down in the audience, sitting beside World Series hero Shanty Bruke of the Austin Aerosols, is the young delivery boy who tracked down our killer here singlehandedly in the Midtown Hospital, just after the hideous slaughter. This brave young man, in capturing the most gruesome murderer since Adolf Hitler, has captured the hearts of all America as well. Let's really show him how much we all love him, folks! C'mon up here, Jesus… Ladies and gentlemen, **Señor Jesus Bodega!**"

The orchestra played "Rose in Spanish Harlem" and the audience applauded as a short, skinny teenager with shiny black hair loped down the center aisle and mounted the steps two at a time, his shoe cleats clacking on the wooden stage. His rented tuxedo was several sizes too large, and he kept his hands in his pockets to keep his trousers up. Freeing his right hand momentarily, he let Art Pastel shake it, then turned and grinned proudly at the audience.

"Well, Jeez," said the master of ceremonies, "how's it feel to be a hero?"

"Preety swell, Ar'."

"Now, as we all know, you spotted our friend Lewd in the hospital deep freeze, right?"

"Ri', Ar'. I foun' heen dere, an' he hair froze whi'."

Pastel grinned toward the cameras. "I think what Jesus means is that Lewd's hair was covered with white frost."

"Firs' I thin' he cover by whit crean, then I reco'nize dee som beech."

The audience exploded with laughter and in the control room, Monteczuma shook his head: "Som-beech. Pastel better ditch that greaser before he really blabs a nasty."

On stage, Art Pastel was already ushering the youngster over toward the witness platform. "Great, Jesus. Now if you'll just take a seat on our Official Witness—"

"An' den," Bodega went on as he was led across the stage, "dee beeching cops, dey make me late for wor'."

"We're running late ourselves, Jeez—"

"Den, my bozz, he's fire me!"

"Terrific, Jesus, just sit over here and—"

"I loss my sheeting hob!"

In the control room, Monteczuma yelled, "Cut that wetback's mike before we all lose our sheeting hobs!"

"Magnificent, Jesus," Art Pastel was saying, above the howling laughter of the audience, "just great! Couldn't happen to a nicer guy! But, you'd better sit down now, because I see our Guest of Honor here is getting a little green around the gills, and I just happen to have the perfect remedy waiting right backstage. She's our last Official Witness, folks, and believe me she needs no introduction— her assets are all clearly visible! Get ready to drool, fellas, 'cause here she is— Hollywood's Hedonistic Hellcat— **Miss Carisse Crosse!**"

A statuesque, voluptuous redhead oozed out of the wings and posed extreme stage left, provocatively smoothing the transparent golden fabric of the gown which clung desperately to the explosive contours of her legendary lulus. The orchestra played "Caress Carisse," from the motion picture of the same name, while the erogenous starlet propositioned the whole world with her eyes, laving the searing oval of her lusty lips with her lascivious tongue. A number of distinguished men in the audience stomped their feet and yowled like coyotes.

The pandemonium continued as she slowly slunk across the stage, stroking her hypnotic, undulating hips, and permitted Art Pastel to lick her hand; then she turned and greeted the audience with a second standing ovulation.

Though her pose remained quite motionless, her awesomely molded alabaster flesh seemed to be in constant flux, an elusive, microscopic dance, with every minute cell responding frenetically to the throbbing drum of life resounding deep and desperately within.

On stage, the twelve marines of the Gung-Ho Guerrillas remained at rigid parade rest, their faces impassive, eyes glued firmly upon the starlet's bountiful buttocks. Jesus Bodega rolled his eyes and made loud kissing sounds with his lips. Chaplain Levitsky skipped three lines of scripture. Lewd Noogie stood staring at the floor; he tried putting his hands into his trouser pockets, but there were no pockets in the black silk uniform.

Art Pastel waited for the tumult to settle, then addressed the actress, quite openly ogling her magnificent mammaries. "Carisse, it's a real treat to have you **both** on the show." The audience roared, as production assistants jumped up and down in the aisles, waving rubber hoses. "Seriously, honey, how's Hollywood?"

"Just perfectly, Art."

"I hear you've just finished a new picture. Can you tell us a little about it?"

"Yes, Art. It's called *Repent Thy Passion, Doggy-Fashion*, and I portray a perverted evangelist who falls in love with a Saint Bernard."

"The lucky dog."

"Thank you, Art."

"It sounds like another Oscar winner, Carisse. In fact, we have a fellow right here who literally can't wait to see it!" The emcee turned, smiling, toward the Condemned Man, who was standing just right of center stage, gazing dumbly over his shoulder at the electric chair. "Hey, pal, c'mon over here and join the living!" Lewd stared blankly at Pastel for a moment, then the master of ceremonies stepped over and took him by the arm. "Don't be afraid, buddy, no one's gonna hurt you!"

The Condemned Man grinned spasmodically and allowed himself to be led to center stage beside Carisse Crosse. As he turned to face the audience, his arm pressed into the pneumatic depths of the starlet's right breast.

" 'Scuse me."

"Think perfectly nothing of it," Carisse assured him, running her hands up across her silken rib cage, her thumbs brushing the bulbous perimeters of her glorious globes.

Art Pastel shook his head in amazement. "Say, you sure are a fast worker, aren't you, chum?" He looked into the cameras. "This guy doesn't even wait for an introduction! What d'you think of our young **spark** here, Carisse?"

"He's wonderfully cute, Art." She stood two inches taller than the Condemned Man, and as she eased herself into his side, his upper arm became captured in the downy grasp of her capricious cleavage.

"Careful, Carisse," warned the emcee, "he's a regular live wire when he gets turned on— remember those nine kids."

"I **know** it," breathed the starlet excitedly, blowing hot wet air into the Condemned Man's ear.

Lewd blushed and stared at the floor.

Art Pastel nudged him. "Go ahead, pal, say hello to the gorgeous doll— we all know you're just **dying** to!"

The Condemned Man raised his eyes, staring at the actress's milky breast tops a moment before realizing what they actually were, then looked up quickly at her eyes, and finally settled his gaze somewhere in the area of her chin.

"Hullo."

Carisse pressed her upstage thigh warmly against his. "I certainly feel likewise," she whispered, touching a finger lightly to his chest, gently stroking his left nipple.

"C'mon, Romeo," urged the master of ceremonies, "you can do better than '*Hullo*'. Most guys would give anything to be in your shoes right now. **Say** something to the lady."

Lewd studied his shoes a moment, then looked back to

the actress's chin and said softly, "I seen you inna pitcher."

Carisse smoldered with ecstasy. "Why, how perfectly darling," she panted, hovering her moist, quivering lips beside his ear and teasing his ear lobe with her tempest tossing tongue.

The Condemned Man shuffled his feet and wiped his ear.

Art Pastel nudged him and winked. "What a way to go, huh?" The emcee glanced at the flashing timepiece above the electric chair; it read 11:29:50. "Hey, tempus fugit! I hate to interrupt you two love birds, but we do have bills to pay around here, you know." He reached off camera and returned with an object which he handed to the Condemned Man. "Here-make yourself useful." He adjusted the object in Lewd's hands so that everyone could see that it was a bottle of Sparkle Wax. "Ever use this stuff, buddy?"

The Condemned Man studied the bottle a moment, then slowly shook his head. The master of ceremonies gazed triumphantly into the cameras. "There you are, folks —now you know what can happen to you if you don't use Sparkle Wax!" Production assistants rubber-hosed the audience into peals of laughter. "How 'bout you, Carisse? Is there a Sparkle shine in your kitchen?"

"Enormously, Art. I love it for those hard-to-get-at places, such as corners and under kitchen appliances, as it... as it says right on the bottle, Art: Sparkle Wax Is Never Lax!"

"What more can I say, ladies and gentlemen? In Hollywood, the stars wouldn't shine without *Sparkle!*" Pastel took a few steps stage right and the cameras panned with him, revealing two buckets, two wax applicators and two small sections of vinyl flooring. "Now, here we have two identical squares of kitchen tile, and we're gonna ask Carisse to wax the first with Sparkle, while our Guest of Honor uses another leading brand on the second square."

In the wings, Tully Keyster shook his head and turned away from the stage in disgust. *Fart-bag fag.* The warden had consumed a bit too much champagne. He strolled through the semidarkness, trying to direct his thoughts to what he was going to talk about on stage. *Evening, folks, welcome to Achen State.*

"Hi, Daddy Bear."

"Why, Jen! What're you doing back here, muffin?"

"Just watching." She gazed wide-eyed at the stage, chewing on several strands of her honey-colored hair. "Isn't Art Pastel omega omee?"

"That sow-suckl" blurted Keyster. **"That homo-wart grease—"**

"Shhhhh!" Ralph the stage manager appeared from the darkness near the light board, glowered at the warden, then disappeared again.

Tully leaned close to his daughter's ear and hissed, "Lookit, young lady, if that crab fag so much as even **farts** in your direction, I'll…" Glancing down the front of her gown, the warden noticed an object hidden in his daughter's youthful cleavage. "What's that?"

"What?" She followed his gaze to her bosom. "Oh, nothing." Primly, she covered the area with her hand.

"Nothin', my dingus, missy— give it here." She turned the object over to him. "A cigarette? For the love of suck, muffin, you ain't sneakin' off and smoking weeds behind my back are you?"

"Negative, Daddy Bear. Really it's not…"

"Next thing I know, you'll be wantin' to drink beer and go out with boys! Wait till your old lady finds out about…"

"Shhhhh!" demanded Ralph Goliones, ominously.

"Okay, okay," the warden hissed, "don't get your muff hot." He shook his head, looking at the cigarette in his hand, then stuffed it into his jacket pocket. Gazing down upon the innocent countenance of his little girl, Tully sighed with exasperation. "Smoking. Lord love a frog, where'd I go wrong?"

"So here he is now, ladies and gentlemen— The Michelangelo of the Scissors— Mister Bruno!"

Applause echoed through the chamber as Art Pastel introduced the internationally renowned men's hair stylist, a husky, middle-aged man with silver hair. Mister Bruno wore a red smock, a black beret, and carried a pair of tarnished scissors.

The barber looked around impatiently, snipping the air with his scissors. "Well, what're we waiting for? Let's cut some hair, before I get nervous."

Pastel took the Condemned Man's arm. "Step right up, buddy there's only one chair, but there's no waiting!"

Two of the Penthouse Pixies wiggled out of the wings, pushing a black barber's chair on wheels, and a third dancer emerged toting a tray of tonsorial implements. The two honorary nurses stepped downstage to assist, as the chair was wheeled to center stage and the Condemned Man sat upon it, a black silk cloth tossed over him and snapped about his neck. Carisse Crosse stood beside Lewd and held his hand, as Art Pastel announced, "Okay, Mister Bruno— he wants it long on the sides and bald on top!"

Brandishing his twelve-year-old scissors and a broken comb, the Michelangelo of the Scissors began carving clumps of hair from the top of the Condemned Man's head. "Slide down in the chair, your head's too high! The head has to be the right height, because I'm a genius and I'm gonna give you a haircut you'll never forget! See that little twirl I give the scissors when I snip? That's the secret, that's my famous Curvilinear Clip, of which I'm the only barber in the world that does it."

Pacing back and forth backstage, Warden Keyster contemplated his television debut and searched his pockets for a cigar to calm his nerves. *Crumb suck.* All he came up with was the cigarette he had taken from his daughter, so he lit that up instead.

On stage, Mister Bruno had sculpted a perfect circle of scalp on top of the Condemned Man's head, which he now covered with creamy lather and attacked with a flashing straight-edged razor. "I usually don't give a shave, but for you I make an exception." Soon the gleaming pate was toweled dry, scented with cologne and sprinkled with powder; then, the hair-sculptor swept off the barber cloth and announced, "I'm a genius, tell your friends about me, I'll give them a discount." He marched toward the wings.

"How 'bout it, folks?" shouted Art Pastel. "Let's hear it for the great Mister Bruno!" The APPLAUSE sign produced impressive results. The emcee and Carisse Crosse both stepped behind the barber chair and looked down at the Condemned Man's shaven head. "Well, Carisse, what d'you think? Is it better than the statue of David?"

The starlet traced her finger teasingly across the smoothly shaven surface and cooed, "Fantastically, Art. I just adore bald-headed men!" She leaned over and planted her juicy lips smack in the center of the powdered pate, which immediately began to blush crimson. Pastel watched her hot mouth pump electric vibrations into the Condemned Man's skull.

"Careful, gorgeous– you're not gonna leave anything for the chair!"

Miss Crosse slowly unglued her magnetic mouth from the Condemned Man's head, leaving a scarlet oval of lipstick in the center of his scalp. "He's just sooo adorable!" Stepping a bit to the side of the chair, she bent far forward, gazing at the Condemned Man and at the same time providing the world with a breathtaking moment of the deepest Carisse.

In the control room, Monteczuma watched his Number-Two Monitor, which showed the actress bending toward him, her explosive, torpedo-nosed tits but a hairbreadth of becoming launched. It had to be a split-second decision: would the detonator tips of those torpedoes slide free of the golden cloth that barely covered them? "Take Camera Two!" the director ordered, gambling they would not. One billion television viewers were treated to an extreme closeup of Carisse Crosse's renowned bosom, dangling completely exposed, except for the bullet-hard nipples themselves, still covered by the shimmering bodice of her gown, but threatening to dance free at any second. "Man, what a shot!" crooned Monteczuma. "Please, God, just don't let those dugs pop out!"

The audience was uproarious. Men left their seats and tried to climb onto the stage, but their wives pulled them back. Art Pastel let the gimmick run until the dramatically proper moment, then stepped over and took the starlet's arm, escorting her to an upright position. "Hey, c'mon, Carisse, let's keep the death toll down to one, shall we?" The audience roared, and Pastel took this opportunity to dismiss the actress, who slunk over to her witness seat amidst tumultuous applause as Lewd was taken off the barber chair and the hair cutting apparatus was struck from the stage.

Art Pastel and the Condemned Man were left standing alone center stage. The Condemned Man's face had turned gray. "Our pal here looks a trifle under the weather," observed the emcee. "What's the problem, buddy? Suffering from that **burning** sensation? Well, cheer up and look at the bright side of all this. For one thing, you don't have to go to work tomorrow!" The audience shrieked; the Condemned Man picked cut hairs from underneath his collar. "Our buddy here has had quite a busy day, folks, so we thought you might get a kick out of watching this short film capturing some of the highlights of what they call Zero Day on Death Row."

Off in the wings, Warden Keyster took one last drag on his cigarette, inhaled deeply and stepped on the butt. His foot moved lightly, as though it had no weight at all. His temper was completely under control now; in fact, he felt remarkably free of tension, the most relaxed he'd felt all day.

Tully, you old son-of-an-aitchbone, you're tougher'n a dyke's dugs. You got the world by the big back squat. Get out there and show 'em what you're made of— guts and gonads. He saw the four wrestlers troop by on their way to the stage. *You're next, Tully. The whole world's watching, and you're only fifty-three years old— a spring clam, for slut sakes. The perfect age to run for Governor.*

"And now, ladies and gentlemen," Art Pastel was saying, "in answer to the Condemned Man's last wish, we take great pleasure in presenting— live on our stage tonight— an Australian tag-team match, featuring our guest of honor's four favorite professional wrestlers! Introducing, Team Number One: Baron von Buster Block... and the Silly Savage!" Good natured applause greeted the two wrestlers. "And, Team Number Two: the Horrible Hydrogen Bum... and the monstrous Frank N. Stein!" The audience laughed and applauded as the second pair of combatants pranced on stage.

The Penthouse Pixie dancing girls gathered downstage right and joined hands, spreading out to form a three-sided wrestling ring, the open side toward the audience. "This will be a one-fall match," announced the emcee, "and the wrestlers are advised to keep off the ropes!" The audience chuckled as the Silly Savage ran his hands up and down a dancer's arm, whooping a fertility chant.

"Keyster?" Ralph Goliones prowled through the backstage darkness, paging the warden in a loud whisper.

"Where's Keyster?"

"Here I am!"

"Shhhhh!" Ralph took the warden's arm and escorted him toward the stage. "You're on next, so I want you to stand right off stage here till Pastel gives you your cue, understand?"

"Sure, sure," Tully agreed, complacently, "don't frazzle your nates, son— everything's under control." The warden stood on the edge of a dream, gazing out at the stage, oblivious to the pandemonium currently being caused by the frenzied wrestlers. His eyes were focused on his destiny: GOVERNOR TULLY KEYSTER. Someday, maybe even the White House.

Entranced, Tully next envisioned Hollywood's hopeless hunt for an actor capable of portraying the title role in *The Tully Keyster Story. By buns, no fag-face actor's gonna nate-slime the name of Tully Keyster— nosirree. I'll play the geeking part myself!*

Tonight, all the warden's dreams were coming true.

Merlin Trump carefully adjusted the knot of his silken cravat, then stepped back and peered at his image in the bar mirror. "Sharp as a tack." Moving slowly to the closet, he withdrew a gray tweed topcoat with a black fur collar, and draped it over his arm. Pausing, he pondered the garment, then shuffled over to the window, eased it open a crack, slipped his fingers outside and wiggled them in the frigid night air. "Yep, she's winter all right." Returning to the closet, he selected a gray slouch hat, with matching gloves and scarf. Depositing his garments on the bar, the old man rummaged about until he came up with a dusty briefcase, which he wiped off with a paper towel. Picking up his experiment logbook, Merlin gazed once more at the recipe for Groundhog Cocktail before reverently tucking it away inside the briefcase. "Oh, hotsy-totsy," he whispered, brushing a tear from his eye.

He washed his hands, dried them with a paper towel, then wrapped the soiled towels in a sheet of newspaper, tied the parcel with string and packed it in the briefcase. As an afterthought, he also packed two bunches of carrots, a celery stalk and a three ounce vial of olive oil.

Gathering up his garments and briefcase, he looked around to be sure everything was in its proper place; then he shuffled to the door, where he turned to peer about the room a final time. "So long, Labor Gang... and thank you kindly." He left the attic garret, locking the door carefully behind him, and descended the winding stairway to the third floor of the mansion.

Strolling along the deeply carpeted hallway, the old man paused briefly in the dim light to wink at a white-marble statue of a water sprite. He trudged down the stairs leading to the second floor landing, and hesitated outside his wife's bedroom door. Setting down the briefcase, he gently raised his hand and touched the door twice with one finger. *Fast asleep, God bless her.* He picked up his briefcase and descended the long spiral staircase to the main floor.

Upon reaching the bottom, Merlin stood quietly for several moments while he caught his breath. Then he moved slowly to the suit of black armor and hitched the handle of his briefcase to a hook protruding from the iron man's breastplate. "Hold this for the Chiefie, if you kindly please." He slipped into his outer garments, adjusted the brim of his hat, and reclaimed the briefcase. He took a five dollar bill from his pocket and tucked it into the metal man's face mask, then put his finger to his lips and winked. "Shhh."

Shunning the front door, Merlin tiptoed toward the back of the house, passing the television room where his daughter sat in the dark watching four wrestlers cavort among a troupe of squealing, scantily dressed females. Toy sat with her back to the doorway and did not see her father; nor did Merlin see her in the darkness, as he winked at the television set and put his finger to his lips, before ambling on through the dining room, into the pantry, and down the cellar steps. The basement was pitch-dark. The old man paused at the bottom of the stairs, waiting for his night eyes to warm up, watching colored balls of light float before his face. He patted his briefcase. *This is it, m'boys she said. The job 's done.* "Thalia, m'dear, is that you?"

As soon as he began to discern outlines in the dark, he trudged slowly to the workbench, pulled over an old chair and climbed up on it, raising himself to sufficient height so he could withdraw the long iron bolt. Climbing down from the chair, he eased the heavy work bench aside, revealing the huge, rusty iron door. Merlin searched his pocket for keys to open the heavy locks but, finding none, he tried pushing on the massive portal and it swung open silently. *Who forgot to lock the door? Wait till your mother hears about this.*

Merlin stepped across the threshold and peered about the pitch black wine cellar, then he carefully slid the workbench back in place and closed the heavy door, bolting it from the inside. *They'll never catch the Chiefie— not in a month on Sunday.* The darkness was almost total, yet the old man moved about as though the room were bathed in light.

The only object whose presence he seemed unaware of was Arthur's life-sized medical dummy; this stood squarely in Merlin's path and he walked right into it. "Sugar!" The wood-and-bone dummy toppled and crashed to the concrete floor, its various organs clattering in every direction. "Shhh! Golly Neds, you'll wake the dead!" The old man stood in the darkness, waiting for the commotion to settle, then gingerly nudged the fallen dummy with his foot. "Road block, is it? Ambush?" Kneeling, he touched the skeleton's bony hand. "Hesperus, it's a someone! Mercy-dory, I kindly beg your pardon! If I may be so kind as to help you to your feet..."

Raising the disassembled dummy, he propped it against

a wine rack and brushed off its rib cage, now devoid of organs. "No damage, just send me the bill, my..." He peered at the absurdly tilted head, sans jawbone and eyeballs. "Why, is it you, Arthur, m'boy?" He patted the cold, hollow skull. "Mercy Neds, are you thriving?" His fingers touched the empty rib cage. "Go put a raw egg in a glass of beer, you're too skinny ."

Merlin showed the dummy his briefcase. "Arthur, my good old chip off the old block, we're right back on the old mappy! The Eighteenth Amendment is full of prunes!" Gazing about, he touched his finger to where the dummy's mouth had once been. "Shhh! Mum's the coast." He sidled up to it and whispered, "No aqua vitae, that's the ticket. House O' Trump Groundhog Cocktail, and the feds can't touch us, m'boy, and I don't mean Mayberry." He nudged the dummy emphatically then stepped away and said loudly, "Those people moved, you say? Don't tell me! Moved, did they? Why, can you de-magine that?" He winked at the dummy and whispered, "Little pitchers have big ears." They stood together in the silence a moment before Merlin smiled and patted the dummy's cheek. "Tell your mother the old Chiefie couldn't wait. The job's all done, Labor Gang, and he's tired."

The old man shuffled off between the long rows of empty wine racks, blowing air through his toothless gums, which was as close as he could approximate whistling. In the most remote corner of the cold, dark cellar, he stepped up to a rack built against the cobble stone wall and reached between two wooden members, pulling out another long iron bolt. With little effort, he slid the empty rack aside, revealing a second, smaller iron door. This one was also unlocked, but Merlin found it difficult to push open. "Give us a hand, m'boys she said. Do the best you can, that's all you can do." The rusty portal grumbled and gave way. "You're a gentleman and a scholar, and that's for sure." Merlin slipped through, dragging the wine rack back to its original position before forcing the heavy door shut again.

He stood in a low, dark tunnel. At the other end, about thirty yards away, a dim light was visible; as the old man trudged toward it, he heard the patter of tiny feet scampering off ahead of him, saw little red eyes peering up at him from the damp black floor.

"Groundhogs."

Something wrapped itself around his foot and he stooped to pick it up. It was a strip of gossamer material, shredded with age. Merlin raised it to his nose and sniffed gingerly, breathing in a dank, musty odor.

"Strawberries," he decided at once, then looked about him and called softly, "Thalia?" He folded the remnant carefully and tucked it away in his overcoat pocket, continuing along the passageway until he reached another metal door, this one with small louvers in it, permitting diffused light to seep in from the other side.

Merlin carefully raised the iron latch and eased the portal open, peering outside for several moments before stepping through and shutting the door quickly behind him.The door closed with a click, and the old man tried it to make certain it had locked itself from the other side.

He was standing on an old abandoned subway platform. Only a few dim emergency lights illuminated the empty underground platform; on the tile wall was an elaborate mosaic sign which read 91ST STREET.

"Coast's clear." Gazing around with satisfaction, he moved to the edge of the platform and peered up the tracks; no train was in sight. There were noises, however, emanating from the opposite direction, and Merlin looked down the tracks to see the twinkling lanterns of a subway maintenance crew working a few hundred yards away. "Labor Gang."

He returned his gaze to the direction from which the trains came; far away up the dark tunnel, two dazzling silver eyes rumbled toward him. "Right on the old timetable, m'boys." He glanced back at the unobtrusive metal door through which he had just passed. It was painted green and on it, in white letters, were the words SUBWAY MAINTENANCE. "A pretty penny, but worth it."

The speeding train bore down on the abandoned station, prepared to roar right through without stopping, as trains had done for more than forty years, but the motorman saw the lights of the maintenance crew working farther down the tracks, and began to slow up. As the train pulled into the station, the construction crew flashed it a red signal, so the motorman brought his rig to a halt right beside the platform.

The conductor, gazing absentmindedly from his window at the middle of the long train, saw a passenger waiting on the platform and, without thinking, flicked the levers which opened the doors of the train. The passenger boarded and the doors were closed again before the conductor realized what had happened. He peered at the platform sign and gasped. "Jesus Christmas— this is Lewd's Landing!"

The shaken conductor left his little booth and trotted up the aisle to the next car, where an old man sat holding a briefcase in his lap. "Hey, did you just get on this train?"

"Shhhhh!" The old man put a finger to his lips and winked. "Mom's the world, ain't it?" He dug into his pocket and slipped the conductor a five dollar bill. "Keep it under your hat— the job's done— the Chiefie's goin' home." Merlin reached into his coat again and took out a small wad of bills, leaning toward the conductor and asking confidentially, "How much is it to the end of the line?"

Tully Keyster stood in the wings and watched the four wrestlers leave the stage. The backstage monitor showed a commercial running; as soon as it ended, the warden would make his entrance.

Reaching into his jacket pocket, Keyster withdrew a small mirror and studied his face with satisfaction. *Go get 'em, Tully.* He set his jaw and the image in the mirror became the archetypal Administrator of Justice— impartial, emotionless, efficient. The warden grinned, and suddenly a different being gazed out at him through the looking glass: the Eternal Father— authoritative, sagacious, yet benign— the face his daughter had dubbed Daddy Bear. Furrowing his eyebrows, Keyster glowered at the mirror and came face to face with the Gar Mountain Monster— ferocious, ruthless, hideous. Which Tully Keyster would the world see tonight? The warden set his jaw; he grinned; he glowered. He floated.

The clock on stage read **11:44:00** when the commercial ended and Art Pastel announced to the world, "And now, ladies and gentle men, it's time to turn the festivities over to a man who has a certain way about him that just burns people up!"

Standing off stage, the warden put away his mirror and adjusted his bow tie. *This is it.*

"If you think your electric bill is high, you oughta see this guy's!" Pastel continued. "Folks, let's say hello again to the head man here at Achen State Penitentiary. Here he is now— **Warden Tubby Kisser!**"

Tubby Kisser? The warden stood frozen at the edge of the stage, spaced out and beginning to glow. *Tubby Kisser?!* The applause continued and he did not move. Behind him, he heard a voice hiss, "For Chrissakes, get out there!" Two hands planted themselves firmly against his back, propelling him stage-ward. Stumbling into the bright lights, Keyster flapped his arms to keep his balance. A hand appeared before him and he clutched at it desperately, managing not to fall.

The warden found himself standing face to face with Art Pastel, shaking his hand. Pastel was smirking and the Playpen rocked with laughter. *TUBBY KISSER!* The name flew like a banner headline before the warden's eyes, and he began to squeeze the emcee's hand with all the strength in his 263-pound frame. Pastel began to wilt and Keyster squeezed harder, determined to break the maggot's hand.

In the control room, Roland Montezuma watched in disbelief. "Am I going crazy, or are they Indian wrestling down there?"

Finally, Art Pastel grunted through clenched teeth, "Warden... say hello... to the **whole world.**"

It slowly dawned on Keyster where he was. He turned his head toward the audience and the look on his face twitched from Gar Mountain Monster to Daddy Bear. **"Why, howdy, folks! Welcome to Achen State!"** He glanced at Pastel and continued to crush the emcee's hand as he announced **"Keyster's** the name— *Tully* **Keyster,"** then he released the pressure of his grip, leaving Pastel's hand all mottled and misshapen; the pain brought tears to the star's eyes, and it was all he could do to retain a smile until he reached the wings.

Meanwhile, the warden was swiftly regaining his composure. "Tonight, most of you out there will be witnessing your first wienie roast— ah... execution— so I figure a couple words might be in order before we strap our con into the Whoopie Seat." He stuffed his hands into his jacket pockets, glanced at the ceiling to collect his thoughts, then leveled his gaze on the camera lens. "Now, the only profession older than prostitution, is criminal punishment. Back in the days of the cavemen..."

In the control trailer, Montezuma realized that Warden Keyster was not following the script. "Oh-oh, that fat bastard's winging it." He glanced at the clock, which read 11:46, and switched on his headset. "Hang loose, everybody — we might have to improvise some cues for the next nine minutes, till Pastel comes on again." In his monitors he watched the warden continue his discourse; behind Keyster, forgotten, stood the Condemned Man. Montezuma looked at the tech director and nodded his head. "So far it's been a breeze— but I got a feeling the honeymoon's over."

Off in the wings, Pastel paused to examine his hand and wipe the tears from his eyes. Nothing seemed broken. How could he get even? What could he do that would really hurt Keyster?

"Mr. Pastel?" Lilly, the elderly make-up assistant, smiled sweetly and held up a powder puff. "May I powder your face?"

"Here, honey," the star cupped his hand over his crotch, "powder this." He bolted off through the semidarkness, bound for the sanctuary of his dressing room. Suddenly, Art Pastel stopped cold in his tracks; before him stood the most beautiful girl he had ever seen.

On stage, Warden Keyster was amazing himself with the brilliant insights issuing from his mouth. "...Then, the goody-goodies come up with a new toy— Criminal Rehabilitation, they call it. But I call it *Rat Crap*. Anybody thinks my cons are sick in the head is an A number-one Sunday Sucker, pure and simple. Why, my staff shrinks say cons are better adjusted than most so-called decent people — and then I get these roach-brained do-gooders tellin' me my goons are antisocial because they're emotionally disturbed or socially oppressed, if that don't scratch your crabs. And alla time the cons are stringin' along, playin' them for a sap, yuckin' their hornies off behind their backs."

Backstage, Ralph spoke to the director over his headset. "What about it, Rally— should I cut him off?"

"Hell, no. So far, it's better than the script."

In the wings, Art Pastel stood before Jenny Keyster, paralyzed by her gaze. Finally, he lowered his head and tried to walk around her, but she reached out and touched his arm, stopping him dead.

"Criminals are born, not made," explained Warden Keyster. "And Darwin taught us we gotta wipe out all the murderers and rapists before they pass on their fag-forsaken genes." The audience broke into thunderous applause and sounded its noisemakers.

"Karoo, Mr. Pastel," sighed Jenny, "I really think you're thermal!" She pressed the tip of her breast against his arm. Pastel's breath caught in his throat; the young girl's proximity made him tremble. He tried to smile at the admiring blue eyes, but their radiance was too intense. He averted his glance and stammered, "You... ah... you look a little like my... sister."

"True-tell?" Jenny picked a piece of imaginary fluff from the star's lapel and brushed her downy breast against his arm. "Is she pretty?"

"She... she's beautiful." Pastel blushed.

"Omega-karoo, what an omee thing to say!" Jenny laid her head upon his shoulder and returned his compliment with a hug.

On stage Warden Keyster was leading the Condemned Man out of the way so that everyone could have an unobstructed view of the electric chair. "This, folks, is a Hot Seat, invented in the 1880's by a dentist, of all geeking things, back when they knew a thing or two about dealing with slime-suckers. The cons got a whole shebang of nicknames for it— Harm Chair, Barbecue Pit, Devil's Doorstep, Queasy Chair— but, as someone once remarked, 'A rose by any other name...' "

In the wings, the warden's daughter was leading the emcee out of the backstage traffic. "If I let you crash off without dropping me your autograph, I'd just go crambo!"

They stood close in the semidarkness and Pastel searched his pockets for pen and paper. "I... ah... I'm afraid I don't have any..."

"Not like that, fuddle," the girl cooed, "like this." She lifted his right hand, captured his index finger with her silken lips and danced her playful tongue across the tip. Withdrawing the moistened finger from her mouth, she placed it to the bare flesh of her chest, just above her throbbing heart. "Sign here, deva-doll."

Tully Keyster was now sitting comfortably in the electric chair, his legs crossed, holding the audience in the palm of his hand. "My cons call this Tully's Throne. This little baby was built for Achen State by a fella named Ferguson Fohat at the Electro-Services Corporation back in nineteen-thirty-six. Better'n two hundred aitchbones have been toasted on Tully's Bun Burner, and not a single part has been replaced on this mother since she was delivered. Yessir, they don't build 'em like this any more."

Art Pastel shakily moved his finger tip across Jenny Keyster's smooth, cool flesh.

"Course," Warden Keyster admitted, "they've spiffed it up a bit for the show, but it's still the same old chair that's sent some pretty famous bums off to their just desserts. Fellas like Rhino DeBussy, Fingers Bodance, Lucky Lexanovsky, Mad Lenny Gouda— I could go on all night."

"Mega-thank, deva-doll," whispered Jenny, as Pastel crossed the last *t* at the hollow of her left shoulder. To further illustrate her gratitude, she rose to her tiptoes, wound her arms about his neck and softly planted her moist, open lips on his.

"Now, when a con gets the chair," the warden was explaining, "we call it Ridin' the Thunderbolt. In a couple minutes, when our friend here's time runs out, you'll see me pull that switch over there, and that'll cut loose a jolt of juice hot enough to singe the hairs off a hippo's hornies. Y'see, only a small current— maybe a hundred volts— is enough to cook a guy, but because the body is highly resistant to electric current, we have to pump a whole muff load into him just to drive it through from head to foot. The principle it works on is a lot like your electric light bulb, with the Condemned Man acting as the filament. We feed 'im a grand total of two thousand volts for a period of two minutes— or enough electricity to light every

Christmas tree in Zenobia for a month." The audience was visibly impressed.

Jenny's hot, electric tongue slithered into Pastel's mouth. The emcee's entire body trembled violently and his hands clutched at her honey-blonde tresses.

Nearby, two seamstresses paused to shake their heads with disgust, and several leering stagehands lounged about on packing crates, grinning lasciviously and passing around open bottles of champagne.

The warden climbed out of the electric chair and glanced up at the flashing chronometer, which read **11:52:09**. "Well, I guess it's time to put my bird in the oven." He turned to the Condemned Man, who was staring white-faced at the timepiece. "Let's go, cream puff." The warden led Lewd to the black grotto. "Watch out for that first step— it's a *killer*." The audience laughed and Lewd jerked his head toward the laughter, squinting into the lights and smiling weakly. He climbed onto the black platform and stood with his back to the audience, until Keyster turned him around. "Now we sit in the chair— isn't that the way we play the game, buster?" Lewd Noogie snapped his head up and down spasmodically, but made no move to sit. "What's the matter, too stiff to sit down?" The warden planted a beefy hand in the middle of Noogie's chest and shoved him into the chair. "In a couple minutes, you'll be too stiff to get up."

Jenny eased her mouth from Art Pastel's and studied his face to see how far out she'd taken him. The emcee raised his eyelids and gazed at her with wonderment; then he whispered, "Toy Boat," and lunged at her again, devouring her wet ripe mouth.

On stage, the two honorary nurses were helping Warden Keyster strap the Condemned Man into the chair— "Just to keep him from floppin' around too much." As the starlets bent over, their almost completely exposed bosoms dangled before Lewd's face. "Take a good look," advised the warden.

"There won't be nothing like that where you're goin'."
The nurses stepped back when they were through, and
Keyster bent over to examine the straps, presenting his
ponderous fundament to the audience and cameras.
"There, that looks pretty good."

"Not from here it doesn't," frowned Monteczuma in the
control room.

Jenny tore her mouth from the star's sucking vortex,
aware that the stagehands were giggling nearby. Pastel
clutched at her once more, but she held him off, so he just
stood gazing at her with helpless longing. Then she gently
took him by the hand and led him off into the solitary
darkness behind the lighting board.

Warden Keyster was adjusting the steel cap atop the
Condemned Man's head. "We call this thing the Pope's Cap—
beats the roach outta me why. Anyway, underneath it we
stuff this here small sponge— it's been soaked in a brine
solution, just to give the current a little goose goin' into
the brain. Then, down here..." he knelt to attach the metal
clamp around Noogie's right calf, "this gadget completes
the circuit." He stood up and brushed off his hands. "Now,
when that jolt of juice rams through him, you'll see his
body leap upward. This is a natural reaction— I guess you
could say it makes him want to jump right out of his skin.
You folks watching on TV will probably be able to see how
all the body hair is singed right off as the flesh starts to
sizzle."

In the wings, Ralph Goliones knocked on Pastel's
dressing room door to inform the star that he was due on
stage in exactly two minutes. There was no response.

Behind the lighting board, in the humming darkness,
the warden's daughter unbuttoned the emcee's shirt and
fluttered her tiny finger tips over his bare chest. Then she
took hold of his dumb hands and led them around her to
her firm, pert buttocks.

Returning from the star's empty dressing room, the

anxious stage manager approached the stagehands who were swilling champagne. *"Where's Pastel?"* Ralph hissed. The men just giggled and shrugged their shoulders.

Warden Keyster had taken a small, telescoping silver pointer from his pocket, and was now explaining the flow of the electrical current and its effect on the Condemned Man's body. "The juice jumps into the skull, here," he tapped the metal cap with his pointer, "and immediately cooks the brain into a blob of senseless jelly. Yessir, one jolt from this baby and the old gray matter ain't what she used to be."

Art Pastel's hands were under Jenny's gown now, kneading the hard mounds of her buttocks, lifting her from the floor and sucking her velvety lips with his voracious mouth. Her arms slowly settled around his neck; drawing up her silky knees, she wrapped her legs about his thighs.

The stage manager combed through all the dressing rooms, restrooms, closets, hissing frantically for the missing emcee.

"Folks," Warden Keyster was saying, "this here's the official sawbones at Achen State, Doc Pettibone. His job is to make sure we get the job done right. After the juice goes off…"

In the control trailer, Monteczuma ran his hands through his hair. "It's eleven-fifty-five— Pastel just missed his cue. We're in trouble, Ralph."

The stage manager was outside the building, prowling through the parking lot. "Pastel! Pastel!" He clicked on his headset. "No dice, Rally."

"Keep looking," ordered the director. "Stand by, everybody— this is gonna get hairy."

Throughout the Playpen, the crews of Pastel Productions swigged champagne, wondering what all the fuss was about. On the band stand, Ulloch Tugg fumed because one of his songs would have to be cut. On the stage, Tully Keyster had everything under control; the realization flashed through is mind that Pastel was supposed to be singing a song by this time, but if the fag snake never showed up it would be too soon for the warden.

Off in the wings, Art Pastel released the girl's buttocks and ran his hands over the bare flesh of her shoulders and back. Jenny captured his hands and peeled them from her; stepping away from him, she gazed into his hungry eyes as she reached up behind her and began to undo the bodice of her gown. Pastel awaited the sacred revelation, panting and transfixed.

"Now, our chaplain back here is of course praying for the soul of the Condemned Man, a fat load of good it'll do 'im." Keyster put his arm around the priest's shoulders. "Oh, don't stop, boy— you're doing a bang-up job."

> *"...then shall be brought to pass*
> *the saying that is written,*
> *Death is swallowed up in victory.*
> *O death, where is thy sting?*
> *O grave, where is thy victory?"*

"Well, now," the warden grinned, "I don't know about the victory part of it, but our boy's got one bee-muff of a sting comin' up in about four minutes, eh, chaplain?"

Behind the lighting board, in the sultry glow of a red emergency bulb, Jenny Pye Keyster paused a moment for dramatic effect, then let the silken bodice of her gown peel away, totally exposing her from the waist up. Art Pastel's breath rattled in his throat as he ogled the glowing crimson flesh, ebbing and flowing before his eyes like gossamer mist— drifting crimson clouds, rippling down across a subtly contoured angelic chest, then puffing into a pair of fleecy swells whose crests were capped by bell-button uppity-dugs. Foaming at the mouth, the berserk superstar crushed her to him with a gurgle, slobbering over her silky shoulders as she darted her tongue into his ear, making him jerk as though hit by speeding bullets. He kissed her throat, licked her shoulders, bit her hair and danced his hands upon her breasts, kneading the soft bulges and tweaking the gumdrop nipples, trying to steal them from her candy chest.

On stage, the chronometer read **11:57:13**. "Well," said Warden Keyster, "I guess it's about time for the Condemned Man's Last Words. How 'bout it, cream puff— wanna say night-night before we turn off the lights?"

Lewd Noogie's ashen face was bathed in sweat. He flicked his gaze from side to side and his Adam's apple bobbed, but no sound issued from his mouth.

Keyster shook his head. "Scared stiff." He reached into the grotto, grabbed the Condemned Man's cheeks and shook his head. "C'mon, for sow sakes, speak up— we ain't got all night."

Noogie cleared his throat, tried to speak, then licked his parched lips and tried again. "Ah... so long... Mom, an' Fi... an'... an' all." He looked down and tried to bring his hands together, but they were strapped to the arms of the chair. "That's about it."

"Atta boy," said the warden. "Have a nice trip." Keyster began fastening a black hood over the Condemned Man's head. "And Happy New Year."

Art Pastel's jellied knees buckled and he sank downward, dragging his flapping tongue down across the girl's chest and into the fragrant valley between her breasts. Then his arms locked about her hips and he straightened up again, lifting her from the floor and pressing her back against the warm lighting board as his moaning mouth mashed her left breast, sucking the hard nipple like a souped-up vacuum cleaner. Floating on the crest of a girlish dream, Jenny let her head loll back; her arms drifted languidly upward and she tangled her wrists in the ropes overhead, imagining that she was strung up there and at his mercy.

11:57:54.

Warden Keyster walked stage right and mounted the platform where the large circuit breaker was located. "Hold your hat, maggot— this is gonna take your breath away."

In the control trailer, Monteczuma was snapping out emergency orders. "Ralph, if you don't turn up Pastel in thirty seconds, forget it. Have Freddy Fredella announce the countdown on the offstage mike. Ulloch, your music cues stay the same. Lights, when Keyster throws the switch..."

The Playpen audience was spellbound as Warden Keyster explained, "Now, at ten seconds to midnight, we'll all have a little countdown, from what I understand." He pointed across the stage toward the large sign headed R.I.P. and listing all the names of the deceased Noogies. "With each second of the countdown, one of them names will light up, then, at twelve o'clock, right on the gnat's no-no, I'll flip this here switch. The juice'll go on, the New Year's celebration will get going, and I don't know what all else. Course, this ain't exactly the way they planned things, but just leave everything to old Tully— I ain't had a bad burn yet."

A blast of sunlight flashed against Jenny's eyelids as she dangled from the ropes, glued to Pastel's mouth. Drifting on a current of ecstasy, she gently opened her eyes and gazed into the brilliance, which momentarily blinded her.

Ralph Goliones trained his high-powered flashlight on the passionate couple for several moments before realizing he had found Art Pastel. Then, without a word, the stage manager grabbed the emcee by the back of the collar, tore him away from the half naked girl and propelled the delirious man toward the stage.

"Artie?" whispered the bewildered girl, seeing only a blotch of colored light wherever she looked. "Where are you, deva-doll?"

The emcee checked his forward momentum and did an instantaneous about-face, loping back toward Jenny, grunting with passion. The stage manager intercepted him, grabbed his lapels and shook him frantically. "Jesus goddamn Christ, you're three minutes late for your cue!" Pastel stared at him dumbly for a moment, then spun about and sprinted for the stage, straightening his clothing. Ralph clicked on his headset and rasped, "Got him, Rally— he's heading for the stage now."

"Nice," said Monteczuma.

The stage manager directed his flashlight beam toward the dazzled girl dangling from the ropes, her youthful breasts hard and red from being sucked. *"Jee-zuss,"* he whispered.

The girl gazed blindly at the bright light, eased her grip on the ropes and slipped to the floor. "Artie?" The light clicked off, but its afterimage hovered in the dark before her eyes as she groped about. "Artie, don't crash me, deva-doll. Where are you?"

"Here I am," whispered a masculine voice, as hands ran over her naked flesh and a hungry mouth closed over her right nipple.

11:59:13

Art Pastel emerged from the wings, adjusting his French cuffs and smoothing back his hair with trembling hands.

Warden Keyster, stationed at the switch, continued his running commentary to the cameras, noting the star's entrance with inner annoyance. *Here comes fag-face.* "Now, some of you might think this here switch is just a dummy. Well, you're dead-clam wrong. When I pull this handle—"

"That's right, Warden!" broke in Art Pastel, suddenly aware that just thirty seconds remained until midnight. "You mind the switch, while we all say goodbye to our Guest of Honor!" He danced to the grotto and lifted the edge of the Condemned Man's hood, revealing a chalk-white face and bewildered eyes. "How 'bout it, bubbie, any last words?"

Warden Keyster sighed and shook his head. "We been through all that leech-dung, Pastel. Now, get your nates away from the chair, unless you wanna go with him." The warden raised his hand and clasped the large black handle, watching Pastel drop the Condemned Man's hood and stumble backward from the electric chair, grinning in terror. *He's really shook*, thought Keyster with satisfaction. *Play pen Palsy.*

Recovering once again, Pastel turned to the audience and proclaimed, "Well, then— I guess we're ready to ring out the old and ring in the new! How 'bout it, folks?"
The audience emitted a stifled roar. Everyone sat on the edge of his seat, eyes bulging, breath held with anticipation. The atmosphere was electric.

On the bandstand, Ulloch Tugg pointed his baton, and a drum roll began.

In the control trailer, Monteczuma was speaking into his headset. "Ralph? Ralph, where the Christ are you, now? It's fifteen seconds to finale, Ralph..."

Backstage, Ralph Goliones was impervious to the sound of the director's voice calling to him through his earphone. He was trying desperately to push down Jenny Keyster's pantyhose, while she was opening his belt and zipper, whispering, "Oh, Artie— hurry, Artie!" On stage, the chronometer flashed **11:59:45, 11:59:46,** and Art Pastel shouted, "C'mon, everybody— let's all join in and give it a big countdown!" As the timepiece flashed **11:59:50,** the emcee yelled, **"Ten!"** He was joined by the dancers, the boys' choir and the orchestra, which played a resounding chord. At stage left, the huge electric R.I.P. sign lit up the first name: **AARON ABBOTT NOOGIE.**

"NINE!" The entire audience joined in and the orchestra played a higher chord. The second name on the R.I.P. sign lit up: **BAILEY BAINBRIDGE NOOGIE.**

The tumult penetrated the darkness in the wings, and Ralph Goliones suddenly tore his mouth from Jenny's hot nipple and jerked his head toward the stage. "Jesus Christ, I gotta go!"

"EIGHT!" **R.I.P. CADBY CADDOCK NOOGIE**

"No, Artie— please don't go away!" pleaded the young girl, clinging to him.

The stage manager tried to peel the tenacious arms from around his neck. "Leggo!" He started to run toward the stage, but his trousers fell down and he stumbled to the floor, with Jenny landing on his back.

"SEVEN!" Viewers at home joined in the count, their eyes glued to their screens. **R.I.P. DACEY DAG NOOGIE**

"SIX!" **R.I.P. EACHAN EARL NOOGIE**

"Goddamnit— *shag off!*" hissed the stage manager, trying to buck Jenny from his back as he crawled from behind the lighting board on his hands and knees.

"FIVE!" **R.I.P. FABIAN FABRON NOOGIE**
Ralph lunged to his feet and wrenched free of the girl, hiking up his pants as he jogged toward the stage.

"Artie!" called the bewildered girl.

"FOUR!" The orchestra continued to climb the scale.

R.I.P. GABRIEL GABLE NOOGIE

"THREE!" **R.I.P. HACKETT HADDEN NOOGIE**

Jenny climbed unsteadily to her feet, groping blindly in the direction of her lover's departure. Her disheveled blonde tresses covered her face; her head seethed with frustrated passion and with each step she felt the squishiness between her legs. "Artie?" was her plaintive call.

Breathing heavily and licking their lips, the stagehands nearby ogled the half naked girl as she moved, unsure, unseeing, toward the stage.

"TWO!" Now the whole world shouted.

R.I.P. IAN IGNATIUS NOOGIE

"ONE!" R.I.P. CORBIN GILBERT NOOGIE

Jenny Keyster paused at the very brink of the stage, astounded by the Playpen din, her hair still covering her eyes, her breasts still naked and red from being sucked.

"ZERO!" proclaimed the universe.

The Marines fired their weapons in thunderous salute; in ten-foot letters, the words **HAPPY NEW YEAR** lit up across the backdrop; the BBS Orchestra erupted with "Auld Lang Syne"; the last name on the R.I.P. sign ignited— **LEWD NMI NOOGIE**: throughout the entire world, no one drew a breath. But Tully Keyster did not pull the switch.

"PULL THE GODDAMNED SWITCH!" roared Roland Monteczuma, springing to his feet in the control trailer. *"PULL THE SWITCH!"*

Warden Keyster's hand was frozen on the handle. His gaze was frozen on a half naked woman standing in the wings across the stage. His first thought was a simple one: Son of Smut— look at that set of dugs. Then he noticed the violet gown. The woman's hand went up and parted the hair that covered her face. Tully Keyster's heart stopped beating. *Why... that's Jen. That's my little girl!* Time stood still.

Standing beside the grotto, Chaplain Levitsky thought it strange that he could hear nothing to indicate that the chair had been turned on. He looked up from his Holy Book and peeked around the corner of the grotto; the Condemned Man's body was tense and quivering, but there was no promised sizzling sound. Suddenly the priest found himself gazing toward the wings, at Jenny Keyster's half nude body.

The viewers at home saw the prison chaplain clutch his Bible and sink to his knees at the Condemned Man's feet.

On the bandstand, Ulloch Tugg peered over his shoulder. "What ees?" He was directing the orchestra through a nostalgic rendition of "Auld Lang Syne," and the hall was deathly silent. Through his earphone he could hear

Roland Monteczuma shouting at the stage manager, who was babbling about a naked lady. *Hokey Smokers*, thought the musical director, signaling his orchestra to silence.

The Playpen guests were in suspended animation, half risen out of their seats and ready to explode. They did not understand the cause of this delay, since Jenny Keyster stood just out of their line of sight.

Art Pastel was paralyzed as well, gazing at the offstage apparition with a mixture of desire and terror.

In the control trailer, Monteczuma was shouting, **"Ralph, goddamn you, if you don't get on that stage and throw that switch, I'll beat your fucking ass up around your eyebrows!"**

Ralph Goliones was trying to find a way to get on stage without having to go past Jenny Keyster.

The chronometer read **12:00:10** before Jenny became fully aware of her plight. She gazed miserably at the mortified Art Pastel, then softly in the silence uttered, "Ohh, Artie..." and turned and fled into the backstage darkness.

Artie? Warden Keyster snapped his gaze toward Art Pastel. *OH, ARTIE?* Tully's eyes filled to overflowing with sudden, hideous wrath. His immediate impulse was to murder Art Pastel, but this compulsion was quickly overridden by a higher value in the Keyster Ethic: Tully was Executioner first and Father second, so he could not vacate the switch until his duty was complete— and thus the warden's wrath became displaced. Peering at Pastel with terrible eyes, bulging and mad, Keyster bellowed from the very bowels of his soul: **"DIE!"** His gaze riveted on the master of ceremonies, the warden slammed down the switch with all his might.

An awesome sizzling sound erupted from the golden chair. Lewd Noogie's body lurched upward against its restraining straps. The audience exploded with a tumultuous roar of release. Ulloch Tugg directed his orchestra to resume playing.

"Thank God!" sighed Monteczuma in the control trailer. "Cue balloon releases one and two!"

Five thousand colored balloons cascaded downward from the ceiling, each imprinted with the slogan BETTER DEAD THAN YELLOW, and on the television screen appeared this credit:

Courtesy of DAUGHTERS OF DEAD HEROES

The balloons drifted down among the Playpen guests, who pushed them impatiently aside; their only desire was to watch without distraction as the Condemned Man burned.

On stage, Tully Keyster held the switch down so hard his knuckles were white. **"DIE, MAGGOT!"** the warden boomed.

Lewd Noogie's brain began to boil.

"Keyster's gone berserk!" shouted Monteczuma. "Cut his mike and keep all cameras off him! Take Camera Two!" The switcher punched up a shot of the electric chair, the Condemned Man's body writhing and jerking against the straps, Art Pastel standing nearby and grinning stupidly, and Chaplain Levitsky kneeling with his eyes closed, clutching his Bible.

"DIE, FAGGOT! DIE, ROACH!"

The director shook his head. "Pastel's mike is picking up that raving fat-ass! Cut it!" he ordered. "Cut *every goddamned mike on stage* if you have to! Camera one, pan the audience!"

The Playpen revelers were beginning to loosen up again — dancing in the aisles, kissing one another, sounding noisemakers, swilling champagne.

The Condemned Man shit his pants.

Warden Keyster was completely in the hands of instinct. His thoughts were not in words— his seething mind filled instead with colored flashes, mostly red and black.

His psyche teetered between Executioner and Father. The demands of the Executioner weighed heavier at first, so he remained at the switch, crushing down the handle that sent lethal current throbbing into the Condemned Man. To the warden, however, the act was more of an evil curse directed at Art Pastel, and he held the handle down a full minute before deciding that this was a poor substitute for the usual brand of Keyster vengeance. The balance tipped from Executioner to Father, and at that instant Keyster abandoned the switch and leaped toward the petrified emcee, bent on annihilation.

Unfortunately for the warden, the circuit breaker was equipped with a spring-action handle, and as soon as he released it, it sprang open, cutting off the electrical current to the chair. The Condemned Man's body quit flopping; the chair stopped sizzling. At once, the warden's psychic balance swung the other way again, for his burn was not complete. With a strangled roar, he pirouetted in mid-charge and lunged back toward the switch, smashing it closed again with all the strength in both his arms.

The current ripped anew into the Condemned Man's body, which resumed its writhing and jerking against the straps. Desperately, Keyster tried to fix the handle in the ON position. Holding it down tightly for several seconds, he then released his hold and watched it spring right open. The power in the chair went off. Tully smashed the handle down again and the current surged back into the Condemned Man's body. The enraged warden slowly eased up on the handle, and the handle eased upward just as slowly; the current snapped off once again.

"AARRAAGGHH!!" Keyster pumped the handle up and down with all his might, bashing it closed again and again, trying to make it break in the closed position. The Condemned Man's body bounced up and down with each jolt that shot through it.

Art Pastel stood nailed to the stage beside the sizzling,

quivering body in the golden chair. The acrid stench of burning flesh and human feces drifted to the emcee's nostrils, and he gazed toward the cameras, whining, "I didn't do it, Mommy... I didn't make the poopy."

In the control trailer, Montezuma saw in his monitors that the star was speaking on stage. "Cut to Camera Three! Turn on Pastel's mike!" By the time these things were done, however, Pastel had lapsed into silence once again. "We blew it. Eugene, hang loose on those sound pots— I might want them open or shut on split-second notice, you grab?"

"Everythin's copacetic," yawned the drunken sound technician. The picture transmitted across the airwaves showed the black grotto, the Condemned Man sizzling in the golden chair within, Art Pastel, the prison doctor and his honorary nurses standing nearby, the Chaplain Levitsky kneeling at the Condemned Man's feet. At that moment, Levitsky also became aware of the putrid odor emanating from the chair, and looked up at the body cooking beside him. The priest's eyes rolled back and he flopped right on his face in front of the electric chair.

"Sweet Jesus!" Montezuma gasped. "Take Camera Two! Ralph, get your ass out there and drag that asshole off the stage!"

"Right, Rolly," replied the stage manager. "By the way, don't forget you still have another five thousand balloons to drop."

"Christ, I did forget! Cue balloon releases three and four!"

Camera two showed the home viewers a shot of the stage left witness area, where Fila Noogie, Governor Black, Carisse Crosse and Jesus Bodega were seated. As the falling balloons drifted toward the stage, Miss Crosse jumped up to catch one, leaning over the delivery boy's back to reach for it. As she stretched upward, both her ponderous breasts wobbled out of her gown and into the full view of one billion people. Jesus Bodega, spying them hovering just above his head, mistook them for balloons and grabbed them.

"Oh-oh!" shouted Monteczuma, "Boobies! Camera Two, pan left— *fast* Ralph, boobs loose on stage— get 'em back in the bag!" Camera Two panned left just in time to pick up Fila Noogie planting a hot wet New Year's kiss on a reluctant Governor Angus Black. Her right hand was groping him.

"Oh, no!" Monteczuma spun toward the switcher. "Punch up an audience shot, quick!"

Formally attired men and women were knocking over audience chairs, chasing after the falling balloons. Couples were locked in passionate embraces; champagne glasses arced through the air, bursting with crystal showers on the stage and against the electric chair.

At the switch, Warden Keyster had torn off his bow tie and was now wrapping it around the circuit-breaker handle, trying to tie it in a closed position.

The Condemned Man's exposed flesh— his hands and right leg was beet— red.

At center stage, Ralph and the prison doctor each grabbed one of Ryder Levitsky's arms, while the two starlet nurses each took hold of a foot. As they headed for the wings, they had to step over Fila and Governor Black, who were wrestling on the floor; then they passed by Carisse Crosse as she struggled to make the delivery boy release her bulbous breasts. "Uh, Miss Crosse," the stage manager said in passing, "would you mind putting your... ah..."

"Don't tell *me*," exclaimed the sex symbol, "tell *him*!"

At two minutes past midnight, the orchestra finished playing "Auld Lang Syne," as dictated in the script. The electrocution was slated to end at that time, as well, but Tully Keyster was beyond time now, still trying to tie the switch in the ON position. In the control trailer, Monteczuma ran his hands through his hair and switched on his headset. "Ulloch, go on with the finale— Keyster's liable to fry that bastard all night."

The orchestra erupted with a resounding fanfare, then was joined by the massive, magnificent pipe organ on stage, as the Homeless Boys' Choir began to sing "The Battle Hymn of the Republic."

> *"Mine eyes have seen the glory*
> *of the coming of the Lord:*
> *He is trampling out the vintage*
> *where the grapes of wrath are stored..."*

The TV audience saw a view of the glittering stage, with champagne goblets shattering around the smoking electric chair. The honor guard from the Gung-Ho Guerrillas stood tall and unflinching; the Penthouse Pixie dancing girls turned their heads aside, wiping their eyes and swallowing often; the little flower girl downstage on the orchestra side leaned over the apron and vomited. The Condemned Man began to melt.

> *"He hath loos'd the fateful lightning*
> *of His terrible swift sword,*
> *His truth is marching on."*

Warden Keyster finally managed to tie the circuit breaker in the closed position; then he bounded from his platform toward Art Pastel, who backed away several steps before taking full flight around the back of the grotto.

"Holy Christ!" Monteczuma shouted. "That goofball's loose on stage! Cut to the audience again!"

"Camera One's gone inoperable," announced the tech director. The Number-One Monitor was black.

Camera Two panned the audience, whose members seemed to be so deeply engaged in drunken revelry they no longer paid any attention to what was happening on the stage. Members of the television crews were seen romping among the dignitaries, swilling champagne and smooching the women.

Monteczuma looked at the tech director. "I want every man who leaves his post fired on the spot, is that clear?

Now, get out there and put the fear of God into those assholes." The show director studied the chaos evident on all his monitors. "I don't like the look of this."

"Glory, glory Hallelujah!
His truth is marching on."

On stage, Warden Keyster was chasing Art Pastel around and around the grotto, screaming obscenities. The dancers scattered in fear and confusion. Suddenly, a middle-aged woman ran up the steps from the audience and flung herself between the berserk warden and the sniveling emcee. Both men stopped for a moment, dumfounded, when they saw her. Keyster was the first to spring back into action, attempting to sweep the woman aside and pounce on the paralyzed Art Pastel.

The woman latched onto the warden's lapels and he dragged her along several steps while she shrieked up at him, "Don't you dare! Don't you dare! *Don't you dare lay a hand on my son, Tully Keyster!"*

The warden paused a moment, peering down at her as though she were some sort of crazy animal attached to his chest, then he lunged once more for the unmoving Art Pastel. This time the woman reacted with awesome fury, whacking him across the face several times with both hands until Keyster just stood there and looked at his wife in disbelief.

Anita Keyster held her husband and looked him squarely in the eye, speaking as gently as the situation permitted. "Tully, listen to me and try to understand. I'm sorry, dear— I hate to have to tell you here like this... I hoped I'd never have to tell you at all. My real name is

Thalia Trump. Arthur here is my son, my own flesh and blood." The warden regarded her as though she spoke a foreign tongue. "But... my Jen..." he heard himself explain, "this man raped my little girl."

"Tully, Jenny is Arthur's half sister." Anita's gaze wavered away from her husband's. "One more thing, dear— I might as well make a clean breast of it— I... never divorced my first husband."

In the control trailer, Roland Montezuma saw in his monitors that things had settled down considerably on stage. Someone informed him that the unidentified intruder was the warden's wife. "Christ, if I knew how easy she cools him down, I'd have had her on stage all night. Camera Three, gimme a medium shot of everybody center stage."

In the TV room of the Trump mansion, Toy Boat bolted from her chair and stood frozen several moments before uttering the first word of her own devising in twenty years:

"Mother!"

She watched Thalia Trump turn away from the deflated form of Warden Keyster and stand face to face with her son. Then Toy, along with one billion other viewers across the earth, watched Art Pastel make pee-pee for his mother, right in his pants.

Roland Montezuma rose out of his seat, staring at his Master Monitor in disbelief. "He's pissing his pants! Pastel's pissing his pants on camera!" Desperately, he scanned the monitors in search of an air-able shot. The Number-One Monitor was still dark; its camera was a handheld job stationed in the audience, and the preliminary report was that a guest had poured a goblet of champagne into one of the unit's exhaust vents. Camera Two was a dolly-and-crane rig, also in the audience, but that seemed to be going haywire as well, its picture out of focus and gyrating wildly. Camera Four, which looked down upon the audience from the ceiling, was still operational. "Punch up Camera Four!"

the director ordered. "Zoom in and pan the audience!"

Number Four zeroed in and began to pan the hall. "My camera's overheating," the cameraman complained.

Tuxedoed gentlemen were seen pouring champagne on one ano her's heads. Throughout the hall, scattered fist fights had broken out and were rapidly becoming drunken brawls. Two woozy women in wrinkled gowns had commandeered the Number-Two Camera and were swinging it about, aiming it at passing revelers as though it were a gun in an amusement arcade. Men and women roamed the hall in carnal abandon, passionately embracing at random, harpooning each other with lustful tongues, clutching at jerking buttocks; the men were violently kneading buxom breasts, stuffing hammy hands into the soiled bodices of costly gowns; the women were hotly chafing anonymous crotches with their hands, their groins, hips, buttocks, thighs— anything they could throw at their objectives.

Quite naturally, the more attractive individuals became the preferred targets of this tremendous outpouring of raw genital energy. Four men surrounded a Broadway sexpot enthroned upon an audience chair; one stood behind her with her head tilted back, his mouth glued to hers; two others had worked her well-known knockers out of her gown and were sucking them voraciously; and a fourth man knelt between the lady's legs, the top portion of his body hidden beneath the full-flowing skirt of her gossamer gown. Her arms hung limply at her sides in the time-honored attitude of a goddess permitting her worshipers to adore her.

Many men, however, were still more interested in making war than love, and the bloodshed continued to spread, creating a drain on the masculine population of the hall, and leaving a large number of wanton women wanting. Of these frustrated females, some simply ganged up on the most virile specimens available, but the majority were left to seek consolation in each other's arms, deep kissing and massaging crotches and breasts. The floor was strewn with fallen bodies, passed out drunk, beaten unconscious, or just trying to get into one another's pants.

"Punch up Camera Five!" shrieked the appalled director.

Camera Five, situated at the rear of the hall, zoomed in over the heads of the debauching guests and began to pan the stage. Enfolded in the arms of his long-lost mother, Arthur Trump stood pathetically, dissolved in tears and pissing his pants. Warden Keyster had slowly sunk to the floor and now just sat there, gazing at his wife holding Art Pastel. Fila Noogie and Governor Black were writhing on the floor of the stage, his trousers unbuckled and her skirt pulled up around her waist. Jesus Bodega and Carisse Crosse were in a passionate embrace, his face wallowing between her wobbling woo-woos. The soldiers of the honor guard had succumbed to the allure of the dancing girls, who were sickened by the onstage stench and were in no condition to resist the horny GIs.

The stage was filling up with white smoke; the electric chair had now been sizzling nearly twice as long as had been scheduled, and acrid billows were pouring from behind the circuit breaker, the golden chair and from Lewd Noogie's body itself. Adjacent to the huge hall, in the tiny generator room, the tandem units began to shudder and smoke as well, but the attendant electricians were too drunk to notice or care.

"Punch up Camera Three!"

Camera Three, situated at the south wall, picked up a shot of Ulloch Tugg, the BBS Orchestra and the Homeless Boys' Choir, still thundering through their majestic rendition of the "Battle Hymn of the Republic."

> *"As he died to make men holy,*
> *let us live to make men free.*
> *While God is marching on.*
> *GLORY, GLORY, HALLELUJAH!*

GLORY, GLORY, HALLELUJAH!"

With each towering "GLORY," a mammoth military cannon erupted from the rear of the orchestra. The tremendous pipe organ on stage was blasting at maximum horsepower, and both orchestra and choir were striving for absolute ultimate decibel output.

"GLO-RY, GLO-RY, HAL-LE-LU-OO-YA!"

Suddenly, with a momentous, incredible roar, the entire band stand collapsed, sucking eighty-three shrieking choirboys and musicians into a smoking black pit.

On his Master Monitor, Monteczuma watched the BBS Orchestra and the Homeless Boys' Choir self destruct before his very eyes. The director flopped back in his chair and scanned the monitors numbly. "This isn't a Death House," he uttered softly, "it's a Madhouse." He drew a shaking hand across his eyes and clicked on his headset. "All cameras... focus on the fucking ceiling— I gotta have time to think." He tilted his head back and closed his eyes. *There goes my Emmy.*

The bandstand catastrophe failed to dampen the spirits of the partygoers; few even seemed to take notice. The onstage pipe organ now boomed out the hymn alone, though its powerful console was beginning to smoke rather badly. Out in the generator room, a spinner flew off the governor which kept the two roaring units in sync, and they began to whine crazily, turning faster and faster. Remote control electronic equipment throughout the Playpen began to tremble and smoke, and the technical director began to fear a power failure.

Off stage in the wings, a group of drunken stagehands had Jenny Keyster pinned face down over a humming electrical console, her legs dangling down one side. The skirt of her violet gown was wrenched up over her waist, her pantyhose had been torn from her body and a dirty rag was stuffed in her whimpering mouth. An ape-like stagehand was planted between her slender legs, his soiled hands squeezing her firm, white buttocks, his greasy thumbs digging into the tops of her supple thighs, spreading apart the soft, damp, honey-tufted labia, his dungarees unzipped, his thick, swollen penis buried wetly in her to the hairy hilt. He rammed with all his might, ground against her yielding thighs, gaped his mouth, rolled his eyes and shot his thick white victory into the depths of her delicate belly, feeding it to her in hot, fast squirts. The rest of the men encircled the moaning girl, holding her down and feeling her up, watching their comrade pump his silver syrup deep inside her. Their fat, fleshy flagpoles loomed from open flies, each waiting its turn to carry the colors.

The first stagehand withdrew his soggy saber and staggered backward, wheezing dreamily, as another man shuffled into position for sloppy seconds. The second stagehand waited while his buddies pinned the shuddering girl firmly against the hot surface of the smoking electrical console, then aimed his throbbing turgid torpedo at the helpless, foundering vessel and yelled, "Fire One—!" driving his massive missile clear up to the young girl's cervix with a single thrust.

The console exploded.

One thousand lights throughout the hall exploded. The light board exploded. The pipe organ shrieked its highest note, and exploded. The sound consoles, speakers, microphones and headsets exploded. The cameras exploded. The flashing chronometer, which read **12:03:53**, and all the other electrical signs exploded. As if disintegrated by a nuclear bomb, the BBS Control Trailer exploded. The electric chair exploded, the circuit breaker exploded, and then the two screaming generators, pregnant with power too great to contain, exploded.

With a blinding flash, the entire hall was gorged with

white-hot primal energy; next, the concrete walls burst outward as if punched with omnipotent fists, and the massive iron ceiling came bashing down. In a matter of seconds, the electrical cataclysm was complete; then, the more mundane, infernal blaze began the leisurely task of cleaning up, consuming debris with a patient holocaust of yellow flame and purple smoke. There were no survivors.

If you enjoyed

PLEASE

Post a review on Amazon.
Whether you write a dissertation or just a few words, you are helping to support this author's popularity and income.

Please help spread the word.

ABOUT THE AUTHOR

Robert Shiarella, as a youth, aspired to become a master oyster-shucker. Failing that, he attended Penn State University, where, sadly, no courses in oyster-shucking were offered, so he obtained a Master's Degree in Radio, TV and Theater. He subsequently held many jobs, including acting and directing Off-Broadway and in summer theater, as well as Casting Coordinator for NBC New York, and Articles Editor for Argosy Magazine. Deciding to do something "more practical," he studied with several famous gurus throughout India and Nepal, thereafter becoming a freelance writer and Director of the World Yoga Center in Manhattan.

When his first and only novel, *Your Sparkle Cavalcade of Death*, was published, readers suggested that he should "do therapy." Misinterpreting their suggestions, he actually became a Jungian Therapist, having studied at the Jungian Institute in Zürich, Switzerland. His non-fiction book, *Journey To Joy*, is a textbook on Siddha Meditation and the Oriental Philosophy of Kashimir Shavism.

With the republication of *Your Sparkle Cavalcade of Death*, Robert now sees endless vistas opening out before him; although mostly out of his window in Connecticut, accompanied by his daughter, Princess, a sultry, silky, white Angora Feline Diva.

If you liked the book

YOUR SPARKLE CAVALCADE OF DEATH

ROBERT SHIARELLA

You'll love the audiobook!

Unabridged, with Sound Effects and Music

Performed by

Jon Koons

Available from <u>audible.com</u>

Spring 2021

Metamorphic Press

We Only Print
Good Stuff!

Irreverent Humor
(first time
in print
since 1976)

Irrelevent Humor
from award
winning author
Marvin Kaye

Humorous
SciFi
YA!

Historical
Fiction

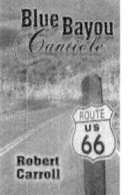

Classics

Stories for
Adults

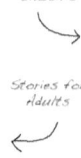

Stories for
Kids

Inspirational
Pads and
Journals

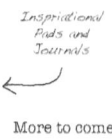

More to come!

metamorphicpress.com

www.ingramcontent.com/pod-product-compliance
Lightning Source LLC
Chambersburg PA
CBHW021446240626
47153CB00001B/313